DEFINITELY

THE COMPLETE SERIES

ELLA MILES

Copyright © 2018 by Ella Miles

EllaMiles.com

Ella@ellamiles.com

Editor: Jovana Shirley, Unforeseen Editing, www.unforeseenediting.com

Cover design © Arijana Karčić, Cover It! Designs

FREE BOOKS

Read **Not Sorry** for **FREE!** And sign up to get my latest releases, updates, and more goodies here→EllaMiles.com/freebooks

Follow me on BookBub to get notified of my new releases and recommendations here→Follow on BookBub Here

Join Ella's Bellas FB group for giveaways and a **FREE** copy of **Pretend I'm Yours**→Join Ella's Bellas Here

MAYBE, DEFINITELY SERIES

The Definitely Series is a spinoff series of my Maybe Series. While the Definitely Series can be read without having read the Maybe series, it is best read after the Maybe series.

MAYBE, DEFINITELY SERIES:

Maybe Yes
Maybe Never
Maybe Always

Definitely Yes
Definitely No
Definitely Forever

DEFINITELY YES

1

SCARLETT

WHY ARE there no hot men in this bar? I sigh. *Why are there no hot men at any bar—ever?*

I take a sip of my gin and tonic as I scour the room, looking for anyone who will do for tonight. This bar used to be the best bar in New York City to pick someone up for a one-night stand. Now, it is just another bar to add to my list of has-beens.

It's a shame really. This bar has everything. It's clean; it has a live band every night, not just on the weekends; and the bartenders here know my drink order without me having to order. It used to be full of life, full of energy, but now, it is nothing more than an overpriced bar with crappy music and no hot men.

As I glance around the large bar, I don't count more than six other people in the bar, only two of which are men. One is too old—my best guess, mid-forties—and the other, I doubt he's eighteen.

"It just ain't what it used to be, is it?" Todd says.

"No, it isn't. I hate to say this, but I'm going to have to find a new bar," I say.

Todd wipes off the counter in front of me. "I hate to say this, but me, too. The tips aren't what they used to be. And if my favorite tipper leaves me—"

"Your only tipper and most attractive customer," I say, smiling.

Todd flashes me his smile that is missing one front tooth. "Only tipper. I won't be able to survive on the measly salary this place pays me. I guess it is off to find greener pastures."

"Yeah, I guess." I frown as I finish off the last of my gin and tonic.

Todd immediately places another glass in front of me, making me smile.

"Thanks, Todd."

"You bet, Scar," he says.

I take the full glass and raise it to my lips, sipping the perfect, cold liquid that I find myself needing more and more after a long day of work. I love what I do, but running Beautifully Bell Enterprises, the fashion and beauty company I own, is exhausting by the end of the day. I need something cold to relax me and a hot man in my bed to reenergize me for the next morning.

As much as I love spending my evening talking with Todd, it's not enough. I need more. I need thrills and excitement to invigorate me. To make me excited to wake up the next morning. I used to have that every night when I was twenty-five and a model. I always knew the hippest bars to find an attractive man. Half of the time, I didn't even have to go to a bar to find a man. The male models I worked with that day would more than do.

Now, at thirty-two, I've found that it is harder to find a good man for one night. I don't model as much anymore. I just don't have time with my fashion empire. And then men my age are beginning to become more and more interested in more than just one night. They want marriage and babies and the whole package. I'm just not ready for that yet.

That leaves me with the twenty-something-year-old men who are practically still babies themselves. Men who are excited about the idea of one night only. Men who don't care that I'm older than them. Men who like being controlled by a more domineering woman.

My phone buzzes against the table, and I turn it over to see who messaged me.

Kinsley: Emergency! Can I meet you tomorrow? Have news!

My heart races when I see the words *Kinsley* and *emergency* in the same line.

My best friend has been through too much in the past. It's been almost ten years now since she found out her family was money launderers, smugglers, and killers. Ten years since my best friend almost died at the hand of her own grandfather. Now, she's living her happily ever after here, in New York City.

But seeing her text message has me worried that something has happened again. It's after midnight, and my best friend is never awake this late on a Thursday.

I type frantically.

Me: Where are you? Do I need to call the police? What's happening?

I stare at my phone, gripping it much too hard, as I wait for the message to get sent and read.

Come on, come on, I think as I frantically bounce my legs up and down, hoping that she will respond quickly. *I should have just called her, but what if she is stuck in the back of a trunk somewhere? Then, if I called her, it would let her kidnappers know that she had a phone? What if her mouth is taped shut with duct tape, and she can't speak? What if—*

Then, I watch as three dots appear on the screen, indicating that she is typing a response. My phone buzzes in my hand as the message comes through.

Kinsley: LOL. Sorry, didn't mean to scare you. There is nothing wrong. I'm completely fine. Just have some happy news that I can't wait to tell you tomorrow! We've been having trouble with finding time for each other lately, so I just wanted to make sure you knew that I really need you to drop everything and just be my best friend tomorrow.

I shake my head at my friend.

Me: Chica, you just about gave me a heart attack, and then you wouldn't have been able to share your news with me. Just name the time and place, and I'll be there tomorrow.

Kinsley: Eileen's Cheesecake. 1:30 p.m.?

I laugh at her message. *Since when does my friend think it is a good idea to skip lunch and just go straight for dessert? Sounds like I am finally rubbing off on her.*

Me: Done.

I smile, excited to take a break tomorrow to go be with my best friend. It has been a while since I have seen her. *Three months? Or is it four?*

Even though we live in the same city, we might as well live on different continents. With my busy schedule, it's too hard to find time to see each other. Especially since Killian, her husband, doesn't like the idea of us going out to pick up guys for me at night. I need to change that.

I pull up my calendar on my phone. *Shit.* I have meetings all afternoon. *Not anymore,* I think, smiling. I hit Delete on every single one that starts after one o'clock and then type in *Afternoon with Bestie,* starting at one thirty p.m. instead.

I open my email and type a quick message to my assistant, Preston, to cancel everything and reschedule for later. I also tell him to make sure I have an hour or two in the afternoon at least once a week to make time for my friends. I've worked hard enough these last ten years. I think I deserve an hour or two break to actually enjoy the money I make and spend time with my friends.

I should also think of planning a vacation soon. Maybe see if Kinsley and Killian would want to tag along. I'm sure I could find plenty of men to enjoy my time with if we went to a beach in the Caribbean or Mexico. So, I tell Preston to find a good time in my schedule to do that, too. I hit Send, knowing that Preston is going to hate me when I come into the office tomorrow, but he can handle it. It's my business, and if I decide I need a break, then I need a break.

I feel better already as I take another sip of my gin and tonic. I might not be going home with a man tonight, but at least I can go home, feeling good from the alcohol and knowing that tomorrow is going to be a good day.

I finish my fourth drink.

"Another?" Todd asks although he knows I usually stop after four, my usual limit for feeling good without overdoing it.

"A shot of tequila and then another gin and tonic."

Todd raises his eyebrows at me, but doesn't question me as he goes about making my drinks. "What's got you in a better mood?"

"My best friend has good news that she is sharing with me tomorrow."

"I thought I was your best friend," Todd says, placing the shot and glass of gin and tonic in front of me.

"Best guy friend." I wink at him. I raise the shot glass. "To my best guy friend."

Todd smiles, and to my surprise, he raises his own shot glass. We clink the glasses together and then both down our shots. The tequila burns in the best possible way as it goes down my throat.

My phone buzzes again, and I expect to see a message from Kinsley. Maybe she wants to meet up tonight after all. I doubt she will be able to keep her good news to herself any longer. But it's not from Kinsley. In fact, I have no idea who it is from. I open the text message.

Unknown: I want you, just for tonight. I want to make you feel things you have never felt before. I've been watching you all night, Beauty. You're exactly what I want.

I stare down at my phone, confused as to what is going on. I glance over at Todd, assuming it is a prank, but he is deep in conversation with the older gentleman who is now sitting at the bar instead of at one of the pub tables.

Hmm...

Me: I think you have the wrong number.

My phone buzzes again almost immediately.

Unknown: I have the right number, Beauty. I want to shred into pieces that little red dress you're wearing that hugs your overwhelming curves. I want to tame that mane of long, wavy brown hair. I want to feel your tan legs wrapped around my waist until you dig your black pumps into my back so hard that I have to punish you for the pain you have caused me.

I bite my lip as I stare at the seductive message I just received. A message that seems like it is meant for me. The woman he is describing fits me to a T. I uneasily shift in my seat at the thought of having a stranger stalking me. Someone has been watching me, but I can't deny that the thought of a sexy man trying to seduce me via a text message turns me on. It does—more than I would ever admit to this stranger.

I pick up my gin and tonic and spin in the barstool until my back is to the bar, trying to act as casual as possible as I scan the room. But I don't see anyone new who could be sending this. I sigh. *And how would a stranger get my number anyway?*

Todd.

I turn back around and wait impatiently for Todd to find his way back down the bar to me.

"Did you give my number to any strange men?"

"Nope. Why would I want to give any other man a chance to snag my girl?" He smiles.

I wonder if Todd really thinks that way or if it's just a joke in the same way we tease each other about our choice of TV shows. Todd isn't bad-looking. The only odd thing about him is his missing tooth that he told me he'd lost when playing ice hockey. To some women, that would even be a turn-on. He's about my age, but he's just not my type. Not dangerous enough. And I see him more as a friend than a lover.

I look back at my phone. *If Todd didn't give this person my number, then who did?*

Me: Who is this? Who gave you my number?

Unknown: It doesn't matter who I am. All that matters is, we both want the same thing. One night of danger, passion, and mystery. One night that will forever be burned in your memory. One night that will ruin you, so every time you fuck another man, you will think about tonight and wish he were me. Wish he could thrill you the same way that I could.

I read his message, and it's like he has been reading my thoughts. It's exactly what I want. It's what I *need.* But I still don't know exactly what he is proposing. I begin typing to ask him that very question, but I receive his message first.

Unknown: Will you meet me in my room on the top floor of the Waldorf, Beauty? I want to fuck you until you're so sore that you can't walk without thinking about me tomorrow.

My eyes widen as I read his text. I'm supposed to go to a hotel room without even knowing who he is. He could be planning on raping me. He could kill me.

Or he could give me the best night of my life.

I begin to type, *No,* but then stop. *Why am I even considering this? This is crazy! I can't go.*

Kinsley would kill me if she found out. I wouldn't have to tell her though. It would just be one night, and then I would never see this man again. Whoever he is.

He picked the Waldorf, one of the nicest hotels in New York City. He has money.

What if he is that old man sitting down the bar from me? I glance over at him. I study his jeans and button-down shirt. There is nothing fancy or designer about his clothes. His watch is a knockoff. And he's drinking cheap whiskey. He couldn't afford a hotel room like that.

I could ask Todd to go with me. Check out this man and let me know if he's okay first. But that would take all the excitement out of it.

I reach into my purse, making sure the pepper spray I bought after Kinsley had gone missing is still there. It would be my only defense.

I do a lot of kickboxing to stay in shape. I've taken some self-defense classes. Being a single woman, living in New York City, I felt I needed some level of protection. But I know my skills would be no match for a man who is prepared to rape or murder. If he has a gun, I'm fucked. If he surprises me, I'm fucked. If there is more than one man, I don't stand a chance. It doesn't matter how many classes or how strong I am for a woman; most men are still stronger than me. I shouldn't even be considering it.

I hear the door open, and warm, humid air fills the room. I turn just in time to see a tall, dark man leaving. A man in a suit with tousled hair on top of his head. He looks like any typical businessman my age who works in New York. But there is one thing not typical about him. He turns to look at me just before the door closes, and for a split second, I see the danger lurking in his eyes as he stares at me like no man ever has. A danger that pulls at my heart.

I glance back down at my phone and hit the Delete button until I erase, *No*. And then I type, *Yes*, and send the text.

2

SCARLETT

FUCK, what am I doing? I walk back and forth in the hallway on the top floor of the Waldorf. I pace in front of the hotel room he texted me after I said yes.

My heart is beating loudly in my chest and races even faster each time I take a step closer to the door and then slows as I walk past it again. Everything in my body is screaming that I shouldn't do this. If I do this, it could be the last thing I ever do. But, somewhere underneath all of that, my body is screaming to knock on the door. To go get the fuck of my life. That, after building a business from the ground up, I deserve this. That I deserve to live a little on the dangerous side.

And, I already said yes. I'm here. I know I won't be able to leave now without knocking on the door. My curiosity, if nothing else, is what is going to get me killed. But at least I'll die without regrets, knowing that I lived my life on the edge instead of in fear and pushed myself to my limits.

I stop in front of the door and knock loudly three times, showing the man on the other side of the door that I'm a confident, strong woman whom he shouldn't mess with. Not a weak, meek woman who is just doing this because she has no other options.

I wait, but the door doesn't open. Instead, I feel my phone buzz in my pocket.

Unknown: Open the door.

I put my hand on the handle and turn, not expecting it to actually open. It's a hotel room. I don't have a key. It shouldn't open. But it does. I push the door open, hoping to see my stranger. Instead, all I see is darkness.

I step inside, feeling for the light switch on the wall. I find it just as the door swings shut behind me, latching loudly, causing me to jump. As the darkness surrounds me, I flip the switch, but the lights don't turn on. Panic engulfs me as I continue to flip the switch up and down, but no light comes on. I blink rapidly, trying to see past the darkness, but I can't. My hands are clammy as I dig in my purse to pull out my phone for light when I hear his voice.

"Stop."

I freeze. *How can he see me? How can he see what I'm doing when all I see is darkness?*

He must be in the room though, not more than a couple of feet away from me. His voice sounded close. His eyes have probably had time to adjust, while my eyes can't see past the darkness.

I don't know why I listen to him. I don't *take* orders from men. I *give* the orders. I pick up the guys; the guys don't pick me up. I'm my own boss. Men don't control me.

But, for some reason, this man's voice makes me stop. It was so deep and commanding that it makes me want to do whatever he says because behind the voice is a promise that, if I do listen, I will get everything I've ever wanted and more.

But his voice is not enough to keep my own voice at bay.

"Who are you?"

"A man," he answers.

"What's your name?" I try again.

"It doesn't matter."

"Have I met you before?"

"No."

"Do you know who I am?"

"Yes."

I gasp. He knows who I am.

"I don't think it's really fair that you know who I am, but I don't know who you are. I can't even see you," I say.

"It's not, but if I tell you or show you who I am, it will ruin this," he says.

This time, I feel his breath on my neck, causing me to shiver. He's not the man I saw leaving the bar. He's probably hideous or old. That's why he's hiding in the darkness.

"What do you want?"

He laughs, and the deep sound sends more shivers running through my body.

"I thought I made that perfectly clear. You."

"Then, what are you waiting for?"

He chuckles again. "I chose wisely, Beauty. But I need to hear you say it first. I don't fuck women unless they tell me to first."

I don't hesitate. I just say, "Fuck me."

A moment passes as I breathe slowly in and out, waiting for him to make his move. I would make the first move, except I can't see him. And I kind of like the idea of giving up control to a man, not knowing what is coming next, just for one night.

I only get one breath in before my hands are pulled roughly up. Rope narrows around them, binding them together. It's tight enough that I know there is no way I'm ever getting out. He quickly pulls me forward from the hallway and into the next room. I don't know what room this is. I can't make out anything in here either. All I can feel is my arms being jerked rapidly up over my head.

I pull on the rope that must now be tied to something above me because it doesn't give at all. I panic slightly. I've never been one for pain. I've never been one for BDSM. I like my sex full of pleasure without pain, but it seems my stranger is into kinkier things.

I should tell him to stop. That I can't do this. That I need to back out.

"Relax, Beauty. I'm not going to hurt you," he says. "Seeing you in pain isn't what gets me off."

I close my eyes and then slowly open them, trying to push the fear out of my body. Trying to trust this complete stranger. I push most of it away, but there is still a little bit of fear left. Just enough that it amplifies the excitement and anticipation.

"I need you to listen to me, Beauty. I need you to do exactly what I say, and you won't get hurt."

I listen carefully to his words. Each word is dripping with lust and need. Each deep word makes my panties wetter and my nipples harden. Each word makes me think I might have made the right decision.

"Answer me, Beauty. Will you do exactly what I say?"

"Yes," I answer as my voice cracks.

"Good girl."

I feel his body heat as he moves up behind me, but doesn't touch me. He takes his time with studying me, just building the anticipation, before he touches me again until I want to beg him to touch me. I don't. Instead, I wait to see what he is going to do.

Too much time passes. I bite my bottom lip as I wait, but it does nothing to calm my beating heart. I want him. I've never wanted another man so badly in my life. I want this stranger that already has my heart beating too fast and my stomach in knots.

Finally, I feel his hand sweep my hair off my neck, and his lips land on the back of my neck, kissing me softer than I was expecting, showing me that he isn't going to hurt me. My mouth falls open as I breathe heavily, trying to keep my composure but knowing that it isn't going to last. Soon, this stranger is going to turn me into a sex-needing goddess who can't control herself.

"This dress, Beauty, fits you perfectly, but I'd rather see it on the floor," he says.

His hands drop my hair and then travel over the thin straps of my dress, stopping just above my swollen breasts. My nipples harden, begging him to give them attention, just beneath the thin material. His hands capture my breasts, pushing them together, and I let out a gasp at his sudden touch.

His hands grab my dress in the center and then pull hard, ripping the dress in half, down the front. The thin straps that were holding it on my body come undone. I feel the dress fall to my feet, and then I'm standing, naked, in front of a complete stranger.

I've never been insecure about my body. In fact, I've modeled nude for several magazines before. I love how my body looks. Voluptuous but strong at the same time. Sexy. I've been naked in front of strangers before, but being naked in front of a man I've never seen, one I'm giving up complete control to, this is different. I've never felt this exposed before in my life.

I bite my lip, again, as I wait for him. I feel his eyes going over every inch of my body even though I can't see him.

"You're sexier than I realized, Beauty."

"I know. I want to see how sexy you are, too."

"You don't get to see how sexy I am. You just get to experience it."

"But—"

And then his lips are on mine, shutting me up.

He's right. I can feel how sexy he is from how he kisses. The way his tongue moves around my mouth, massaging my tongue, before his mouth sucks on my lips, drawing me into him. I can feel the stubble from his upper lip brush against my lip, as he pushes his tongue into me further. It makes me think back to the few images I have of the stranger leaving the bar.

It has to be him. He has to be that stranger.

I let the image of that stranger mix with the clues this stranger is giving me of what he looks like. He's tall; I know that much from how he is kissing me in a downward motion, making him taller than I am, even with my heels still on. He's confident and aggressive, yet gentle.

As he kisses me, he gathers my hair into a ponytail on the back of my head and pulls firmly, forcing my head upward, giving him a better angle to kiss me. His body presses against my naked body. He's still dressed. I feel buttons on my breasts, a belt, and a cock pushing against my belly, hidden behind fabric that feels like dress pants.

I pull against the rope, wanting to tangle my hands in his hair, as he kisses me. I want to explore his hard muscles with my hands that I feel against my body. This man works out because all I can feel is hard muscle pushing against me. I can sense his strength in the way he pulls my hair. And I want to feel him. But, no matter how hard I pull against the rope, my hands don't move. They stay high above my head.

When he stops kissing me, I say, "I want—"

"I didn't give you permission to talk, Beauty. No talking. Just feel."

I sigh. I want to talk, to tell him what I want even if he is more than meeting my needs. I'm used to being able to tell a man what to do and how to do it.

I try to be quiet as his mouth returns to mine. It's easy at first as I lose myself in the kiss and as his hand travels over my breast, making me crazy with need, to the point that I forget I'm supposed to be quiet.

"Jesus Christ...I..."

Something hard and round is being shoved into my mouth and then is fastened around the back of my head.

"No more talking, Beauty."

I swallow, trying to get used to the ball gag that is now in my mouth.

He took away the last thing I had control over—my voice. Now, I have nothing left. I can't control my own movements. I can't control what he does to me. I can't control my voice. I've given up all control to this stranger. Everything of me is now his.

I don't know what he is going to do next. I thought my eyes would adjust to the darkness by now, but they haven't. My ears, on the other hand, seem to have gained super-hearing powers now that all my other senses have been dampened. I hear him walking behind me. I hear the rustle of his shirt as he takes it off, exposing what I can only imagine are devastating muscles that I'm dying to see. I hear the loosening of a belt, followed by the drop of his pants.

I suck in a breath, waiting to feel his cock at my entrance. Waiting to feel his hands on my breasts. Waiting to lose myself in him.

Time passes slowly as I wait, and I know he is doing it on purpose. The longer he waits, the crazier I become, the more I don't care that he is a complete stranger. I don't even know his name or what he looks like or what his intentions are. All of those thoughts drift out of my mind until the only thing I care about is him fucking me.

By the time he speaks to me, I've already become completely lost. Lost in the adrenaline firing through my body—a feeling that, no matter how many men I've had, has never felt like this. He wouldn't even have to touch me again, and I would still consider this one of the top sexual experiences I have ever had.

"Spread your legs," he says, his voice commanding.

I spread my legs apart without hesitation.

It doesn't make sense at all, but I've never felt stronger than while standing here, naked, in front of this man who keeps calling me Beauty. I've never felt more empowered even though I don't have any control. I have all the control because, without me saying yes, this would have never happened. And he knows that, at any second, I could turn that yes into a no.

"Good girl."

He's quiet for a moment. And I don't feel him touching me. I have no idea what he's doing, but the waiting is making me mad. I pull against the rope again, but it remains firmly against my skin. I can't do anything but try to slow my breathing and wait and imagine what he is going to do to me, how his cock is going to feel inside me.

"So wet, Beauty," he finally says.

His words make me pant around the ball gag because that is about all I can do in this position.

My eyes narrow, trying to search for his that I know must be locked somewhere between my thighs where moisture has been gathering quickly ever since he stripped me bare. I'm surprised when his hand doesn't immediately go there. Instead, his hand starts at my neck and trails down to my breast and then stomach. He takes his time with savoring the curves of my breast and the smoothness of my stomach. He goes lower, and my legs shake gently.

Finally.

He stops just short, and I let out a small whimper.

"Patience, Beauty."

I can feel his mischievous grin. He knows exactly what he is doing to me even though I can't see it.

God, how I want to see him. When I go home, I want to be able to replay this in my head, but I won't be able to visualize him. Not really.

His body presses against me as his lips devour my neck. I silently scream from the intensity that his touch invokes inside me. All he has done is fucking kiss me, and I'm already losing my mind.

Who am I kidding? My mind was lost the second I got that text message.

His hard, thick cock presses against my stomach, and I lose it. I can't wait any longer. I'm done with his slow torture as his hand finds my breast and squeezes my nipple between his fingers. I lift my leg around his body, pressing my entrance to him, hoping he will get the hint that I'm ready. *Now.*

He slaps my ass—hard. I whimper loudly. He promised he wasn't into that kinky, painful stuff. But I find that, despite the pain, the slap turned me on instead of off, like I would have expected.

"That was for disobeying me. Now, spread. Your. Legs."

His voice, although commanding, is also wavering. I can hear the need dripping from his every word.

I smile inside because I can already feel him giving up a little bit of his control. I've just pushed him to the edge, and now, there is no way he is going to be able to regain his control in the way he wanted.

I lower my leg and slowly spread my legs. He reaches his hand down and touches my entrance. My legs shake as his fingers slowly slip in and out.

"Jesus," I moan through the ball gag.

He removes his hand, and I take one defiant step forward, despite his earlier threats. It's just enough so that his cock is pressed against me again, enough to make him lose the last thread of control that he has been holding on to.

He growls as he grabs my ass, and then he lifts me into the air and brings me down onto his hard cock.

Oh. My. God.

My legs automatically wrap around his body, holding on for dear life. But I quickly realize that he can more than hold my weight as he thrusts inside me, burying himself inside me, in what feels like a challenge that he's somehow won. I've never been fucked like this in my life, and after this, I never want to be fucked any other way again.

"Look at me, Beauty," he says.

I open my eyes, not even realizing when I closed them. Probably the second he entered me, and it was the only thing left I could control. I see him staring back at me, inches from my face, as he continues to torture me below. I'm so close, and the way he is devouring me with his eyes might be my undoing.

In the darkness, I can't tell what color his eyes are, and I don't really care. *Jesus Christ, I don't care.* I could stare into his devastatingly dangerous eyes all night even if we weren't entwined together at the moment. But being able to see this one part of him, as he fucks me, is too much.

He continues staring at me. He continues fucking me, holding on to my ass to keep me from falling, while his other hand reaches up and removes the ball gag from my mouth before dropping it to the floor. I thought, the second that it was gone, I would have all sorts of words to say to this man. But I have no words. All of my words are gone. I can't think of even the simplest of words to say to this man. All that escapes my mouth are a mix of groans, whimpers, and, *Oh my God*s.

Not that he gives me a whole lot of time to speak anyway. His tongue buries itself inside my mouth, like he has been kissing me his entire life. It feels like we have been doing this our entire life. He doesn't feel like a stranger, considering he knows the curves of my body and exactly how to kiss me. The way he knows just how to read my mind. There is only one man in my life who knows me that well.

How did I not see it before?

I pull back from his lips. "Jake?"

He laughs. "I don't know who Jake is, but if I'm reminding you of another guy, then I'm not doing my job right."

That's when everything changes. His intensity. His growls. The way he slaps my ass as he pounds into me. I don't wonder if he is Jake again. I don't really care if he is or isn't. And I can no longer think straight.

Our breathing picks up. Our moans get louder. And our bodies collide faster.

Until I'm coming, and he is shooting his load inside me.

"Fuck, Beast!" I scream as I come.

He doesn't put me back down immediately. Instead, our eyes stay locked on each other as we both try to quiet our breathing. Eyes that I will never forget, that will haunt me all my life.

I quickly realize I can't keep looking at him. I have to forget about this night. If not, I will never move on. This was one night to get lost in and then forget. I can't take it with me.

He slowly lifts me off his cock and then lowers me to the ground. He holds on to me until I've steadied myself on my heels.

And then he's gone.

It gives me time to repeat to myself over and over again, *This is just a dream. This didn't really happen. I didn't just let a stranger fuck me. I have to forget.*

When he returns, I don't know what to expect. If he's looking for another fuck, it will have to wait. My arms ache from being tied over my head, and I can barely stand. I'm exhausted. I need a break before it can happen again—and it *needs* to happen again.

When I feel his hand between my legs, I tense. "I can't—"

"Hush," he says.

That's when I realize what he is doing. He's cleaning me up.

Strange, this man is. Dangerous. Controlling. Dark. Mysterious. And caring? It seems out of character for him.

When he has finished, he removes the rope from my arms. I slowly lower them, afraid that I'm going to collapse from exhaustion. He's got me covered though as he quickly scoops me up in his arms. He carries me to a bed and then places me on it. I don't argue. I don't say anything as he covers me up. I'm too tired to do anything but sleep.

I feel the mattress move as he climbs into bed with me. I'm

shocked when his arms go around me. I wouldn't have thought he was the snuggling type, but there is more to my beast of a man than I thought there was.

I feel his cock press against my ass, already hardening, and I freeze. I can't. Not yet.

"Sleep, Beauty. You're going to need your rest for what I have planned for you next."

I take a deep breath, relaxing. "Good night, Beast."

I drift quickly into sleep. I don't worry about what this stranger has done to me or could do to me in my sleep. I don't worry if he used a condom or not when he came inside me. I'm on birth control, and I'll get tested later. I won't be doing anything this stupid again anyway. And I don't wonder if the man holding me is Jake or another ex or a complete stranger. I don't think. I can't because he's taken even that from me.

3

BEAST

EARLY LIGHT PEEKS in through the blinds, telling me that it is time for me to go. I shouldn't have even stayed for as long as I did. Every minute that passes is another minute that she might wake and find out who I am. Despite how much I want to roll her over and fuck her, I can't. She won't want to fuck me, not after what I did. Not after she realizes who I am.

Still, I can't help but look at my beauty sleep. *So peaceful, so beautiful* are the only words I can think of that describe her. No, that's not right. I can think of a lot of fucking words. *Dangerous. Strong. Intelligent. Smart-mouthed. Disobedient.* And incredibly *stupid* for trusting someone like me.

I don't know what the hell she was thinking. If it weren't me that she'd said yes to, I would have taken her aside and yelled at her until she realized how stupid she was to trust a complete stranger so easily. I could have killed her. I could have done anything I wanted with her. *So stupid!*

I glance down at my sleeping beauty one last time. It has to be the last time. I can't do this again. I can't risk it. I promised myself, if she said yes, then that would be it. That I wouldn't see her again.

And I have to keep that promise to myself.

I slip out of bed and slowly put my clothes on. A small part of me hopes that she will wake up and see me. A small part hopes that I am wrong. That when she sees it is me, she will be happy and want more of me instead of running away in fear. I know that will never happen though, and even if she woke up and saw me and still wanted me, I couldn't let her be in my life. She deserves better than me.

I finish dressing, and then there is nothing left to do but say good-bye and never look back. I stand over her, thinking back to last night. I never woke her again to fuck her. That might have been my biggest fucking mistake, not taking her again while I still had my chance. I couldn't though. Watching her sleep was all I could do. She was too perfect to wake.

I think back to what she called me last night. *Beast*, I think it was. I frown. I don't know why she picked that name for me. It's far too tame for what I am. I wish I were just a Beast. I wish that were all that I was.

I reach down and tuck her gorgeous hair behind her ear so that I can get one last look. Her plump lips still bear the tiniest bit of stain from her red lipstick. I want to stay around and hear her sassy mouth speak to me again. I want those lips wrapped around my cock as I shoot my load down her throat. I want those fuckable lips crushed on mine.

Never again.

I don't tempt myself by kissing those lips. If I do, I will never leave.

Instead, I turn and walk out of her life. "Good-bye, Beauty."

4

SCARLETT

I WAKE up to an empty bed. Not surprising. I didn't figure Mr. Mysterious would stick around long enough for me to see him in the light of day. I sigh as I lie in the comfy hotel bed. I don't want to get up. As soon as I do, last night will be nothing but a memory. A *really* good memory.

I smile and know that this smile isn't going to leave my face for the rest of the day. I glance at the clock. It's six thirty. I slept in thirty minutes later than I usually do. I have an hour to head back to my apartment, shower, change, and make it to the office by my usual seven thirty. Or I could call in sick and stay in this bed all day, reliving last night, until I'm supposed to meet Kinsley. I am the boss after all.

What good is it, being the boss, if you can't take a break whenever you want?

I hear my phone vibrating nonstop though, and I know it wouldn't be fair to my employees to stay in bed all day. *And what good would it do anyway?*

He's clearly gone, never to return to my life. It was a one-night stand. Nothing more.

Except it was everything more.

My phone stops for a second but then begins buzzing again. I hop out of bed and instantly regret the motion. *Fuck, I'm sore.* I wasn't expecting that after only one round of fucking. I've certainly gone more than one round with a man before, but none of those times left me feeling this sore.

I push through the feeling and search for my phone. It buzzes again, and on a chair in the corner of the room, I see my purse sitting neatly along with my clothes from last night. Not that I can wear those after he destroyed them. *Shit.* I'm going to have to call someone to get me clothes to wear out of here.

I'll worry about that later.

I grab my phone out of my purse. I already have five missed calls from Preston. More than a hundred unread emails. And a dozen or more text messages from various employees needing answers to their questions. I smile though when I see one from Kinsley.

Kinsley: Can't wait to see ya in a few!

I type my quick response to her, ignoring the rest of the messages until I at least get into work.

Me: Can't wait either! I have some hot news of my own.

Kinsley: Yes! It's been too long since I've gotten to live vicariously through your sex life. I always feel bad about sharing my married hot sex.

I sigh. It's not that I don't like hearing Kinsley's sex stories, but they always revolve around the same man—a man whom I have to see multiple times a year and spend holidays with. It is a little hard to enjoy my Thanksgiving dinner with them after she's told me that Killian fucked her over the dining room table when she was trying to prepare for dinner.

I stop texting Kinsley and look at the dress that is neatly folded on the chair. I unfold it to see how much damage is done and if I can salvage it at all. My mouth drops when I see the dress. The rip is completely gone.

I'm stunned, trying to think back to last night. *He most definitely ripped the dress in half. So, how did it magically get back in one piece? Did I just dream up the whole encounter last night?*

I look closer, and that's when I see a tag sticking out of the top of the dress. The bastard bought me a new version of the identical dress to the one I was wearing. I don't know when he found the time to do that last night.

Or did he do that earlier, even before I said yes? Was he prepared for any scenario?

I shake my head as I put on my dress and text my driver the address to pick me up so that I can go home and change before heading into work. My driver, George, replies right away. He's more than used to picking me up in strange places. If I were smart, I would just carry a change of clothes in my purse for this exact situation, but there is nothing like going back home and showering in my own shower. I love my shower. And, most of the time, the men end up in my bed, not the other way around.

I run my hand through my wild hair as I look around the room for any signs of who the man was. *Who was my beast?*

I don't see any signs though. It's like he wasn't here. I walk into the living room, and I know it's where he fucked me, but there are no signs of anything that happened here either. The rope is gone. The furniture is perfectly in place. It doesn't even smell like sex in here. But it doesn't stop every feeling from last night from cropping back into me.

I walk to the door and open it without glancing back. I can't glance back. If I do, I will spend the rest of my day in this room, dreaming about a man I can never have again. So, I leave without a good-bye.

My phone rings, and this time, I answer Preston, knowing that work is the only thing that has a chance of distracting me.

"You're late," Preston says as I walk into my office.

I smile at my neurotic assistant. I know I'm not more than ten minutes late. Although unusual for me, it is not a big deal. I reach for my latte that is already sitting on my desk and take a sip. It's already starting to get cold from sitting on my desk for the last ten minutes, not that I really care.

"We have a meeting in twenty minutes with possible new financial managers. Later, you have several meetings to decide on whom the new financial managers are going to be. The designers want you to approve your new eye-shadow line. You need to decide on the final design for the box the shadows will go in.

"Then, you have about a million emails that you need to get through in thirty minutes because you have to meet with the models for the fall line to ensure they are up to your standards.

"You have a lunch with the designer you hired to help with the men's line.

"You have to prep for interviews you have with several magazines first thing tomorrow morning.

"And then you have—"

"Take a breather, Preston. That's why I hired you—to ensure that I am everywhere I'm supposed to be. I don't really need to hear every detail of my schedule for today. Just make sure I'm there. And I already told you to cancel everything after one p.m."

Preston's mouth drops. "I didn't think you were serious. You've never canceled anything before, and you really can't cancel anyway. You have—"

"I have nothing after one today."

Preston's eyes grow large. "Scarlett, that really can't happen. You have—"

"Nothing after one today," I say more sternly.

"But you have to prep and then—"

"I don't need to prep. I've done hundreds of interviews before. I think I can handle tomorrow's without meeting with Cynthia to prep. My lunch meeting is fine, as long as it is done by one. And anything I have scheduled for later, you can handle. That's why I pay you the big bucks."

Preston frowns, although he knows everything I said is true.

If I didn't show up for work for the next year, he could handle everything just as well as I could—if not better. He's been my right-hand man from basically the start. He's the one who keeps me sane and going at work. He knows what decision I'm going to make before I do.

His only flaw is his confidence in himself. As an assistant, he's great. He keeps me in line and will do everything and more. He will stand up for me, no matter the situation. But, when it comes to standing up for himself, the guy lacks balls.

Even when I increased his salary to almost half a million a year, he tried to talk me out of it. He thought I was crazy for giving him that much money, said he was an assistant and I shouldn't pay him that much.

What he doesn't realize is, he is more than just an assistant. He's *me* when I'm gone. If only I could give him the confidence to actually be me, then I wouldn't have to work the crazy hours that I do. Starting work at seven thirty and then not getting off until ten, just in time to hit up a bar, and then start it all over again is not exactly what I imagined doing all my life when I started this company. I hate to admit it, but I imagined I would be married with kids by this point in my life. Even if I enjoy the one-night stands and putting myself and my company first, I still thought that was where I would be at this point in my life. And if I ever want a chance at having a family at some point, I'm going to need someone I can depend on.

"But I just can't—"

I glare at Preston. "You can. Whatever decisions need to be made after one today are yours to make. I don't want a text message asking me which color is better for the font on an ad. I don't want a phone call saying there is an emergency in shipping. I don't want an email asking if I want to do a press interview. Whatever it is, you handle it!"

Preston sighs. "Yes, Scarlett."

I smile. "Now, let's get to work, so I can go see my best friend."

"The first firm of financial guys are here," Preston says, poking his head into my office.

I sigh as I look at the emails that have piled up on my computer. I've barely even made a dent in them, and now, I have to pause to take a meeting that I don't really care about.

"Okay, let them in," I say, standing from my desk and trying to apply a smile to my face.

I hate interviewing new financial guys. They are always so boring, and I'm afraid they are totally going to burst my happy bubble that I'm in after having the best sex of my life. The fake smile on my face easily turns into a real smile as soon as I let a few memories from last night creep back into my brain.

The rope around my wrists. The feel of his rough hands on my breasts. My legs wrapped around his body.

"Miss Bell, my name is Dustin Morgan, here with guys from Morgan Real Estate. Is now a good time to meet with you?" a man who is suddenly standing in front of me says.

I look from him to Preston, who is standing next to him. He rolls his eyes at me because he knows I was just zoned out when I went back to my one-night stand. It isn't the first time that has happened while I've been at work today, and I know it won't be the last.

"Sorry." I try to lighten the smile on my face, but I can't. "Yes, now is a good time. I'm Scarlett Bell. Nice to meet you..."

"Dustin Morgan," the man says, smiling and extending his hand to me.

I shake it and study the man who looks close to my age. He's wearing an expensive suit, and he has dark black hair and a tight smile.

"These are my associates, Kristopher Bryant and Felix Guild."

"Nice to meet you," I say to both of the men before shaking each one's hand.

His associates seem quiet in comparison to Dustin. I glance to Kristopher, who is good-looking, but there is nothing special about his suit and blond hair. I peek at the last man, Felix. He looks at me with such intensity in his eyes that my heart stops just a little.

I glance back to Dustin, unable to look at Felix without fearing for my life.

At any other time, these three hot men standing in my office would have my full attention. I would be deciding which one I would hire and which one would be in my bed tonight. Not right now though. Now, I can barely concentrate on them because, if I hit on any of them, I know none of them would be able to live up to my experience last night. So, why even bother?

We all take our seats, and then Dustin begins droning on and on about why I should choose his company over any of the others. Thank God for Preston, who keeps the conversation going and asks all the important questions, because I am barely registering any of their words.

I'm back with Beast in the darkness, and that's where I stay for the rest of the day until I leave to go see Kinsley.

5

SCARLETT

GEORGE DROPS me off at Eileen's Cheesecake at one thirty p.m. exactly. My smile brightens when I see my best friend already seated at a table with a large cheesecake placed in the middle. I quickly walk over to her, and she stands and immediately hugs me.

"I'm so glad you made it. I wasn't sure until I saw that you were actually here," Kinsley says.

I frown. "I told you I would be here, so I'm here." I glance down at the table as I take a seat opposite her. "I see you've already taken the liberty of ordering an entire cheesecake. I know this is supposed to be about us catching up and all, but I don't think that, even in our best days in college, we could have finished off an entire cheesecake between the two of us."

Kinsley smiles. "I'm hungry, and I will eat an entire cheesecake if I want to. You wouldn't deny a pregnant woman something she was craving, would you?"

I scream, and within seconds, I'm up and out of my seat, crushing my best friend with a hug. "You're really pregnant?" I half-ask and half-squeal.

Kinsley laughs. "Yes, I'm really pregnant, but I would appreciate it if you didn't tell the whole world yet."

"My best friend is pregnant!" I scream to the two other people seated at a table outside the small restaurant.

A few passersby stop and look at me like I'm crazy, but I don't care. She's pregnant.

I go back to my seat, not able to contain my excitement. "How? When?"

Kinsley laughs again. "I think you know how. You see, when two people love each other, the husband sticks his—"

"Stop!" I laugh. "You know what I meant. I thought you said you didn't want children. I thought that was what you and Killian decided was for the best after..." I let my voice trail off, not able to bring those memories back, but it doesn't damper Kinsley's smile.

"That's just what we told everyone to keep them from asking questions or pressuring us. We've been trying to get pregnant again for a long time. And, now, it's finally happened, and I'm far enough along that we should be safe this time."

"How far along?"

"Three months to the day," she says, smiling.

"Three months! Why didn't you tell me sooner?"

"I had a doctor appointment yesterday that gave us the okay to tell everyone. That's why I haven't wanted to see you these past few months. I knew, if I saw you, I wouldn't be able to keep this a secret."

"Well, I'm happy for you and Killian. If anyone deserves it, you do," I say, beaming.

Kinsley slices the cheesecake and places a slice on each of our plates. We each take a bite of our cheesecake at the same time, and we both moan as the rich, cheesy goodness fills our mouths.

"Do you know if it's a boy or girl yet?"

Kinsley smiles. "Nope, and we aren't finding out until the baby is born."

I frown. "Really? I don't think I could handle not knowing. Don't you want to know, so you can decorate and buy gender-specific things? How am I supposed to know what to design and make for my little niece or nephew if I don't know if it is a boy or girl?"

Kinsley laughs in between mouthfuls of cheesecake. This might not be the most nutritious meal for a pregnant woman, but if I get my way, Kinsley is going to be eating food like this all the time, so my niece or nephew will come out all plump and cute-looking.

"After waiting years and thinking my time was almost up for this to happen for us, I think we can wait to find out the gender. All we care about is that the baby is happy and healthy."

I frown. "What do you mean, time was almost up?"

"I'm thirty-two, turning thirty-three in just a few months. By thirty-five, any pregnancy is automatically considered high risk. I've been through enough miscarriages and shots in my ass from in vitro that I wasn't going to risk a high-risk pregnancy on top of all my other issues. I was running out of time."

I nod, letting that sink in.

We are the same age. I haven't thought about settling down with a man for a long time. The last serious boyfriend I had was in college. I thought I would end up married to him, but after we broke up for the millionth time during our senior year, we never got back together. I thought, eventually, I would find someone who would convince me that the whole marriage thing was what I wanted, but so far, the single life has been good to me. I know plenty of women who have had kids in their late thirties or early forties. I never thought it would be an issue until I saw my best friend struggle with infertility issues for years. Just because it happens later in life for some women, it doesn't mean it could happen to me.

But do I even want kids and a husband?

"So, what about your news?" Kinsley asks, studying me.

I lay my fork down even though I'm only halfway through my delicious cheesecake. I'm not sure I really care to eat anymore.

"What news?" I ask.

Kinsley laughs. "The man who had you smiling like an idiot before you found out my news. Who's the guy?"

I freeze, not sure I should really tell Kinsley about last night. She will overanalyze it and convince me it meant something. Persuade me I should text him and ask him out. Convince me that last night could lead to love instead of being what it was—a one-night stand that I will never forget. He has probably already moved on to his next catch for tonight. I'm nothing but a distant memory to him.

"He was nobody. Just another stupid one-night stand."

"I don't believe a word out of your mouth, Scar. Now, spill. That's what you would tell me to do if things were reversed," Kinsley says.

I study her as my smile returns to my face. It was an amazing night, and if I don't tell her, I might burst. Even if it means I will have to deal with her opinions about it being something that it was not. Even if she thinks it was stupid of me and dangerous.

"Okay, okay," I say.

Both of our faces light up with excitement. We're like two school-girls who are about to talk about their crushes.

"So, I was sitting at this bar—"

"Two Hundred Sixty-Nine Bar," Kinsley interrupts me, already knowing which bar I'm talking about.

I smile. "Yes. I was sitting there, and of course, no men were at the bar. I mean, *none*. I was drinking my sorrows away, knowing that I wasn't going to be bringing any men home to my bed, when I got a text message."

Kinsley leans forward, listening to my every word. "Who was it?"

"I don't know. The message was from an unknown number. I didn't think the message was for me. But it was."

"What do you mean? Who was it? It had to have been someone you knew if they had your number. Don't keep a pregnant woman in suspense. Just tell me!"

I laugh. "I don't know who it was."

"You didn't ask his name at any point during this?"

"Of course I did. But he didn't want to do names. He just texted me to meet him at the Waldorf, and I did."

Kinsley frowns. "I should so lecture you for meeting a complete stranger in a hotel, but since you are still alive and well, I won't. But don't do it again. My baby needs his or her Aunt Scar."

Kinsley rubs her stomach, and I smile.

"Duly noted. I will not meet a complete stranger in a hotel room again."

"What did he look like?"

"I don't know."

"What the hell, Scar? Did you fuck this guy or not?"

My smile widens at my friend's use of a cuss word. She doesn't cuss often, but when she does, it is by far the most adorable thing on the planet.

"It was dark."

"And you didn't think to turn the lights on?"

"Of course I did, but having the lights off made it better. More mysterious. He took control from the second I entered the room, and I sort of liked it. It was the best fuck of my life, Kins."

Kinsley sits back in her seat. "So, are you going to see this mysterious-best-fuck-of-your-life guy again?"

I sink into my chair, hating my answer, but having to say it anyway because I already know the answer to that question. It's an answer that I've been avoiding since I woke up this morning.

"No, I'm not going to see him again."

To my surprise, Kinsley doesn't have a reply to that.

Who I am kidding?

She completely has a reply but just isn't telling me.

"Come on, tell me what you are thinking, oh wise one."

Kinsley smiles. "I'm not saying anything. This is something you are going to have to figure out on your own."

I sigh and then look up, and I see Killian walking toward us with a serious grimace on his face.

"Hey, Kill! Congrats on finally knocking up your wife," I say, getting out of my chair to give him a hug.

He hugs me, and when I let him go, I see the tiniest bit of a smile slip onto his lips.

He turns to Kinsley, who hops out of her seat and smiles at her husband. He instantly smiles back and takes her into his arms, possessively holding her while he holds on to her stomach.

"You have a good meeting, babe?" Kinsley asks.

"Not really, but seeing you makes everything better, princess," Killian says to his wife. Then, he firmly kisses her on the lips.

My heart warms every time I see them together. And, now, they are having a baby. God, they are such grown-ups. And they couldn't look happier.

It's what I want, a little voice in my head says.

I shake my head. *No way. I love running my empire. I love...*

Except what if running an empire isn't enough anymore?

Maybe that's why, even when I find a new man to fuck every night, it is never enough to keep me satisfied for more than a day.

Except last night was enough. If I had that every night, I wouldn't care if I were married with a baby on the way.

But most one-night stands are not like last night.

What if I want marriage? What if I want to have a baby before it's too late? What if I want everything Kinsley has?

I sigh. The problem is, I don't really know what I want, and I hate that because, usually, I know exactly what I want. I always thought, when I was ready to settle down and start a family, there would be a clear sign pointing me that way.

Maybe Kinsley being pregnant is that sign?

6

BEAST

My phone buzzes, and I jump to pull it out of my pocket, hoping that it's her. I glare at my phone when I see that it's not her.

I answer the call but don't bother saying hello.

"We have a job for you."

"I thought I was already in the middle of the most important job I could have."

"Yes, well, now, we have another for you."

"What's the pay?"

He laughs. "Really? You used to never care about pay. It used to be all about the thrill of the chase. Thrill of doing something you love. I didn't know you had changed so much."

He damn well knows why everything has changed. I'm not going to sit here and fucking explain it to him.

"What's. The. Pay?" I spit my words out.

He laughs again. "Come in and find out for yourself, but you know she's not going to be happy if you turn the job down."

I end the call. I don't need him fucking reminding me how pissed *she's* going to be if I don't take the job. I already fucking know.

So much for having an easy, relaxing day.

I walk over and pull a suit out of the closet. Even when I'm supposed to have a day off, I never get a day off. After these jobs are over, I need to take a vacation. I need to forget about my fucked up life for a while and just disappear. Maybe think about changing professions even.

In the meantime, I have to find a better way to deal with this tension.

I pull out my phone and text something I shouldn't.

7

SCARLETT

UNKNOWN: *I know you are thinking about me.*

Me: *I am not. I don't even know who this is.*

Unknown: *You're thinking, "How could a stranger turn me on so much? How could a stranger know me so well?"*

Me: *You're right. It's because I don't think you are a stranger at all.*

I turn my phone off. He shouldn't be texting me. I thought it was only supposed to be one night. I can't let him think that it is going to be anything more. I can't let him pull me back into the temptation of having him more than one night when I know it's not going to lead to anything else but dissatisfaction with every other man.

Not after I've realized I want more than just one night with him. In order to satisfy my thirst for him, I would need night after night after night for years. And, even then, I'm not sure I would have enough of him. And if I can't have that, then I want something more meaningful than one-night stands that will never live up to him. I want something that could lead to marriage and babies. That might be the only way to forget about him.

"Scarlett!" Preston says as he knocks on the door to my office.

I motion for him to enter. He does, and I watch as the door swings shut behind him.

"Why is your phone turned off?"

I stare down at my phone that I just turned off and laid on my desk. "Because I'm trying to ignore a one-night stand who won't go away."

Preston rolls his eyes. "You can block people's numbers, you know. You don't need to turn your phone off."

"What's up?" I ask, not willing to tell him that I can't block his number. I don't have the self-control to do that because I want him to text me.

"You have a meeting with the new financial guy in five minutes."

"What financial guy?"

Preston slumps into the chair in the corner of the office. I raise my eyebrows at him. I've never seen him so flustered on the job before. He is always the epitome of professional.

I stand up from behind my desk and move to the chair next to him, taking a seat. "What's going on, Preston?"

"I can't handle this! You can't just leave me in charge on such short notice again. Do you know how many decisions I had to make yesterday? About a million."

I laugh as Preston continues rambling.

I know the feeling. I make about a million decisions a minute.

"I just can't handle it. This is not what I signed up for when I took this job as your assistant. I am supposed to be *assisting* you, not making the decisions myself. I've taken a whole container of Pepto and antacids, trying to calm my stomach. But I'm a nervous wreck.

"I had to finalize the colors for your new eye shadow, pick the model who is going to be featured in your new makeup ad campaign, interview a financial manager since our last one retired, plan your schedule for today without you. It's just..." Preston whips his head to look at me. "I have a life, too, you know. I have a girlfriend whom I promised to take out to a late dinner, but I had to cancel on her, and—"

"Wait!" I raise my eyebrows at him. "You have a girlfriend?" I spit out without even thinking.

I always just assumed Preston was gay, like ninety percent of the men who work for me. He's a petite, scrawny-looking man, whose favorite thing in the world is fashion. He usually wears skinny jeans and a tight-fitting shirt. Depending on the trends, his hair changes just as fast as his clothes, but right now, he is a blond, his hair spiked up in the center with the sides shaved. Occasionally, I've even seen him wear a little makeup.

I had no idea he had a girlfriend.

Preston rolls his eyes at me. "I know, I know. You thought I was gay. I'm not."

How many times have I gotten completely naked in front of this man because I thought he was gay? How many dirty details from my sexual encounters have I overshared with him?

I shrug. *Oh well.*

"It's not that exactly. It's just...I have never heard you..." I stop when I see Preston staring at me, like he knows I thought he was gay, and there is no point in denying it. He's right, so I stop. "Okay, you caught me. I thought you were gay, but to my defense, you never corrected me or talked about a girlfriend before."

"That's because we have only been dating for two weeks, and I don't think it is very professional to bring up home situations at work."

I smile at my workaholic assistant. "You must think I'm a terrible boss then because that is all I talk about."

Preston shakes his head. "You're the boss. You are allowed to talk about anything you want."

"So are you! Preston, you've been with me for almost eight years now. I don't think of you as just my assistant. I think of you as one of my closest friends. You've spent Thanksgiving with me for the last three years, for God's sake. Please stop acting like you are just like any other employee. Get some balls, and get over not being able to make decisions. You can so make decisions as well or even better than me.

"Now, tell me about this new girlfriend."

Preston blushes, but then his phone buzzes in his pocket, and he jumps up. "The new financial guy is here. I'll see him in."

I sigh and get up as well. I slowly walk over to my desk, not excited to hear what the new financial guy Preston hired has to say. I'm sure he's great. I know Preston wouldn't hire anyone who wasn't anything less than amazing. Still, talking with financial guys is not the highlight of my day. I would rather think about clothes and makeup or, better yet, how I'm going to find me a husband. Not talk about the business's finances, which I already know are better than fine.

"I want a rain check though on hearing about the girlfriend, Preston!" I shout to him as he leaves my office.

I glance down at my phone that is still dark, sitting on my desk. I consider turning it back on and checking to see if *he* texted. From just thinking about what he might have texted me, my nipples harden to attention beneath the white dress I'm wearing that scoops low in the middle. My finger hovers over the On button when a knock sounds at my door.

The door swings open again, and Preston pokes his head in.

"This is Mr. Jake Walton, senior financial manager," Preston says.

My mouth drops as Jake appears in my doorway. *What the hell? This has to be a joke.*

I haven't seen Jake since I broke it off with him in college.

Jake, on the other hand, doesn't seem surprised at all that I'm who he is visiting today. He smirks a little when he sees me staring at him with my mouth half-open, and then his eyes lock on my hard nipples that are very visible beneath the thin white material. He probably thinks they are hard because of him and not because of a possible text message from a stranger. Never in my life had I wished more that I had worn a bra.

"I've got it from here, Preston. Scarlett and I go way back," Jake says.

Preston stares in horror from Jake to me. He knows he has fucked up, but I can't let him think that. I want him to feel confident in his decisions. I'm sure Jake is a very competent financial manager. In the future, I just need to give Preston a list of all my ex-boyfriends and one-night stands, so he doesn't accidentally hire one again.

Preston mouths the word, *Sorry*.

I shake my head, doing my best to smile at him, and then he slumps out of my office, closing the door behind himself.

"Well, that was deceptive. There are other ways to get a girl to go out with you, you know, Jake. You can't just trick my assistant into hiring you and think that I will go out with you."

Jake grins again as he takes a seat in the chair in front of my desk even though I didn't invite him to. "Are you finished?"

"What?"

"Are you finished? I didn't come here to ask you out. I have a fiancée. My firm assigned me to your company after Lloyd Mayor retired. And I was supposed to have an interview with you yesterday anyway. I thought you would take one look at me and want someone else. That's why I requested this meeting with you personally today. I didn't want you to think I was taking advantage of you not being at the interview yesterday."

He has a fiancée, is all I hear. He has a fiancée.

The man's a dick. He came here, and that is the first thing out of his mouth. He has to flaunt it to me that he has a fiancée while I have nothing.

My inner voice reminds me, *That isn't true.*

I have an entire company while he, I'm sure, makes decent money while working at a financial firm, but it is nothing compared to what I have.

"So, are you okay with me being your financial manager?" Jake asks.

I fold my arms over my chest as I study Jake. He looks almost exactly the same as he did in college. Light-brown hair tamed nicely on top of his head; brown eyes that say, *Take me home to mama*, without an ounce of danger lurking behind them; clean-shaved face; and a nice suit that could use a little more tailoring to show off his muscles that seem to have gotten larger since the last time I saw him.

"Yes."

Jake smiles, and I see the tension that I must have missed seep out of his eyes. He thought I would say no. Like I have a chance of that happening now. I have to at least appear that I am over him. Because I was. Before he walked in that door, I was completely over him. I have barely thought about him since I broke up with him during our senior year of college. He's too perfect. He always wanted the American dream—married with two kids on the way. A wife who would stay home with the kids. I didn't want any of those things back then.

But now...

Now, that might be exactly what I need to move on from the best sex of my life. It might be exactly what is missing from my life.

I crook my head to one side as I look at him. He's good-looking; he always has been. And even though I don't ache for him to rip off my clothes and take me like animals do, even though I don't remember the sex to be anything special, I still want him. I want the dream. I think back to the first time I saw him in college. I was getting out of a class and he was horsing around playing touch football with several guys in the open field between buildings. I remember stopping to watch. Half of the men were shirtless after all. But it wasn't just his body that caught my attention. It was his confidence, his smile. After I saw that I didn't give him a choice but to go out with me. He was and still is an all-around good guy. He's the exact type of guy who can give me my own happily ever after. Instead of daydreaming about one-night-stand guy, I should be convincing Jake to marry me and give me everything I never knew I wanted.

"Marry me?" I spit out without thinking.

Jake's eyes widen when I say the words, but he doesn't laugh or immediately tell me no. He's too nice of a guy to do either of those things.

"I have a fiancée," he says again, like that's a reason for not being able to say yes.

He hasn't married her yet, and as far as I'm concerned, he must not be that into her if he is here with me. If he didn't want to jeopardize his relationship with her, he wouldn't be here with me.

"So?" I run my tongue over my bottom lip.

He glares at me. "How about I take you out for dinner as two friends, and you can tell me what's going on?"

My lips curl up into a tight smile. "Yes."

8

BEAST

ME: You want more than one night. Admit it. You want more. You want to take my cock between your fucking lips until I shoot cum down your throat. You want to know how it would feel to take me in your ass. You want it all. Admit it.

"Are you listening? Put your damn phone away!" my boss shouts at me.

"Yes, sir. I'll arrange a meeting for the day after tomorrow, and the job will be done by the end of the week."

"Good. Don't fuck this up, son. You've fucked up too many things already."

I glare at him. "I'm the best. That's why you are sending me."

"You are also the only one who has royally fucked up everything before."

I abruptly stand up, knocking my chair backward. "Then, send someone else if you think I'm a fuckup. I quit!"

I storm out of his office and head toward the stairs. I need to take the stairs down the ten flights to try to cool off. Plus, I know I won't make it out of this building without him sending someone to remind me why I can't quit. Because he owns me.

Fuck.

I look down at my phone and begin typing again. I thought just texting her would quiet the desires she spurs inside me. I was wrong.

9

SCARLETT

I DON'T BOTHER CHANGING for my date with Jake tonight. I already know the white dress that I'm wearing is perfect for seducing a man. From the stares I have gotten all day from the few straight men who work for me, I know it's a hit. And I don't want Jake to think I'm desperate because I'm not. I'm the furthest thing from desperate.

I didn't even think about *him* as I went about my work today. Okay, that's not true. When I wasn't thinking about Jake, I was thinking about the mysterious stranger who shouldn't have texted me back. I still haven't turned my phone back on to see if he sent me any other messages, but it didn't keep me from thinking about him every second I got.

I'm thinking about *him* as I contemplate turning my phone back on when I hear Jake's voice stir me back to reality.

"It's eight thirty. You ready for dinner yet, or do you need to work some more? I'm fine either way. I have plenty of work to keep me busy if you aren't ready yet."

I glance at the clock on my office wall. *How did it get so late so fast?* I still have hours' worth of work, but I should call it a night. I run a hand through my hair, loosening it from this morning even more.

"Yeah, I guess I should call it quits," I say even though I feel like I should work longer, especially after ducking out yesterday to spend time with Kinsley. "I just need to tell Preston that I'm heading out, and he should go home," I say.

Jake nods, and I walk past him to Preston's office, which is next door to mine.

His door is already open, so I just have to poke my head in. "Go home."

Preston lifts his head from the computer he is working on. "I will soon. I just need to—"

"No. Go home to that girlfriend of yours, and take her on that date you missed because of me."

Preston nods but doesn't get up from his computer. I walk over and unplug it, not caring what damage is done to the computer or what info he will lose that he didn't save.

"Shit, Scarlett. I was working on your schedule for tomorrow. I still need to send a couple of more emails."

"No, you don't. Go home, Preston."

I wait and watch as he gathers his things and then leaves with a scowl on his face. I walk back to my office, passing Jake, who is standing in the doorway with his arms folded over his chest, smirking at me. I ignore him as I walk to my desk to grab my purse and things.

"You're one bossy boss. Should I be worried you are going to boss me around, like you did him?" Jake teases.

I glance up at him. "Yes," I answer honestly because I already know I'm a bossy woman.

He steps forward. "You are the most intimidating woman I know. It's one of the reasons you and I never worked out. You're too much woman for me, Scarlett."

I bite my lip as he says my name. He's one of the few people who always called me Scarlett instead of shortening it. No matter how long we dated, I was always Scarlett, never Scar.

"I'll work on the intimidation thing."

Jake laughs. "Yeah, you work on that."

"I will."

He laughs again. "You can't change who you are. You're bossy, controlling, intimidating, and sexy as hell. That's who you are, Scarlett."

I smile as I walk past him.

"What's the devious grin for?" Jake asks.

"You called me sexy. That means, there is hope yet."

"Now, just wait a minute. I didn't mean—"

I wink at him. "Come on. Let's go on our *date*."

"Scarlett, I already told you, it's not a—"

I turn and suddenly kiss him on the cheek, shutting him up.

I'm going to marry him. He might not agree yet, but he is exactly what I need—stable, ambitious, settled. He wants to get married and have babies, and he already knows everything about me. He's exactly what I need.

10

SCARLETT

"So, where are you taking me?" I ask.

"I was going to leave it up to you. You never let me choose where we went before. Why would I think tonight was going to be any different?"

I frown. I know that I'm bossy and usually in control, but maybe I always took control because he never did, no matter how much I desperately wanted him to.

"Well, I'm letting you choose everything we do tonight. I don't want to have to make another decision the rest of the night. I'm leaving everything up to you—from where we go to what I order to whether or not you take me home and fuck me later."

Jake frowns and gives me a dirty look at that last one.

"Relax. I said you get to decide that one," I say, winking, as we head out of the elevator of Beautifully Bell Enterprises.

It doesn't wipe the frown from his face or relax his tense shoulders beneath his suit that isn't the least bit wrinkled, despite him working in it all day long. I glance down at my own dress that has a few wrinkles in it and even a small stain near the hem that I don't know where it came from. Even his ordinary life is perfect compared to mine.

"So, where are we going?" I ask again as we exit the building. I consider calling my driver to come take us somewhere, but I'm going to let him guide our evening, so I don't.

Jake thinks for a minute, considering where, and then throws out the name of one of the most expensive steak houses in New York City.

I raise my eyebrows at his suggestion, but he's the one deciding, so I just answer, "Sounds good to me."

We begin walking two blocks before I can't stand waiting for him to figure out that we sure as hell aren't walking the thirty blocks from here to that steak house.

"Are you going to hail a cab, or do I need to call my driver?"

"Neither. I'm driving."

"You own a car? In New York City? Who does that?"

He smiles. "Me."

He turns us into a parking garage and walks over to a black Honda Civic.

I sigh. Of course the man I want to marry doesn't even have a nice car.

I climb into the very sensible car as Jake climbs into the driver's seat. It's not that I need a man to have lots of money and expensive things. Despite running a beauty and fashion empire, I'm not overly materialistic. Okay, I am, but I can buy my own nice things. I just want him to buy nice things for himself, too. Especially when I know how much I am paying him, so he can easily afford more than this car on the salary I am paying him alone. And I know I'm not his only client, so he makes more than enough to own a nicer car.

"Nice car," I say in a snarky voice.

"Thank you," he says, ignoring my snark.

The car ride to the restaurant is long. Neither of us talks, and Jake doesn't bother turning the radio on to drown out the silence. He probably enjoys the silence, thinks it's calming. I hate the silence. I consider taking out my phone and seeing if I have any more messages, but I don't. I'm going to give Jake everything I've got.

When we pull up to the steak house, Jake valets his car. I smile when I see the valet, who is used to parking expensive Mercedes and Teslas, climb into his car to go park it.

Jake holds open the door to the restaurant, and I walk inside. We are seated at a table almost immediately. The waiter comes over shortly after we are seated. "Can I get you anything to drink?" the waiter asks, looking at me. I turn my attention to Jake. "I'm letting my date for tonight decide," I say, smiling as sweetly as I can.

"Excellent. Sir, what are we having? I can recommend some wine, if you would like," the waiter says.

That's when I realize that Jake might not order wine or alcohol at all. I don't think I can survive tonight without a drink. I need a drink. *Order the wine*, I think over and over in my head. I hope that Jake will get the hint that wine is what I need.

Jake smiles at me. "No need for recommendations. I was here about a month ago when I proposed. If I remember correctly, your Stag's Leap Cask 23 wine was an excellent choice. We will share a bottle of that."

The waiter's eyes brighten. "Congratulations," he says to the two of us before he runs off to get us our wine.

I smile as Jake frowns at how his plan backfired so magnificently. He brought me here to remind me that this is where he brought his fiancée. To make me jealous. To make me realize that he is serious, and it will never happen between us. He didn't count on the waitstaff playing right into my hands though.

"So, what is your fiancée's name?"

"Karissa."

"And? Give me details. How did you meet? What does she do? How'd you fall in love? Favorite sex position? Something."

To my surprise, Jake smiles at the last one. Maybe he is capable of lightening up a little bit.

"She's in finance as well. We met when she joined the firm as a financial analyst almost three years ago. She is now the best financial manager—after me, of course. While at a company retreat in Florida about six months after she joined, we fell in love. And doggy style is definitely my favorite."

I spit my water out when he answers my last question. Maybe he isn't as sweet and innocent as he used to be. Maybe there is a layer of danger lurking beneath what he shows the world.

The waiter brings us our wine, and then Jake orders us each a steak, and I'm surprised he remembers how I like it. I taste the wine, and it is delicious.

"What about you?"

I give him a confused look.

"Have any guys found themselves under the control of Scarlett Bell, or have you stomped on any hearts lately?"

"I don't stomp on men's hearts."

"You stomped on mine," he says suddenly, to my surprise.

"I'm sorry."

He shrugs. "It's old news. What I want to know is, why did you suddenly propose to me in your office? What's going on?"

I take another sip of my wine, so I don't have to answer him.

"Scarlett?"

"I've just finally realized it's what I want. I want everything that you have. I want to be married, I want kids, I want to be in love. I always thought having the amazing career would be enough. It's just not enough anymore."

Jake sits back, smiling and nodding. "You deserve all of those things."

"I just can't have those things with you?"

He nods. "I'm not that guy for you. I wish I were. If you had asked me three years ago, I would have said yes so fast. You were the one who got away, Scarlett."

"It's not too late," I say, hopeful, even though I know it is. It's too late. I shouldn't even be asking him to consider me when he has already proposed.

"It's not too late for you to find Mr. Perfect, Scarlett. It's too late for us though."

I sigh. "I know. I just have no idea how to go about finding Mr. Perfect, as you called him."

Jake laughs. "I wouldn't worry about that. As soon as the world finds out you are looking for something more than just one night, guys will be lining up to marry you. You are quite a catch, you know, even if you are intimidating."

"Thanks."

We finish eating while talking about nonsense things. The weather. Trips we have both enjoyed. Our careers. We don't mention my lack of a love life or his fiancée again.

"I can pay," I say when the waiter drops off our bill.

"Not a chance," Jake says sternly to me. "This was my last chance to take out the famous Scarlett Bell. I'm not letting you pay even if you are worth millions more than me."

I smile. "Thanks, Jake. I'm going to head to the ladies' room then. Excuse me."

He nods as I leave the table and head to the restroom. I immediately pull out my phone and turn it on. I have four missed text messages from *him*. I read through to the last one.

Unknown: Admit it, and I'll give you what you want. Admit it, and I'll find you.

Unknown: I know I'm already consuming your every thought. I know you want me to rip off that white dress you're wearing today. I saw your nipples piercing through the thin fabric. Your nipples grew hard because of me. I'm not a patient man. Just say the word.

Unknown: I know what you are doing. You are trying to resist the temptation. You are trying to pretend like the other night didn't happen. You are wrong to try. You can't resist. That night was just the beginning. I can give you so much more.

Unknown: He's not right for you. He wouldn't know what to do with a woman like you, Beauty. Just tell me yes, that you want me to remind you why you can't get me out of your head. Just tell me yes, and I will show you a whole new world you've never conquered before. Just say yes...

Me: Yes.

11

BEAST

BEAUTY: Yes.

Beauty: Where should I meet you?

I can't help but smile at my Beauty. She came to me last time, and now, it's my turn. It's my turn to capture her in the dark. And I can't wait to have her with Jake in the next room. I can't stand watching her go home with him, not until I have her first.

I walk deliberately past him, but he doesn't even glance up from his phone that he is staring at with a frown on his face. I've been watching him all evening, and I don't understand why he hasn't already made his move.

If I were here, having dinner with her, it wouldn't have lasted long. I wouldn't have been able to keep my hands from her hands. I wouldn't have been able to keep from undressing her with my eyes. And she wouldn't have been able to resist my look, knowing that I was going to undress her the second I got out of here. We wouldn't have lasted five minutes at dinner without needing each other again.

I turn my back to him and keep walking, forgetting about that bastard. I have more important things to worry about at the moment. Unlike him, I don't plan on squandering this moment. I plan on taking her. I plan on controlling her. I plan on devouring her.

I head straight to the restroom I know she's already in, most likely fantasizing about where she's supposed to meet me. I push the door open to the women's restroom, immediately turn off the lights, and lock the door behind me.

She doesn't scream, like most women would. Instead, she stiffens. She knows it's me, despite not seeing me, but she doesn't say a word. She doesn't have to. I already know what she's thinking. I know what she wants, and I plan on giving it to her.

"Miss me, Beauty?"

I watch in the mirror and am able to make out the faintest of her movements despite the darkness. My eyes, I suspect, adjust faster than hers. I've always been able to see easier than most in the dark. I watch as she runs her tongue across her lower lip, and then she slowly and deliberately moves her tongue to her upper lip, like she thinks I need some enticement before I fuck her. She doesn't need to know I'm already more than enticed, and I know just what to do.

"You didn't answer me, Beauty. Did. You. Miss. Me?"

"Yes," she breathes, slightly turning her head in my direction.

What I didn't expect is what she does next.

She doesn't bother turning around to face me as her hands move to the straps on her dress, lowering them down her shoulders. Her hand then moves to the back of her dress. She grabs the zipper with one hand and the top of her dress with the other, and then she begins to slowly pull the zipper down her back. I can't take my eyes off of her hand as she lowers the zipper until it stops just above the curve of her ass. I'm entranced by the small of her back as she slowly reveals her smooth skin to me. I can't take my eyes off of her.

I thought I knew this woman, but seeing her undress herself without me even asking might be the sexiest thing I've ever seen.

I growl when the dress drops to the floor in a heap at her feet. She's not wearing underwear again.

God, this woman, I moan silently to myself. *This wonderful, competent, sexy woman.*

She is going to be the death of me. And I'm going to enjoy dying slowly at her hands.

I walk over to her and immediately place my hands on her body. My hands continue moving all over her body, exploring, studying, learning every curve. I grab her neck, pulling her backward, so that I can kiss her while my hands find her breasts. She moans so softly in my grasp that I can barely hear her. It's like she's in a trance the second I touch her. And only I will be able to break the spell I've started.

"Haven't you learned yet that I'm the one who's supposed to tell you what to do?"

"Then, tell me," she says.

I gather her hair in my hands and pull so that her ear is right against my lips. "Put your hands on the counter and spread your legs."

She touches her throat, like she is trying to catch her breath, as my words seem to go in one ear and out the other. She doesn't move to obey me. But she won't get what she wants if she doesn't obey me.

"Now, Beauty." I slap her ass to remind her that I don't like being disobeyed. "Or I won't be able to give you what you want."

She stumbles forward, just barely grabbing ahold of the counter to keep herself from falling. She quickly regains her composure though as she spreads her legs and arches her back so that her ass is high in the air, begging me to give her what she wants. *And who am I not to give her everything she desires?*

The door to the restroom pushes against the lock, and I watch as Beauty jumps when she hears someone at the door. I smile because I know now that her heart isn't just racing for me; it's racing at the thought of getting caught in the act. I can see her short, shallow panting speed up as she waits for me to fuck her. I can see the liquid dripping down between her legs, begging for me to enter her. And I know, with each second that passes, she is going to grow heavier with need.

I begin slowly undressing, deliberately wanting to take this slow, but I know that I don't have enough time to enjoy her like I want. I undo my belt buckle on my pants and take my cock in my hand, quickly pulling a condom over my shaft. A cock that has been begging for her, begging to feel her wrapped around it again since that night.

I find her eyes in the reflection in the mirror. I know she can't really see me. I know her vision isn't good enough yet in the darkness to make out more than the whites in my eyes, although after a few more minutes her eyes will adjust. But I can see her. And her eyes say everything. Desire. Need. Longing. Wanting.

Jesus, the look is enough to undo a man.

I tangle my hand in her hair, pulling gently to ensure that I can keep looking at her gorgeous big eyes as I enter her. My cock rubs against her ass, begging for entrance. As I rub against her, she tilts her ass higher, begging for me to take her already.

I shouldn't do it. I shouldn't claim her ass, not like this. Not before ample prep. Not when I promised that I wouldn't hurt her. But my need to conquer all of her beats out the pain I might cause her since tonight might be my last chance to have her this way.

I don't give her any warning other than the tug of her hair as I drive my cock into her ass. She's tight—*God, she's tight*—as I drive inside her. I lock eyes with hers, looking for any hint of fear or pain, but there is none, only increased desire. Her lips are parted, and her cheeks are flushed, but I read nothing that says she hates me or wants me to stop.

"Good girl," I say as I begin moving inside her.

"Oh my God," she says.

Her words would be enough to undo me if I hadn't expected them and had already stopped to prevent myself from becoming completely undone.

I move again, and this time, it's with ravaged, fast-paced, unable-to-control-myself-any-longer thrusts. She matches me thrust for thrust, unable to control herself as well.

There is no speaking. Neither of us could if we wanted to. There are barely any groans or moans escaping her lips, most likely for fear of being heard. There is just us moving as one until we are both coming as one.

I collapse on top of her back, not able to keep myself from feeling all of her against my skin, if only for a second.

Fuck, I don't understand what this woman is doing to me. I don't understand how, even after I just had her, I still want her. That's never happened to me before. I've fucked countless women and never even thought about looking back after I left. But I know, after leaving her, it's going to be hard not to look back.

But I have to. This has to be the end. I have a job to do, and she would just complicate things.

I remove myself from her and find her dress on the floor as I tuck myself back into my pants. She stands slowly.

I toss the dress to her. "Get dressed, Beauty."

"You know, one of these times, you should let me be in control," she says with a grin slowly spreading over her face.

"Not a chance." *Because this isn't happening again.*

I unlock the door and walk out of the restroom before she has a chance to say something that'd make me change my mind.

12

SCARLETT

"You've got that goofy grin on your face again," Preston says as he walks into my office.

"So?" I ask, still smiling. From last time, I know that it's not going to disappear easily. I take a sip of my latte as I wait for Preston to continue.

"So your not-a-date with Mr. Walton turned into another one-night stand to add to your endless list?"

I frown. "No. He's engaged. I don't break up people who are serious about each other."

Preston sighs. "So then, who was it?"

"One-night-stand guy from before," I say.

Preston raises his eyebrows. "Really?"

"Yes. What's so shocking about that?"

"Nothing," Preston says, smiling. He begins to walk toward my door to exit.

"Is that all you came in here to say? To ridicule me for smiling about a guy I had sex with more than once?"

"No. I came to tell you that Mr. Walton requested an appointment with you this afternoon. Apparently, you made quite the impression on him."

I roll my eyes. "Please refer to Mr. Walton as Jake. And I did not. As I said before, he's engaged. And, as you might well have already guessed, Jake and I dated before, and it didn't work out. There's nothing between us."

"Sure, there's not." He disappears before I can say more.

Damn it! What could Jake want?

We've already discussed the business situation, so I doubt he has more to say there. I think for a minute. Probably has to do with taking time off for the wedding. I let whatever it is with Jake go. I have too much work to do today to worry about him—or my mysterious stranger, my Beast.

I just know there's not a chance in hell I'll be able to get him out of my head today, no matter how hard I try. I take out my phone and text him because I can't stand it if that was our last time.

Me: If it's possible, last night might have been better than the first. But I'm greedy. I want more. I want my chance to control your body like you have controlled mine. I think it's your turn to say yes.

I immediately turn my phone off after I send the text. He will text me later, and I will be happy to see his response. But, if I leave my phone on, I will be constantly checking it, and I won't get any work done. Instead, I will just have to settle on dreaming about his response.

I balance a pile of eye-shadow palettes in one hand with a stack of designs in the other as I walk with Preston back to my office. I feel my phone buzz in my pocket, and I immediately think it's *him*.

I realized quickly that having my phone turned off did nothing to help keep Beast out of my thoughts. And it annoyed Preston to death because he couldn't forward my calls to me. So, I ended up turning it back on. The only downside is, now, every time it buzzes, I think it's *him*.

"Preston, can you—"

"Already on it," Preston says as he reaches into my back pants pocket and pulls out my phone. "Miss Bell's office. Preston speaking."

Preston casually says his speech as we continue walking toward my office. I frown because I know it's not *him*. He's never called me before, only texted.

"Yes, she's right here," he says.

I sigh as Preston holds the phone up to my ear. "This is Scarlett."

"Miss Bell, we need to set up a meeting for you to approve the new lipstick colors," Teresa, head of my beauty department, says.

I give Preston a dirty look because this is something he should be handling, not me. But I answer anyway, "I have a meeting that I need to get to right now, but I can meet you in about an hour. Sound good?"

"Yes, Miss Bell, that will work fine."

"Good-bye."

Preston removes the phone from my ear. I'm just about to rip into him when we reach the door to my office, and I see Jake sitting somberly in the chair across from my desk that's angled so he can watch the door waiting for me to enter. I don't know what's happened, but I've seen that face before—on the day I broke up with him—and I know it's not good. I feel the eye-shadow palettes slipping from my grasp, dropping to the floor, one by one, until I'm only holding one. The designs in my other hand scatter to the floor as well. I don't care about either as I step forward toward Jake, who is looking down at the ground.

He looks up as I approach.

I attempt to smile, but it's fake. "What's wrong?"

Jake looks from me to Preston and then back to me, but he doesn't answer.

"Preston, can you give us a minute?"

Preston is already on the floor, trying to gather up the dropped eye shadows and designs. "Just give me one sec—"

"Now!" I say firmly.

"Okay, okay." Preston leaves the items on the floor and shuts the door behind himself, leaving me and Jake alone.

"What's wrong?" I ask as I walk around to the other side of my desk and take a seat, trying to give Jake some space.

"Karissa broke up with me."

My mouth drops open, but I don't know what to say. I feel horrible, as if it has anything to do with me. *It can't though, can it? We didn't do anything wrong.*

I wait for him to say more. I wait for him to explain. He doesn't though. Instead, he just stares at me with bleakness over his face.

"Why?"

Jake frowns.

"It wasn't because of me, was it?"

"No," Jake says.

I wait for more, but he doesn't give me anything.

That's when I realize that Jake might be uncomfortable with having this conversation in his boss's office, and that is the last thing he should be worrying about. He shouldn't feel like I'm his boss—at least not right now. Right now, I'm a friend who is comforting her friend. Nothing more.

I get up from my desk without saying a word to Jake. I walk past him and open the door leading out into the hallway.

"I need you to cancel the rest of my day."

"What? Why? I can't do that again." Preston gets up from behind his desk, trying to do his best to convince me to stay.

"I can't. Jake needs me."

"What could he possibly need you for?"

"His fiancée just broke up with him."

"Oh," is all Preston says. Then, he laughs.

"What's so funny?" My voice is stern, not finding the fact that Jake's fiancée just broke up with him funny at all.

"There was no fiancée. He just made that all up to get into your panties."

"Just cancel my plans for the rest of the day." I walk out the door and back to my office before Preston has a chance to change my mind. I poke my head back inside my office. "Come on, Jake, let's go. I'm taking you for drinks."

13

SCARLETT

"I'll take a beer," Jake says.

I shake my head at the bartender.

"We'll both take a double scotch on the rocks," I say to the bartender. I turn to Jake. "Beer isn't strong enough to get the job done today, I don't think."

"You're probably right. Since when did you start drinking scotch though?"

The bartender sets both of our drinks on the bar, and I pick up the scotch. It's not as bad as I remember it being.

"Right now," I say as I smile.

Jake attempts to smile again this time, and it isn't as pathetic as the one he gave me in my office. I watch as he takes a sip of the golden liquid. I watch Jake swallow, and his Adam's apple bobs up and down as the liquid goes down his throat. I'm supposed to be here to cheer Jake up, but instead, all I can think about is how I wish I were kissing that throat. And it doesn't help that being in a bar reminds me of the first time I stepped foot in a bar with Jake ten years ago.

"Really? You got me a beer?" I ask.

He smiles bashfully as he slides the beer to me across the small pub

table that we are both standing at. I grab the bottle and lift it to my lips.
"Good thing I'm not like most girls and can actually drink beer."

He raises his eyebrows at me as if he isn't sure.

I raise my beer and he does the same clinking the bottles together. "To a
fantastic first date," I say.

He nods and then I put the beer to my lips. It's not that I don't like beer
I just prefer a stronger drink. You get drunk faster with less calories that
way. I chug the beer until the bottle is empty and then slam it on the table.

Jake looks up at me with a goofy grin on his face. I glance at his bottle
that is still mostly full.

"You're going to have to drink up for what I have planned for you
tonight," I say.

His grin wavers just a little. "And what's that?" he says leaning into
my ear.

"You'll see," I say with a wink.

I shake my head putting the memory away. That night didn't end
in sex like I thought it would. Jake was too much of a gentleman. It's
what made me fall for him. Looking at him now I know I have zero
chance of getting lucky tonight too. I shouldn't even be thinking
about it. I'm here to make him feel better, not hit on him.

Jake finishes about half of his drink before I ask him again, "So,
what happened?"

"I don't want to talk about it."

"Yes, you do. You need to talk about it. It's the only way you can
move on."

"I didn't have to talk to anyone to move on from you."

I close my eyes as the sting sets. "I'm sorry for everything I put
you through. Really, I am."

He takes another sip of his drink but still doesn't say anything. I
sigh and take another sip of my own scotch.

He's not going to say anything. He's not going to let me help him. I've
hurt him too much.

"Karissa broke it off because she said I work too much. She
doesn't want to be married to somebody who doesn't put her first."

Jake shakes his glass and watches the ice rattle around in it. "She's wrong."

"Of course she is. I could see yesterday that you put her before your job," I say.

Jake looks from his glass to me. "That's not why she's wrong. She's wrong for saying she broke up with me because I didn't put her before my job. She broke up with me because we were wrong for each other. We have been for a long time."

I take another long sip of my scotch, each sip tasting better than the previous one.

"She broke up with me because she thinks I'm in love with someone else."

I shouldn't ask what I'm about to ask. I shouldn't say anything or do anything when Jake is obviously hurting and obviously getting over a very recent breakup. But I have to know.

I look at my glass, not able to meet his eyes, as I ask, "Is she right? Do you love someone else?"

Jake moves his hand under my chin and forces me to look at him. He forces me to look into his deep eyes as he says, "Yes."

I shouldn't do what I'm about to do. I should give him time to digest what happened. I should give him time to mourn the loss of his relationship. I should give him time to fight for her.

I can't wait though because he could be everything I've been looking for.

My hands go around his neck, and I pull his lips the remaining few inches to mine. I kiss him. And he kisses me back. As soon as his lips touch mine though, I know it is a mistake. The kiss is nice, better than nice. The kiss is great. But I realize, as soon as our lips meet, that neither of us is thinking about the other. He's thinking about *her*. And I'm thinking about *Beast*. I know that this kiss doesn't compare to any kisses that either of us has had in the past.

I slowly remove my lips from his and keep my eyes closed as I whisper, "I'm sorry. I shouldn't have done that."

"Don't be sorry. I want..." He doesn't finish his sentence as his lips are back on mine, attacking me, begging me to make his pain go away.

I give in. I kiss back, hard and fast, trying my best to erase *her* memory from his mind. I bite and nip at his lip, brutally trying to make him focus on me instead of her. I thrust my tongue into his mouth, trying to wipe her away.

It doesn't work. Her memory seeps back, and I can tell by the way he's kissing me that he's not really here; he's still with her.

And I'm still with Beast.

I don't care though. I will let him kiss me for as long as he needs. He deserves that after I broke his heart. He deserves to have the chance to lose himself in me.

I let him continue to kiss me until the kisses change. Once they change to something more aggressive, demanding more than just a kiss, I realize it's time to stop. I push him away, slowly and calmly, so as not to cause him more pain.

"I won't be the woman you fuck tonight to make you forget about her."

Jake nods.

We go back to our respective drinks, trying to comprehend what just happened and what should happen now. Neither of us has an answer, so I order more drinks, like that's the answer. We drink more. We sit in silence longer. We gaze at each other longer, both wanting to find a hotel room to fuck in to wash the others away even though we know we could never be a part of each other's future.

"Do you have a place to stay tonight?" I ask.

"I was just planning on staying at a hotel for tonight, and then I'll start to look for an apartment in the morning." He sighs. "That is, if she won't take me back."

"Do you think there's a chance of that happening?"

He looks at me with such sadness in his eyes. "No. She won't take me back. And I shouldn't want to take her back."

I nod. "You can stay at my place tonight."

"I don't think that's a good idea."

"Sure, it is. I have a spare bedroom. We are both adults and can control ourselves." I smile. *For now*, I add to myself.

Jake nods. "Thank you."

We finish our drinks, and I pay the tab, despite Jake's protests. I text my driver, George, to come pick us up, and then we walk outside the bar into the warm night sky. We have been drinking for hours now, but no matter how long we drank, it didn't wash away his pain, like I'd hoped it would. I can still read his pain all over his face. And there's nothing I can do to help him.

George pulls up in the blacked out sedan, and we silently climb in. George doesn't question which strange man he's driving back to my apartment. He's done it more than enough times to make assumptions about what we're doing. Even though it's not about that.

Jake doesn't say anything to me as we ride back.

George pulls up in front of my apartment twenty minutes later.

"Shit. I forgot to ask if you needed us to stop by your place first, so you could get some things."

Jake shakes his head. "That's not necessary, but thanks."

I frown, but don't push it. If he says he doesn't need anything, he doesn't need anything. We climb out of the car and walk up to the entrance of the massive apartment building. I love this building. It has Old World charm while still having all the best modern conveniences.

Tom, my doorman, holds the door open for us. "Good evening, Miss Scarlett, sir," Tom says to both me and Jake.

"Good evening, Tom," I say, smiling.

Jake barely acknowledges Tom, only nodding his head in Tom's direction before walking past him.

"Thanks, Tom," I say.

In the center of the apartment building, Jake and I walk onto the elevator, and then I press the button to the top floor. I watch Jake out of the corner of my eye and see when he notices that I live on the top of the building, his eyes widening just a little.

Maybe inviting him to my apartment is a bad idea?

I don't want to emasculate him when he sees that my apartment is probably ten times nicer than his. I just want to give him a place to sleep, so he doesn't have to worry about his fiancée.

We step out of the elevator when it stops on the top floor, and I pull my keys out of my purse. I walk to the single door on this floor and put the key inside to unlock it. I push the door open, holding it for Jake, and I flip on the light switch that turns on all the lights in the living area.

When Jake enters, he says, "Holy shit, Scarlett. This place is fucking amazing."

I smile as I look around my apartment. There are floor-to-ceiling windows that cover two stories, making my living space look huge and grand. All of my white-colored furniture helps to make the room seem even that much more spacious. The stainless steel appliances in the kitchen along with the white cabinets and white-colored granite really make the room pop. A spiral staircase in the center of the room, leading up to my bedroom that overlooks the space, finishes what can be seen from the entrance.

"I know. It's pretty great, right? Who would've thought I would build an empire big enough to allow me to afford a place like this on my own? Everybody thought I'd just be living on my parents' money at this point or be married to some rich guy who could afford a place like this."

Jake steps into the center of the room and looks around. "You're wrong, Scarlett. Everybody thought you would have this and that you would get it on your own." He looks at me. "At least, I did."

I suck in a breath at his words. I don't believe him for a second, but it's nice to hear that somebody believed in me, even back then.

"Here, let me show you to your room," I say.

I lead Jake to the one guest room on the main floor. I open the door and click on the lights to the spacious room that contains a king-size bed, a sitting area, a closet, and its own private bath.

"I think this will do just fine," Jake says with a sly smile on his face.

"Good," I say.

I walk back to the living space, and Jake follows. I don't really know what to do at this point. It's about ten o'clock at night, well before my bedtime, but it's not like I can just go upstairs and sleep. It doesn't seem like Jake is ready for sleep either.

"Would you like another drink?"

Jake nods as he makes himself comfortable on the white sectional in my living room. I walk to my bar in my kitchen and pull out the one bottle of scotch I have. I pour a healthy dose of scotch into two glasses. My hand shakes slightly as I pour. Except, when I hand Jake his glass of scotch, that's exactly what the gleam in his eyes says he wants.

And who am I to resist that look?

I take a seat on the sectional, as far away from Jake as I can get, and begin sipping on my scotch. I'm hoping that, if we drink enough, we will each just slip into a coma, so I won't have to tell him no and break his heart again. I'm afraid he thinks the reason I brought him up here was to sleep with him even though I've already told him no. I'm afraid he thinks that he can convince me to change my mind. And maybe he can.

"You really are amazing, Scarlett. You have done so well for yourself. It is just incredible."

"Thank you. You're pretty amazing yourself."

"Not like you," he says.

"You went after your dream, the same as me. It doesn't matter that I make more money."

"You're right. I did. But my dream wasn't just about becoming a financial manager. My dream always included the wife and the kids and the happily ever after. So, I don't quite have my dream yet, unlike you, who has already accomplished everything that you've ever dreamed of having."

I pause. "You think I have everything that I've ever dreamed of?"

"Yes. Don't you? You've built an empire. What's left to do?"

"I want the same things you want. I want to be married, have kids, have the happily ever after."

He narrows his eyes at me. "You said that before. But I didn't really believe you then. Since when did everything change?"

"Since I realized that I was missing something in my life. When I come home, I don't have someone to share my life with. I don't want to have to keep going to bars every night to find a stranger to hook up with. I want more."

Jake studies me, but doesn't move or say anything. He just studies me, like he doesn't believe me.

And maybe he shouldn't when the primary reason I broke up with him was because things were getting too serious. He wanted more, and I didn't.

Could it be that, now, we both want the same thing? Could it be that we are both now single and have a chance to have that with each other?

A slow grin forms on his face. "You know, Scarlett, I can't get my deposit back."

"Your deposit for what?"

"The deposit for my wedding."

"I'm sorry. That sucks. We should plan a big party to have instead of your reception."

He nods. "We could. But I have a better idea."

I look at him, confused, not understanding what he's saying.

"Will you marry me?"

I suck in a breath.

He shouldn't have asked me that. He shouldn't have asked me unless he was completely serious because I already know my answer to that question. I already know what I want. I know that Beast will never give me anything long-term. He won't even agree to more than one fuck at a time. And my only shot at being happy is to settle down and forget about men like him.

So, I simply say, "Yes."

14

BEAST

I STRAIGHTEN my tie before I walk into the corporate headquarters of Fledge Real Estate Group. As much as I hate to admit it to my boss, I love jobs like this. They are why I get up in the morning. Exciting. Thrilling. Controlling. And the day ends in destroying someone else's life.

What's not to love?

I make my way toward the receptionist's desk in the center of the main floor.

"Hello. How may I help you, sir?" the young woman behind the desk says, smiling at me a little too brightly.

I don't bother smiling back as she takes in my perfectly tailored suit that fits me like a glove, showing off the muscles lurking beneath. Her eyes stop when she sees the bulge in my pants, and she brightens, hoping that she will get a chance at seeing my cock in person and not just beneath my pants.

Not a chance.

She's my usual type. Young, blonde, nice rack. But I don't want anyone anytime soon. Not after Beauty destroyed me for any other woman.

"I'm here to see Brett Fledge."

"And your name, sir?"

"Julian Vulture," I say.

She nods as she finds my name on Brett's schedule for the day. "His office is on the six floor. You can take the elevators behind me. I will let the receptionist on his floor know you are on your way up." She hands me a name tag. "Here's a visitor's tag. You can head on up now."

I take the name tag and walk past her desk. Then, I crumple the tag in my hand before letting it drop to the floor. I'm not wearing a damn name tag. I press the elevator button and then climb on. Alone. *Thank fucking God.* I don't want to deal with strangers right now.

I press the button for the sixth floor and then ride in peace as I make my way up to Brett's office. I climb out and am immediately met with another young woman sitting behind a desk.

"Mr. Fledge is in another meeting right now, Mr. Vulture. You can take a seat over there," the woman who isn't as hot as the receptionist downstairs says, pointing to a couch in a small waiting area.

I glare at her. "I don't like waiting."

Her eyes widen in shock. I doubt anyone has ever said that to her before. Brett is always the big dog when people come to visit him here. There is never any worry about making people wait to see him.

"I'm...I'm sorry, sir. I don't..."

I roll my eyes at her blubbering. "It's fine. Just ensure that Brett knows that I don't like waiting."

"Yes, Mr. Vulture. I will let Mr. Fledge know."

I nod and watch her walk back behind her desk. I pull my phone out of my pocket. I ignore the missed messages from my employer and employees, and instead, I go to my guilty pleasure.

I text her.

Me: Your begging won't get you anywhere, Beauty. I'm the one in control. I decide when or if we fuck. I decide how. Your only job is to obey me. But, after I saw you with him, I'm not sure we can ever be together again.

I press Send and then wait. She doesn't answer immediately. I didn't expect her to. But she will eventually. She always does.

"Mr. Vulture, Mr. Fledge can see you now," the woman behind the receptionist desk says.

I get up from the uncomfortable, tiny couch that I know is meant to weaken his adversaries before he lets them into his office. It doesn't work with me.

I follow the woman to the office door that sits just on the other side of her desk, like he needs a guard to watch over and protect him.

The woman knocks on the door and then opens it. "Mr. Vulture, sir."

She holds open the door for me, and I step in. Brett stands from his desk and walks over to me. He extends his hand to me, but I don't take it. He lets it slide back to his side.

"Thanks, Jeannette," Brett says to the woman, who leaves us be.

He motions for me to take a seat in a chair opposite his large wooden desk. I do, and he takes a seat back in his chair behind his desk.

"Your name suits you, Mr. Vulture," Brett says.

I nod. "It does, Brett," I say, letting him know I won't deal with formalities of calling him by his last name.

Brett frowns. "I knew I shouldn't have even taken this meeting."

"You shouldn't have, but you did. So, let me say what I have to say, and then neither of us has to see each other again."

"Fine. Let's hear it."

I smile and pull the paper out of my briefcase. I fling it in front of Brett.

"What's this?" he asks.

"The agreement you are going to sign that will give me control of Fledge Real Estate."

Brett's frown deepens. "Like hell it is!" He tosses the paper back in my face.

I crack my neck back and forth, not the least bit fazed. This is always the initial reaction. Now, it's my job to close. "I would reconsider if I were you."

"Fledge Real Estate is not for sale! I don't know what the hell you are thinking, coming in here and demanding that I sell my company."

I smirk. "That wasn't me *demanding*. It was me *asking*."

"This meeting is through." Brett presses the button on this phone to call Jeannette back in here to escort me out.

Like I said before, *Wuss*. He can't even throw me out of his office on his own.

"We are not finished."

I pull out my phone and find the inappropriate pictures. I smirk as I look at the pictures of Brett—a middle-aged man with a beer belly, tied up, with two women all over him. Brett is supposedly happily married to his wife of fifteen years with two young kids at home.

I slide my phone across his desk. "Look at the pictures."

He does. "You bastard."

I smirk, but don't disagree. I am a bastard. I'm also much worse.

"Now that I have your attention—"

"You can't do this. It's illegal."

"I can do this, and I don't deal with such things as legalities. I take what I want. It's as simple as that."

"What do you want? What do I have to do to keep these pictures from going public?"

I've won, I think. *That was simple.*

I slide the paper he threw at me earlier back across his desk. "You agree to our terms. You will have more than enough money to live off of, and we will get your company."

"Why would you want a real estate company? That's absurd. I shouldn't sell for so little."

I nod. "I think you are forgetting the additional payment of those pictures not being all over the six o'clock news tonight."

Brett's mouth drops. "You wouldn't."

"You have until five p.m. to sign the paper, giving me full owner-ship of your company. If you don't, those pictures will be all over the six o'clock news."

I reach over the desk and snatch my phone back out of his hands. I pick up my briefcase and exit his office. I dial the number. "It's done."

15

SCARLETT

Fuck! Fuck! Fuck! What the hell did I just do?

I just said I would marry my ex-boyfriend after his fiancée had just broken up with him. I'm not even over Beast yet, and I've already decided on having a future with Jake even though he isn't over his ex.

After I said yes, Jake and I spent the rest of the evening drinking, kissing, and imagining our future lives together. At some point in the night, we drank enough that we both passed out on the couches.

Now, the morning light is streaming in through my windows, and I realize what a stupid fucking mistake it really is.

How could I be so stupid? How could I say yes to marrying someone I hadn't had a relationship with in over ten years?

I get up from the couch, careful not to move too fast, as Jake is still sound asleep on the other half of the sectional. I tiptoe up the stairs to my bedroom and shut the door before taking a sigh of relief. I can't face Jake right now, not until I get my shit figured out.

I walk to my bathroom and flick on the lights before I head to my shower and turn it on full blast. I quickly strip off my clothes, like stripping it off will erase everything that happened in the last twenty-four hours. I know it won't, but it makes me feel like it could. I quickly step into the shower and immediately feel relief as the hot water pours over me.

I let the water drown out any memories from the last twenty-four hours. I just focus on how the water feels as it pours over my head. Amazing. Refreshing.

When I stand in the shower so long that I don't even remember what got me upset in the first place, I turn the water off. I grab a towel and wrap it around my body before stepping out of my waterfall-like shower that looks more like a cave filled with gorgeous rocks.

The door slamming downstairs though reminds me that Jake is still here. It reminds me that I said yes to a question that I never should've said yes to. Reminds me that I royally and totally fucked up.

I get dressed quickly, putting on a pair of jeans and a tank top, not caring that it's a workday and that I should show up in something a little nicer than jeans. I run a comb through my hair but don't bother blow-drying it, nor do I put on any makeup. I can't remember the last time I went outside without fixing my hair or makeup.

Once dressed, I run downstairs, hoping to solve whatever happened with Jake. To erase what happened last night and blame it on the alcohol we both drank. Blame it on Jake's broken heart. A broken heart that he still has a chance of fixing with Karissa.

But, by the time I get downstairs, Jake is already gone. He didn't leave a note. I check my phone, but there are no new messages from him. He just left, like last night didn't even happen.

Maybe it didn't. Maybe it was all a dream.

I glance at the clock on my phone. It's only six thirty a.m. I still have plenty of time to get ready and make it into work on time. Properly. So, I head back upstairs, change out of my jeans, and put something more appropriate on along with doing my hair and makeup.

And then I head into the office, like last night didn't even happen.

"Glad to see you made it into the office today. I was beginning to think that you decided to take another day off," Preston says.

I roll my eyes at him as I unlock the door to my office. "I'm five minutes late, Preston. I don't think that's enough to worry about me not showing up to work."

"Well, after you were pulled away from work two times now, I wasn't sure if you would show up again this morning. I wasn't sure if you'd be able to face your one-night stand at work."

I pause in my tracks. "Jake is here?"

"Yes," Preston says slowly, like he thinks I'm crazy.

I contemplate on how to handle Jake. I wasn't sure if he would show up to work today between what happened with him and Karissa and what happened between me and him. I thought it would be too much for a man. I guess I was wrong.

"Can you have Jake meet me at his earliest convenience?"

"Sure, just as long as the meeting doesn't end with you running off again and leaving me here to do all your work."

"Relax, I'm not running off again. But, even if I do, you have been doing a great job, so much so that I might even think about giving you another raise."

"Please don't. I don't need any more responsibilities. I just want to be your assistant."

I sigh and continue to my desk where a mountain of papers and designs are covering it. My phone is flashing the number of messages I've already received. I can understand why Preston can't handle this. *I* can barely handle this.

"Just tell Jake to meet me when he can. I promise, I won't run out early on you today, and if I do, you'll get to leave early, too."

Preston narrows his eyes at me, trying to determine if I'm telling the truth or not. Trying to figure out if he should prepare himself for another afternoon of running the company by himself. I don't think he believes me, but he leaves me alone, so I can get started on the papers in front of me and the messages on my phone.

An hour later though, I hear a knock at the door.

"Come in!" I shout, not bothering to get up, assuming it's Preston.

It's not. At the door stands Jake, looking sexier than ever. He hasn't bothered to shave, so there's a nice amount of stubble covering his neck and chin. His hair is in a less than perfect mess on top of his head. And he's wearing the same suit from yesterday.

"Having second thoughts?" he asks as he shuts the door behind himself.

Yes, I think. That's not what I say though. Instead, I say, "No."

"Good." He walks over to me and grabs my hands. He pulls me into a standing position.

I have no idea what he's doing, so I just go with it. He tucks a strand of loose hair behind my ear and reaches behind my neck, forcing my lips onto his. The kiss is sweet, chaste. There's nothing dangerous about it. Nothing that stirs an inner desire inside me. It's just nice.

When he breaks away, I ask the only question that's on my mind, "Why did you leave this morning then? I thought you had changed your mind."

A smile forms on his lips. "No, I had a few things I needed to take care of. But I meant it when I said that I wanted to marry you. I always have. I've spent my entire morning thinking about you, dreaming about you. Haven't been able to get any work done."

"Me neither," I say even though that's not true.

I've been able to get some work done, and the only reason I couldn't was because I was worried that I'd said yes to a stupid question. Wondering why, when I'd said yes to this good nice man, that I was still thinking about my much more dangerous man. A stranger who wants nothing more than a nice fuck with me, but only on his terms.

"Are you free this evening?" Jake asks.

I force a smile onto my lips. "I usually work till nine or ten. After that, I'm free."

"Good. I'll pick you up from here around nine?"

"Yes. I can't wait."

Jake pulls me into one final kiss before he leaves. The kiss just leaves me feeling even more confused than before. It was nice, but I still want more than nice.

As soon as Jake leaves, I pick up my phone and ask Preston to come in.

He comes in the office almost immediately. "You are not going anywhere."

I shake my head. "What are my plans for lunch today?"

He looks at his phone that holds my schedule for the day. "You don't have a meeting until one thirty p.m."

"Good. Can you see if Kinsley is free to meet me for lunch?"

He frowns. "Sure."

"Thanks."

I think I know why Jake wants to take me out tonight, and it's not something that I can handle without talking it out with my best friend even if I don't usually take her advice. I just need to be reassured that I'm doing the right thing. Because, right now, I'm torn between a dangerous life filled with hot sex that I can never control and might never get again and a nice man, albeit a little boring, who could give me the kids and a happily ever after.

"Wow, I get to see you twice in one week. That's a record, I think," Kinsley says, laughing at her little joke.

I frown. I'm not ready to deal with jokes when I have things a lot more serious on my mind that I have to deal with. Kinsley notices as she takes a seat across from me in the booth at one of our favorite Italian restaurants. I study her stomach as she takes a seat and notice a small bump that's beginning to form. It makes me happy to see her with a baby on the way, and just looking at her reminds me that I could have that, too, if I marry Jake.

"What's wrong?"

I take a deep breath. "I think I'm engaged."

Kinsley raises her eyebrows. "You think?"

I rest my head in my hands, trying to make it all go away. "No, that's not true. I'm engaged. All that's left is the ring that I'm pretty sure he's about to give me tonight."

Kinsley's mouth is open. "How do you get yourself into these messes? Who's the guy? You've been dating somebody and not telling me? But I thought, just earlier, you were talking about—"

"It's Jake."

"Oh."

"Oh what?"

"Nothing. It's just that I always thought, after you two broke up in college, you would never get back together."

"Me, too. But he sort of just showed back up and asked me to marry him after his fiancée broke up with him."

"Oh."

"I really wish you would stop saying that."

Kinsley's cheeks blush a bright shade of pink. "Sorry. I just don't know what else to say. I'm happy for you. I can't believe you're getting married!"

"See, that's the thing. I'm not sure I'm getting married yet either."

"Then, why did you say yes?"

"It's complicated."

"I think you need to start at the beginning and explain everything."

"Are you ready to order?" our waitress says, interrupting us.

"I'll have the Caesar salad."

"And for you?" the waitress asks, looking at Kinsley.

"I'll just have the salad as well."

I shake my head. There's no way my pregnant best friend is only getting salad for lunch.

"She'll have the lasagna as well," I add.

The waitress nods and hurries away before Kinsley can protest.

"I shouldn't eat the lasagna. I'm already gaining weight a little too fast."

"Nonsense. You're allowed to splurge a little bit now that you're pregnant."

Kinsley smiles. "Now, what's going on?"

"Basically, I want what you have, and Jake is the best option for me to get that."

"But?"

"But there's no spark. I want more than just a nice guy."

Kinsley nods. "Sometimes, it takes a little while to get a spark though."

"Maybe. But what if it never happens?"

"It will. It just sometimes takes a better foundation first before the spark happens."

"I guess. It didn't take long though for the spark to happen with my one-night-stand stranger."

Kinsley shakes her head, like I'm ridiculous. "There is only a spark because of how you met. If you had met like normal people and gotten to know each other first, before you had sex, there wouldn't have been a spark either. The real spark only happens after you get to know someone and find love."

I nod. It makes sense but doesn't fully ease my worries.

"So, what are you going to do?" Kinsley asks.

"I'm going to marry Jake, and I'm gonna forget all about my one-night stand." Even as I say it, I'm not sure I will be able to.

"Good."

Our waitress brings our lunch, and we quickly dive into the deliciousness. About halfway through, Kinsley gets up to use the restroom, and I take a moment to check my phone. I have another text message from Beast.

I want to read it. I want to get the thrill, the rush, that I get every time I do. But if I'm going to marry Jake, I have to delete his number. I have to block his number to keep him from texting me. I'm just about to do it when Kinsley returns.

I glance up and look at a pale Kinsley, who doesn't look very good.

"You okay?" I ask, worried that I'm going to have to take her to a doctor or something.

"Yes. Just being pregnant is no fun. The morning sickness never ends. I told you, I shouldn't have had the lasagna."

She pushes the lasagna away from her, and I laugh. I put my phone back into my purse, forgetting about the reason that I got it out.

"You sure you want to be pregnant soon, just like me?"

I look at Kinsley, who looks a little green and pale, but happy. That's what I want—to be happy, just like her. "Yes, I'm sure."

16

SCARLETT

I HAVE Preston bring me some options of dresses that I can wear on a date tonight. That's the benefit of owning a fashion company. There are always hundreds of new dresses at my disposal to wear anytime I want. And the benefit of still having a model's body type is that I can wear any of the dresses that the models wear, which means I have an endless supply of dresses to choose from. I try on a dozen before I find the dress that's perfect for tonight. It's black with a low V neckline, a large slit up the side, and a fairly exposed back. I fluff my hair and redo my makeup as the clock nears nine o'clock when Jake is supposed to pick me up.

"You need anything else?" Preston asks.

"I don't think so." I shake out the nerves in my shoulders and arms.

Preston walks over to me and grabs ahold of my shoulders, trying to calm me. "You look great, and I think saying yes to a man you're so clearly infatuated with is the right decision."

"Thanks."

"Just make sure he signs a prenup before you marry him."

I roll my eyes. "I don't think that's necessary."

"Oh, it's necessary. And you are making him sign a prenup. You're worth a lot more than he is."

"This isn't about money. I trust him."

"Honey, don't ever trust a man."

I nod although I don't agree.

"You're beautiful," Jake says, staying at the door.

I turn to look at him, and my jaw drops. Jake is standing in the doorway in a full suit, combed hair, and a clean-shaven face. I'm glad I changed.

"Thanks. You're pretty good-looking yourself."

"You ready?"

I nod, unable to say any words. Maybe this is what Kinsley was talking about. Maybe this is the moment the sparks start flying.

Jake walks over to me and holds out his arm, which I immediately take, loving the way my hand feels wrapped around his hard biceps.

"You two have fun now," Preston says.

I shoot a dirty glance at him.

Nerves begin forming in my chest as Jake leads me out of my office. We get stares from several of my employees as we walk. I feel anxiety, knowing that, tomorrow, everyone in this office will know that we are engaged. When that happens, there will be no backing out without completely stomping on his heart again and destroying his image in front of everyone.

I already know what they're thinking. They're thinking that I'm the one who broke up his first engagement. I didn't, but there is no way to remove those thoughts from their heads. It's done. So, now, we have to live with that.

Not that I really care about what they think. All I care about is not hurting Jake and also finding happiness.

To my surprise, when we exit the building, a limo is waiting. Jake really went all out tonight. That makes me even more suspicious, thinking that he is going to propose for real. By the end of the night, there might be a ring on my finger. And, this time, when I say yes, I have to be absolutely sure.

Jake helps me into the limo before climbing in himself. The door shuts, and I glance at him and see him staring at me so intently with a hint of love already in his eyes. That's when I am a hundred percent for sure that saying yes tonight will be the right thing. That's all I want—someone to look at me like they love me. God, it's been so long since anyone has ever looked at me like that—not that I have seen anyone long enough to know the feeling. Kinsley loves me, but she doesn't really count. Not even Preston really looks at me that way. No one-night stand or other ex has ever looked at me that way. Jake's the guy for me.

"So, where are we going?"

"It's a surprise."

I smile. "I like surprises."

"I know."

I lean over and kiss him, giving the kiss everything that I have. And he gives me everything he has in return. It's perfect, almost too perfect, but I push that thought out of my head. Instead, I just enjoy the kiss. Enjoy the thought that, after tonight, I'll get to kiss this man anytime I want. He's mine.

We stop kissing when the limo comes to a stop.

I glance up, and that's when I see we're parked outside my building. "What are we doing here?"

"You'll see."

The driver gets out and opens the door for me. I climb out, followed by Jake. Jake holds his arm out for me again, and I take it. He leads me to the elevator and presses the button for the top floor.

I look at him, confused. *Is he just taking me to my apartment? Maybe he thought I needed a chance to change?*

Although, by what I'm wearing, he should know that I don't need to change.

I don't question him now. I don't want to ruin the surprise.

We step out onto my floor, and I begin to pull my keys out of my purse, assuming that we are going to my apartment. His hand grabs mine at the wrist, stopping me from digging any further into my purse. He shakes his head back and forth.

I stop. "What?"

He just smiles. "This way."

I follow him past the door to my apartment and down to the end of the hallway where there's an emergency exit door.

"We can't go out the door," I say with a worried look on my face. I don't want to actually set the alarm off again. It only happened to me once when I went out to smoke, but man, was it embarrassing. That experience alone got me to quit smoking.

"Sure, we can."

I watch in horror as he puts his hand on the door, and to my surprise, the alarm doesn't go off.

"What did you do?"

He just smiles and grabs ahold of my hand. He pulls me through the door and up the stairs to the rooftop. The rooftop is supposed to be closed. But it's obviously not closed because sitting on the top is one single table with two chairs. At the center is a gorgeous arrangement of red roses.

I look to Jake. "How did you do this?"

He shakes his head. He walks me over to the table and pulls out a chair for me. I take a seat. I can't believe he's done all this.

He takes a seat opposite me. "If I remember correctly, Italian is your favorite," he says.

A waiter appears and places a basket of breadsticks on the table along with a bottle of champagne.

I nod and smile. It is my favorite, and I don't have the heart to tell him that I had Italian earlier today. I watch as Jake pops open the bottle of champagne and pours each of us a glass. He lifts his glass, and I do the same.

"To forever," he says.

"To forever," I repeat as we clink our glasses together. I take a sip of the bubbly liquid. *Perfect.* "This is really nice. Thank you for doing this. I can't remember the last time a guy took me on this nice of a date."

He frowns. "Well, get used to it because I'm going to take you on a lot of dates like this. You deserve it more."

"I'm not sure about that." I take another sip of my drink, trying to distract myself from the thought that I know he's going to propose for real at some point tonight, but it's not something that I want to spend the whole night anxiously thinking about. So, instead, I change the subject. "So, what have you been up to over the last ten years? Give me all the highlights."

He nods. "I graduated with my finance degree but then decided that wasn't what I wanted to do. So, after working for a couple of years in finance, I went back to school with the intention of getting a law degree."

"Really? You have a law degree?"

He laughs. "No."

I quizzically look at him.

"I never finished. Only lasted about a year."

"I'm not sure I believe that. Jake Walton always finishes what he's started. Always. At least the Jake that I knew."

He sits back in his chair. "It was hard to quit. Once I realized it wasn't what I wanted to do and that I was just in it to try to get the degree that I started, I realized it was stupid for me to waste my time and money on something that I didn't love."

"Do you love finance?"

He thinks for a moment. "I didn't at first, but I realize I'm really good at it. That I can make a good living at it. I'm not sure if it's love, but it makes me happy and gives me the freedom to spend my spare time doing things I really love."

"And what do you really love?"

"I love my family. I love spending time with my siblings and their nieces and nephews. I love watching sports. I love just having time to myself to relax."

I nod. Jake hasn't changed much in the ten years that we've been apart.

"What about you? What do you love?"

I think for a minute, not really sure how to answer the question. It's obvious that I love all things about fashion and beauty. I wouldn't have started my own company if I didn't. But I don't want to give such an obvious answer.

"I love spending my time doing something adventurous, something new. Something that really gets my blood pumping. But, most of all, I want to spend my free time starting my own family."

I see the shock that forms over his face at those last words even though I'm pretty sure I told him this last night. Although he might have been too drunk to remember. I don't think he thought that I wanted a family. I think he thought that marrying me would mean giving that part up. But hearing me say the words confirms for him that I really am ready to get married, that I really do want to start a family.

"How soon?" he asks.

He doesn't have to clarify what he means. I already know. *When do I want to start a family?*

I smile. "As soon as possible. I would start tonight, if you would let me."

He spews a little of the champagne out of his mouth. He wasn't expecting me to say that I wanted him to fuck me tonight, to impregnate me, to make me his in every way of the word.

"Do you think that is possible?" I grin as I say the words.

I watch him swallow hard, trying to gather himself.

"I think that can be arranged."

Our first course is brought out and placed on the table. A simple garden salad. We both dig in.

After a few bites, Jake asks, "How many?"

Again, he doesn't have to specify what he means. I already know. *How many children do I want?*

"I've never really thought about it before. As many as we can take care of."

He nods and smiles. "Sounds like a plan to me."

And that's when I realize, that's exactly what we are doing. Planning. It's not something that I particularly enjoy doing. I don't even really do it at work. I don't plan for the future. I make the future be what I want to happen. But I guess that's what being in a relationship with another person is. Planning. Sharing. Compromising.

But I can't believe we are doing it before he's even officially asked me to marry him. It's not something that I thought I would ever do.

"I just need you to answer something for me, Scarlett. What changed? What changed in the last ten years since I knew you? Because the woman I knew before would never have agreed to anything that I'm saying."

I think for a moment, not really sure what to say. I know my answer is important. I know that, if I don't say the exact right words, this might never happen. So, I take my time to say the words, knowing they have been there all along, "Nothing's changed. This is what I've always wanted. I've always wanted a family. I just wasn't ready to have one until now."

A slow smile spreads across Jake's face. He stands up and walks over to my side of the table.

I freeze. *This is it.*

Instead of kneeling down, like I expect him to, his lips crash on mine in a perfect kiss. I kiss him until he controls my whole mind, so all I think about is this kiss. Until all I want is to continue kissing him forever.

He does not continue the kiss that long though. Instead, as he pulls away, with the kiss lingering on my lips, I keep my eyes closed, trying to keep the memory within me.

"Scarlett," he says.

I open my eyes and see him kneeling in front of me. I swallow hard, washing down any nerves that I have.

He grabs ahold of my hand and says, "Scarlett, I know that it's been almost ten years since our last official date. I know that, since then, our lives have taken us on vastly different paths. I know that rebuilding a relationship will be far from easy or quick. But I don't want to wait to start the journey with you. I don't want to wait to make sure that this is the right thing because I already know it's the right thing. Scarlett, will you marry me?"

"Yes."

I watch in amazement as Jake produces a box containing a large oval-shaped engagement ring. It's beautiful, elegant, and simple. I know from the size that it cost a pretty penny. He places the ring on my finger. I can't decide if I should study it more or throw my arms around Jake. So, I do both.

"You like it?"

I release him, so I can look at him. "I love it."

"Good."

Jake begins to go back to his seat, but I'm not done with him yet. I grab the collar of his shirt and pull him to me, devouring him with my lips and tongue.

I need him now. I need him to erase every man from my lips. I need him to erase every man from my body. I need to feel like he is the only man in my life. Because, from this moment on, he is.

He accepts my challenge as his kisses intensify with mine. His hands tangle in my hair as my fingers begin to pull at the buttons on his shirt. I need him undressed, so I can have him right here on the rooftop. I move my kisses from his lips to his smooth neck.

He groans as I do. "Fuck, Scarlett."

His moans and cursing just make me want him that much more. So, instead of unbuttoning his buttons one at a time, I grab each side of his shirt and rip it open. He growls when I do, just like—

I step back and look at Jake.

"What?"

"I have to ask you something."

Jake pants hard as he waits for me to ask the question that I'm not sure I should be asking. If I ask him and I'm wrong, then for no reason, I will have just brought up the fact of how recently I've had sex with someone else. But if I'm right, then all my dreams are about to come true.

I take the chance. "Did you fuck me in a hotel room a couple of days ago? And then again in a restaurant restroom?"

Jake raises his eyebrows in complete shock. A grimace comes over his face. And redness flushes his cheeks.

He's pissed. I was wrong.

"What are you talking about?"

"Nothing. I was wrong. Let's just enjoy the rest of our dinner."

Right on cue, the waiter brings us two giant plates of pasta and sets them on the table with a smile. I smile at the waiter. Jake, on the other hand, doesn't.

He begins pacing back and forth on the rooftop, trying to decide if he should be angry with me or not. I don't feel that there's any reason he should be, but then again, I'm not Jake.

"Let me get this straight. You fucked a man in a hotel room and a restroom, and you thought it was me. How's that possible?"

I sigh, realizing he's not going to let this go without an explanation. "Because it was dark, and he was a stranger. Just now, when you growled, it gave me a flashback to then. So, I thought, maybe it was you."

"So, you just said yes to me even though you let a man fuck you a couple of days ago?"

"Yes."

"I don't understand you! What the hell were you thinking?" Jake storms back and forth on the rooftop, unable to stand still.

My voice rises. "I was thinking that I would have a good time since I didn't have a boyfriend or fiancé. And, when you asked me to marry you, I realized that was what I really wanted. You of all people should know that, Mr. My Fiancée Just Broke Up with Me the Same Day I Officially Asked You to Marry Me."

He runs his hand through his hair as he continues to pace, not seeming to listen to any of my words.

"Will you please just sit down and finish our dinner?"

He stops and looks at me, but from the look of pain and anger on his face, I can tell that he can't just sit down. He can't just let this go.

"I can't. I'm sorry." He turns around and walks toward the exit.

I stand from the table, planning on running after him. "Wait!"

Jake turns for just a second. "No. I just need some space."

I freeze in my tracks, a foot away from the table, and I watch the man I just said yes to walk away from me.

How the hell did I fuck this up so much?

I sit back in the chair instead of running after the man who just put a ring on my finger. I hope that, if I stay here long enough, he'll just come back, so we can fix this.

I pull the ring off my finger and stare at it as my own anger boils inside me.

Who is he to get mad at me for sleeping with another man so soon before I said yes to him? Who is he to get mad when he was supposed to marry another woman just a couple of days ago?

I don't deserve this. I deserve better.

I pull out my phone and text.

17

BEAST

I STARE at the woman sitting across the boardroom table from me. She's one of the most ruthless competitors I've ever faced. This job is going to be harder than I thought. Of course, I've done my research on her. She's ruthless, tough, and smart.

Tania Griggs smirks at me with her arms folded across her full chest. She's a good-looking woman, and she knows how to use it to her advantage, especially in a world where she deals mostly with men. That's not going to work with me. Her good looks are not enough to convince me to put my guard down.

"I see that we don't have a deal then," I say.

"You would be right, Mr. Bolt," she says.

"That's too bad," I say, getting up from the table. And it truly is now that I'm going to have to find another way to do my job. I don't accept defeat. If I did, I wouldn't have this job.

Tania stands as well. "I need to speak with Mr. Bolt alone for a moment," she says to the men on either side of her.

They all nod and begin exiting the room. I raise my head toward her.

Maybe I was wrong about her. Maybe she does want to come to a deal.

"Change your mind and don't want your board to know, huh?"

She smiles as she walks around the table toward me. "So sure that you can get me to change my mind? Typical man. No, I have a different proposition for you."

I narrow my eyes and frown, not liking this at all. I don't give up any control unless it's to my benefit, and I know whatever she proposes won't be to my benefit.

"What's the proposition?" I glance at my watch. "I have other places I need to be."

She smiles and adjusts the tie around my neck before letting her hand slide down my hard chest. "I think you and I would make quite a pair. You obviously have a good business sense; otherwise, you wouldn't be after my company. So, how about, instead of trying to steal my company from me, you come work for me? I could use a good partner, and I mean that in more ways than one," she says, winking at me.

I forcefully remove her hands from my chest as I glare at her. "I don't need a partner. I work for myself. And I guarantee, by the end of this week, your company will be mine."

She just laughs. "I don't think so. You don't work for yourself. You have someone you have to answer to, but if you came and worked for me, you wouldn't have anyone to answer to."

"No? I would have to answer to you. And I don't answer to other people. I control my own life. And, like I said before, I want this company, so it will be mine. Simple as that."

She sighs. "Too bad. There were a lot of things I wanted to do with you."

She moves out of my way, and I walk past her. I walk to the elevator, press the button, and then wait. I feel my phone buzz in my pocket, so I pull it out and smile when I see Beauty's name flash across my screen.

I open the message.

Beauty: I shouldn't want you, and I'm not going to have you again, but it doesn't stop me from imagining all of the things that we could do together if we had one more chance. I could suck your cock, take it down my throat.

You could take me against a window, so the whole world could see. There's the ocean and the beach. I can only imagine what you could do to me there. In the back of the car or in a dirty alleyway. I can only imagine how good it would feel to have your cock inside me again. I can only imagine because I can't have you again since you won't say yes. That's all you have to do. Say yes, and meet me here at my apartment. I'm sure you already know the address.

My cock instantly hardens at her words. Her words are exactly what I want to put this whole disaster of a day behind me. I need her, and from the sounds of it, she needs me just as much. I begin texting her back.

She said she was at her apartment. Having her there will be easy enough.

My phone buzzes, interrupting my text message.

I growl in frustration but answer anyway, "Yes?" My voice is short and harsh.

"Is it done?"

"Not yet. It will be."

"That's not acceptable. We need it done tonight."

"It will be." I end the call and then delete the message that I started. Beauty will have to wait.

I step into the elevator and contemplate my next move. But I realize there's really only one move.

I step off the elevator and onto the main floor. I dial Tania's number.

To my surprise, she answers on the second ring, "I knew you wouldn't be able to resist calling me. Change your mind so soon?"

"I'm picking you up in thirty minutes."

I can practically hear her smiling on the other end of the phone.

"Thirty minutes is a little early for me. I was thinking more like an hour."

I shake my head even though she can't see me. "Thirty minutes or nothing." I'm tired of playing this woman's game.

"Thirty minutes, it is."

"You're late," I say as I pick Tania up from her office.

She rolls her eyes. "So, where are you taking me, Gerard? I mean, are you simply taking me back to your apartment? Because I'm fine with that. I'm not the type of woman who needs to get to know you first. I know exactly what this is. It's one night to fuck and get our sexual frustrations out of the way, so we can come to an agreement."

I nod. "That's the plan."

I begin walking.

Tania hurries after me. "Are we not going to take a cab?"

"No."

"So, you live close?"

"No."

"So then, what are we doing?"

I ignore the woman and keep walking. She has made today a living hell. And she's the reason I can't go see Beauty right now.

"Gerard, where are we going?"

I freeze at her insistence. I can't take this woman anymore.

I push her into a dark alley. "Right here."

18

SCARLETT

I RUB MY EYES, not caring if I smudge my makeup. I know, from not getting any sleep last night, that I already look like hell. Dark circles have formed under my eyes. My eyes are red, and my body is tired. I'm a mess. And all because of two stupid men.

One man, I thought was a nice guy. He could have been a perfect husband, father, and eventually lover. He's not a nice guy though. He's mad at me for something that he is just as guilty of. I'm an idiot for thinking that we could rush into a relationship and just pick up where we'd left off. There is a reason we broke up in the first place, and this is it.

And another man, I already knew he was a dangerous, dark man. He didn't give a fuck about me. I texted him over and over again last night, but I never got a response. He never came for me.

He's a dick, and Jake's a bastard.

And I'm all alone now. And that's the way I plan on keeping it. I don't need a man. I just need to be alone. I need to work. I need to go back to having fun.

I walk into my office building, more determined than ever to just focus on my work today.

"Congratulations," a woman in accounting says as I walk by.

I smile and nod even though I have no idea what she's congratulating me on. Maybe it has something to do with getting one of the best designers in the business on board. It doesn't seem that weird until I walk past another woman who also congratulates me, followed by another. By the time I make it into my office, I'm thoroughly confused.

I take my desk just as Preston enters my office.

"Congratulations."

I look up at him and frown. "Why is everyone congratulating me?"

He incredulously stares at me. "Funny."

"I'm serious. I have no idea why the whole office is congratulating me."

"Because you said yes to Jake."

I frown. "How does anybody know about that?"

"Because it's office gossip. Jake told one person, and now, everybody in the whole office knows."

"But it's not the truth. I'm not engaged."

"What do you mean, you're not engaged? Jake showed me the ring yesterday. You didn't say yes?"

"No, I did."

Preston laughs. "Honey, if you said yes, that means you're engaged."

"I said yes, but then he stormed off when I told him that I slept with a complete stranger only a couple of days previously. So, that effectively put a kibosh on the whole getting-married thing."

Preston looks at me with confusion on his face. "I think the two of you need to have a long discussion because I'm pretty sure Jake still thinks you're engaged."

I sigh. I don't want to deal with this. I don't want to deal with him. After the crazy week I've had dealing with two deranged men, I just want to bury myself in my work. "Well, he'll have to wait. I'm sure I have a mountain of paperwork to catch up on, and I know my afternoon is booked solid."

"Maybe this is one of those times when you should cancel your afternoon? I can handle it, I promise."

"No. I want to. And I don't want to deal with Jake right now."

"Are you sure?"

"Yes. And make sure Jake doesn't visit me. If you could help put the kibosh on the rumors about our engagement, that would be helpful."

Preston sighs. "I don't think that's a possibility, but I'll see what I can do."

"Thank you, Preston." I fire up my computer and watch as the emails pour in. I could easily lose myself in the emails for several days, and that's exactly what I plan on doing.

"Can we talk?"

Damn it! I was hoping I could avoid Jake all day, but he's found me.

"No."

Jake slips into my office anyway and shuts the door behind himself.

"I told you, I don't want to talk right now. Have a meeting in about twenty minutes that I need to prepare for. It'll have to wait."

"I can be fast."

"I don't want to hear it, Jake. Last night was a mistake."

"You're right. Last night was a mistake. But it was *my* mistake, not *yours*. I'm the one who fucked up."

I look up as Jake walks closer. Not knowing what he wants, I glare at him, hoping that he'll go away.

"I'm sorry. I messed up. I shouldn't have gotten mad at you for sleeping with another man when I've been sleeping with another woman for the past few years. It wasn't fair of me. And I regret it. I am a dick."

"*Dick* doesn't even begin to cover it. You're a bastard and a jerk."

He smiles. "Yes, I am all of those things. But I want a chance to prove to you that I can also be better than that. I can also be the man you want to marry."

"Doubtful."

"Just give me a chance. This weekend, let me make it up to you."

"I really think we both just need to give it a rest. Just go back to being friends and see where it leads. I don't want to force this."

"I don't want to force this either. But we're not forcing it if it feels right. Just give me one more chance. I promise, I'll make it right."

"Just like you made it right when you spread the rumors in this office that we were already engaged?"

"As far as I'm concerned, we are. But I will re-propose hundreds of times if I have to. I'll propose every time I mess up. Because you deserve it."

"How about you just don't mess up?"

"I'll work on that."

"Good."

Jake grins. "Still come with me this weekend?"

I sigh, hating that I've already let my plans of keeping men out of my life fall to the wayside. "I'll go with you this weekend. But we are not engaged. And, if you fuck up again, we're going back to just being friends without a shot of being anything more."

"Agreed."

"Now, go. I have a lot of work to do."

Jake nods and leaves without saying another word. Just as he does, my phone buzzes. I look down and see Beast has texted me.

Beast: God, you're so fucking sexy, Beauty. I want to do all of those things to you. I want to come hunt you down and demand you give me all of those things. I'm so sorry I couldn't come to you last night. I worked late and didn't see your message till this morning. I'm ready for you now. Please tell me I'm not too late. Because I don't think I can continue living without knowing what it's like to bury my cock down your throat. Just say yes, and I'll come hunt you down. Just say yes.

Really? How is it that both men can fuck up so easily one second and then both at the same time decide to try to make it up to me in another second?

I really can't deal with both of them right now. So, I'll just deal with them one at a time. I'll deal with Jake first. And then I'll move on to Beast.

I just have a feeling, by the end of this, I'm going to leave with a broken heart and no one but myself to blame.

19

SCARLETT

EARLY SATURDAY MORNING, Jake picks me up in his Honda Civic. He takes my overnight bag from me and puts it in the trunk as I climb into the passenger seat. He didn't tell me where we're going or what we're doing, so I'm just wearing jeans and a T-shirt, but I have plenty of options in my bag, prepared for any situation.

As he climbs in, I don't bother asking where we're going. I already have a pretty good idea. His family lives maybe two to three hours from here. If I had to guess, that's where he's taking me. He already knows that I love his family. I'm guessing he thinks he can just get me around them again to make me realize how much I want him. He's probably right, but I'm not about to admit that to him.

He begins driving in silence, so I flick on the radio, needing some sort of music to drown out the silence.

After a song or two, I say, "It's not going to work, you know. You can't just use your family as a way to try to make me like you again."

"That's not what I'm doing."

"Isn't it?"

"No, it isn't. I just want to take you somewhere I know you will have a good time. Without any pressure and to see what happens."

I yawn and stretch.

Jake reaches into the backseat of his car, pulls up a pillow, and tosses it at me. "Sleep. You're got a two-and-a-half-hour drive to sleep. And you looked like hell yesterday."

"Thanks for the compliment."

"I'm sorry, but you did. I'm guessing it's because you didn't sleep after what I had done."

I frown. I don't like that he thinks the reason I didn't sleep had anything to do with him. "You aren't the only reason I had trouble sleeping. There's a lot going on at work right now, and all this bull-shit is just distracting me."

Jake nods. "Just sleep, and you'll feel better."

I don't argue with him anymore because I really do need sleep. I move the pillow off my lap and put it in the corner between the head-rest and the window. I recline a little bit until I'm comfortable, and then I close my eyes as I rest my head on the pillow. Sleep over-whelms me quickly.

"I want you, Beauty. I want you on all fours."

I shiver at his words, but do what he said. I move to all fours and arch my back, giving him a good view of my ass. I feel him up behind me, but he doesn't enter me immediately. Instead, his head moves between my legs, and he takes my pussy into his mouth.

"Oh. My. God."

I feel his lips turn up into a smile as I moan. His tongue twirls around my clit with perfect accuracy. He's definitely a skilled man who knows what he's doing. His rough scruff on his face just adds to the friction and makes me go wild with need for him.

I want him. Desperately.

"I'm going to—"

As soon as I say I'm about to come, he instantly stops. I pant hard from getting so close to coming and then having it ripped away from me.

"Please," I beg.

He obliges. I feel him thrust inside me as his balls hit my clit over and over. His hand comes up and finds by breast. It's exactly what I want; it's exactly what I need. He builds me up over and over, each time just stopping short of letting me come.

"Please," I beg again and again.

"Patience, Beauty."

He doesn't relent though. Instead, he builds us up over and over and still denies us each time. I can't take it anymore. I reach my hand down to my clit, intending to make myself come whether he wants me to or not.

When he realizes what I'm doing, he flips me over in one movement and pins my hands high above my head. He is not going to let me come without his permission. He enters me again and begins the slow torture all over again.

"Please, Beast," I beg again.

"Open your eyes."

I do, and I see my Beast standing over me. It's exactly who I thought it was. A tortured man I shouldn't love. That I shouldn't want. A man more dangerous than even I could have imagined.

"Come now, Beauty."

I open my eyes and pant from my intense dream.

"You okay?" Jake asks.

I nod.

"That was some dream you were having. You were panting hard, and every once in a while, you would mumble something about a beast. Didn't make sense to me. Does it to you?"

"No," I lie even though it makes complete sense.

It's just one more reason I should choose Jake over Beast. Jake is safe. Beast is dangerous. But it doesn't keep me from wanting to know if the danger would be worth it.

20

SCARLETT

JAKE'S PARENTS' house is anything but typical. It's beautiful and large, and despite being over fifty years old, it's been completely renovated. His parents live near a large lake in Upstate New York, making it one of the most beautiful and serene houses I've ever been to.

As I climb out of Jake's Civic, all I can think about is how peaceful it is here compared to the city. Even compared to the house I grew up in Las Vegas, it's larger and more serene here. If I didn't love the hustle and bustle of New York City so much, this is where I would choose to live. It's exactly where I'd pick if I needed a break from my life.

It's exactly what I need right now. And Jake knew that.

Jake walks around to the trunk of his car and pulls our bags out. He slings them over his shoulder like they weigh nothing. I smile a little as he does it. It's a good reminder that there are plenty of muscles beneath his polished exterior.

Jake begins walking toward the door of his parents' house and motions with his head for me to follow. I do.

Before he can get to the front door, his mother and father run out and embrace him in a hug. I smile and take it in. It must be nice to have parents who care about him so much. His mother looks up after she has finished with her hug, and she sees me. Her eyes fill with a warmness that I haven't felt from any mother figure in a long time.

"Scarlett, honey, it's so good to see you again. Thank you for coming to our anniversary party," Evette Walton says.

She walks over with open arms, and I embrace her. I get a deep breath of what smells like brownies mixed with her motherly perfume, something I haven't smelled in a long time, probably since the last time I embraced this woman.

"It's nice to see you, too, Evette," I say.

Larry walks over next and embraces me in a similar hug with stronger arms to hold me tighter. "I see you made it okay."

I nod and smile.

"Well, come in, come in. Jake, you guys can share your bedroom. I have it all made out for you," Evette says.

When a slow grin forms over Jake's face at the thought of sharing a bedroom, I give him a dirty look.

"I'll just show Scarlett to my room then," Jake says, winking at me.

I don't want to share a room with Jake this weekend. Not when I'm so annoyed and angry with him.

"That's fine, dear. You guys have about an hour before guests will begin to arrive for the party. Plenty of time to freshen up," Evette says.

I swear, she winks at her son.

I sigh. I guess I have no say in how this weekend will go if Evette and Jake are already teaming up against me. I'm sure it's only a matter of time before Larry joins. So, I might as well give in to them and just enjoy the weekend.

I follow Jake into the house, and my jaw drops a little. It's just as beautiful as I remember. I was only here once before. We didn't stay long, just one night, and we didn't share a room then. It was just after we'd started dating, and Jake had had to fly back here for his brother's wedding. I'd decided to come along, needing a break from school.

And that weekend was just as much of a break as this one is going to be.

Still, even though I've been here before, I forgot how warm it felt inside. I forgot how it felt like a home.

I follow Jake up the curved staircase that overlooks the entrance. The hallways are filled with family pictures of him and his brothers and parents. As we climb up the stairs, I stare at the pictures before my eyes, watching as Jake grew from a naked baby into a striking man.

"You coming?" Jake says when he notices that I stopped to stare at a picture of him at college graduation.

It's the Jake that I know best. Young and carefree, but determined. Now, he's grown into quite the accomplishment.

I nod and continue to follow Jake up the stairs. We walk down the hallway, which is filled with more pictures of him and his family, before Jake opens the door to the bedroom that I haven't been in before. His bedroom.

My eyes widen as I look around the room. It still looks like what I would guess his boyhood room looked like. It's like his parents haven't changed the room at all since he lived here. They haven't turned it into a guest bedroom or gym, like most parents would. It's still the same. The only sign that anything has been replaced is a large king-size bed, sitting in the center, instead of what used to be a twin.

Jake places our bags on the floor as he quietly looks at me. He doesn't say a word. He just leaves me be as I begin to inspect every inch of his room. More pictures of him and his brothers sit in the room. Posters of Angelina Jolie plaster his walls.

I smile. "I didn't picture you as an Angelina fan."

Jake smiles and nods, but doesn't say anything. I don't think he wants to distract me from continuing to inspect his room and from him studying me. I walk over to the shelves of old trophy after trophy —from basketball and football sporting events. I run my hand over the cold, dusty metal that contains a lifetime of Jake's boyhood. I pick up a picture frame of Jake with his arm around a girl in a prom dress. I smile, seeing how happy he is to be taking the girl. I imagine, she's a nice girl, unlike me.

I frown and replace the frame back on the shelf where I found it.

"What's wrong?" Jake asked.

"Why me? You should be with a good girl, like the girl in the picture. Not someone like me."

Jake walks over to me and puts his arms around me, pulling me into a tight hug that's so similar to his father's. "You're exactly what I want. Strong, determined, sexy. And you're enough of an adventure to keep me busy and entertained for more than a lifetime."

I don't smile as Jake lets me go, but I don't argue with him either.

I walk to the bed to pick up my bag. "I should get changed if the party starts soon."

Jake nods. "You can have the bathroom, and I'll get changed here. And don't worry about tonight; I'll sleep on the floor. I don't want to rush anything."

I force my face into a tight smile now as I walk to the bathroom that's off of his bedroom. I close the door behind myself. I'm thankful that Jake doesn't want to rush anything, especially when I'm still angry with him.

But maybe that's the problem—that Jake doesn't want to rush things. That he is too nice. Maybe I want him to push me beyond my limits and show me how much he wants me, despite my protests. Maybe I want a little more roughness, a little more mystery, a little bit of not-so nice.

I try to push those thoughts out of my head as I rummage through my bag to find a dress that I packed. I pick the sexiest black dress that I brought and put it on. My boobs look fantastic in this dress, and my legs look long and lean. And, when I put on the black pumps that go with the dress, fix my hair, and apply a little red lipstick, Jake won't be able to resist me.

The question is, do I have the balls to wear this dress in front of his parents, knowing full well that they will know exactly what I'm planning for later?

A wicked grin creeps up my face. Yes, I do.

Maybe twenty minutes later, when I exit the bathroom, Jake is already gone. Probably already downstairs, helping his parents set up for the party.

I walk down the stairs. Maybe, if I get lucky, I'll be able to corner Jake and give him a taste of what I want to do later. Instead, I get lost in the house. Not literally lost, but my mind wanders as I stare at the pictures of the family. As I stare at the furniture that's a little too worn in a house this nice, yet somehow, it works because I know it contains memories of the family enjoying time together. The house is just a little too dusty because they don't bother to hire maids to clean it. I continue to walk around the house, lost in my own thoughts, for I don't know how long, before I hear voices coming from what I remember to be the kitchen.

"Can I do anything to help?" I ask as I enter the kitchen.

Evette looks up from her station at the kitchen and warmly smiles at me, but it's not her reaction I'm worried about. It's Jake's. He drops the salad bowl he was holding, and I watch as the glass shatters into pieces on the floor, lettuce scattering. His mouth falls open as he looks at me, showing his shock at what I'm wearing.

It takes him a second to regain his composure, and then he raises an eyebrow at me, as if to say, *You sure you're going with that tonight?*

I smile. *I'm sure*, I silently say back.

"Let me help you with that," I say, walking over to Jake.

I get down on the floor to help them pick up the salad and broken glass, giving him a perfect view of my breasts, as he bends down next to me.

"Thanks," he says as we finish cleaning up the kitchen mess he made.

I try to hold back my giggle because I know what the thanks is for, and it's not for helping him clean up the floor. It's for the bulge in his pants that has been forming ever since I walked in the room.

I move my attention from Jake to Evette, now knowing that there's nothing I can do with Jake for several hours. I'm not going to do anything with him at least until his parents' party is well underway, and our services are not needed.

Evette is arranging cookies and brownies. She most likely home-baked the desserts. Another stark difference between her and my mother. My mother would never be caught cooking anything in the kitchen.

I begin helping Evette arrange the dozens of cookies on the fancy silver platters that she has set out.

Larry calls for Jake to help him move some tables outside, and then it's just me and Evette left in the kitchen.

"It's good to see you and Jake back together again."

I try to figure out what to say to this woman without lying to her. I don't want to lie. Technically, Jake and I aren't together yet. Also, I don't want to tell her I technically accepted his proposal.

"I'm happy to be here," is what I settle on.

The truth is, I am happy to be here. It's nice to have a weekend away from work and to really get a chance to see if Jake and I could ever work.

"I know you and Jake have a lot to figure out. And there are reasons you didn't work out before. I'm sure those reasons made sense then. I'm just not sure they still make sense now. I know you're still trying to figure out what you want, and I understand that, but give him a chance. He's not a bad boy."

"I will," I say honestly. Because that's what I plan to do.

Her last line has me worried though because she's right. Jake's not a bad man. There's not a bad bone in his body. And I'm afraid I need a little bad boy every now and then.

The doorbell rings, and Evette rushes around the kitchen.

"Let me finish. You go see to your guests," I say.

"Are you sure, honey?"

"Yes."

"Thank you," Evette says as she removes her apron, fluffs her hair, and hurries from the kitchen to the front door.

I finish placing the desserts on the trays and then carry them outside to the table set up with the other food. People are already beginning to gather together outside in the backyard. I remember the yard was my favorite thing about the house. It is large, filled with large oak trees that look older than any of us. There are a couple of gazebos on the property, and now, there are dozens of tables for people to grab food or a cocktail from. The only staff I see are a couple of bartenders manning the bar. The rest are just people who love the Waltons and want to help them celebrate.

It's amazing to see the mix of people who have come out to celebrate—young and old, wealthy and not-so-wealthy friends, family, and acquaintances. All the people here fell in love with the Waltons the second they met them. Because they are nice people, people who you want to be around because they remind you of your own home.

I scan the crowd, looking for Jake, and I finally see him talking with what looks to me like old high school buddies. I leave him to it and walk over to the bar where I order a glass of wine.

"You're my kind of girl. Bar's the first place I always stop, too," Larry says as he stands at the bar next to me.

I turn and smile at Larry as he orders a whiskey on the rocks.

"Glad he traded up from Karissa. Those two never made any sense together, if you ask me," Larry says.

"Thanks," I say hesitantly.

I'm not sure if I like the fact that they already like me better than Karissa. They barely know me, and I still believe that Jake deserves better, someone nicer. All I deserve is...

"Let me introduce you to some of my friends," Larry says.

"I'd be happy to meet your friends."

Larry leads me over to a group of older men, and we begin chatting about everything from my job to politics. It's easy to talk to these men. And it helps me get lost in the evening of drinks, good food, and good friends. Even if they aren't my friends.

The only problem is, I've barely spent any time with Jake.

I see him across the backyard, talking with his mother. I give him the most seductive look I can. My eyes scream with need for sex. I bite my lip a little too hard and then seductively run my tongue over my bottom lip. I nod toward the house, telling him to follow me. So, I begin walking toward the house with the intention of going to his bedroom and waiting for him to follow me and be the bad boy who has to be buried inside him.

21

BEAST

FUCK. What am I doing here?

That's the question I've asked myself about a dozen times since I followed Scarlett and Jake to his parents' house. Since I threw on a suit and hid among the crowd of people at his parents' crowded anniversary party. Since I was allowed on the property, despite not being on the guest list. The security here is nonexistent. Basically begging me to follow her here and show her how wrong she is to be with him.

Because she is fucking wrong.

I know she shouldn't be with me, but Jake Walton is the absolute worst man for her. He's not strong enough for her. He's far too nice. And he won't challenge her like she needs to be challenged.

Then, why the hell is she here? That's the question that keeps playing in my head now. *Why the hell is she here? Is she really that desperate?*

I don't know, but I'm about to get some answers.

Scarlett makes her way toward the house, and I know it's my only chance to get her alone. I know it's risky. I know that, by following her, I risk her finding out who I am. But I have to go after her. I have to have her. She hasn't answered any of my text messages, and I simply can't wait any longer. Now that I know that she's been with Jake, I want some damn answers.

Scarlett walks into the house, and I walk in just a few seconds behind her. I glance behind me to see if he's following her. He isn't. He's too tied in a conversation with his mother and her friends. It'll be at least a good twenty minutes before he can get away. More than enough time to do what I need to do.

I follow Scarlett as she slinks through the house to the stairway and goes up the stairs. I wait until she's made it all the way up the stairs and into his bedroom before I follow. I run up the stairs, taking them two at a time, anxious to get to her.

I pause for a second at the door.

Here's where everything could go wrong. If she sees me before I have a chance to turn the light into darkness, then I'll be fucked. Whatever the hell this is will be over. But if I don't open the damn door, I won't get to fuck her.

It's really not a decision.

I push the door open and am happy to see the lights are still off.

"I wasn't sure if you would come," she says.

Her dress is already off and lying on the floor. She's completely naked, standing in his bedroom in almost complete darkness, just a few beams of light sneaking in through the blinds. The light is enough that I know she'll see me if I move toward her even one step. So, instead, I wait for her to come to me, just like I imagine that damn fucker would do.

She takes my bait and walks toward me where I wait in the darkness, her curves swinging back and forth in the few beams of light that are slipping through the blinds. My mouth runs dry as I watch her, and it's a good thing because it prevents me from speaking even though I want to.

I want to demand her to turn around and show me that tight ass that I fell in love with last time. I want to control her and tell her to get on her knees and suck my cock, like she promised in her text. I want to control her, but I can't. Not until I have my lips on her.

Because, when she realizes that it's me and not him, she will have a chance to say no. But as soon as I have my lips and my hands on her, I know she won't be able to resist.

She walks closer and closer until she's just an arm's length away from me. I reach out then, unable to wait any longer, and I pull her fully into the darkness. She lets out a quiet whimper as her body becomes pressed against my chest. I wish I'd thought to remove my clothes while waiting for her to come to me because, right now, I need her skin against my skin.

Our hands grab ahold of each other as our lips find each other again, our tongues tangling together. I feel a desperation oozing from her that I haven't felt before. A desperation for her to get exactly what she's been missing these past few days without me. Something that I know he hasn't been giving to her. She wants to be controlled. She wants to feel that rush of adrenaline. She wants me. And I'm more than happy to give her that.

Kisses tangle together until I have no idea how many times we've kissed. Hands tangle together in hair and clothes. Our bodies cling together, fighting to become one again, if only for a few moments.

Goddamn, she is worth the risk.

Her hands move inside the collar of my shirt, trying to get at my skin. I love her hands there, but I want her on her knees more. I want to see her gorgeous big eyes looking up at me as she takes my cock in her mouth. I want to see her expert tongue moving around me before I reward her by taking her against the window of his bedroom, so if anyone looked up, they could see an outline of a woman being fucked.

"On your knees," I say.

She freezes, and I think it's because she wants to tell me that she wants to be in control this time, just like some of her text indicated. I can't let that happen now, not when she's been with him. I need to be in control now.

She pushes her hands against my chest and takes a quick step backward and then another. "Beast?"

I take a step forward, but stop short of letting myself into the light. I thought, once I kissed her, she would forget that she came here to fuck Jake instead of me. I was wrong. But there's no point in denying that now that she knows it's not Jake.

"Yes."

"I need you to leave," she says.

She gathers up her dress and slips it back on before I have a chance to capture the image of her naked body in my head forever.

"No."

She shakes her head at me with anger on her face. Her nostrils are flared, her cheeks are bright red, and her hair is a mess on top of her head. And, God, I've never wanted to fuck her more than I do right now.

"You need to leave. Now."

"No. I need to talk to you. Now."

She takes a step forward, and I take a step back, afraid that she might see me.

"You. Need. To. Leave. Now."

"That's not happening. Not until I have you first."

She huffs. "Why are you both such complete idiots?" she says mostly to herself as she runs her hand through her hair. She walks back and forth in the room. "I don't want you. We're through. I'm with Jake now."

Anger boils inside me at the thought of them being together. Really, at the thought of her being with any man other than me. "He's not good enough for you. You shouldn't be with him."

"Then, whom should I be with?" she challenges.

I want to say *me*, but I don't because she deserves better than me. My silence gives her, her answer.

"Because it sure as hell isn't you," she spits at me.

"Anybody but him."

"You don't get to tell me what to do."

"I have before."

"Yeah, well, that's over."

I sigh, hating her words. They are the worst words I've ever heard. But I have no idea what I have to do to convince her that, at this moment, I would do almost anything. I don't care about my job. I don't care about my life, outside of this room. All I care about is her and having her and wanting her to want me back.

It doesn't make sense. I've never wanted a woman to want me before. I prefer to just control them and tell them what they want, and they almost always seem to oblige. Beauty though, she's different. I love the challenge and her defiance.

"You should go," she says again—this time, her voice soft and defeated.

"No."

"Jake will be here any minute. You should go before he throws you out of the party."

"I don't think Jake's coming."

Scarlett doesn't argue that fact though because she knows, deep down, that he isn't coming. But she will say anything to get me to leave, and I know she doesn't have the willpower to leave me on her own.

"What do I have to do to have you again?"

She just shakes her head and ignores me.

"Answer me," I say, more commanding.

"You can start with showing me who you are."

I don't know why, but I wasn't expecting her to say that. I thought she liked the mystery and not knowing who I was. I thought that was part of the excitement for her.

"Why?"

"Because maybe I would like a relationship with you beyond text messages and you randomly showing up whenever the fuck you want to fuck me and nothing more. Maybe I want to date and see where it goes."

"I don't date. And fucking is as far as this goes."

"Then, show me who you are. Show me why this is as far as we go."

It's what I want, too. God, I want to be able to fuck her in the light of day instead of the darkness. For once, I want to hear her say my name. I want to gain her trust completely. But I know, as soon as she sees me, she'll be gone.

She waits for a moment longer to see if I answer, and when I don't, she walks past me, leaving me alone in the room. In the darkness. Leaving me alone with the one request I can never answer.

Who am I?

22

SCARLETT

I SLAM the door shut to Jake's bedroom, and then I begin running down the stairs, trying to get as far away from the bastard as I possibly can. Trying to erase his kiss from my lips. Trying to forget about the fact that I kissed Beast again when I swore I wouldn't. I swore I wanted Jake, not Beast. And I know that, on some level, when he walked in the door, it wasn't Jake, and still, I kissed him anyway.

What is wrong with me? Why can't I let that one night go? Why am I okay with settling for nice? Why am I okay with either one?

Because I'm tired of being *alone.*

I continue walking toward the back of the house, intending to go back outside and enjoy the party, like nothing just happened. I can't though. For one, I look like I just had sex. My cheeks are flushed, my hair is unkempt, and my lipstick is smeared. I would feel too guilty, walking around like that with these people. Too guilty to face Jake right now. I don't exactly have any other place to go though.

I stand at the door that leads back outside to the party, trying to figure out where I could go. The lake is just down the hill from the house. If I could just make my way down there before anyone spotted me, there would be far less people for me to deal with.

I open the door and scan the crowd for Jake. I see him, still in deep conversation with his mother and her friends. So, instead of going left toward him, I go right. I skirt the edge of the party, smiling politely when anyone notices me, but I make my way down to the lake, only stopping once to grab two gin and tonics to take with me down to the water's edge.

I make it to the edge of the water just as the sun is setting over the lake. I hike my dress up and remove my heels before I take a seat on the sand and stick my feet into the lake water. I don't care that the dress is now ruined. All I care about is drinking on the edge of the water, alone, so I can figure out what the hell I'm going to do with the two men in my life.

First though, I down the first gin and tonic and mix that cup with the still full cup. And then I just stare at the sun setting, trying to forget what just happened.

The sun goes down quickly though, and then I'm left in the darkness with only the light from the moon and the flicking of lights from the party behind me. Without those lights, I'd be sitting in the darkness. Just like Beast.

I feel a tear trickling down my cheek. I let it fall. I let myself feel the pain. Even though I don't know why I'm crying.

Beast.

My dark stranger.

My lover.

I didn't realize how much I cared about Beast. How much I wanted there to be a chance of *more* with him. From the first moment I met him in the hotel room, it wasn't just one night for me. My heart has been begging for more and more and more. Never going to be satisfied until I at least get a chance to be with him. But, after tonight, I know that there isn't going to be a chance.

Beast isn't a *more* kind of guy. His secrets are more important than giving us a chance together.

Maybe tonight was for the best. Because, tonight, I can finally let him go, knowing that we will never have a shot.

So, that's why I let the tears that I almost never let out fall. I don't remember ever crying like this, except for ten years ago when I was told that Kinsley was dead. After that, it was only tears of happiness when I found out she was alive. After that, I haven't cried for myself because I have never gone through anything nearly as painful as she has.

Right now, I let myself cry. And cry and cry. Because my heart is broken.

I realize now that, when I said yes to Beast, I gave him half of my heart. And, when I said yes to Jake, I gave him the other half. And, now, I have nothing left.

But maybe Beast confirming that there can't be anything more set half of my heart free? Maybe, once the tears are gone, I can reclaim that half of my heart and decide if I want to keep it for myself or give the rest of it to Jake?

I wipe the tears from my eyes and try to forget about Beast. It should be easy to forget about somebody I didn't even know. I didn't know his name, the shade of his eyes, or what he did for a living. I didn't know any of the important things about him. All I know is that he likes control, he has intensity in his eyes, and he seems to know me better than I know myself. If only he were able to share something with me, anything, show me some sign that he wanted to do more than just fuck me, then maybe he would've been enough. But he's not enough.

I take another sip of my drink as my thoughts turn from Beast to Jake. Jake's caring, nice, a good man. He's everything I should want in a husband and father to any of my children. The only problem is, he doesn't get my heart pumping. And he takes things far too slow. He hasn't even tried to have sex with me yet. Not really. Even when I try, he doesn't seem to want to push forward. Even though we've had sex in the past, albeit it was ten years ago.

I could just forget both men. I could adopt or try surrogacy and have kids by myself. I could do it. Then, I could have the family without having to deal with either of the two men. Or any other man. I could have my own family, and then I wouldn't be alone again.

"Hey, stranger. Is this seat taken?" Jake says as he walks up behind me.

I wipe my face again, making sure all the tears are gone. I slightly turn my head so that I can see Jake. "It's all yours."

I watch as Jake sits beside me on the wet sand. He kicks off his shoes and rolls up his pants legs before sticking his feet into the water.

"Here, I thought you could use another drink." He hands me another gin and tonic, and I take it from him.

"Thanks," I say, smiling at the drink.

Jake even remembers my drink order.

Why the hell don't I see that he's clearly the best choice?

"Sorry I didn't spend much time with you at the party. I thought it was best to give you some space," Jake says.

"I understand. I'm still trying to figure out a few things myself."

"Like whether you want to wear this ring again?" Jake holds up the ring he proposed to me with.

I nod, surprised to see the ring in his hand. I try to think back to where I put it. I remember packing it in my things, but I don't remember taking it out.

"Did you go through my things?"

Jake nods. "I thought you might have had the ring. I thought that, if I could just find the most opportune moment to give it to you again, this time, you would say yes, and it would stick."

I take the ring from his hand and hold it in mine, staring at the sparkly diamond. "And you think now is the most opportune time for me to say yes?"

Jake frowns. "No. I just realized, I don't want to trick you or trap you into marrying me. I want you to want to say yes, no matter if I asked you to marry me in the nicest restaurant in New York City or in front of the city dump. Or after I blurted it out after a night of heated passion. Or while sitting on the edge of the lake in my parents' back-yard. I want you to want to say yes because you love me and want to marry me, not because you just want to get married, period."

I take a deep breath in. And then I hand him the ring back. "I want that, too. I'm not able to say that yet. I can't give you a definite yes. I can't give you that. So, hold on to this until it doesn't matter when or how you ask me, until you know I won't be able to help but say yes because I'm desperately in love with you. Not in love with the idea of marriage."

Jake's frown deepens as he takes the ring back and tucks it back into his pocket. "So, where do we go from here?"

"You ask me out. I already know my answer to that question. And it doesn't matter how you ask me; my answer would still be the same. No matter if you asked me in the fanciest restaurant or next to the city dump or while sitting on the edge of the lake in your parents' backyard, I already know my answer to that question."

Jake's grin is larger than I've seen it in a long time, and his smile actually reaches his eyes. "Scarlett, will you go out with me?"

I smile and give him a shot at the other half of my heart that I just reclaimed. "Yes."

I reach my hand to the base of his neck and pull him into a kiss. It's a tentative kiss on both of our parts. He's trying to figure out exactly where he stands, and I'm trying not to compare it to the kiss I had earlier today that wasn't from him. Still, the kiss is nice and exactly what we both need at the moment.

We pull away at the same time—both keeping our eyes closed, both still holding on to each other, just no longer kissing.

"Let's go to bed," I say.

I hear him swallow nervously.

I know the right place to have sex again for the first time in ten years is not in his parents' house, so I put his nerves at ease. "Just to sleep. I'm exhausted."

"I don't have to sleep on the floor?"

I let out a small giggle. "No."

23

BEAST

I DRIVE FAST, needing to get somewhere so that I can get a release soon since she wouldn't give me what I needed. I don't understand why I feel like this. And why I won't just go out and pick up another woman. That's the simple solution. Find a new woman. Fuck her. And then get back to my job.

It's not that simple though. My cock doesn't get excited anymore whenever I see any other woman. I don't dream or fantasize about other women, just *her*. I can't do my job properly because, even when I'm in the middle of doing the job, I'm thinking about her.

My mind is a mess, but I'm afraid my heart might be worse. Because my mind can be controlled. I can tell my mind over and over again that she's not worth it. I can remind my mind that being with her would effectively destroy my life. Because that's what I'd be doing —killing us both. My mind isn't the problem.

My heart though...that's another story. I don't understand what my heart is feeling. I don't understand how my heartbeat speeds up when I'm around her. I don't understand why my heart begs me to tell her my name. I don't understand how my heart expects me to give up everything for her. That's something that I have no idea how to control.

I drive faster and faster in my black Mercedes-Benz that has blacked out windows so that nobody can see who I am. Nobody knows who I am. Not her. Not my employers. Not my employees. Not my friends. Not even my family. Nobody knows who I really am and what I really want.

And the only person that I want to know who I really am is Scarlett.

I almost miss my turn because I'm already distracted again, thinking about her. I turn sharply at the last minute and listen to my tires squeal. I swerve into a parking spot before killing the engine and climbing out. Every time I put a step on the ground as I make my way to the building, I take a deep breath, trying to calm myself. It's no use.

I'm still thinking about her with every step. I'm thinking about her plump red lips. Her long mane of hair. Her legs that go on for miles. I think about the strong woman who controls her own empire, who controls her destiny. But, for some reason, she gives the control to me every time I fuck her. I have a feeling she would give more control to me if I would just tell her who I was.

I make it to the door and swing it open as my breathing has now turned into hard pants instead of calming breaths, like I intended. I feel sweat forming on my forehead, threatening to move and sting my eyes. I wipe it off as I walk to the man behind the desk.

"You okay, man? You don't look so good," he says.

I glare at him. "I'm fine. I need an hour." I pull out my wallet and throw some cash on the table.

The man wearing the name tag that says, *Jimmy*, nods and takes my cash. I walk to the shooting range behind him. I don't bother with the stupid safety goggles or ear protection. I don't have to bother stopping in a locker to get a gun, like most people would. My gun is always on me. I pull my pistol from the back of my pants along with the ammunition I always carry.

I straighten my arms and fire over and over and over at the target of a man across from me. I perfectly hit the target in the head every time. I move my aim from the head to the heart and fire another dozen shots. Each shot perfectly pierces the heart. I continue doing this for an hour until that hour turns into another hour and then another. Until I have no idea how long I've been here.

But it does give me the release I've been needing all day. It gives me the control when I have none over my life. When I've finally had enough, I begin putting the gun and remaining ammunition away into the back of my pants.

"I could watch you shoot all day. I've never seen a man shoot with such accuracy. I know you're not a cop or a military guy. And I know you don't work for any faction of the US government," Jimmy says from behind me.

I turn and look at the older man who runs the range. I haven't ever been to this shooting range before, and for this very reason, I tend not to go back to ranges more than once. I don't want the employees to get to know me. I don't want them to know my story. But no one's ever questioned me before because I only come once and then never return.

"And why do you say that?"

The old man smiles at me. "Because you're the best shot I've ever seen. And no training from any government facility would make you that good."

"I didn't train at a government facility, but that doesn't mean I don't work for the government now."

"Whatever you say. I don't care whom you work for. I just wanted to let you know that you're welcome back anytime you want, no questions asked. You don't have to worry about hiding who you truly are. I respect you for whatever you are."

I nod, but don't bother saying thank you. "See you around, Jimmy," I say. I walk out of the building and back to my car. I don't intend on coming back again. It's too risky.

I start the ignition in my car and then drive quickly out of the parking lot. I glance at the clock in my car. I was there for almost four hours. Enough time to give me plenty of perspective on my current situation. I can't have her, but the only way I'll be able to let her go is if I find somebody that should be with her. Someone who can take care of her and cherish her in the way that she should be cherished.

I'm not convinced Jake Walton is that man yet. Maybe, after I meet him in person, I'll change my mind. I just need to arrange the meeting.

I dial the number, and the phone connects to my car speakers as I wait for him to answer, so I can schedule the meeting.

24

SCARLETT

WHEN I HEAD BACK into my office on Monday morning, I feel refreshed. I feel *over* whatever the hell happened between me and Beast. And I feel ready to give Jake the real shot that he deserves. But, most importantly, I'm ready to get back to work and my normal life.

"Good morning, Preston," I say happily as I walk into the office where Preston's already waiting for me.

"Good morning," he says back. "Somebody's in a happy mood today."

"Yep. I had a good weekend, and it gave me some perspective on my life. I'm excited to get back to work today."

"Good, because we have a lot of fucking work to do."

I walk over to my desk and take a sip of my latte that Preston always makes me every morning. "Where do we start?"

Preston smiles, happy that I'm more focused on my work than I've been in a long time. "We start with picking the models you want to use for our national makeup campaign."

I smile. Being a former model myself, it's one of my favorite parts of the job. Picking models to represent my brand. Making girls' dreams come true because that's what I'm doing when I pick a model. I never pick someone who has tons of experience or an actress who wants to make an extra buck by modeling. I always pick somebody new and fresh and give them a new chance at their dream.

"Let's go then," I say.

Preston nods and begins walking to our offices on the main floor where we interview models and do some test shots.

By the time we get there, Jamie, my casting director in charge of finding our models, has already begun explaining to the models how the process works and getting everything organized. She's the best at what she does, and she is one of the most organized people I know. It's why I love her.

"Are you ready to start?" I ask Jamie.

Preston and I take our seats behind the long table that serves as a desk for the three of us while we do the interviews.

"Of course. It's eight o'clock, and we always start on time," Jamie says.

"Good, because we have a full schedule today," Preston says.

"When do you not?" Jamie asks.

Preston just shrugs. "Never."

"All right, we need models one through five," Jamie says.

The models begin lining up on the makeshift catwalk, and Jamie takes a seat next to us. I glance down at the five models' headshots, each one of them gorgeous in their own right. Each one of them would probably do a great job in working for us. But we only need one out of the more than a hundred who showed up today for the job. Jamie tells them to start walking, and they do, one at a time, down the catwalk.

I smile and watch as each of them walks. A couple of them shake a little as they walk, most likely from nerves. One even stumbles in the heels she is wearing. Only two of the first five look confident. I focus in on those two as they walk. Either one of them would do. But I also know from experience that there will be a couple of confident ones in almost every bunch. And those are the ones that I'll have to choose from. We don't have time to train someone who isn't ready yet.

When they finish walking, we ask them to line up. Then, we

begin asking them basic questions to see how they do with talking and interacting with the camera since that will be a part of the job while shooting a commercial.

"Why do you want this job?" I ask.

We get the standard answers from most of the girls.

"I've always dreamed of being a model."

"Your makeup line is my favorite."

"You're such an inspiration, and I'd love to learn more from you."

And then one stands out from an unexpected girl. The one who tripped and almost fell. The one who I almost immediately counted out. "Because I'm the fucking right person for this job. I'll work harder than anyone else. And I want to be the next Scarlett Bell. And I will be whether or not I get this chance."

I jot down a note on her headshot. Number three. Emmy Bitton. I know without looking at any of the other women that she will be the one I choose. That Preston and Jamie will fight me on it, claiming that another one was better, stronger, more confident. A better fit for the job. That's not what I look for when I look at models. I look first to see if they are a star in the making. I look for someone like me or someone like my best friend, Kinsley. I look for someone who will change the world, and I know that Emmy Bitton will. And it's not because she just told me that she would. Saying that you're going to do something is just the first part. The actual following it up, that's the key to actually getting what you want and actually changing the world. I have every faith that Emmy will do it even if I don't give her this chance.

We spend the next hour and a half going through model after model, and just like I expected, Preston and Jamie both like another one.

"It's got to be number twenty-five. She was, by far, the best. She has the best face for beauty and more confidence than even you, Scarlett," Jamie says.

"No, no! It's got to be number seventy-two. Did you see how she handled that walk? Flawless," Preston says.

I watch them bicker back and forth, not really adding anything because I already know who we are going to choose.

"What do you think, Scarlett?" Jamie asks. "Number twenty-five or seventy-two? Or did you have someone else in mind?"

"Number three."

I watch as Jamie and Preston dig through their files and notes, trying to find the girl I'm talking about. I hand them my headshot of the girl to refresh their memories. It's easy for me to find because she's the only girl in my Yes pile.

"She's pretty enough, I guess," Preston says. He looks at the picture of the blonde woman who wore her hair in long curls, reminding me of how Kinsley used to wear hers when she was a model. "But she has that small scar on her cheek that will be hard to cover with makeup. And didn't she stumble? I think you got the wrong girl, Scarlett. She's not confident enough."

I point to the girl. "She's our girl," I say.

Preston and Jamie frown at me at the same time.

"Are you sure?" Jamie asks.

"I'm sure."

"I'll make it happen then," Jamie says, standing from the desk and gathering her things to make the call that will change this woman's life forever.

I gather up my things, and Preston and I both walk back to my office. We make it back upstairs when I see Jake standing in my doorway, his arms folded across his chest, with a dumb-looking grin on his face when he sees me.

"So much for getting work done today," Preston whispers in my ear.

I laugh at Preston. "We'll get plenty of work done today. I'm sure Jake just wants to say hi."

But I glance over at Preston, who's eyeing me suspiciously, not believing a word I'm saying. Maybe I'm wrong. Maybe Jake isn't here just to say hi. Maybe he does want to steal me away today and play hooky. Maybe he does want to show me a wilder side.

Jake automatically kisses me when I get close enough to him. I frown, not liking that his kisses are automatic already.

"What's up?"

"I just came to see how you were doing today. I missed you."

"We just got back last night and slept over at my apartment again. I don't know how you can miss me," I say, laughing.

"I'm not sure either, but I do." Jake's large smile returns to his face. "So, do you have any lunch plans or evening plans? Because I don't know how I'm gonna make it through the day if I don't know when I'll get to see you next."

I glance over at Preston, and he's rolling his eyes at Jake's cheesy words.

I want to go out to lunch with Jake, but I can't. I know I already have plans. "Can't do lunch. Already have a meeting lined up. But how about drinks with me and Preston and Preston's new girlfriend?"

I glance over at Preston, who nods like that can be arranged.

"Sounds good to me. As long as I can see my favorite girl, I'll be a happy man."

"Preston will let you know the time and place to meet us."

Jake wraps his arm around my waist and pulls me to him into a kiss, this one more passionate than the first.

"I would say, get a room, but you two might actually do that, and then I'd be left to make all the decisions—*again*," Preston says.

We both pull away.

"I'd better get back to work. My boss is quite the tyrant," I say jokingly.

"I'd better get back to work, too. I wouldn't want my boss to think I was lazy or anything," Jake says.

Jake leaves and heads back to his office, leaving me and Preston alone.

"Funny, I'm not your boss, just your assistant," Preston says.

"You could've fooled me," I say.

Preston shakes his head. "Just get to work before I fire you," he says with a smile on his face.

I finish sending my last email of the day and then holler to Preston, who is sitting in his office, just around the corner from me, "I think it's time to call it a day."

A few minutes later, Preston walks into my office. "Sounds good. My girlfriend, Kathy, said she could meet us there in a half hour."

"Good. I can't wait to meet this girl. And Jake?"

Preston frowns. "Sorry, forgot to tell you that Jake had to cancel. Said he had a late meeting and that he would meet you back at your apartment later."

I frown. I didn't think Jake would work harder than I did. I guess I was wrong. I guess I'll have to wait to see Jake later.

"Let's go then," I say.

Preston nods, and we head out of Beautifully Bell Enterprises to my waiting driver, George.

"How are you doing this evening?" George asks as we climb into the car.

"Pretty good. My date canceled on me tonight, so I am playing third wheel with Preston and his girlfriend."

George raises his eyebrows. "You have a girlfriend?"

Preston rolls his eyes. "Why does everyone keep asking me that?"

George and I both laugh.

George says, "Sorry. I guess I thought that—"

"Yeah, I know. You thought I was gay," Preston says.

"No. I thought that you were a mama's boy and a workaholic, so you wouldn't have time for anyone but yourself," George says.

Preston's phone rings, and he answers it, confirming George's statement that he is a workaholic.

I glance at my own phone and frown because I haven't gotten any text messages from Jake or from Beast. I don't know which one stings more. I thought Jake would text me that he was sorry he couldn't come. I hoped that Beast would have changed his mind and said that he was ready to tell me who he was. That I was worth risking whatever he'd be risking by telling me who he was.

George stops the car in front of a new bar that Preston wanted to try out. We both climb out and walk into the bar. We find a small booth table while we wait for his girlfriend to arrive. The waiter comes over and asks for our drinks. We each order a gin and tonic.

"So, when is Kathy supposed to get here?" I sip on the gin and tonic the waiter just brought us.

Preston nervously glances down at his phone. "She's not coming out."

"What? Why?"

"Work."

"And I thought we were the workaholics. Who'd have thought our significant others would be working harder than us?"

Preston shakes his head and takes a drink. "Good thing we have each other when our significant others don't work out."

I nod. "So, what do you think about Jake?"

Preston stares down at his drink, like it's the most interesting thing in the world.

"What is it?" I ask.

"Nothing. I just always pictured you with somebody who was more your equal."

"How is Jake not my equal?"

"I don't know, Scarlett. He's just not."

I swirl the ice around in my drink, but I know exactly what he is talking about. Jake isn't my equal. Opposite maybe but not equal.

But don't they say that opposites attract?

"So, is Kathy your equal?"

Preston shrugs. "No, but she's fun to fuck."

I laugh and spew some of my drink at that. *Who knew Preston had it in him?* "You're such a man, Preston."

He nods.

I glance around the bar that is getting busier by the second. The bar is almost completely full of men.

"If I weren't dating Jake, there'd be plenty of men for me to choose from here," I say.

Preston nods. "It is quite a hopping bar."

Just as he finishes speaking, loud music comes on, and barely dressed men begin dancing as the crowd squeals and shouts in excitement.

"Oh my God, Preston. It's a gay bar."

"It is not," Preston says. But then he laughs when he realizes it's true. "Sorry."

"Don't be sorry." I enjoy the view of half-naked men.

"Come on, let's get you home before you turn a gay man straight," Preston says.

"Hello?" I shout into my apartment as I open the door.

I don't get an answer. I walk into the living room and flick on the lights. I smile when I see a half-naked Jake passed out on the couch.

I bite my lip as I study his hard, muscular chest that I swear has gotten even more muscular since college. He always did have a good body. I walk over to him, still staring and not ashamed to admit it.

"Jake," I whisper.

He doesn't wake.

I try again, "Jake."

Nothing.

I sigh. If he stays like that on the couch, he's going to have a wicked crick in his neck in the morning. And I can't really resist his half-naked body at the moment. I bite my lip, considering what I'm going to do, but I already know.

I kneel on the floor next to the couch as my lips move to his hard chest. I start at the top, on his hard pecs, kissing each part of his smooth muscles and each crevice between his abs. I kiss softly at first, trying not to disturb him so that I can just enjoy his body.

But then my kisses become harsher and more aggressive, trying to wake him. Trying to get him to want me. To fuck me.

He moans softly as I begin kissing lower and lower on his stomach, but he doesn't wake up. A devious thought creeps into my mind. I know he wants to take this slow, but the speed we are going is ridiculous. And I can't wait much longer.

He's wearing athletic shorts, and I begin pulling gently at the waistband. He still doesn't wake. I pull harder until his shorts and underwear are pulled down, and his cock springs free.

I bite my lip again, staring at it. I thought, by now, he would have woken up.

Do I really have the balls to do what I'm about to do?

Yes.

I move my lips to his cock and began sucking. He moans as I do, but that still doesn't fully wake him up. So, I suck more, harder, faster. I love having his cock between my lips. I love that I can bring him pleasure, even in his sleep. I move my hand to his shaft and begin pumping up and down in rhythm with my lips.

His moans intensify until I'm sure he's about to come, but then he says, "Karissa."

I freeze, not sure what to do. He said her name, not mine. I know he's asleep, and I shouldn't hold him accountable for anything he's said, but it still hurts. It hurts that he still thinks of her, even in his dreams.

Jake's eyes suddenly fly open, and the smile on his face turns to terror. "Scarlett," he says in shock. "What are you doing?"

I slowly remove my lips from his cock and pull his waistband back over him.

I shake my head. "Nothing. It was nothing. Forget all about it. Go to bed. We can talk in the morning."

"Scarlett, wait. I didn't mean...I didn't know..."

I'm already halfway upstairs to my bedroom by the time Jake tells me to wait.

"It's really okay, Jake. I understand completely. I'm just tired now. I think it's best that we both just go to sleep."

"We can talk in the morning?"

I nod. "Sure."

I continue up the stairs, trying to forget about Jake. I open the door to my bedroom and close it behind me. I try to forget about what just happened because it was an honest mistake.

But, instead, all I keep thinking is, *This will never work*.

We don't belong together. He belongs with her, and I belong with Beast.

The only problem is, the people we're supposed to be with are too stubborn and stupid to realize that they belong with us.

25

BEAST

I KNOCK on Jake Walton's door. He agreed to meet me at his personal office at the financial firm he works for. Not in his office in Scarlett's building. I'm thankful because, if we had met in the same building as her office, it would have been too hard for me to resist the temptation. And, if I go see her again, I won't be able to resist.

"Come in," Jake says.

I open the door and let myself into a small office. I take everything in the second I walk through the door. I take in the white walls that he hasn't bothered to paint or decorate. I take in the standard desk that looks as boring as he does. I take in the picture frames sitting on the desk that look to be of his family, the only personal items he has in the office. I take in the neat pile of papers and almost spotless computer.

And then I take in the bastard sitting behind the desk. He's sharp-looking, despite his suit not being of the expensive type. His hair is nicely combed, and his face still looks clean-shaven, despite being late in the evening. He looks like a boy, not a man. He's young-looking, nice, and boring.

The very opposite of me.

"Nice to meet you, Mr. Hackett," Jake says as he stands from his desk and extends his hand to me.

I take his hand and shake it. I find his handshake to be far too weak for someone in the business world. I frown. "You, too, Jake."

Jake takes a seat. "So, you prefer to be called by your first name, Raymon?"

I take a seat opposite him. "No. I prefer to be called Mr. Hackett, Jake," I say, making sure to use *his* first name.

Jake narrows his eyes at me in return, but otherwise, he gives no impression that he finds my request unusual. "What can I do for you, Raymon?"

I smile, impressed at least that he has the balls to use my first name when I clearly told him to use my last. "I heard you're the best. I recently acquired a real estate company and would love your help in running the numbers on the company and making sure everything is in order."

Jake nods. "Have to be honest with you. Even though I am the best, my schedule is currently pretty busy. I recently took on several clients that will be taking up a lot of my time, and I'm not sure if I'll have time to put into the work you'd need me to do."

"Are you referring to your new job, working at Beautifully Bell Enterprises? Or are you referring to your recent relationship with the owner, Scarlett Bell?"

Jake glares at me, giving me such a heinous look that it should have me running scared out of his office. His look doesn't scare me though. His look just shows me how much of a weak man he really is. Because, if I were Jake and had any real claim to Scarlett and another guy came in and threatened that, there'd be no way that I'd just be sitting in a chair, giving him a dirty look. That man would already be ripped to shreds.

"It's none of your business. How do you know that anyway?" Jake says.

I lean back in my chair and smile. "I have my ways. And none of them are *your* business."

"I think we're through here," Jake says, getting up from his chair.

"Almost. I just have one final question."

Jake frowns, but hears me out anyway. That's a mistake.

"There are rumors that you don't do enough to satisfy Miss Bell. There are rumors that there is another man in her life other than you. Any idea if they are true or not?" I say with a smirk on my face.

I expect a sharp right hook to my jaw. I expect more cursed yelling for me to get the hell out of his office. I expect some sort of pain to be dealt by the hands of this man who is supposedly in love with Scarlett. Instead, I see a man raging with anger pick up his phone, and dial a number.

I raise my eyebrows, curious as to what he's doing. Because what he's doing is not on the list of things I would expect.

He begins talking, "I need security to come escort Mr. Hackett out of my office and make sure he's not allowed back on the property again."

My smile lightens. This man has more control over himself than I expected. The only problem is, he has no control over Scarlett. As much as he would like to lay claim to her, she's not his. She's *mine*. Or at least, she will be.

"No need. I'm leaving," I say with a grin on my face.

26

SCARLETT

I HEAR the knock on my apartment door, and I light up with a bright, albeit a nervous, smile on my face. Jake's sister is bringing her two young kids over for me and Jake to watch while she and her husband celebrate their anniversary in New York City.

When Jake said he would be watching his niece and nephew, I got excited because it meant I could see how he was around kids. It meant I could see how I would be around kids. Something that I haven't been around since...well, never. I don't have any siblings, and I didn't spend much time babysitting when I was younger.

I get up from the couch Jake and I have been sitting on while both working on our respective computers until the kids get here. Now, I'm on my feet as Jake walks to the door and opens it to his sister and niece and nephew.

"Good to see you, Nina. I missed you at the anniversary party," Jake says to his sister, wrapping his arms around her and the two kids in her arms. "Where's your husband?" he asks.

"Good to see you too. I was hoping we could have made it to mom and dad's anniversary party, but then Claire was sick. And he's holding the cab for us," Nina answers.

She hands the rambunctious toddler with light-blond hair into

Jake's hands. He takes him, happily throwing him up in the air, like he's nothing, and then catching him and spinning him around. The child squeals and laughs, as he seems happy to see his uncle.

Nina walks to the kitchen, still holding the brown-haired baby in her arm along with what I assume is a diaper bag slung over her shoulder. She sets the diaper bag on a counter in my kitchen and then walks over to me and hands me the baby. "This is Claire," Nina says.

I awkwardly hold the baby in my arms as she begins playing with my hair and pulling on my necklace. I try to keep the smile on my face. I try to keep the terror away, but I'm sure it's plastered all over my face. And I'm sure that Nina must be questioning her decision to leave her children with me even though Jake will be here as well.

She doesn't seem to care that she is leaving her kids in the hands of someone who knows nothing about kids. She walks back to the door and then pauses briefly. "We will be back around ten to collect the kids. If you need anything, you know my cell number. The kids will probably pass out around nine. Thanks again." And then she's out the door.

I look down at the baby in my arms and have no idea what to do. *Do I talk to her? Do I just hold her?* I should've brought some baby clothes from my line, and then at least we could've played dress-up.

"Balls," the toddler named Troy says.

I have no idea where he sees balls. I assume his mother packed some toys for him, so the balls he is referring to are probably in his bag that she dropped off.

I begin walking over to the bag, still holding the baby in my arms, and I look for any toys for Troy. Troy, on the other hand, has a different idea as he begins climbing up onto my kitchen table. I now see what he meant when he said *balls*. He grabs the decorative balls out of the container on my kitchen table. Jake laughs and grabs the boy before he is able to climb all the way up.

The tot doesn't seem to care though, as he laughs more in his uncle's arms.

"You hungry?" Jake asks Troy.

Troy nods. "I want chicken nuggets."

"How about pizza?"

"Cheese?" Troy asks.

Jake nods.

"Okay," Troy says.

Jake goes over to the boxes of pizza that arrived just shortly before Troy and Claire. He begins fixing Troy something to eat while I just continue to awkwardly stand and stare at the baby.

After Jake gets Troy settled at the table with his pizza, he walks over to me. "Here, I'll hold her for a while, and you can eat your pizza." He has a smug grin on his face.

"What? What's so funny?" I ask.

He shakes his head, but continues to smile anyway. "Nothing. You're holding the baby like she is a priceless piece of art. Like, if you dropped her, she would break. You're not holding her like a baby."

I frown as I look at how I'm holding the baby tightly so that I don't drop her. I don't really see the problem with how I'm holding her. "If I drop her, she will break. What's wrong with the way I'm holding her?"

Jake takes Claire from my arms and holds her against his body. "Nothing. You're just funny."

I decide to let it go. I grab a slice of pepperoni pizza and take a seat next to Troy at my table.

I watch Jake wrinkle his nose, and then he checks her diaper. "I need to go change Claire's diaper and then make one quick phone call. You two going to be okay?"

"Yes," I say at the same time as Troy says, "Yes, Uncle Jake."

Jake smiles at both of us before he grabs the diaper bag and then heads to the spare bedroom to change her diaper and make the call. I turn my attention to my pizza and to Troy. I know I should say something to him. Ask him a question or entertain him somehow, but I have no idea what to talk about.

"I want ice cream," Troy says.

"You can have ice cream after you finish your pizza."

"I want ice cream now. No pizza."

I glance at his pizza. He's only taken two, maybe three, bites of his single slice.

"Once you finish your pizza, you can have ice cream," I say again, thinking the child will understand because I'm sure it's something his parents have said to him before. Boy, am I wrong.

Instead, Troy screams at the top of his lungs as tears fall from his eyes. "I don't want pizza! I want ice cream!"

I pat his back to try to get him to calm down, but it doesn't work. I glance toward the door to the bedroom Jake disappeared into to see if there are any signs that he is coming back anytime soon. There isn't. I'll have to handle this.

"Shh, it's gonna be okay. You can have ice cream soon."

"No, now!"

"How about you eat your pizza, like me?" I take another bite of my pizza, trying to pretend like it's the most delicious food in the entire world.

Troy doesn't buy it though. This time, he screams and begins knocking his hands and feet against my table, making it shudder with each knock of his hands. The high-pitched squeal along with the thrashing is enough to drive a person mad. I have no idea how to calm him down other than to give in and give him the ice cream he wants.

"Okay, okay. I'll get you ice cream."

I get up from my chair and go to the freezer. I pull out the chocolate fudge pops we bought for him. I unwrap it quickly and hand it to Troy, who immediately stops crying as soon as he has the chocolate goodness in his hands. I sigh in relief and take a seat back at the kitchen table, hoping I can at least finish my one slice of pizza before I have to deal with the next crisis with him. That doesn't happen though. Instead, Troy decides he doesn't want us at the table anymore, and he jumps up before I can grab him.

"Troy, you have to sit at the table while you eat your ice cream."

"No!" Troy says as he runs to my living room and climbs up onto my white couch to eat his chocolate ice cream.

"Troy! Come back here right now," I say as I get up from the table, intending to get him to sit back down at the table.

But he squeals again when I try to grab him and bring him back to the table. And I know I'm not going to win. So, instead, I grab as many napkins as I can and my plate of pizza, and I join Troy on the couch where there's already two chocolate stains forming. I sigh. I wanted a new couch anyway. Because I don't have any faith that those chocolate stains are coming out of my white couch.

I hear the bedroom door open, and I turn to see Jake walking back in with Claire in his arms along with a bottle. He laughs when he sees me and Troy.

"Troy, did you finish your pizza?" Jake asks.

"No." The boy looks down as redness fills his cheeks. "The lady said I could have ice cream."

Jake curiously raises his eyebrows at me, as if wondering what happened, but he just smiles and laughs and shakes his head at me.

"Troy, you need to finish your ice cream in the kitchen, and then you need to finish your slice of pizza."

"Okay," Troy says sadly as he makes his way back to the kitchen.

"How did you do that?" I ask.

Jake shakes his head as he sits down on the couch next to me. "He was just testing you to see what he could get away with."

I sigh. "And I failed big time."

Jake nods.

"It's my turn with Claire. You handle Troy," I say, knowing I have no chance at getting Troy to do anything I say.

Jake nods and hands me Claire along with her bottle. I hold her the same way Jake just was, cradling her in my arms, and then I take the bottle and hold it into her mouth. She begins to suck from it, and I sigh in relief because she is much easier to take care of than Troy was.

Jake stands up and heads to the kitchen, leaving me and Claire alone on the couch. She feeds from the bottle quietly, and I realize that she's really no trouble at all. I can handle this.

A few minutes later, Jake walks over, holding on to Troy's hand.

"I'm going to give Troy a bath and try to wash the chocolate off of him."

I glance at Troy, who is truly covered in chocolate, all down the front of his shirt, his hands, and his face.

I nod, happy that I don't have to tackle bath time with a toddler.

"You and Claire going to be okay?"

"Yes," I say, looking down at the baby who is about to fall asleep as she feeds from her bottle. "I think we will be fine."

"Good. If you need anything, we'll be in the bathroom."

I watch as Jake leads Troy to the guest bathroom. I can't help but smile at the two of them. Jake is really good with him. Better than I expected.

I glance at Claire, who is just finishing her bottle. I remove the bottle from her lips, assuming she's done. Evidently, she wasn't done because she begins screaming shortly after.

"I'm sorry. I'm sorry," I say, hurriedly putting the bottle back into the baby's mouth. "Here you go."

But Claire doesn't want the bottle anymore. Apparently, she just wants to scream. I put the bottle down next to me and try to hold her closer to my body to get her to stop screaming. It doesn't work. I quickly stand up and begin trying to rock or bounce Claire in any way that might be calming. It doesn't work. I try singing. It doesn't work. I try bouncing in any sort of movement I can. But nothing works.

I try checking her diaper, just like Jake did, but that doesn't seem to be the problem. *I* seem to be the problem because I have no idea what to do.

So, I just continue walking around the room, trying to calm the baby that doesn't seem to be able to be calmed.

Until Jake walks back in the room with a cleaned up Troy and a goofy smile on his face. He walks over to me, and I immediately place Claire in his arms.

"I can't get her to stop crying," I say.

Jake nods and begins bouncing Claire up and down a little, but it doesn't work either. He then places her head against his shoulder, and he begins patting her on her back. She immediately burps and begins to calm down. My eyes widen.

"She just needed to be burped," Jake says.

Of course she did, I think to myself.

Of course, the woman who has never been around babies has no idea what to do with a baby after feeding it. I sigh and plop back down on the couch. Jake takes a seat next to me with this sleepy Claire in his arms, already looking like she's asleep the second he sits down.

"Troy, can you grab the remote that is sitting on the coffee table, and then I can put a movie on for you?" Jake says.

Troy grabs the remote and brings it to his uncle before climbing up on the couch next to him. Jake quickly puts on a movie for Troy, and Troy snuggles in next to Jake. Claire is sound asleep in his arms. And I'm left sitting by myself, feeling like there's no way I could ever have kids by myself. The only way I could ever have kids is with a man like Jake. Because I have no idea how to handle kids.

I snuggle up to Jake's other side and close my eyes, ready for the day to be over. Ready to get back to my office tomorrow where I feel like I have some semblance of control. Ready to get back to my office tomorrow where I know what the hell I'm doing. Because, right now, I feel clueless.

27

BEAST

IT's a stupid mistake that I've only made once before. But I have to be sure. I have to be sure that she is worth risking my life for. I have to see her in the daylight, face-to-face. I have to see her and see that she really wants me and not him. Because I'm already sure that he's not good enough for her. I'm just not sure if she believes that she's better than him.

I walk into Beautifully Bell Enterprises along with my team of two men. None of my men know why we're really here. They just think we are here on another job. Scouting out another woman. Another company. They don't know that this job didn't come from the boss. They came for me, and it has nothing to do with what our boss wants. It only has to do with what I want.

Thankfully, my men trust me and will do whatever I ask, whenever I ask. No questions asked. I guess that's the one perk of my job.

We walk up to the floor where Scarlett's office sits.

Scarlett's assistant called back to tell us her decision if she was going to take our financial advice or not and use us in the future. But I managed to arrange the meeting so that she could give us the decision in person. I already know her answer though. I already know she chose Jake as her financial manager, and that's fine. I'm not here to try to convince her to use my company instead.

I already know that she's a smart businesswoman who doesn't need our financial advice. Her assistant tried to tell us her decision over the phone, and I said that we needed to be told in person that she wouldn't be needing our services. It was just an excuse to see her again.

Nerves creep up inside me as we walk closer and closer to where I know her office is. I know this is a risk. I know that, when she sees me this time, she might recognize me. She might realize who I am. Even the last time was a risk, but she hardly looked at me then. It was obvious she was still blissfully thinking about our night together and not thinking that I could be in the same room as her.

This time though, she knows me better. She might recognize my voice. She's seen my eyes. She knows my body. And I know, inside her head, she's formed some sort of image of what I look like, and if that image at all matches what I truly look like, then I'm fucked. Because this is not how I want her to figure out who I am. This is just me figuring out what I want.

So, I let my men take the lead as we approach her office. Dustin, my more trusted man, knocks on her office door, and her assistant comes out and leads us into her office where they've been waiting.

Scarlett begins shaking everyone's hands. It's when I realize that I'm going to get to touch her skin again. I silently wait my turn until she gets to me. When she does, I keep my eyes from hers as I feel her smooth skin against my rough hand. She doesn't treat me any differently than any of the previous men, and it's when I know that she doesn't recognize me.

I watch Scarlett walk back behind her desk, and Preston takes a seat next to her.

"When you contacted us for a follow-up, Preston really should've told you that it wasn't necessary for all three of you to come back down here again. I just wanted to inform you of our decision and say thank you for being so kind. I think you are a fantastic firm, but we decided to go in a different direction."

I want to speak, but I don't. I know that the more I limit my voice, the less likely it is that she will be able to recognize me. So, I don't speak.

Instead, I let Dustin speak, "It's really not a problem. We wanted to come down here and make sure that you didn't want to take us up on our offer. Because we believe that we could really help you take your business to the next level."

Scarlett smiles at Dustin, and I lose it. I want her smiling at me, not him. I scoot my chair on the hard floor, causing it to make a loud scraping sound. But it gives me the attention I want. It gives me Scarlett's eyes back on me and not him. She warmly smiles at me for just a second and then turns her attention back to Dustin.

"I really appreciate it, Mr. Morgan. I really appreciate all that your men have done. And, if I ever decide that I need help with growing the business, I will gladly take you up on your offer. At the moment, I feel that we have one of the best financial managers in the world, and I feel like he's going to do a fantastic job. If I change my mind though, you will be my first call because you have my confidence that you are the best man for the job. You were just beat out slightly by another."

She stands, and I know the meeting is over. I know that this is my last chance to assess her. To determine if she's worth it. But I already know my answer. I already know that my heart is racing. I already know that, just by coming here, I've risked everything, and I've already made up my mind. She's worth the risk.

Scarlett begins shaking each of our hands again. I wait my turn for one last touch of her skin before I do the stupidest thing I've ever done. Risk my life.

She gets to me, and this time, I don't look down.

I look right into her eyes. "It was a pleasure, Miss Bell."

I shake her hand, and she looks at me with a hint of confusion on her face.

"It was nice speaking with you as well, Mr. Guild."

I turn and follow my men out of her office, hating the name that fell from her lips when she was referring to me. I hate that the only name I've ever heard fall from her lips, other than Beast, is a fake name. It's not my real name. But I don't know if my real name falling from her lips would be any better. I just want to hear the one name she's adapted for me from her lips again as I claim her and make her mine. I just want her to call me Beast again.

28

SCARLETT

I RUN. I run faster and faster, trying to escape the darkness. But the darkness continues to find me, continues to chase me, until there is nothing left of me.

But I keep running anyway. I keep running, trying to escape the darkness I've found myself in. I try to escape even though I know there's no use. I've let the darkness into my heart, and now, there's no way to get it out.

Kinsley has been taken from me. I let the darkness consume her. I let the darkness take her from me, and now, I'm alone. And she's in danger. And there's nothing I can do to save her. Still, I run to try to save her.

The darkness pushes Jake away. Keeping Jake away from me but keeping him safe. He tries to pull me back to keep me from running, but still, I keep running.

The darkness consumes Preston's soul. It intertwines in his head, scaring him with the thoughts that the darkness is taking me away from him. That I'm in danger even if I'm not. Preston pushes me to run while still being scared and thinking I shouldn't.

Worst of all, Beast is affected by the darkness. It's so connected to him that it's hard to tell what's the darkness and what's him. I run because Beast tells me to run. But he doesn't tell me why I am running.

Me. The darkness pulls at me, and I go willingly. I run.

All of us are connected through the darkness. Through a past and a future that I don't understand. Still, I try to connect the pieces. Kinsley. Jake. Beast. Preston. And me. They're all connected. I just don't understand how.

I open my eyes and stretch, trying to put the strange dream I just had behind me. It was just a dream. And nothing really happened in the dream. I was running. I remember that. I remember everyone who's important in my life appearing in my dream. I just don't understand what any of it means.

I try to push the dream out of my head because today's going to be a good day. Today, I'm taking Kinsley out to plan her baby shower. I know it's still early, but I want to throw her the best baby shower that's ever been thrown. And I know that it's going to take a lot of planning. Plus, I'll take any excuse not to think about the men in my life and just focus on my good friend for at least an afternoon.

I head to my shower and take my time in getting ready. Showering, dressing, and doing my hair and makeup. There's no reason to hurry today. I don't plan on going into work. I'll just answer some emails from my computer. And all that's waiting for me downstairs is Jake.

He's been staying with me since his fiancée kicked him out of their apartment. He just hasn't been sleeping in my bed with me. Yet. He said he was going to look for another apartment, but I know we've both been stalling, not wanting him to get a new apartment until we decide if this thing between us is really going to work out or not. If it does, he can just stay here with me.

When I finally finish getting ready, I head downstairs. I look around my living room for any signs of Jake, but there's none to be found. I frown. I'm so used to seeing Jake greet me at the base of the stairs every morning with coffee and breakfast, just like he used to do when we were in college. In fact, I have gotten a little spoiled from having him live here. It looks like, this Saturday morning, he's either sleeping in or decided I'm not worth the effort.

I head to the kitchen to make myself breakfast when I see a note on the counter along with a paper bag. I pick up the note and read it.

Scarlett,

I had to go meet with some clients today for work. I wasn't sure what time you'd get up, but the coffee should still be hot in the pot. There are also some bagels in the bag. Have a good day with Kinsley.

With love,

Jake

I smile as I read the note, happy that he didn't forget about my breakfast. Happy that he remembered to take care of me. I glance at the bottom where the words, *With love*, stand out. It's not weird that he wrote it. Lots of people I know write that at the end of notes. It doesn't mean he's *in* love with me. It doesn't mean he *isn't* in love either.

I sigh and place the note back on the counter, trying not to read too much into it. I'm not ready for him to love me yet. All I want is a few dates to see if there is more to him than just being able to care for me. Because, although it's nice, I don't need anyone taking care of me. I've been taking care of myself since I was thirteen. What I want is a partner, lover, challenger.

I fix my breakfast and get my computer. I decide to eat outside on my balcony this morning while I work. My phone buzzes in my pocket, and I pull it out to look at it. When I see whom the message is from, I drop my phone. I watch it clank against the hard floor.

Shit.

I stare at the phone on the floor, thankful that it didn't shatter, although I'm sure it has a few good scratches on it now. I want to pick it up, but I don't.

It's from Beast. I'm afraid of what the text says. I'm afraid he's just going to go back to texting me, like nothing happened. And I can't give him that without more. I'm also afraid that he's going to say he's willing to give me more even though I've already closed off my heart to him. Even though I've already decided on Jake.

So, I just stare. As my heartbeat races. Faster. Faster. Faster. Until I can hear my heart pumping in my chest. Until my breathing becomes loud and uneven. And until I'm afraid I'm going to give myself a heart attack if I don't pick up my damn phone.

I slowly bend down and cautiously grab the phone, like it's a scared dog that might bite if I'm not too careful with it. I study the phone for a second, and as I look, there seems to be a few scratches on the screen and back. But, somehow, the screen managed to stay unshattered.

I unlock my phone and hover over the message from Beast. I could just delete it. I could forget this ever happened.

I shake my head. *No way in hell.*

I open the message and read.

Beast: I was wrong.

That's all the bastard says. *I was wrong.*

I read his words over and over, trying to find the meaning behind them. There are too many things that he could mean with that statement, and I don't even know where to begin. He could be wrong about letting me go. He could be wrong about telling me who he is. Or he could be wrong about wanting me in the first place.

I consider texting him back to ask him what he means. But I'm afraid I won't get a straight answer. He's obviously not ready to tell me what he's wrong about. He just texted me to drive me crazy until he's ready to tell me.

I want to throw my phone over the balcony and watch it shatter on the sidewalk below. I don't, as much as I want to. I want to forget he ever existed. I want to erase that night from my memory. I want to go back in time and say no instead of yes. Maybe then I wouldn't have to feel this pain every time he texts me. Every time he does, it affects my life. Because that's what he's doing when he's texting me. He's pulling me back away from the decision I've made to be with Jake yet not giving me everything I want with him. He's an asshole.

My phone buzzes again in my hand, and I jump because, despite how much I hate him, I hope it's him. I hope it's him texting me more than *I was wrong.* When the phone buzzes again though, I realize it's not a text message; it's a phone call. From Kinsley.

I hit Answer. "Hey, babe!" I say as happily as I can, trying to forget all about Beast.

"Hey! You ready? I know I'm a bit early, but I'm excited," Kinsley says.

"Yes! I'm absolutely ready," I say. I begin cleaning up my breakfast and my computer as I continue holding my phone against my ear.

"Good. I'm waiting for you downstairs."

I laugh. "I'll be right down."

I quickly clean up, get my purse, reluctantly stick my phone into my purse, and head downstairs to meet my best friend. When I get off the elevator, Kinsley is standing at the bottom with a huge grin on her face. I merely wrap my arms around her.

"You have no idea how excited I am!"

I smile. "What? You're excited? I couldn't tell," I joke with her.

She playfully hits me on the shoulder. "I know. I'm sorry. Killian's just driving me nuts."

I frown. "What? Now, what did Killian do?"

Kinsley rolls her eyes at me. "No, nothing like that. He's just being overprotective of me and this baby. Will hardly let me do anything around the house anymore. Won't let me go to work. If it were up to him, he'd put me on bed rest and never let me leave the house again."

I laugh. "He's just trying to protect you and make sure you and the baby are safe."

"I know. It's why I love him. I just need a break from him."

"Good. Because I need a break from all men."

Kinsley laughs. "Good. I can't wait to hear all the juicy details."

"Before we start in on all the juicy details, we should get going. We have the cake shop to visit. The caterer. We need to talk decorations. And, of course, to visit several baby shops. All in one day."

Kinsley nods, but I can tell the excitement isn't going away anytime soon. That she really needs today. That she really needs a break from her husband and to just be able to relax for once. And that's exactly what I plan on giving her.

"You okay having my driver, George, drive us?" I ask.

"Yes!" Kinsley squeals, unable to say anything without showing her excitement.

I smile and grab her hand. "Let's go."

We walk out of my building and over to where George sits, waiting for us.

"Good morning, girls," George says as he opens the door for us to climb into the car.

"Good morning," we both say back.

We both climb in as well as George.

"Where to?" he asks.

I glance at Kinsley and then down at the clock in the car, reading the time. It's only nine o'clock, but I know exactly where Kinsley's going to want to go first. Her favorite part of this baby-shower planning.

"Cake shop first," I say.

George smiles at me, and then he pulls the car away from the curb and begins driving us. Kinsley smiles brightly beside me, unable to contain her excitement.

"So, tell me about these damn men you are trying to forget about today."

I sigh. "I'd rather not. I just want to forget they exist and have a good day with my bestie."

"I want to—" Kinsley grabs ahold of her stomach as a pained look comes over her face.

I turn and grab her shoulders, trying to comfort her. "Are you okay?"

I meet George's eyes in the mirror and see that he's prepared to take us to the nearest hospital. Kinsley takes a deep breath and then another and another. Ignoring me, just focusing on her breathing. Time is moving slowly, and I'm worried that something is seriously wrong.

My eyes move back up to George, and I'm about ready to tell him to head to the nearest hospital when Kinsley says, "I'm fine. I just didn't eat breakfast this morning, and I'm pretty sure this little one is telling me he or she is hungry. I'll be fine after I get some cake in me."

I study my friend for a couple of moments more until she's breathing normally again, and that goofy smile has returned to her face.

"George, can you—"

"Already on it, Miss Scarlett," George says.

I glance up with a smile as I see that George is already pulling us into the drive-through of the nearest Starbucks. That's why I love George so much. He can read my mind, and he knows exactly what I want before I even have to ask it. He knew I'd want to make sure Kinsley got breakfast before I took her to the cake shop.

After a quick Starbucks run to get Kinsley a breakfast sandwich, we're back on the road, driving toward the cake shop.

Between bites of her breakfast sandwich, Kinsley says, "You still never told me about the men you're trying to forget about. What's going on?"

"It's nothing. Nothing I want to talk about anyway."

Kinsley takes another bite. And, with a mouthful, she says, "Tell me what's going on. It will make me feel better."

I narrow my eyes at her, afraid she's going to take this pregnancy thing and use it to her advantage. I need to be better prepared in the future to deal with her scheming. But, for right now, I'll give in to her. Right now, I'll give her exactly what she wants, as she knows I don't want to see her in pain or upset.

"I just want both men to be something they're not. I want Jake to challenge me more, to live a little more dangerously. And I want..." I stop, not sure what to call Beast in front of Kinsley.

"You want your one-night-stand guy?"

"I want him to want more than one night. I want him to want a real relationship and to care for me just a little bit. Is that too much to ask of the two men in my life? For one of them to step up and be the complete package?"

Kinsley puts the rest of her sandwich on her lap and shakes her head. "No, it's not too much to ask of them. And if neither one of them can give you that, perhaps it's time to let both of them go."

I nod, knowing she's right. "I'm just tired of being alone. I'm ready to move on with my life."

Kinsley wraps her arms around me, and she holds my head tight to her chest. "You're not alone, Scar. You have me and always will. And you'll have a niece or a nephew to keep you busy soon."

I smile and pat her belly. "You're right. After this baby is born, I'll be spending all my time with him or her. I won't even be thinking about men."

The rest of the day, we don't talk about men. We don't talk about Killian, Jake, or Beast. We don't even talk about Preston. We just focus on each other, and the baby's party we are planning.

We test about one million cakes at the cake shop. Finally, we settle on three flavors—wedding cake, strawberry shortcake, and chocolate-cookie filling.

At the caterer, we decide on a full buffet filled with everything from tacos to Italian to burgers. Kinsley said we should just pick one. But there was no way I'd let her pick just one, not when we are celebrating her baby. She deserves the best, and that's exactly what I plan on giving her.

We discuss some decoration options and things that Kinsley likes and doesn't like. But I don't want her to be heavily involved in the decorations or activities for the baby shower. I want to plan some things that will be a surprise to her. She'll just have to wait to find out what I have planned.

The last stop for the day is a cute boutique where she can begin registering for gifts for the baby. This shower isn't going to happen for at least three months, but still, she needs to start registering for gifts. Mostly because it's one of the most fun parts about a baby shower.

"This is going to have to be the last stop. I'm exhausted. My feet are swollen. My back is killing me," Kinsley says.

I smile at her. "You know it's only going to get worse from here, right? You're not even halfway through yet. Just imagine how exhausted you will feel a few months from now."

"Don't remind me."

"We don't have to go. I can just have George drive us back to your apartment. We can schedule another day to come to this boutique."

"No, no. I want to look at the cute onesies and baby shoes and things."

I wrinkle my nose. "Babies need shoes? Doesn't it take them a few years to learn to walk?"

Kinsley laughs. "Not a few years. A few months to one year. And the shoes aren't for walking. They're just cute. I thought you of all people would understand accessorizing and just looking cute."

"I understand looking cute for cute's sake. Just curious."

I follow Kinsley into the boutique, and I'm amazed by the smells and sights I see the second we're in the store. It smells like baby in here.

And, immediately, when I look around the store, it gives me all sorts of ideas and plans to start my own baby line. Kinsley immediately walks over toward the clothes section, and I follow. We go through every dress in the store, oohing and aahing over our favorites. I already know I will be getting her baby basically this whole store, plus whatever I end up having designed for the baby.

"This baby is going to be the most spoiled baby on the planet," I say.

"I know. Between you dressing my baby and Killian giving it everything that it could ever want, I'm afraid our baby is gonna turn into one spoiled brat."

"The baby will just be the most well-dressed baby who has everything they could ever imagine. It will be the most loved baby in the entire world."

"Maybe you're right."

"Of course I'm right. I'm always right."

"I'm going to go to the restroom. Be right back," Kinsley says.

"I'll be right here, salivating over all the adorable little things, as my ovaries burst with need, wanting a baby."

"You do that. My evil plan is working," she says.

"What do you mean?" I call after her.

"I just knew, the second I got you around all this baby stuff, that you would want to have a baby yourself. And having a baby would be a million times more fun if you were having one as well," she says before walking away from me.

I roll my eyes because I don't want to let her know that she's winning. That she's already won, and she's already convinced me that I want a baby, too. Because it's something I've been thinking about forever. Even through all the one-night stands. I just can't have one alone, and I'm not sure either of the two men in my life is the right choice.

I get lost in my head, thinking about all the designs that I want to discuss with my design team when I get back to the office, while Kinsley's in the restroom. I walk over to one of the cashiers and ask if they have some paper and a pencil. She gladly hands them over to me, and I began sketching some ideas that have been floating around in my head of things that could work for a baby line.

I get so lost in sketching and designing that I don't know how long Kinsley's been gone. When I notice I've done about a half-dozen designs, I stick the papers into my purse and begin scanning the store, looking for Kinsley. I don't see her anywhere.

I walk over to the cashier. "Have you seen my friend?"

The cashier shakes her head. I begin walking again, but don't see her. The boutique is pretty small, so it's not like she could be hiding anywhere. I walk to the restroom and push the door open. My mouth drops open as I see Kinsley lying on the floor, holding her stomach.

"Oh my God! What's wrong?"

"My stomach," is all she can get out as she moans and twists her body on the ground.

I rush to her side and grab her hand that she begins to squeeze tightly. My purse drops to the floor, and I dig out my cell phone with a shaking hand.

"I'm scared," she whispers.

And I panic. I don't know what the fuck is happening, but I know it's bad.

"Just squeeze my hand, and everything's gonna be okay. I'm going to make everything okay."

Kinsley moans louder as I grab for my phone again. I unlock it and see that Beast texted me again. I ignore it, not giving a fuck about what he has to say. I dial 911 and hold the phone to my ear.

"Nine-one-one. What's your emergency?"

"My friend. She's on the restroom floor in a boutique, and she's in a lot of pain. She's pregnant." I try to keep my voice calm and steady, so as not to let Kinsley know that anything is wrong. Although I know she can hear it. She knows me better than anyone else.

"Okay. Is she breathing? Is she awake?"

"Yes."

"Good. I need you to tell me the address, and then I'll have an ambulance on its way. I need you to just keep her awake and calm. I need you to tell me if she stops breathing or passes out, okay?"

I nod, not able to answer her question.

"Okay?" the operator says more firmly.

"Okay." I tell the operator the address.

Then, I wait as I hold Kinsley's hand until the ambulance arrives with the paramedics. I feel completely useless as I sit next to her, holding her hand, praying like hell that nothing happens to her or this baby. Because I don't know what I would do if something did.

29

BEAST

I SEE MY MARK. I've studied her. I understand her—or at least as well as I'll ever understand another woman. I know what I have to do. I know what I have to do to get her alone. I know what I have to do to take her out.

All I have to do now is report the plan to my boss. Tell her how and when I plan on taking her out. Then, I'll get the go-ahead, and it'll happen. Just like it has happened hundreds of times before.

I don't know why this one is hard for me. I've killed before. Too many times to count. I don't even care about this woman. She's nothing to me. But I feel reluctant to take on this job. To kill this woman.

I shouldn't feel reluctant though. If anything, I should want revenge. And the revenge would be justified because of what she's done to me in my life. I should want to end her life. I should want to end her life in the same way that she ended mine.

Still, as I watch her, my heart fills with pain at the thought of pulling the trigger. I don't know if my reluctance to kill her is because I no longer want to be a killer. Or if it's because of Scarlett. Because I don't want to hurt her. I don't want to be a killer even though that's what I am.

I am a killer.

That's what I do for work. But it's more than just that. It's *who* I am. It's *why* I wake up in the morning. It's *why* I sleep well at night. I kill those who need to be killed. I kill those who have done me or my family wrong.

I kill. And I enjoy it.

Until now...

30

SCARLETT

I HATE WAITING. I have no patience for waiting. I hate giving up that control. But I don't really have a choice. My only choice is to wait.

I rode with Kinsley in the ambulance to the hospital. I held her hand the entire time. Terrified that something was going to happen. I watched as the paramedics worked on her, but didn't tell me what was going on. They just worked tirelessly, trying to solve a problem that I didn't understand.

I stayed with her right up until we got to the hospital. They took her to another room and told me to wait.

So, here I am, in the waiting room, waiting.

At first, I had something to do. I called Killian and told him to get here right away. When he got here, he spoke to me briefly. He spent the rest of the time arguing with doctors until they finally let him go back to see her. I haven't seen him since, and they haven't let me go back yet or given me any updates on how she's doing.

I spend the rest of my time staring into space. I consider texting Jake to let him know that I need him. That I need him to come be with me, to comfort me. But I'm just not sure if him being here would actually bring me any comfort. So, I don't text him—at least, not yet.

I still have an unread message from Beast taunting me. Every time I open my phone, I see the red little number one on the Messages app, telling me I have a missed message. Telling me that Beast has something to say to me. Telling me that, if I would just open it, he could finally give me the answer I'd been wanting all along. Or he could twist the dagger that's already in my heart.

It's been hours now since we showed up at the hospital. Far too long for me to just sit and do nothing. I have to do something.

I open my phone. I open a new message and text Jake.

Me: Kinsley's at the hospital. I'm not sure what's wrong yet. Just waiting.

I give Jake a chance to prove to me that he's the guy for me. But I also want to give Beast the same chance. So, I open the unread message.

Beast: I want to tell you who I am.

I don't know if it's the emotion from the day finally getting to me or if I really care that much about knowing who Beast is. But I cry when I see the message. I ugly cry. The kind of crying that you usually do when you're alone in your bedroom. Not the kind of crying you do in a public hospital, especially not one that deals with loss on a daily basis.

A nurse immediately comes over to me, thinking I got some horrible news about a family member. She sits next to me and places her hand on my back. "If you need someone to talk to, there are pastors and ministers that I could arrange to talk with you. Or I could just talk to you?"

I shake my head. "I'm sorry." I wipe my eyes, trying to stop the crying. "Really, I'm fine. I just got some happy news, and that mixed with my anxiety and feelings of not knowing what's going on with my best friend. It caused the tears."

The nurse nods in understanding, but doesn't stop rubbing my back until the tears have fully diminished. "That's pretty normal. People cry here for all sorts of reasons. My advice is to just cry and get out. Don't hold the emotion in."

"Thanks," I say.

I take a few deep breaths, and then the nurse leaves me alone. I go back to my text message.

Me: Kinsley, my best friend, is in the hospital. I don't know what's wrong with her, but I'm afraid it's serious. I'm here, waiting.

I close my phone after sending the text message to Beast. And then I wait. I wait to find out what's wrong with Kinsley. And I wait to find out if either of the men will prove to me that I should be with one of them. Or if I should be alone.

I don't have to wait much longer to get at least one of my answers.

"Scarlett," Killian says.

I look up and see Killian standing over me with tears in his eyes. His face is red and puffy. He looks like he's just gone through hell and back. I jump up, needing to know that she's still alive. Needing to know that she's okay.

"Is she..." I ask, unable to finish that sentence.

I was told my best friend died once before. That pain was unbearable. If I'm told that again, I don't think I could survive, no matter if either of those men showed up to help me.

"She's..." Killian takes a deep breath, like he can't quite get it out, and then I wrap my arms around him as we both cry again. "Alive," he whispers into my ear.

But it doesn't stop our sobs or my feeling that something is wrong. I know, if he's been crying, there is something wrong. We just cry and hold each other for a long time. For too long. Neither one of us wants to let go. Neither one of us wants to go face what I'm afraid just happened.

"She needs you to go see her, Scarlett. She needs her best friend. I did the best I could to help her. And I'm not sure how much help I'm being when I'm in just as much pain myself," Killian says.

We slowly pull away from each other.

"I don't know if I can help her." My voice is shaky. *I'm not strong enough for this.*

"Yes, you can. You're one of the strongest people I know. Now, go help your best friend," Killian says sternly, giving me the intense glare that he always does whenever he's around someone who isn't Kinsley.

He's right. I am strong. And I have to be strong for her.

I leave Killian standing in the waiting room, and I walk to the room number he gave me. I knock softly on the door and immediately open it, not waiting until I lose my nerve to go in. I see Kinsley lying in a hospital bed, connected to all sorts of machines and tubes. I quickly walk over to her and throw my arms around her, holding her in a strong, tight embrace.

I feel her tears dripping onto my back, and I feel my own tears dripping down my face and onto hers. We hold each other for a long time. Longer than I held on to Killian. I don't ask her what happened. I already know. I know from the look on Killian's face. I know from the look on hers when I entered the room. I know from the way she's hugging me.

I won't ask, not unless she needs to tell me. Not unless she needs to say the words out loud in order to heal.

I don't bother with words at all really. I know that no words I could say at this moment would erase the pain that she's feeling. Because I can feel the pain that she's feeling with every ounce of my being as I hold on to her. It's horrible pain. It's the worst kind of pain. It's the most intense pain ever felt, even worse than when I thought I had lost her.

We hold on to each other for who knows how much longer. Killian eventually comes into the room and sits behind his wife, holding on to her as well. We both just hold her until she's finally ready to speak.

"It was a boy."

Our sobs deepen at her words. I try to think of something to say, but I can't.

"His name was Wesley."

We sob some more.

We let the pain consume us.

We let the love for a child that we will never get to meet surround us.

I want to run. I want to run away from all the pain and heartache. Unlike my dream, I don't run though. I stay right here where I belong. I stay in the darkness.

31

SCARLETT

I OPEN my eyes and lift my neck off the arm of the chair that I must've slept on. As I sit up, I feel a shooting pain in my neck. I slowly stretch it, trying to make the pain in my neck go away. It doesn't go away easily, but as I continue to stretch, it does become more tolerable. Tolerable enough that I can sit up in the chair.

I glance around the room, trying to figure out where I am. It's still relatively dark in the room, despite the morning light seeping in through the blinds. I see Kinsley asleep in a hospital bed, and then I remember. I remember the horrible reason we're here. I glance over at Killian, who is sitting in a chair next to his wife's hospital bed, just staring at her.

"Good morning. Do you need anything? Does she need anything?" I say.

"No. At least, we don't need anything that you can get us right now," Killian says, his voice seeming more distant than it did yesterday.

I run my hand through my hair as I stare at Kinsley sleeping in the hospital room.

We both stayed with her all day yesterday and all through the night. And I'm afraid that we didn't do anything to make it better for her or for us. I rub my eyes, and I can still feel the sting from my tears. I can feel the swollenness in my eyes from crying all day and through the night. The pain is here just as badly as it was yesterday. And it's not going away anytime soon.

I know that going to get coffee or breakfast for us isn't really going to help. That the pain will still be here. But it's something that I can do.

So, I get up from the chair. "I'm going to get us coffee and breakfast. I'll be back soon."

I don't wait for Killian to answer me. I know that, even if he does, it'll be a distant speech about how breakfast won't fix anything. And I understand that, but it will give me some purpose. It will give me something to do.

I walk out of her hospital room and close the door, finally feeling like I can breathe a little the second I step out. I lean against the door, put my head in my arms, and just try to breathe. The tears come from me again, and I cry and cry and cry. I hate that I can't fix this for her. I hate that I can't bring back her baby.

It takes a while, but when the tears finally subside a little, I stand off the door and walk toward the elevator. I take the elevator down to the main floor where there is supposedly a cafeteria, according to the signs. I walk to the cafeteria and see that they have all sorts of breakfast items and coffees. I know it's not going to be the best breakfast we've ever had. But I know that even the best breakfast wouldn't do much to heal our souls.

So, instead, I get in line, and I get a few options—bagels, eggs, toast, and fruit. I don't really know if any of us are going to feel like eating, but simple, boring food might help. I put all the items on a tray, followed by three coffees, and then I slowly work my way back upstairs to Kinsley's room.

I have to really focus with each step that I take to ensure that I don't drop any of the food or spill any of the coffee. It's really nice to be able to focus on something so intently that isn't pain. With each step that I take, I become more and more focused. With each step that I take, the tiniest part of the pain becomes erased from my mind, replaced with more and more need to focus. I spill a little bit of the coffee as I take a step, but it just refocuses me more until I forget why we're even at this hospital.

Until I reach Kinsley's hospital door.

Sitting on the floor outside of it is Jake. I give a weak smile at him, thankful that he finally came. He doesn't smile back. He just stands from his place on the floor and opens the door for me.

As I walk past, he says, "We need to talk."

I nod my head at him. "I'll be right back," I say.

I walk into Kinsley's bedroom, surprised to see that she's still asleep. She is always an early riser. But the loss she dealt with yesterday has taken a lot from her. And the nurses gave her some meds to help her sleep last night. Killian is still sitting next to her, right where I left him.

"I brought breakfast. You don't have to eat it. But it's here if you decide to," I say as I set the tray down on one of the tables in her room.

Killian nods but doesn't say anything. I grab one of the coffees and take it with me back outside to speak with Jake.

When I walk back into the hallway, Jake is still waiting for me with the same frown on his face.

"How is she doing?" he asks.

I study my coffee, hating the question. Afraid that, if I let myself think too much about Kinsley, I'll cry again. "Not well."

"I'm sorry."

I nod, trying to keep my words to a minimum.

"How are you doing?"

"Not much better." I look up at him, and I see the sadness in his eyes, but I also see something else that I'm not used to seeing from him. Anger.

"Why didn't you come yesterday?" I ask.

He pauses. "I did. At first, they wouldn't let me come to her room. And I didn't want to text you and disturb you. Eventually, they let me up, but by then, you'd all passed out. I stayed for a while and then went home, determined to come back first thing this morning."

I try to smile at him again, but I just can't. And I'm tired of waiting for him to spell out whatever he came here to say. I've been through too much in the last twenty-four hours to be able to handle anything more.

"Just tell me. Tell me whatever you came here to say," I say, feeling exhausted.

Jake takes a deep breath and then another before he reaches into his pocket and pulls out my phone. My eyes zoom in on the phone in his hands. It's my phone. I must've left it when I went downstairs to get breakfast.

I reach for the phone. "Thanks."

I don't understand why he seems angry to be giving me my phone back.

He doesn't let me take my phone back though. Instead, he unlocks the phone and pulls up something on it before he hands it to me. The screen is opened to message after message from Beast. Each message contains our dirty desires. Each message is filled with my need for more from him. Each message is filled with the truth of need and want.

"Who is Beast?" Jake asks.

I frown as I look at the phone. I can't believe he's going to cause a fight about this now.

"Really? You're going to bring this up now? You're going to do anything but try to be here for me when my heart is completely broken and shattered from dealing with the loss I dealt with yesterday? When I'm this fucking broken? That's when you choose to start a fight over a text message that you shouldn't have seen anyway because you shouldn't have been snooping on my phone."

Jake takes a step toward me. "No, I'm not starting a fight. All I want to know is, who is Beast?"

I take a step toward Jake, letting my anger mix with the pain in such a way that I'm afraid of saying things that I don't mean. No, that's not true. Maybe I'll say exactly what I mean, and the anger and pain won't stop me. I have no filter.

"He's a man I fucked before you. He's a man who brought out

desires I never knew I had. He's a man I've wanted because *you* haven't given me anything other than nice."

"What's his name?" Jake asks.

"I don't know."

He shakes his head. "Tell me his name," he says more sternly.

"I don't know," I repeat again more slowly and just as sternly as his voice was.

I see the anger explode in Jake's eyes.

"Don't fucking lie to me! Just tell me who he is."

"I. Don't. Know."

Jake runs his hands through his hair as he starts pacing back and forth in the hallway. "Do you love me?"

I think for a moment. *Do I love him?* "Yes," I answer honestly.

I do love Jake. At least on some level. My heart wouldn't be in so much pain right now, thinking about not having a real chance with him if this conversation continues the way that I know it's going to.

Jake pauses, listening to my words. "Do you love him?"

"Yes."

"How is that fucking possible? How can you love two men at the same time?"

I shake my head. "I don't know. I just do. Maybe because neither one of you has given me everything I need. All you've given me are parts of yourself, and although I've fallen just a little bit for each of your parts, it's not real. Because neither of you has given me what I need."

"And what's that? How am I supposed to know what you want when you won't tell me?"

"I have told you. You just don't listen."

"I don't know what it has to do with you and me," Jake says, pointing to my phone. "I don't know how we are supposed to keep dating if you lie to me."

"I didn't lie. I never fucked him when I was dating you. It was all before."

"Yeah, you just texted him all the dirty things you wished he would do while you were with *me*."

I feel the tears starting again, but I keep them back. I'm not going to let him make me feel bad. Not right now. Not when there are more important things that need to be handled. This should be a time of us getting closer, not a time of us pulling apart.

A thought Preston said to me earlier creeps back into my mind and I have to know. "Is Karissa real?"

"What?"

I raise my eyebrows. "Is she real?"

"Of course she is real!"

I shake my head. "I don't believe you."

He narrows his eyes at me and I can see him trying to determine how best to hurt me like I've hurt him. I know I've hurt him in the past when I broke up with him the first time. I saw the pain, but I realize now that was for the best. That day was so painful when I realized he wasn't the man for me. I didn't break up with him because I was afraid of commitment. I broke up with him because he was weak. He wasn't strong enough to handle me.

I kiss his ear. "Do me in the bathroom," I whisper into Jake's ear.

He shrugs me off. "No, Scarlett."

I pout my bottom lip. "Oh come on. Live a little."

He gives me a stern look. "No." He lifts the beer to his lips while we stand next to the same pub table we stood at on our first date. Months have passed, but nothing's changed.

I lift my own beer to my lips. I'm not going to let him off that easy. I run my hand through my hair and push my breasts out making sure he can see what he is missing as he stands all stoic and gentleman like across the table from me. Except I don't want a gentleman, at least not in every aspect. I want a man. One that's rough, dangerous, and takes care of me even when I don't need it.

I feel someone pinch my ass, I look over at Jake but his hands are both firmly on the table. I turn to see who the man is that just pinched my ass as he walks past us acting like he didn't just do something wrong.

"Hey jackass!" I shout.

The man turns and looks at me with a smirk on his face.

"Don't grab my ass again!"

He continues to smirk. "Or what sweetheart?"

I wait for Jake to step in. To protect me, take care of me. He doesn't.

I smirk. "Or I'll file a lawsuit against you for sexual harassment."

I see the tiniest bit of fear at that possibility. I would never actually do it, but it was nice that he thought I could. I turn my attention back to Jake who is still standing at the table acting like nothing is going on.

"What was that?" I ask.

"Nothing," Jake says.

"Exactly. You didn't do anything after that man grabbed my ass!"

"What was I supposed to do? Go beat him up?"

"No. You were just supposed to stand up for me."

He sips on his beer slowly trying to keep his composure. He just doesn't realize that he is just giving me more time to get more fed up with him. I've had enough. He's not strong enough for me.

"I want to breakup."

I see the same anger in his eyes now.

"Karissa and I broke up almost two years ago now," Jake says.

I gasp. "So everything you told me was a lie?"

"No, everything was the truth, it just happened two years ago."

"Then why did you lie to me?"

"Because I knew if I let you back into my life you would hurt me again. And I was right. I was weak. I gave in to the temptation and then you fucked me over by fucking another man."

"I can't handle this right now. I just need you to go. We can talk later after this is all over."

I see the same pain in his eyes that I did when I broke up with him that night. But I didn't expect what he says next. I didn't expect that he could say anything that would hurt me so badly.

"It's not like you were the one who lost the baby, Scarlett. I know it's a painful time for your friends, but I can't just pretend like this didn't happen while you get over something that your friend is going through. I need to do this now."

When I look at Jake now, I see who he really is. He's not a nice man, like I thought he was. Because, the one time when he needs to be here for me, he isn't here. In fact, he's making it worse.

"Leave."

Jake narrows his eyes at me. "We're not finished yet."

"We are. Don't call me. Don't text me. I want your stuff out of my apartment by the time I get back there this evening. I don't want to see you again. As far as work goes, you can finish out your contract, but everything should go through Preston and not me. When your contract is over, I want you gone."

I turn around, and I walk back into Kinsley's room, leaving Jake. Forgotten.

And, as much as I thought I loved Jake before, I don't shed a tear when I leave him. Proving that I was wrong all along. I didn't love Jake. I'm not sure if I love any man.

The only thing I'm certain about is that I love Kinsley and her baby with Killian. And that's enough for now.

32

BEAST

HER TEXT MESSAGE plays over and over again in my head.

Me: Kinsley, my best friend, is in the hospital. I don't know what's wrong with her, but I'm afraid it's serious. I'm here, waiting.

I don't know what the message means. And I don't know why she sent it to me. I read the message over and over again, trying to figure it out. Trying to figure out why she sent it to me. Trying to figure out what she wants me to do.

I know it's a test. If I know her at all, I know that's what this is. A test.

I just don't know what she wants me to do. *Send her flowers? Text her something nice to make her feel better? Call her? Tell her I can fuck her to make her feel better? Or come to the damn hospital and reveal myself to her there?*

Despite telling her that I can reveal myself to her, it can't happen at the hospital. It can't happen anywhere in public. It has to happen on my terms.

But I need to do something for her. I want to do something for her. I want to do something to take away her pain. Especially when I know I'm about to drop more pain on her.

So, I've typed out about a million different messages that I could send her. But each variation that I've tried hasn't seemed right. I've spent my entire day trying to figure out what to say.

That's when I realize there is nothing that I can say. Nothing that I say will make her feel any better. All she needs to know is that I'm here for her if she wants me to be. So, that's what I text.

Me: I'll do whatever you need. I'm here for you. If you need me.

I sent the message last night. It's now morning. And I still haven't gotten a response. I've tried to forget about it. I've tried to pretend her lack of response doesn't mean anything. That she's just mourning. That she's just in pain and trying to deal with it herself. And, even if I were there, there would be nothing I could do to help her. Not really.

But, still, her lack of response hurts. It makes me unsure if what I said was the right thing. It makes me unsure if she even still wants me in her life. I won't know until she texts me back. I can't do a damn thing but wait.

My phone buzzes on my coffee table. I jump up from my seat on the couch to get it. I cautiously stare at it until I see her name flash across the screen. I quickly open the message, needing to see what it says.

Beauty: Meet me at my apartment tonight.

She doesn't ask me if I can. She tells me. Tells me where and when to meet but not why or how to get there. She already knows that I know where her apartment is. Or at least she assumes, and she assumes right. I know everything there is to know about her.

And she knows the most important thing about me. She knows that I'll be there.

I knock on her door later that evening. I wait for what seems like an hour for her to answer. But it's in the same way that I answered her when she knocked on the hotel room door.

Beauty: Come in.

I grab the door handle, turn, and push the door open, unsure of what's going to be on the other side of the door. Unsure if this is the last time that she's going to care about me because, as soon as she sees me, she's going to hate me. I push inside the room, and to my surprise, it's completely dark. There isn't even any light coming in through the windows; they have been completely covered with window coverings.

"Beauty?" I call out.

I don't get an answer. I feel my phone buzz again in my hand. I open the message from her.

Beauty: Walk to the center of the room and find the blindfold. Then, put it on.

I read it slowly, over and over. She wants me to give up all my control. Just like I've made her do in the past. The only problem is, I have something to hide, and she doesn't. And, by me giving up my complete control, I'll have no control of when she decides to see who I really am.

I walk to the center of the room, which seems to be her living room, and I find a blindfold lying on her coffee table. I pick it up, feeling the slick silk fabric in my hands. It'll do a decent job of keeping me in the dark although I'll probably still be able to see a sliver of light from the bottom. But it won't be enough to see her every movement. It won't be enough to tell if she decides to turn on the lights before I'm ready.

I tie the blindfold around my eyes, and then I wait. I wait for her to control me.

She makes me wait a long time. My anticipation and anxiety and need for her deepen with each second that passes. I need her. I need her right now. But she hasn't even made it clear if that's what I'm going to get. She might have already figured out who I am. She might be planning on killing me. She might be calling the police. She might be destroying my life. But I don't care. She's worth the risk if I get a chance of having her.

"I need you to make me feel good," she says suddenly.

When I hear her voice, I know she's standing in front of me. I suck in a breath and then let it out slowly. And then I smile because I know that she wants me to fuck her. I can hear it in her voice. That's what she needs. And I'm more than happy to deliver that to her.

"Gladly, Beauty."

I feel her hands on my face, running over my lips, and then they move down my body, feeling every inch of me over my clothes, studying my body with her hands. I don't know if she can see me or if she wants to see me. My guess is, she hasn't, or she would have already run from me.

She grabs my hand, moves me forward, and then lets go. "Undress."

It's one word. One simple word that says so much. It says, *I need you*. It says, *I control you*. It says, *I claim you*.

When she hears the last of my clothes hitting the floor, she says, "Take three steps forward."

I do and then stop. I wait.

"Kneel on the floor."

I do.

"Good boy," she says in the same way that I said, "Good girl," to her so many times before when she'd listened to my commands.

It feels strange, being on this side of things. Feels strange, giving up control. I never thought I would like it. But giving up control to her, I would gladly do it if it meant I got to have her.

I feel her hands touch my face again, followed by her lips. It's an intense feeling since I can't see her. I feel her long hair caressing my face as she kisses me. I reach my hand forward, needing to feel her. Needing to see if she's clothed or not. Needing to feel her body.

I reach out and find her face and immediately feel the fabric that is covering her own eyes. She blindfolded herself as well. She doesn't want to find out my identity tonight anymore then I want to show her.

She grabs my wrist as I reach out for her. "No more touching until I tell you to."

Her grip on my wrist is hard and firm, but I could still reach out and touch her if I really wanted to. I don't though. I listen to her and give her the control she needs.

"Good boy," she says again, her voice seductive, before her lips are on mine again.

Her hands are moving over my body, feeling me for the first time. And I catch my breath as she studies my body with her hands. First, my face that still has stubble from yesterday. Then, my chest. She feels over my heart that I know is beating rapidly. I know she can feel my anxiety and need growing for her. She moves her hand lower to my abs, counting each one with her fingers. Then, to my legs. She takes her time as she learns my every muscle. My every scar. The beat of my heart. When she has finally had her fill, she moves to my cock and roughly takes it in her hands. She studies it, too, even though she's had it inside her.

I let out a low growl when she touches me, needing her to know what she does to me with a simple touch.

Her hands move from my cock to my head. She grabs the sides of my head and pulls me forward. "Make me come with your tongue."

Her hands push my head onto her pussy. And I can't wait to devour her just like she asked. But I know I need to get her there slowly. I know I need to get her to feel every part of this. Forget the pain she's been dealing with for the last twenty-four hours.

I place my hands on her thighs, spreading her apart slowly and firmly in the chair she is now seated in. She lets me. I can feel her breathing. I can feel her pulse in her legs as I lower my head over her pussy. I breathe in and out slowly, letting my warm air move over her sensitive flesh. Trying to get her to focus on my breathing instead of what I'm afraid is still going through her head.

She's impatient though and can't wait for me. She grabs my hair on top of my head and forces my lips to touch her pussy. I can't help but grin at her being unable to control herself.

"Make me come. Now."

I slowly run my tongue around her lips, making circles around her clit. I feel her legs twitch in my grasp, and I know that I'm getting her excited. I continue to slowly run my tongue over her lips, then to her clit, and then back to her lips again—each time, spinning slightly longer and longer on her clit.

"Faster," she commands.

I move my tongue over her faster, and I am rewarded with a louder moan. I can't help myself. I need to feel more of her body, so I move my hands to her plump breasts. I feel her nipples harden. I move her nipples, rubbing them hard between my thumbs and first fingers, listening to more moans as I do.

I move my tongue faster and feel her legs tighten around my head.

Jesus.

I know she's close, but I want to make this last forever for her. I slightly slow my tongue, trying to make this last. Trying to give her as much time to enjoy this as humanly possible.

"Faster!" she screams.

I move faster as she commanded, and I feel her legs tightening on my head harder. I move my hands from her breasts to her legs, forcing her open for me. Forcing her to feel every drop of goodness that she can.

She screams, "Beast!"

It's a beautiful thing, feeling her come around my tongue, even though I can't see her. I can feel her, and that's almost as good.

Beauty doesn't wait until she's come down off her high. And she doesn't give me any warning. She stands quickly and grabs ahold of my body forcing me up. Her lips collide with mine, her hands go around my body, and I grab ahold of her, trying to figure out what she wants, but happy to give her whatever that is. She pushes me back, forcing me into a seat on the couch, and then she makes her intentions known as she mounts me.

"I need you. I need you to erase everything."

"I need you, too, Beauty."

She doesn't waste any time. She slides a condom over my cock, and then I'm inside her. Her hands on my shoulders, she's moving her body up and down over mine. I've never wanted anything more than to see through this blindfold, as I'm sure her breasts are bouncing up and down in front of my face. I want to see the pain disappear from her face. Still, her body moving over my cock is almost more than I can bear. Not being able to see just makes the sensation that much better.

I grab her ass and help her thrust on top of me.

We growl and pant and show how desperate we are for each other until we both come.

She doesn't stop there though. She hasn't had enough, and that's when I realize that the rest of my night is going to be spent here, fucking her. Trying to help her forget the pain.

We fuck on her kitchen table. On the stairs. In her bed. Over and over until she finally passes out in her bed.

When she finally passes out, I take the blindfold off and study her again for the first time today. She's beautiful as she sleeps. Even though I can still see the pain on her face. Even after all we've done all day, the pain is still there. All I did was push it from her mind for a few hours. But I can't think of a better way to spend my day.

33

BEAST

MY PHONE BUZZES, and I see that it's from my boss. I get up from her bed, leaving her to sleep. I don't answer right away. I'll call her back in a minute. I just need a second to gather my thoughts. To study her one last time while she's sleeping. Before she finds out the truth. Before she hates me.

I slowly get dressed as I watch her, secretly hoping that she'll wake up and discover who I am. Maybe if she wakes up before I fulfill my last job, she won't hate me.

She doesn't wake up, and I don't wake her.

I do walk over and kiss her one last time on her lips. Because, the next time I see her, I will tell her who I am. This might be the last time I get to kiss her, so I make it worth it.

Slowly, reluctantly, I turn and leave. I walk out of her bedroom and out of her apartment.

My phone buzzes again. My boss again. I don't answer again.

I will soon enough, but for now, I'm still trying to figure out what all my options are to get out of this mess. I'm afraid the only way I have a shot with her is by quitting. By getting out now before I do something that she won't forgive me for.

I continue out of her building. I can't though. If I don't finish the job, they will hunt us down and kill us both. I just have to finish the job and hope and pray that she forgives me.

My phone rings for a third time, and this time, I answer, "I'm on my way to the office now to tell you the plan."

34

SCARLETT

BEAST: *I want to tell you who I am. Just name the time and place. Or I'll come find you now and tell you. I can't wait much longer.*

Me: *I have a fashion show to attend tomorrow night, followed by an after-party. You can tell me who you are before then, and then go with me as my date.*

Beast: *Fine. Just know that, after I tell you who I am, you won't want to take me as your date.*

I stare at my phone, trying to understand his last sentence. I'm not sure why I wouldn't want to take him after he tells me who he is. But it's something I've been afraid of since the moment he wouldn't show me who he was. There's something wrong. Some reason that he won't just show me who he is.

I've formed hundreds of theories in my head. None of them make sense to me though. None of them have led me down the right track. The most likely scenario is that he is someone from my past, but I can't think of anyone who would fit his description. I can't think of anyone who speaks the way he does or controls me the way he does. I can't think of anyone.

It could be because he's hideous, and he thinks I'd run because of how he looks. But I've felt every inch of his body, and other than a few scars covering his torso, I didn't find anything hideous about him. And, even if he were, I'm not sure it would be enough to make me not want to be with him.

That leaves a third option. He's dangerous. He does something that I don't want to know about. He makes his money illegally. He does something immoral. Whatever it is, I'm sure it's not that bad. I'm sure it's something I can look past or that he could stop doing. It's not like we would need the money. I'm not looking for a man who brings in a lot of money. I'm just looking for a man who will love me and challenge me in the way that I need.

And I have a feeling that, after last night, Beast is that man. Last night was perfect. It showed me that Beast could give me what I needed, even at the cost of him giving up something he needed. And I know giving up control to me was not easy for him. Still, he did it anyway without question. He was the only one who was able to take me away from my pain, if only for a few hours.

The entire time I was with him, I wanted nothing more than to flick on the lights. I wanted nothing more than to open my eyes and see whom he was. I didn't though because last night wasn't about finding out who he was. Last night was about figuring out if he could give me what I needed when I needed it. And he did.

Tomorrow night will be about figuring out who he is and if I can live with whatever it is.

Today and tonight will be about Kinsley.

My driver, George, is driving me to her apartment. Killian needed to go into work for a couple of hours today, and I told him I would stay with her. I think the two of them, despite how much they love each other, need a couple of hours apart. They need a couple of hours to grieve on their own and not blame each other for what happened. A couple of hours not to feel the pain. Even as much as they try to help each other, it's hard because, anytime they look at one another, the pain is always there.

I just hope I'll be able to do something to at least distract her from her own pain.

George pulls up in front of her apartment building. He exits the car and runs around to open my door for me.

When he does, I step out. "Thank you, George," I say.

"It's my pleasure, Miss Bell. And I have to say, you have a hard job ahead of you. But, if anyone can do it, you can," he says.

I give him a tight smile but don't say anything. There are no words to say.

I walk into the building and onto the elevator, going up to the top floor. I'm somewhat surprised that they were still planning on living in an apartment when the baby came. I thought they would have wanted a house that they could turn into a home. I guess I don't know what their plans were for sure, but if I know Killian at all, I know it would have involved a surprise house that he'd bought for her at the last minute.

I swallow the lump in my throat. *How could their life be shattered in a single second? How could it shatter again after all the pain they'd endured? It's not fair. Not fair at all.*

When I reach Kinsley's apartment door, I use my key, not bothering to knock. I step inside. "Kinsley?"

I don't get an answer. I didn't think I would. When Killian left this morning, he said that Kinsley was still in bed and that he didn't want to disturb her. I'm guessing that's where she still is.

I turn right and walk down the hallway to their bedroom. I knock gently on the door. "Kinsley?"

I don't get an answer. I push the door open and see Kinsley sitting in a chair in the corner, staring out the window. She doesn't acknowledge that I'm here although I know she knows that I am here. There is no way she couldn't have heard me.

I try to figure out what I should do. I try to form some sort of plan. I have no idea what I should do. Should I take her out and go to the movies? Go to lunch? Go shopping? I don't think any of these things will make her feel better. But I have to try something.

I walk over to Kinsley and place my hand on her shoulder. "How about you go take a shower? Start there, and then we can figure out what we need to do after that."

Kinsley doesn't say anything. She just continues to stare outside.

I walk around and kneel in front of her. I shake her hands until she's looking at me. "Kinsley, go take a shower."

Kinsley finally sees me and nods. I help her stand and then wait in her bedroom until I see her walk into her bathroom. I hear the water running. I walk back into her living room, trying to figure out what I'm going to do, when I see the mess that is her apartment. Her kitchen is filled with dishes that need washing. Her living room is filled with clutter and clothes. Anything that's been brought into the apartment the last couple of days has just been dropped on the floor. Her bedroom wasn't much better. The bed was unmade, and there was plenty of dirty laundry on the floor.

I don't know what I'm going to do when Kinsley finishes getting ready. But I know what I can do right now. I'm going to clean.

I start picking up items off the floor in her living room. I pick up clothes and put them in her laundry room. Dishes go to the kitchen. And blankets get folded.

After I finish the living room, I head to the kitchen, lost in my own thoughts, forgetting entirely why I'm here, thinking I just need to clean. I turn on the warm water in the sink and begin washing the dishes by hand.

A few minutes later, I see Kinsley walk over and begin drying. Neither of us says anything to each other. We both just become lost in the task. We both just focus on cleaning, and that's when I realize that this is exactly what we need to be doing right now. Cleaning. Because, for whatever reason, cleaning is healing. It's calming and relaxing, and it's exactly what we both need.

We silently agree with one another that this is what we should be doing.

And, after an hour of silent cleaning, the silence turns into gentle talking. Not about anything of importance, just about simple things. The weather, the news, decorations that I like in her apartment.

We continue cleaning until we get to the bedroom door that I don't even think anything about. I just push it open, and a single tear falls from my eye when I see what's behind the door. It is Wesley's room. The room is not completely put together. The unfinished crib sits against one wall. The dressers are still in their boxes. Paint swatches, from grays to greens to yellows, cover the walls since they didn't decide on a color. There are baby clothes and supplies in the corner that still have tags on them.

Still, it is the baby's room, and I shouldn't have opened the door.

I turn around to see Kinsley and try to close the door quickly before she reacts. Before she loses all the progress she's made today.

"No. I need to go in there. I need to clean things up a little bit. I'm not going to get rid of things. We are going to have a baby at some point—whether that's through adoption, surrogacy, or me actually giving birth. It's going to happen. This just wasn't the right time. I need to be able to go into this room. Killian can't. It's too hard for him, but I need to be able to."

I nod and try to keep more of my tears back. Kinsley's going to be strong, so I can, too.

"Okay. But if you're not ready yet, it can wait. There's no rush on healing."

"I'm not rushing. I just...need this."

"Okay."

"Okay."

I hold the door open and watch Kinsley walk inside the room. She takes her time with running her hand over all the furniture. And then she walks over to the corner where the clothes and toys are. She picks up an item of clothing, holds it up, and cuddles it, breathing in the scent of baby that she'll never get to smell because the baby never got to wear it. Because Wesley never got to wear it.

When she removes the item from her face, I see her tears. And I lose it. I go over to her and hold her tightly, and we both cry. Somehow, these tears, so unlike the many tears before, are healing. I know that these tears are tears that we need to cry because, after they're gone, we'll feel a little better. We will be a little stronger. We will know that we can step inside this room and still survive.

"I think that's enough for today, don't you?" I ask.

Kinsley nods, and I lead her back out of the room. I don't really know what to do next, but we need to do something light after what we just went through.

"Want to watch cheesy romances with me?"

"Only if you order me Italian. Lots and lots of spaghetti and breadsticks."

"Deal."

I order her Italian for lunch, and then we both curl on a couch and begin watching cheesy romances for the next couple of hours. It doesn't even begin to take away the pain though. And I'm afraid the pain is always going to be there for both of us. And I wonder if I should have taken Kinsley out of this house, if that would've helped her heal more than just cleaning. Or, at the very least, it might've been more fun.

"Do you want to go with me to a fashion show tomorrow night?" I ask.

Kinsley thinks for a moment. "Are you sure you want to take me? I'm not sure I'll be a lot of fun."

I roll my eyes at her. "When are you ever not fun? Of course I want to take you." I already asked Beast to go with me, but if she says yes, finding out whom he is will just have to wait. My best friend is more important.

"Yes, I want to go," she says.

35

BEAST

BEAUTY: Rain check on tomorrow night. I need to take my friend instead. How about we do something on Saturday night instead?

I hate her message. I hate it. Because there can't be a next night after tomorrow night. Tomorrow night really is my only chance. After she texted me, I put the plan into place. My boss won't let me wait any longer. And I know, after I tell her who I am, she won't want to be with me anyway.

Tomorrow night is when I get my revenge.

Tomorrow night is when I destroy any chances of Scarlett and me ever being together.

Tomorrow night is when my life ends.

36

SCARLETT

"WE LOOK HOT," I say, staring at Kinsley and myself in the mirror.

Kinsley had a hard time with finding a dress that she felt made her look sexy. It was especially hard since she's carrying a little extra weight from being pregnant. And that extra weight makes her think of Wesley. Thank God I was able to find a dress that showed off her curves. It's a black halter dress that hugs her curves and makes her look hot as hell.

I decide to wear a classic red dress, strapless and short.

"You look beautiful," Killian says as he walks into the bedroom. He goes over and gives Kinsley a hug.

She smiles at him as the two hug before he gives her a less than sweet kiss on the lips.

"I don't have to go. I can stay here with you, and we can have a nice dinner, followed by some other things," Kinsley says with a wink at Killian. "I'm sure Scarlett would rather take one of her boy toys anyway."

"First of all, I really don't want to hear that you two are planning on having sex tonight. Second of all, I don't have any boy toys, but if you don't want to come, that's perfectly fine," I say.

"No, it is not perfectly fine. Kinsley needs a night out, and I will be here, waiting to do some naughty things to you that involve chocolate and—" Killian says.

"Oh God! I'll be in the living room. I don't want to hear what you're gonna be doing afterward," I say, leaving the bedroom.

I look through my phone messages on the couch while I wait for Kinsley and Killian to most likely get in a quick fuck before we go. I sigh when I realize I still haven't gotten a response from Beast.

Is he upset that I'm not taking him tonight, like originally planned? Has he not gotten my message yet? Is he not sure if he's free tomorrow night?

I hate that I don't get to find out who he is tonight. But, if I'm honest with myself, I need a night out with my best friend, too. Because, if I were finding out whom Beast was tonight, I would be filled with anxiety. Anxiety does nothing to help healing. Tomorrow night though, I'll be ready. After a night of fun and relaxation, I'll be ready to face whatever he's going to tell me tomorrow.

"Ready," Kinsley says as she walks into the living room where I'm waiting for her.

I laugh when I see her. Her hair is a tangled mess, and she has red lipstick smeared on her cheek. But she looks happy, glowing for the first time in a while.

I get up off the couch and walk over to her. "You're almost ready," I say. I run my hand through her hair, smoothing the tangled mess. I wipe the lipstick off her cheek and then pull my lipstick out of my purse and reapply it onto her lips. "Now, you're ready. Let's go."

We arrive at the fashion event, and I can tell that Kinsley is excited to be back at an event like this. It's been a while since I have taken her to anything like this. Her smile is full on her face, and her cheeks are still flushed from whatever Killian did to her before.

We walk into the building and take our seats next to the runway.

We have front-row seats even though this isn't one of my designers putting this on.

A few minutes later, the show starts, and models began stomping down the runway in various clothes.

"Oh my God, who would wear that?" Kinsley asks when one of the models walks onto the runway with her boobs practically falling out.

"I would! I think it's cute."

Kinsley laughs.

"Oh my God! Is that a penis?"

I turn to see what she's looking at when I see a male model walking down with what I'm pretty sure is his penis hanging out. I laugh. Designers will do the craziest things to get some press the next day.

"Yep," I say, covering Kinsley's eyes.

She laughs and moves my hand away from her face. I smile.

I made the right decision in bringing her here today. This is exactly what we both needed. A night of fun to be ourselves again. To rediscover who we are without men or babies or careers or anything else. Just as women.

The show ends, and we move to the after-party that is being held right next door. We are both immediately handed champagne as the party begins. I should be working tonight. Mingling with other designers and models and people in the business. Trying to spread my name and my brand. I don't though. I don't care about my business tonight. I just care about having fun with Kinsley.

"Let's go check out the appetizers. The shrimp looks delicious," I say.

Kinsley nods and follows. We walk over and pick up a skewer of shrimp that is delicious, followed by another plate of shrimp. Followed by tiny burgers. Followed by ham sandwiches. Followed by cheese fries. It's one of the strangest appetizers that I've seen at an event like this. But it's delicious nonetheless.

I feel my phone vibrate in my purse, and I reach into it,

wondering if it's Killian trying to get me to take Kinsley home so that he can fuck her again. It's not.

Beast: You need to leave. It's not safe.

I stare at the message in confusion. *What does he mean, it's not safe? How would he know?*

Me: Why?

Beast: It doesn't matter. Just go. Now.

"I think we need to leave," I say to Kinsley.

Kinsley wrinkles her face at me. "Why? Is my husband trying to convince you that we need to go home? Because he can wait, you know," she says with a wink of her eye.

"No, it's not Killian. It's just—"

A familiar song comes on, and Kinsley grabs my hand. "We can go in a minute. I want to dance first."

I push away the strange feeling that we are in danger, and I follow Kinsley onto the dance floor. After two songs and a couple of shots, I forget all about Beast's messages. Kinsley and I are having fun, and that's what we need.

"I'm thirsty! Let's go get a drink," Kinsley says after a few more songs.

I nod and follow her off the dance floor. I pull out my phone again and this time it is from Killian.

Killian: I couldn't stay away. I'm on the West side of the building by the bathrooms. Don't tell her yet, but don't be surprised if she sneaks off to the bathroom and doesn't come back. It's just because I stole her.

I smile at Killian's text. We grab drinks, and then Kinsley decides she needs to use the restroom. My smile returns as I scan the crowd as we walk down a long hallway to where the restrooms are. As we walk, a man begins walking toward us and I'm sure it's Killian. The man is a tall, dark man. His hair is slightly messy on top of his head. His dark green eyes pierce my heart as he walks forward. Stubble covers his strong chin and neck. He's wearing a tuxedo that fits him perfectly, better than most men who are attending tonight. It's not Killian.

I can't stop looking at him as he walks toward us. I know this man. I've known this man for ten years. I've seen his picture on the news. I saw the police handcuff this man. I saw him go to jail for life for trafficking people, for killing people. For almost killing my best friend.

I watch this man pull a gun that seems to appear out of nowhere. I watch him aim the gun at Kinsley. I watch him fire before I have a chance to push Kinsley out of the way.

I don't know who screams. Me? Kinsley? An innocent bystander?

I have no idea.

He only fires one shot, and then he turns and walks in the other direction.

I turn to Kinsley. "Are you okay? Are you hurt?"

She grabs her chest and sinks to the floor. I'm afraid he shot her in the chest.

I search her body, but I find no blood. "Kinsley! Are you okay?"

"Yes, I'm okay. He didn't hit me. That was..." she says, breathing heavily.

"Yes, that was Nacio. The man who ran the trafficking ring with your family. The man who almost killed you." Silently to myself, I add, *the killer who is also my Beast.*

I think back to everything Kinsley has told me about Nacio. Everything that I have read in the newspaper about him and what happened to Kinsley. Everything that I've been told, or read, or experienced flashes through my head.

Nacio runs an organization along with Kinsley's Granddad. A terrible organization where they lie, smuggle, and kill for money.

Kinsley pretended to join the organization to try and stop them, but Nacio didn't believe she had the guts to lie, and smuggle, and kill. She needed to be tested.

Nacio shot a woman in cold blood.

Nacio tested Kinsley by telling her she must kill Killian.

...But then Nacio saved Kinsley by killing her Granddad when he tried to shoot her.

Is he really just a killer then?

And then there was that connection. When Nacio was arrested I saw him. Our eyes connected and I saw that there was more to him than just a killer. That he was a man that I felt an instant connection to.

I glance up and see Killian running toward us, anxious to see why his wife is lying on the floor. I don't know why I do it. It might be the worst decision I've ever made. But I need answers. I need to know why he decided to sleep with me. I need to know why he tried to kill Kinsley now when he'd saved her once before. I need to know why, despite being less than a couple of feet away when he shot her, he missed. Because it doesn't seem possible that he could miss. And, even if he did miss, he had plenty of time to get another couple of shots off before anyone could have stopped him.

"I'll be right back," I say to Kinsley. I begin running down the hallway after him as soon as Killian gets close enough to comfort Kinsley.

"Scarlett!" Kinsley shouts at me, trying to get me to stop.

But I don't stop, and I know the fear will keep her from coming after me.

I don't know where he went past the end of the hallway. I don't know where to go. I just run down the hallway and turn right when I reach the end, just like I saw him do. I know there's no way I can catch up to him. I'm in heels and a dress; he was in flat shoes. Even if I were in running shoes, I know I couldn't catch him.

My only chance is that he isn't running. My only chance is that he wants me to find him.

And I do.

I find him just as he is walking out the back of the building and into the darkness.

"Nacio!"

He stops when he hears me shout his name. He slowly turns and sees me. And I can see the pain on his face. Pain that I don't understand.

If anyone should be in pain, it should be me, not him. He's the one who deceived me. He's the one who fucked me even though he knew that, if I ever found out who he was, I'd hate him. He's the killer, not me. *Why the hell is he in pain when it should be me?*

When I see the look of pain on his face, every contradiction to who this man is comes to mind. He's a killer, yet he saved Kinsley almost ten years ago. And I'm pretty sure he just saved her now. He didn't kill her with a bullet even though he could have. And he'd tried to warn us to leave earlier.

He's a killer. Yet he's a man.

And, for some reason, I can't fucking understand why he is a man that I still want. He might not be a good man. He's definitely no knight in shining armor. But I want to give him a chance. I want to understand my beast and understand if he can give up killing.

I watch him study me, and I watch him understand the moment when I realize that I still want my chance with him. That I still want him. My beast. I have so many questions, and I don't even know where to start asking them.

I hear the sirens in the distance, and I know I don't have much time to ask my questions.

But, evidently, he has one of his own.

He holds out his hand to me and says, "Come with me?"

"Yes."

The End

Keep reading for Definitely No...

DEFINITELY NO

1

SCARLETT

WHAT THE FUCK am I doing?

The second I say yes, Nacio grabs ahold of my hand and pulls me out into the darkness of night. We run fast even though I'm in heels. We run, and I somehow manage to keep up. We run through the alleyway in the back of the building and out onto the street. Nacio keeps pulling me, forcing me to run. So, I run and try not to think about what the fuck I'm doing.

Nacio stops abruptly in front of a black Mercedes-Benz. He lets go of my hand and begins walking to the driver's side. "Get in," he says.

I freeze, looking at the car. *What the fuck am I doing?* If I get in the car, he could kill me. If I get in the car, I'd be betraying my best friend. I could be considered an accomplice to attempted murder. I could be found guilty of all sorts of things. I could be destroying my life by stepping into the car.

I can't...

"Scarlett, get in," Nacio says.

I look up and meet his eyes, eyes that are filled with nothing but passion. Eyes that tell me, despite what he does, to trust him, at least this once. So, I do trust him, even though I know I shouldn't. Because I have to find out more. I can't believe that he is really just a killer.

I open the door and climb in as Nacio does the same. Before he even has the door shut, Nacio is pulling out into the street. He drives fast, faster than any person I know. He takes each turn sharply without decelerating at all. I cling to my seat as excitement pulses through me.

You wanted excitement. I suck in a breath. I did, but now, I take it back. This excitement is too much. This excitement is too dangerous.

I squeeze my eyes shut as Nacio takes another turn too sharply, and I'm afraid that he's going to run us into one of the parked cars on the side of the street. When I open my eyes and we haven't scratched the car or collided with another, I let go of the seat I've been holding on to. I glance over at Nacio as his eyes focus on the rearview mirror. I turn around in my seat to look at what he's looking at behind us. I don't see anything.

"Is someone following us?" I ask.

Nacio looks up in the rearview mirror one more time before the light turns red. "No."

The second the word leaves his lips, he glances back in the rearview mirror. I don't believe him. I turn around again, trying to see what he sees, but I don't see anything.

"Is someone following us?" I ask again, my voice calmer.

"No."

"Then, why do you keep looking in the rearview mirror?"

"To make sure no one is following us."

I nod even though he isn't looking at me. He's focused on whoever is or isn't following us. His hand now moves from the wheel and finds mine. He takes my hand in his and begins rubbing his thumb across my palm. It calms me even though I want him to place his hand back on the wheel. With the way he's been driving, he needs two hands to drive, not just one. But it feels good even though I don't know why the hell I'm letting him do it. It calms me.

My phone buzzes, and I jump, letting go of his hand. Nacio barely glances at me, but I can see him eyeing me out of the corner of his eye.

I slowly pull my phone out of my purse. "Kinsley," I say, reading the name flashing across the screen.

I move my thumb over the Ignore button, ready to push it. I can't talk with her right now. I feel bad enough that I left her, but I can't explain what the hell I'm doing with Nacio. I can't explain what I'm doing at all.

"Answer," he says.

"I can't."

"Answer. Tell her you didn't find me. Tell her you just needed some air and you'll talk to her tomorrow. Lie."

I nervously look at him. I've never lied to my best friend before.

I answer the phone. "Hi, Kinsley."

"Thank God you're all right! Where are you?"

I glance over at Nacio. He doesn't reveal at all how he's feeling. He just looks straight ahead, occasionally glancing in the rearview mirror, ignoring me. Giving me no clue of how I should act. Giving me no clue on what I should say.

"I'm sorry I left you. I just needed to make Nacio pay. But I didn't catch up with him. He disappeared before I could find him. And then I was just so upset that I needed some air, so I walked outside."

"Don't be sorry. You just had me worried to death. Killian's here now though. Do you want us to come find you and stay with you tonight? I know that must've been scary for you, and I hate bringing my past into your present. I never wanted you to have to deal with that. I just want you to be safe. Just tell me where you are, and we will come pick you up," Kinsley says.

"No, that's okay, really. You guys should just go home and be together. I can call George and have him take me home. I just need some time to process what just happened anyway."

"You sure? Because we don't mind—"

"I'm sure. I just want to be alone for tonight. I'll call you tomorrow."

"Okay. Be safe, Scar."

"You, too, Kins."

I end the call, feeling like a horrible person. More horrible than I did when I just left her alone. Now, I lied to her. I'm a horrible person. I slowly put my phone back into my purse. I can't look at Nacio. I feel too horrible. I already hate what he's done and who he's turned me into—a liar.

"Where are we going?" I ask. I need to know that I at least lied to her for a damn good reason. I need to know that I lied to find out the truth.

"Somewhere we can talk..." He lets his voice trail off, like he wants to say more but won't.

In my head, I finish the sentence with, *And fuck*. Because that's all we've ever done—fuck. That sure as hell isn't happening. I'm not fucking a liar even though, in the light of day, he makes me even crazier than at night. He's even sexier than I imagined.

His hair is darker and tousled. His eyes are more intense with lust and need. His lips and chin are rougher and sharper than I imagined they would be. His body is every bit as hard and strong as I imagined it would be. Even though I can't see his body because his suit is covering it up, I can tell from the way his suit molds to his body that he is stronger than even I imagined.

Why am I attracted to a killer? I know everything he's done. Well, I know what Kinsley's told me. He's a killer, and there's no telling how many people he has killed since he got out of prison. A prison I thought he was still supposed to be in. Yet I'm still here, and I haven't run for the hills yet. And, now that I know who he is, now that I've seen his face, he doesn't have a choice but to kill me. *So, why the hell am I here?*

I nervously glance over at Nacio. I can feel my heart beating in my throat. I swallow, trying to make the feeling go away, but it doesn't. Nacio glances over at me, and his eyes pierce my soul. He's just as scared as I am. That's what I see in his eyes. He might be a killer, but he is still a man. *And maybe if I can pull enough of the man out of him...*

Nacio breaks eye contact with me almost as soon as he started.

He glances back at the road and makes another sharp right turn. I grab ahold of the seat, trying to keep from falling over sideways.

We come to an abrupt stop. I take a deep breath and then another before I see where he stopped. A hotel. We've stopped at a hotel.

Our doors are being opened, and a hand is placed inside the car to help me out. I slowly unbuckle my seat belt and then take the stranger's hand to help me out of the car.

"Thank you," I say to the valet of the hotel.

"You're welcome, Miss..." the valet says, waiting for me to fill in my last name.

I don't. I know well enough that I shouldn't be telling anybody my name right now.

I walk over to Nacio, who is waiting for me at the door to the hotel. Our hands automatically intertwine, and it startles me. That's not normal. But Nacio just smiles at me and holds my hand, like any boyfriend who's been dating me for a long time would.

Nacio leads me into the nice hotel that rivals the beauty of the Waldorf he took me to earlier. I haven't been to this hotel before. But, from the look of the extravagant entryway, I'd like to come back when I'm not afraid for my life.

Nacio walks us up to the counter. "Your best room," he says.

The woman behind the desk smiles at him. "Our best room is almost twenty thousand dollars a night, sir," she challengingly says to him.

She doesn't think he can afford that much. She doesn't think I can afford that much. Even though I know I can, I have no idea how much being a killer pays.

"Only twenty? Huh, I thought you guys had the best room in New York City. I was wrong. You can't get the best for that cheap."

"I didn't mean, sir...I just didn't want...I mean—"

Nacio watches the woman squirm for another moment before he finally interrupts, "We will take your best room."

The woman nods and begins typing in her computer. "I'll need a name to put on the room."

Nacio nods. "Shane Coleman."

The woman nods and begins typing again. "I just need your credit card, sir," she says hesitantly.

Nacio reaches in his back pocket and pulls out his wallet before tossing a credit card at her. She picks it up and begins typing on her computer again. When she's finished, she slides the credit card back across to Nacio, and that's when I see the name on the card. *Shane Coleman.* My eyes widen as I look at Nacio.

How many fake names does he have? How many fake credit cards? How much of his life is a lie? All of it, I think.

"Here's your room key. You're in room 1501. Take the elevator to your right up to the top floor. You'll need your key to access that floor. Enjoy your evening, Mr. and Mrs. Coleman."

I shake a little when she calls me Mrs. Coleman. I'm not a Mrs. anything. And, with the way my life is going, I never will be. I'm afraid that this might be the last time I see another human.

"We will," he says to the woman, smiling.

Nacio pulls on my hand, and we begin walking toward the elevator.

I walk with him even though I secretly want to yell back at the woman to call the police if she doesn't see me in the morning because that would mean he killed me.

I don't though. For whatever stupid reason, I trust this man who is holding my hand even though he's given me no reason to. I just want answers even if those answers come at the risk of losing my life.

Nacio guides me onto the elevator and presses the button for the top floor. The door shuts, and I bite my lip as the elevator begins going up.

"Relax," Nacio says.

I shake my head. "How am I supposed to relax? How do I know that you're not going to kill me here?"

Nacio laughs. And then he turns me toward himself, lifting my chin so that I'm looking at him. "Is that what you think, Beauty? That I'm taking you up here to kill you?"

I nod slowly.

He laughs again and shakes his head. "Oh, Beauty. If I were going

228

to kill you, I wouldn't have taken you to the nicest hotel in New York City, where there are about a million cameras watching us. If I were gonna kill you, I would've taken you to an alleyway. It would've already been done because, as much as I hate waiting to fuck you, if I wanted to kill you, you would already be dead. I hate waiting to kill someone. I'm not a patient man. I wouldn't wait."

I swallow as I stare at this man. This crazy, confusing man. This man whom I don't understand, but still want all the same.

If only I could convince my body to stop wanting him. If only I could get my heart to stop beating rapidly, to slow down my breathing, to stop my nipples from hardening at the sight of him. If I could just get all those things to stop, maybe I could move on from him. Maybe I could survive. And find a nice guy like Jake. Although Jake didn't turn out to be a nice guy. None of them are. The nice guys aren't nice. But the dangerous guys are dangerous. So, I don't know where that leaves me.

The elevator doors open at the top floor.

Nacio steps off, letting go of my hand. "You coming?" he asks, pausing just outside the elevator doors.

He's giving me another way out. He knows I'm scared. And he's not forcing me anymore. I could press the elevator button for the bottom floor and just go home, like I told Kinsley I was doing. But then I wouldn't have my answers. But then I wouldn't have Nacio, my Beast. Then, I would be all alone.

"Yes." I step off the elevator just before the doors begin closing.

Nacio smiles at me. "Good girl."

I try to smile at him, but I can't, not until I have answers.

Nacio's hand goes to the small of my back as he guides me toward the hotel room. He opens the door, and immediately, I feel such a stark difference from our first encounter in a hotel room.

My jaw drops when I see the inside of the hotel room. It's nicer than my apartment, and I know for a fact that my apartment is one of the nicer ones in New York City. The hotel room is about three times bigger, too.

"Holy shit!" I say.

I take another step or two into the room, marveling at the crystal chandelier hanging overhead. I take another couple of steps and am met with the grand living room that is probably bigger than my whole apartment. The nicest leather couch fills the room with windows at least twice as high as in my apartment.

"I didn't know hotel rooms this nice existed."

"This isn't the most expensive hotel room in New York City, but it's definitely one of the nicest. One of my favorites. The more expensive ones come with things I don't need, like fancy cars, extra butlers, and complimentary champagne. I already have a fancy car, and I don't need a butler or champagne."

I nod as my eyes continue exploring the room, and that's when I realize that he's been here before.

I bite my lip to try to keep myself from asking the question that I don't want to hear the answer to. Because I already know the answer to it. And there are about a million more important questions than the one I'm about to ask, but I can't help it. Once the jealousy starts, I can't just let it go. "How many others?"

I glance up at Nacio standing in the entryway to the living room while I am now on the far side, running my hand across the leather couch.

He narrows his eyes. "Others?"

I nod. "Others..." I don't bother explaining what I mean.

I know he's not dumb, despite how he's acting at the moment. I know he knows exactly what I'm talking about.

He takes a step forward and then another until he's right next to me again. "What makes you think there are others, Beauty?"

I take a deep breath and then another, trying to catch my breath while trying to answer his question at the same time. I realize that I can't do both at the same time with him so close to me. And I realize that this was his plan all along—to ask me a question, so I can't breathe.

"Because you're a man, and there are always others."

Nacio smirks. "I'm not going to lie, Beauty. Of course there have been others. Not here though."

I suck in a breath. I don't know why, but it makes me feel better even though I'm not sure if he's lying or telling the truth. "How do I know you're not lying to me?"

Nacio studies me for a moment. "You don't."

I frown. I have no idea what to say to that. I need someone who tells me the truth. Above everything else. Above the killing or whatever the hell he does for a living. I need him to be honest with me about what he can tell me. *Otherwise, why am I here? If he's not going to give me truthful answers, why am I here?*

"I need answers."

Nacio nods. "Let's go out to the balcony." Without waiting for me to respond, he begins walking out of the living room and down the hallway to the kitchen. Then, he goes through a door that leads out to the balcony.

I hesitate for a second. The balcony would be a perfect place to kill me. Just one push over the edge, and I'd be dead. He could claim that I fell. It would be easy. But I also really want to go out on the balcony because it's probably beautiful out there. I love my balcony, and it's nowhere near as nice as I know this one must be. This one looks like it has a view of the whole city.

So, I walk out onto the balcony. Nacio doesn't take a seat on any of the chairs. He just leans against the edge of the balcony, looking over. I walk up beside him and do the same. Neither of us speaks for a while. We both just look over the edge of the balcony into the night sky. We look over at the beautiful buildings that are still alive with light, despite being so late in the evening. We hear the hustle and bustle of people moving on the sidewalks below. Cabs and Ubers are still driving people around in the city. People are still going nonstop.

Sounds that shouldn't be calming are. I love the city. I love how fast it moves. I love that it is constantly moving, and there's always something to do. That's what calms me. Even when my world is falling apart, other people's worlds are still going on. It's comforting, I guess, to know that.

Nacio and I decide at the same time that it's time to talk. That we can't just look out into the city any longer. I need answers, and he needs to give me some.

Nacio slowly turns to look at me, and I slowly turn to look at him. Neither of us is touching. We are both just leaning against the railing of the balcony. Yet we are still close enough that, if I wanted to touch him, I could. We are still close enough that my heart is beating quickly in my chest from me just looking at him.

"My name is Ignacio Marlow. Nacio, for short. And I'm a killer. But you already knew that."

I nod, waiting for him to continue, but he doesn't. "And?"

He shrugs. "There isn't much else to say. I'm a killer. I used to be a smuggler and a drug dealer and a killer. But I dropped the first two and am now just a killer."

"A killer," I say slowly, like maybe, if I actually say it out loud enough, that the word will change meaning to anything else.

"I tried to kill your best friend and failed."

I stare at his eyes, but I don't believe him. I don't believe he tried to kill her.

"I'll have to go back and finish the job."

"No."

He closes his eyes and nods, thinking that I'm telling him that he can't go back and kill her. That's not what I'm thinking though. Of course he can't go back and kill her.

"I don't believe you."

He opens his eyes and looks at me. "What?"

"I. Don't. Believe. You."

He narrows his eyes at me and takes a step closer. "You don't believe that I'll kill your best friend?"

"I don't believe you'll kill Kinsley."

I take a step forward until we're just inches away from each other. We're both breathing hard. Both feeling something that I can't quite place. *Rage? Anger? Or is it something else?*

"I kill for a living, Beauty. That's what I do. That's what I've done every day since I got out of jail. It's what I did before I went to jail along with several other things that would make your head spin. I'm a killer. And, if my boss tells me to kill Kinsley, then I will."

I study his face that is now red as steam comes out of his nose with every breath. He's mad that I would even question him about being capable of killing Kinsley. But I know he won't.

"I don't believe you."

I realize that I've pushed this man beyond his control. He grabs ahold of me and slams me against the wall of the balcony. He holds my throat firmly enough that I can't move, but not so firm that I can't breathe.

"I will kill Kinsley. You need to understand that. I'm not a good man. And you sure as hell can't change me. This is who I am. The only reason I asked you to come with me tonight is so that you can understand this one point. I'm a killer. I will kill Kinsley, and I will kill you if I have to. Don't give me that chance. Run. Stay away from me. It's your only shot at keeping your life."

Nacio's face is millimeters from mine. His lips hover over mine as he breathes. We both pant, like we just ran a marathon. We are both so worked up, so passionate, so lost with need for one another, that nothing else matters. We are both going to lose it. We are both going to lose whatever tiny shred of control we have over our bodies if we don't watch it.

Nacio realizes this first. He slowly removes his hand from my throat. He slowly backs away from my body until his hands find the railing where he stops and rests, trying to catch his breath, trying to regain his control.

I stay against the wall, keeping my eyes locked on him, trying to understand him. The problem is, I just don't believe a single fucking word that comes out of his mouth. Not one word.

A slow smile spreads over my face.

"Why are you smiling?" he asks.

My smile spreads across my entire face before I speak, "Because I still don't believe you."

"Then, let me try to convince you."

2

BEAST

I GROWL. This woman doesn't know what's good for her. This woman doesn't understand that, as I was holding her throat against the building, I could have squashed her. I could've taken her life with just a squeeze of the hand or a little more pressure on her throat. There was nothing she could've done about it.

She doesn't understand, that's who I am. A killer. She doesn't understand, that has always been what excites me. That's the only thing I've ever gotten excited about in my life. Even when I was involved in smuggling, it wasn't what got me excited. The only thing that did was when I got the chance to kill.

And, now, that's my job. To kill for a living. The only problem is, I'm no longer my own boss. And that's unacceptable.

I can't think about that now. Now, I need to teach Beauty a lesson. She has to understand how dangerous I am. Because, as much as I want her to forgive me and stay in my life, I've realized, in the short time we've been together, that can't be. I won't risk her life, too.

I take a step forward and reach into the back of my pants where my gun sits. I pull it out and watch her eyes widen. I begin dismantling it, ensuring that it can't be used for the rest of the night. "Yes,

Beauty, I could kill you with a single shot. I could shoot you so fast, you wouldn't even know it was coming. You'd just be dead."

I thought the gun would be enough to remind her what I really was. But I can see, even though her eyes are wide with a hint of terror, it's not enough. It's not enough to convince her that I'm a monster.

I take a step forward, getting closer to her, taking my time, until I'm within range to pounce and press her back against the wall with my hand on her throat. "With just a little bit of pressure"—I press against her throat, making it hard for her to breathe—"I could end your life."

I hold my hand there a second longer, letting her feel the pain and struggle that she would feel if I decided to kill her in this way. When I see her eyes begin to water with fear, I let go. But her eyes still read defiance as she coughs and sucks in a deep breath. It's not enough.

I grab her and swing her over the edge of the balcony, holding on to her with my arms so that she's upside down, hanging fifteen stories up. She has nothing to hold on to, except me.

"I could toss you over the edge of this building, like it's nothing. Blame it on suicide. You would be gone in an instant." I pull her back onto the safe side of the balcony, hating and loving seeing her body over the edge. Loving the adrenaline that automatically pumps in my veins at the thought of how I could kill her. Hating that she's not safe though. Hating that her life is in danger.

She was breathing fast before, but now, she's breathing too fast. I can feel the adrenaline pumping through her body. I know that last one scared her. I could feel it in the way she trembled in my arms. I could see it in her eyes. I can see it now in her breathing. I can feel it in how fast her heart is beating and pumping blood to the veins in her arms that I'm still holding on to. So, when she opens her mouth, I already know what she's going to say. That she wants to leave.

"I don't believe you," she says instead.

I don't know who decides it—me or her. I don't know if either of us truly decides or if it is just an automatic thing that happens when two people who have already fucked are left alone in the same room for long enough. Just an automatic response, an automatic need that needs to be filled. But, at the same time, we grab for each other. My hands go to her hips, and her hands find my neck. Our lips collide, and our tongues tangle. We both decide that the entire conversation we just had doesn't matter. Only our need for each other does.

Her hands claw at the tie at my neck, but struggle to undo it. My hands claw the fabric on her hips, needing for it to be gone.

"You have a fucking death sentence, Beauty," I say between kisses that are messy and rough and don't always quite land on each other's lips.

It doesn't stop her from kissing me though. I don't think anything I could do at this moment would stop her. And I don't think anything, short of a gun aimed at her head, would stop me either.

Somehow, I stop kissing her though. I know that we have to stop. I know that, if I fuck her again, it will be all that much harder to leave in the morning. Now that she knows my name. Now that I'd get to fuck her with the lights on. I need to stop before I end up killing her. She realizes that the exact second I decide to stop.

"I don't believe you, Nacio," she spits at me.

I take a step back, trying to put some space between us, as I loosen my tie around my throat, giving myself more room to breathe. She takes a step forward closing the gap between us.

"I don't believe that you would kill Kinsley."

She grabs for me, and I grab her hair, pulling her hard against me, needing her lips to work on mine, sucking that thought from her head. It's a sloppy, messy kiss. When I release her, I hope that thought is gone.

She just smirks and wipes her lips with her thumb. "I don't believe that you would kill me."

Her eyes lock on mine, challenging me to really prove her wrong. Like my little demonstration wasn't enough for her.

"It's the truth."

I watch her hand drop slowly to her breasts that are far too exposed in the dress.

"Don't, Beauty."

"Don't what? If you're gonna kill me, I might as well get one last piece of enjoyment out of you first, right?" Her hands move to her straps as she slowly shimmies them off her shoulders. "I mean, if you're going to kill me, you might as well fuck me first."

She bites her lip as the tight dress begins moving lower and lower. Her hand disappears behind her back, and I can hear the zipper slowly lowering. I can see her breasts straining against the dress, begging to be set free. Her hands come back to the front, grabbing ahold of the dress and slowly lowering it. I keep my eyes locked on her breasts until they are free of the tight fabric.

I let out a low growl when I see her naked body in front of me. She's beautiful and sexy. She's my greatest desire. But I can't fucking have her again. I can't. I'm not fucking strong enough to leave her after this. And I have to leave her. She can't come with me again.

I slowly remove my jacket, intending to give it to her so that she can cover up her naked body. As I do though, I make a mistake. I glance up at her eyes that are challenging me, begging me to give in. I think that's half the reason I wanted to fuck her in the dark. So that I wouldn't have to see her challenging eyes.

I toss the jacket onto a chair in the corner. There is no stopping me now. Not after that. I rip my shirt open and remove it, tossing it in the same general direction where I tossed my jacket. And then I attack.

My hand tangles in her hair as the other finds her breast. And my lips wipe that smirk off her gorgeous lips. I hear her trying to catch her breath between each kiss, but I don't give her time. I just kiss again and again and again.

Her hands claw at my body as I massage her breast. I can barely focus on what I'm doing now as she continues to beg and moan with every touch. This woman...

She, on the other hand, knows exactly what she's doing. Her hands go to my belt, quickly undoing it, followed by my pants until they are in a pile on the floor. Her hand finds my cock that has been hard and begging for her since I brought her on this fucking balcony.

"Fuck me, Nacio," she whispers into my ear.

Now, it's my turn to smirk. Because I know that, this time, she'll be wishing she never said that. I grab my pants, containing a condom I swore I wouldn't use. And then I pick her up, needing her now and not willing to wait. Her legs wrap around my waist, like she's done it a thousand times before even though she hasn't. Her hands clasp my head—not because she's afraid I'll drop her, but because she needs me. Her lips go to mine, distracting me and blocking my view of where I'm taking her.

Still, somehow, I manage to find the piece of furniture I was looking for—the couch that sits in the corner of the balcony, slightly higher up than the rest of the furniture on the balcony. I drop her onto the couch, rougher than she was expecting. She gasps, but it doesn't remove the challenge from her eyes. She still wants me, and I'll more than gladly deliver.

I rip open the condom and roll it onto my cock. She lies on the couch, her legs automatically spread for me, her arms resting on the back. Giving me a perfect view of her body. A body that has curves yet is still strong. A body that I know all too well. A body that trusts me, even when it shouldn't. A body that still begs for me.

I move closer, and her legs spread further, begging me to give her what she wants. I take another step, and I can see how wet she is. Practically dripping with need for me. I take another step until I'm hovering over her body, and I watch her shiver because she needs me.

"Fuck me, Nacio," she says again.

"So impatient to die," I say.

She runs her tongue across her lips. "Impatient to live."

I can't help but smile at her insatiable need for me. And then I sink into her, not giving her any warning.

"Fuck, Beast," she moans.

But I'm not done with her yet. I lift her body off the couch as I climb on. Forcing her higher so that her back is resting on the top of the couch, and her head is hanging over the edge of the balcony. She's not in any danger. Not really. She's not hanging half over, like she was before, but I know having her head tilted back like that while I fuck her will make her think twice about my capabilities. Will make her think twice about how safe she really is.

I kiss her exposed neck as I pump once inside her. "You're not safe, Beauty. Not anymore."

I bite at her neck, needing her to feel some pain and adrenaline. Needing her to feel unsafe. But, instead of finding fear in her eyes, I see more need.

"I was never safe," she says.

I kiss the tiny wounds that I caused on her neck. "You never were safe, but your life is in even more danger now."

She tries to bring her head up to see me as I fuck her. I don't let her. Instead, I force her head back over the balcony. Her hands grab ahold of me, and I can tell that she wants me to pull her back where she will feel safe. But I'm not that guy. I can't keep her safe, especially if she doesn't listen to me. If she doesn't listen to me and she leaves, she'll be as good as dead.

I thrust again and again, and each time, her moans mix with pleasure and fear.

"Please," she begs.

Her begging seems to mean so many things. *Please pull me back over where I'll be safe. Please make me come. Please show me that you're not a killer.*

I only give in to one of those. I change the angle of my thrusts, so my pelvis is hitting her clit. Her moans begin to change from fear to all pleasure.

"I'm not a good guy, Beauty. I can't give you everything you want. But I will give you one thing."

She pants but doesn't answer me. She can barely breathe, let alone think, with the blood pooling between her legs and to her head that's hanging over the balcony edge.

I move faster, knowing that the end is coming soon. Needing it to end soon before she entraps me more in her spell. So, I move faster and faster. Until she is panting and I'm panting. At the last second, I pull her head back to safety, excusing my behavior with the fact that I need to fucking see her come.

"Look at me, Beauty."

She does.

"Now, come for me."

She does, and I do.

"Nacio!" she screams.

I'm sure that every person in New York can hear her. She collapses back on the couch after the waves leave her.

I remove myself from her and begin cleaning us both up while she is barely coherent on the couch. I can't help but smile at her already half-asleep on the couch even though she has no regard for her safety. She has to understand that she isn't safe. But, if my little show didn't convince her, I don't know what will.

I scoop her naked body up into my arms and begin carrying her back inside the hotel room. I make my way to the bed and place her on it.

"In the morning, I want to go with you, wherever you go. I want to know more about you, Nacio."

"No," I say. In her half-asleep state, I'm not sure if she even heard me.

I turn off the lights and then climb into the bed, next to her. I can't help myself as I curl my arms around her. Even though I've done far too much tonight, I can't keep my hands off her. I listen to her heavy breathing, and I match my breathing to hers.

Until she finally breathes, "I don't believe that you won't let me come with you. You will."

I just close my eyes. She will find out the truth soon enough.

3

SCARLETT

I OPEN my eyes from the beautiful dream I was having. A dream where Nacio wasn't a murderer. A dream where we had a relationship. A dream where we acted like normal people and fought like normal people and made love like normal people. It was a beautiful dream, but it wasn't real. And it was far too calm, too simple of a life. As much as I can pretend that's what I want, it isn't. I want more than calm and simple and boring.

I reach across the bed to find Nacio. But he's not there. That's when I get a handful of the cream-colored sheets, not the stark white from the hotel room last night. My eyes scan the room that is so familiar to me.

What the hell?

How did I end up back in my own bedroom? When I fell asleep last night, I was at the hotel with Nacio. *How did I fall asleep in a hotel room and wake up in my apartment?*

I jump out of bed, surprised that I'm clothed in my silk pajamas. I grab a robe out of my closet and throw it on as I quickly check the bathroom for Nacio. He's not there.

I run down the stairs, searching for him. I don't see him. I run through the living room. He's not there. I go to the kitchen. He's not there. I go out onto my balcony. He's not there. I search room after room and come up empty every time. He's not here. I even open the front door and poke my head out into the hallway, looking to see if he stepped out to take a phone call or something. But he isn't there either.

My phone.

I run back upstairs and search for my phone. I find it on my nightstand. There's no text from him. I pull up my messages, and there's nothing there. I begin to look through my messages and contacts, scanning for his number. But it's gone.

Damn it!

He deleted his number from my phone. And I don't have his number memorized. I don't have his number anywhere else.

Damn it! Damn it! Damn it!

I throw the phone down on my bed in frustration.

How could he? How could he walk into my life and completely flip it upside down and then just decide it was time for him to leave, for him to act like he wasn't even a part of my life?

He doesn't get to decide that. Not without talking to me first. I get to have a say in my own future.

I search the rest of the apartment for a note he might have left. For any sign that he was even here. I find none. I find none because he doesn't want to be found. He did this deliberately. He wants me to forget about him and move on. I can't. I can't move on because I still want him. And I still think that he didn't kill Kinsley for a reason. And I hope that reason is because, somewhere inside, he has a heart, that he isn't truly a killer.

I don't know what to do now though. I don't know where to start to find my answers. I don't know where to start to find Nacio. I just know I have to find him. He can't just walk out on me, not like that. I won't let him.

I pick my phone up off the bed, just in case he calls, and I head back downstairs. I grab my laptop out of my office and quickly make a cup of coffee. Then, I take both out onto the balcony. I take a seat on one of the lounge chairs, set my coffee on the table, and place the laptop on my lap. I take a deep breath, as just being on the balcony reminds me of last night with Beast.

Last night was insane. He scared the shit out of me when he showed me what he could do. The ways he could kill me. I know he was trying to scare me, and he did his job. But then, the next second, he showed me how to love—dangerously. And, after that, I don't want any other kind of love.

I open my laptop, not sure of what I'm going to do. I'm just sure that I need to do something. My hands hover over the keys. I decide to start with the simple, the obvious. I type in *Nacio Marlow*.

I wait while the search engine searches for anything on the name. It doesn't take long until hundreds of articles about him instantly pop up on my screen. About his arrest. I've already read these articles though. These are not what I'm looking for. I click on one anyway where there's a picture of Nacio. It's just a picture of his face. It's not a particularly good picture. He's not smiling. He doesn't even seem to be aware that he is getting his photo taken. But still, just seeing the picture confirms that he's real. Confirms that he is what I want. Because just seeing this damn picture has my heart racing, like it never has before. Makes my breathing difficult. He makes everything difficult.

I try to find information about his release or escape or however he landed out on the streets instead of remaining in prison. I search article after article, but I find nothing about it. According to these articles, Nacio is supposed to be in prison for another twenty years. So, I don't know what the hell happened. I don't know if there's another man who looks like Nacio sitting in jail right now. I don't know how he escaped. It's another question about him I will never have answered, just like all my other endless questions.

I try a couple of more searches but give up in frustration when the same articles appear over and over again. There aren't even any new articles from last night.

I pick up my coffee and take a sip, hoping that, somehow, I will find some clarity on what to do next. Nothing comes to me.

My phone rings, making me jump, and I spill hot coffee on

myself. *Shit.* I wipe the coffee off as quickly as I can and grab for my phone that is sitting on the table next to me. It's a number I don't recognize. It could be Nacio. I watch it ring one more time, and then I pick it up.

"Hello?" I say.

And it really seems like an eternity for the person on the other end of the line to answer back.

"Hello, Miss Bell?"

My heart sinks when I hear the man's voice isn't Nacio's. "This is she."

"I'm Officer Gordon Michael. I have a few questions for you about what happened last night at the runway show. Are you able to come down to my office sometime today to answer my questions?"

I sigh. This is not how I wanted to handle my day. I'd rather be doing anything else. But maybe the police will have some answers. I'm all out of options on how to find Nacio at the moment anyway.

"Sure."

"Sorry to keep you waiting, Miss Bell. I'm Officer Gordon Michael. We spoke on the phone," the officer says, taking a seat across the table from me in the interrogation room.

I try to smile at him, but I can't. Instead, I'm giving him a grimace. I don't want to be here, and I especially don't want to be in this damn room. "Am I under arrest for anything?"

Officer Gordon laughs. "No, Miss Bell. I just have some questions for you about what happened last night at the runway show. Since you were a witness to the attempted murder, we thought we should ask you some questions."

I nod. "Then, why am I in this room?"

Officer Gordon frowns. "Because we question all our witnesses in this room."

"You also question all your suspects in this room."

"Yes."

"That's because you don't want me to know if I'm a suspect or a witness, right?"

Gordon shocks me by answering, "Yes."

"At least you're honest. I should probably ask my lawyer to be here, just in case, but since I have nothing to hide, ask away," I say.

I know I should have my lawyer here, but Officer Gordon isn't the only one with questions. And I know he'll be much more willing to talk to me without my lawyer present. Honestly, I couldn't care less right now if I was arrested for what had happened last night. I just want answers.

"Let's start with the event you were attending. You were attending with your friend Kinsley?"

"Yes. It was a fashion event with a runway show and an after-party. I brought one of my best friends in the world, who was going through some hard times, to the event."

The officer nods. "You notice anything unusual at the event?"

"No. Everything up to the attack was normal."

"Can you tell me what you were doing at the time of the attack?"

"Kinsley and I were walking toward the restroom when a man turned the corner and began walking down the hallway, right toward us. We weren't sure who he was at first or what his intentions were. But, once he stopped a few feet in front of us, he drew a gun, fired one shot, and then turned in the other direction."

"And this individual, do you know who he was?"

"Yes, his name is Nacio Marlow."

"What happened after the shot was fired?"

"My friend collapsed on the floor. But I found no blood or wounds on her body. He'd missed. I tried to help her relax and make sure that she was okay."

"And what happened after that?"

"I ran after him."

"And why did you do that? What did you think you were going to accomplish by doing that?"

I think for a moment before answering. This is critical. If he thinks I am on Nacio's side or have anything to do with him, he could arrest me. So, I lie. "I didn't want him to get away. I just needed to follow him and make sure the police got there first."

"And did they?"

"No. He got away. There was nothing I could do."

The officer nods and smiles at me. "What did you do after Nacio escaped?"

"I went for a walk. I needed to clear my head after what happened."

The officer writes some things down, and I can tell that the interview is almost over. That he believes me. There's no reason a woman like me would have anything to do with Nacio.

"Wasn't Nacio supposed to be in jail?" I ask.

"Yes."

"How did he get out?"

"We're looking into that."

"You have to have some theory at this point, right? Some theory on how he escaped? Some theory on why?"

"I'm really not at liberty to discuss that."

"I deserve to know. He went after my best friend, and he could just as easily come after me. I need to know how and why he escaped, so I can figure out how to protect myself until he's caught."

The officer sighs. "We think his family had something to do with his escape. It's something we've been investigating for years now. But we are no closer to having any answers on how he escaped.

"I wish I could say that we could protect you. But we can't. So, hire the best bodyguards in the city and pray like hell that he doesn't want anything to do with you. Nacio Marlow is a ruthless killer. And even your charms won't work on him."

The officer did give me one answer. The police have been working on figuring this out for years, which means Nacio's been out of prison for years. It's something that the police have managed to keep hidden from the public. There have been no news articles about Nacio's escape. Kinsley wasn't notified of his escape. No one was.

"I'll do that."

I stand to leave when the officer says, "Keep that fact that Nacio has been out for years to yourself, Miss Bell. If I find that you leaked that to the media, I'll have you arrested."

He doesn't say why he told me that in the first place, but I know he has his suspicions about me. He's suspicious, and he has every right to be.

I just walk out of the room and give him no reason to look into his suspicions.

4

SCARLETT

I WALK into the office at Beautifully Bell, and watch the stares. Stares from my employees, from clients, from everybody. They all watched the news. They all know what happened. They all know that Kinsley and I could have been killed this weekend. They all know that I'm lucky to be alive. They just don't know the truth.

I keep walking past all of them and head into my office. I plan on locking myself up in my office and working. It's the only way I can keep from thinking about Nacio. If I see one more person look at me like I'm a weak girl who barely survived the shooting, I'm gonna lose it. I'm still their boss, still strong enough to do anything that needs to be done. And I can forget about Nacio for a few hours.

I step inside my office and immediately shut and lock the door. I take a deep breath. I can do this.

I walk behind my desk and fire up my computer. And I watch the emails pour in, as they always do on a weekday morning. This morning though, there are more emails than usual. I sigh. It's going to be a long day.

My door immediately opens, and in walks Preston. "Are you okay? I saw the—"

"No," I answer, not bothering to lie to Preston. I couldn't even if I wanted to. He'd see right through any of my lies.

"Can I—"

"No."

Preston leaves me alone then, and I begin working. But only a few minutes go by before he knocks on my door again and pokes his head back inside.

"What?" I say, a little too snappy.

It doesn't faze Preston though. "You have someone here to see you."

For a second, I think he is talking about Nacio. Then, my mind goes to Kinsley. It's most likely Kinsley coming to make sure I'm okay, protecting me as always. What I don't expect is who walks through my door.

Jake.

He's standing in my doorway, looking sadder than I've ever seen him. I nod to Preston to let Jake in. Preston gives me a soft smile and leaves us alone in my office. Jake takes a step forward and shuts the door behind himself.

"What are you doing here?" I ask.

"I came to see if you were okay."

I nod.

Jake hesitantly takes a slow step toward me. I want to scold him for his behavior. I want to yell or scream at him to get out. I want to do something. But I don't. Instead, I do nothing because I realize that a large part of my anger doesn't stem from Jake; it stems from Nacio. He's the one I'm really mad at.

"So, are you okay?" Jake asks.

"No."

Jake takes my answer as a cue for him to fix everything. I don't want him to fix everything though.

He moves quickly behind my desk and scoops me up into his arms, giving me a tight hug. "I'm so sorry, Scarlett. I should've been there to protect you. I should've been there to keep you safe."

"It's fine. I don't need anyone to protect—"

"Scarlett, I'm so sorry. For everything that I've done. I want you back. And I know I made a mistake, but I want a second chance. You're the woman for me, Scarlett Bell. I want to marry you. I want to protect you forever. Please forgive me."

I take a step back, looking at this pathetic man. A man who thinks I won't survive without a protector. A man who thinks that's why I would take someone back. Like anything less than love would convince me to do that.

"No."

Jake takes a step back. "No?"

"No."

"There's nothing I can do? Nothing I can do to change your mind?" Jake reaches out and softly touches my shoulder.

I close my eyes—not because I enjoy the feeling, but because I'm afraid of showing too much of the truth as to what I'm feeling.

"No. I'm sorry, Jake, but you're not the guy for me. I think you should leave."

Jake nods slowly, and I know he wants to say more. I know he wants to fight me, trying to convince me that I'm wrong and he's right. Nothing he says at this point would make me change my mind. And, honestly, it doesn't have anything to do with Jake. And it has nothing to do with our fight. It has everything to do with a dark stranger I want.

I watch Jake walk slowly out of my office. I know that I probably just broke his heart. Again. But it had to be done.

When Jake has finally left, I take a deep breath and move back to my computer and try to get some work done. I get through three emails before Preston knocks on my door again.

I tightly squeeze my eyes shut to prevent myself from yelling at Preston. It's not his fault. I'm just going to lose my mind if I continue to get interrupted like this throughout the day. Any other day, this would be usual, normal, expected. It would be welcome. Not today though. I'm tired of interacting with people, and I've interacted with only two so far today. I know it's not realistic to be able to hole myself up in the office all day, but that is exactly what I want.

"Sorry to bother you again, but Kinsley is here."

I open my eyes and try to smile. I can't tell Kinsley no. I need to see her.

"Let her in."

Kinsley walks in a second later and runs over to me. I stand from my desk, and my arms go around her. I hold on to her tight and feel the tears from her eyes dropping onto my shoulder. Her tears make me cry, too. It makes me cry that I'm falling for a man who caused my best friend pain.

Shouldn't that be a sign that I shouldn't fall for this man? Shouldn't it be a sign that he is the wrong man for me?

Kinsley slowly pulls away from me. I do the same, and she walks to the chair across from my desk while I take a seat in my chair.

"Are you okay?" I ask the same question that everyone's been asking me all morning.

"No," she says, giving me the same answer I've given to everyone else.

I smile. "We're gonna get through this and come out stronger because of it. Just like everything else you've faced."

"I know we will. What happened is just so surreal."

I nod, encouraging her to continue.

"I just thought that he would always be in prison. I thought I was safe. I thought my past was behind me."

Tears begin dripping down her face again, and I get a Kleenex and hand it to her. She takes it and wipes her eyes.

"So, when I found out that he'd been out of prison for five years now, I was in shock."

"He's been out of prison for five years? How were you not notified about it? How the hell could that have happened?" I ask.

Kinsley shakes her head. "Killian did some digging with the FBI. They've known he's been out of prison the entire time. Nacio bribed some of the security guards, and they helped him escape. He can be charming and rather persuasive when he wants to be."

I nod, understanding. I know exactly how persuasive and charming he can be.

"How scary is that? How scary is it that he has been walking the streets as a free man for five years without any of us knowing? He could have killed me at any time. Instead, he chose last night."

"But he didn't. He didn't kill you. He missed. Doesn't that mean something? After he saved you twice, maybe he isn't just a killer; maybe there's something more to him. Maybe, on some level, he's on our side?"

Kinsley's eyes widen as she looks at me. "Really? You're gonna defend him? What's gotten into you, Scarlett? He's a killer. He tried to kill me twice. Just by luck, I survived twice."

I nod and keep my mouth shut. I don't know why I am defending Nacio to her. There's no reason to.

I watch my office door open again, and in walks Killian. "Are you guys all right?"

"Yes," Kinsley and I answer at the same time, knowing that we can't worry Killian. I'm sure he's already been following Kinsley around every second of every day. I can't have him doing the same thing to me.

"We should be leaving. I know you have a lot of work to do, and I'm exhausted," Kinsley says.

I stand and walk over to her. I give her one last hug before she leaves. "I'm just so happy that you're okay, that you are not hurt. I don't know what I would do without you."

"I feel the exact same way."

Kinsley lets go of me and then walks over to her husband, who merely puts his arm around her, protecting her. Protecting her even though she isn't in any immediate danger.

"Have you hired a bodyguard yet, Scarlett?" he asks.

"No. I think I'll be okay. Nacio wasn't aiming at me; he was aiming at her."

Killian frowns. "You need to hire a bodyguard, Scarlett. If you don't, I will."

I roll my eyes at him. "Fine, Dad, I'll hire a bodyguard."

"You'd better. I don't want anything to happen to you," Killian says.

I watch them leave and don't even make it to my desk before Preston sticks his head back into the room.

"What now?" I ask as I take a seat back in my chair.

Preston doesn't say anything. He just studies me, standing in the doorway, with his arms folded across his chest.

"Preston, I really don't have time for this. What do you want?"

"It's him, isn't it?"

"Preston, I have no idea what you're talking about."

Preston walks toward me and tosses a newspaper on my desk. "It's him. Your one-night-stand guy. It's the same guy who tried to kill Kinsley, right?"

I stare at the newspaper that has a picture of Nacio's face slapped on the front cover. I frown, not wanting to involve Preston in this, but I know I can't lie.

"Yes."

I wait for him to scold me. I wait for him to yell at me and tell me how stupid I am. That Nacio is a murderer. That he could kill me at any second. That I need to go to the police. I wait for Preston to tell me any sort of sensible thing.

He doesn't.

"I don't know why I feel so strongly about him. I know I'm putting my life in danger anytime I see him. I want to go after him though, despite the danger.

"Don't worry though; I can't since he erased his number from my phone. I don't know where he lives. He's clearly on the run from the police. He's gone."

I look up at Preston, who is standing over me with a smirk on his face, still not saying anything.

"What?"

"Nothing. He's hot. I understand the attraction. And, as you said before, he wasn't shooting at you; he was supposedly shooting at her. Or maybe he was just firing a warning shot." Preston turns and begins walking out of my office. "If you ask me, he's begging you to go after him."

"Wait!" I jump out of my chair.

He shakes his head. "I just want you to be happy, Scarlett, and I know that a sweet boy like Jake won't make you happy. So, if you risk your life, just be careful about it."

Preston leaves, and I sink back into my chair.

I look at the picture of Nacio on the paper. He does like hot.

Are you sure you're not gay, Preston? I think to myself, laughing at him calling Nacio hot.

Preston said that Nacio was practically begging me to go after him. But the problem is, I have no idea how to do that. I have no experience in this area. But I do know of one idea that could get him to come after me. I'm just not sure I have the guts to do it.

5

BEAST

I can't get Scarlett out of my head. I thought, after I realized that the only way to keep her safe was to get out of her life, that it would be easy to do my job and forget about her. *But who am I kidding?* Every day, every second is a struggle. A struggle not to run back to her apartment where I left her, scoop her up into my arms, and never let her go again.

I stare at my phone that I'm holding in my hand. It's a struggle not to call her or text her. That's my life now—a struggle.

My phone rings, and I already know who it is, without reading the name that's flashing on my phone. It's not Scarlett. I deleted my number from her phone, so she would have no way to contact me ever again. Trying to prevent the inevitable, I wait as it rings for a second and then third time before I answer.

Finally, when I know the phone is on its last ring, I hit Answer. I slowly lift the phone to my ear.

"Hello?" I say.

"What the hell were you thinking?" she asks.

"I'm sorry. I did the best I could."

"I don't believe you. I don't believe you simply missed like that."

I walk to the window and peer out, afraid that she's hired someone to kill me right now, putting us both out of our misery. I don't see anyone as I peer through the blinds, but that doesn't mean that they aren't there.

"Well, believe me because that's what happened. I missed. Even the best miss sometimes."

"No! You don't miss. You don't fucking get to miss, Nacio."

"Well, that's too bad because I did. I did miss, and now, we have to deal with that."

"No! I have to deal with it. And I have to deal with you."

"What's that supposed to mean?" I ask.

"It means, I should have you killed for what you did. It's what I would do to any of the other men if they'd failed me."

"Then, kill me."

I know she is shaking her head at me on the other end of the line. I can feel the disappointment oozing off of her.

"Good thing your brother can fix your mistake."

I frown. "I can handle it myself."

"No, you can't! You let your feelings or whatever for that damn girl cloud your judgment. You don't get to handle things anymore. I'm giving the job to your brother."

"When?" I ask. I have to know when it's going to happen.

"That's no longer any of your concern. But it can't happen anytime soon, thanks to you fucking it all up."

"When?" I ask again more sternly.

"It's none of your concern. And, if you ask again, I will have you killed."

I glance back out the window, studying the parking lot. I still don't see anyone, but I believe her. If I argue with her too much, she will have me killed. I have no doubt about that. So, I stop asking her about it.

"Then, why did you call, other than to yell at me?"

"I have another job for you."

"No."

"You don't get to tell me no. I'll have someone call you with the details."

She ends the call without a good-bye, leaving me to wonder how soon she would have me killed if I just ran and didn't do the damn job. *How far could I get before she had a bullet put between my eyes? Not far enough.*

6

SCARLETT

"Sorry, Miss Bell," the investigator I hired says.

I sigh. "Thank you, Heath. I appreciate your work even though you weren't able to find him."

"Let me know if you need anything else. I'd be happy to help out in any way I can. Sorry I couldn't do more. Do you need anything else from me at the moment?"

"No. Thanks though."

I watch as Heath leaves my office.

Plan A didn't work. The investigator wasn't able to find Nacio. Now, on to Plan B.

I pick up my phone and dial Jake's number. I wait for him to answer, and I don't have to wait long.

"Scarlett?" Jake answers.

"Hi, Jake. I changed my mind."

"What? Why?"

"It doesn't matter. I want to go out on a date with you and give us a second shot."

"Are you sure, Scarlett? I mean, I just talked to you three days ago, and you didn't want anything to do with me. What's changed?"

"Yes, I'm sure. I want to go out tonight. If I have Preston send you the address of where to meet me, will you be able to meet me?"

"Of course, but—"

I end the call without saying good-bye. I don't want to give Jake any reason to question me.

I know what I'm doing is bad. Wrong. I know that I'm just using Jake to try to get to Nacio. But, after Jake hurt me, it doesn't feel so wrong to hurt him back. Plus, he'll never know why I want him to take me out on this date. He'll never know why I'm taking him to the hotel where I first met Nacio. Jake will have no idea. He'll just think that I'm giving us another shot when there is absolutely no chance of that.

"Preston!" I shout.

Preston hears me and walks into my office. "Why were you just talking to Jake?"

"It doesn't matter." I write down the address to the hotel where I fucked Nacio in the dark. I hand the piece of paper with the address to Preston.

Preston looks at it. "What's this?"

"Just make sure that Jake knows the address and can meet me there around eight tonight."

Preston suspiciously eyes me but doesn't question me further. "Sure. I'll make sure it's done."

"Thank you."

"Thank you for meeting me," I say.

"Of course. You know I would do anything for you, Scarlett." Jake reaches up and tucks a loose strand of my hair behind my ear. "I'm just trying to understand why you wanted me to meet you at this hotel. There's not a restaurant here. There is barely a bar," he says.

"It has a bar. And I don't want to eat tonight. I thought that maybe"—I take a step toward Jake and press my breasts that are barely contained in my tight red dress against his chest—"we would want to do other things after a couple of drinks."

Jake's eyes widen when he realizes what I'm insinuating. That I want sex. That I'll let him fuck me tonight if he plays his cards right.

"Let me buy you a drink then," he says, clearing his throat.

I smirk as he places his hand on the small of my back, and he guides me from the lobby of the hotel to the bar. We each take a seat at the bar. I watch as Jake removes his navy-blue jacket and places it over the back of the chair. I put my purse over the back of my chair and pull out my phone, placing it on the bar in front of me. If my plan works, Nacio will be texting me within a matter of minutes. And I plan on seeing his text message the second he sends it to me.

The bartender moves down the bar until he gets to us. I can read his name tag that says *Kevin*. He's good-looking—tall with nice hair and a sweet grin. But he does nothing for me. Even when he eyes my cleavage and his eyes show lust for me, it doesn't turn me on in the slightest.

My eyes dart to look at Jake to see if he notices the man staring at me. To see if this man makes him jealous. He seems oblivious though. He doesn't have a clue as to what is going on. He doesn't have a clue that I could easily say yes to Kevin instead of him. Either man would probably do for what I want to do tonight, which involves fucking—just not with either of them.

I sigh. It's another reason I don't like Jake. He doesn't even become jealous when other men look at me. I want a man who wants me, who feels like he owns me and would do anything for me. Not a man who is just satisfied to sit next to me and buy me a drink.

"What can I get you?" Kevin says, his eyes still locked on my breasts.

"Gin and tonic," I say.

"Beer," Jake says.

I resist the urge to roll my eyes at Jake. Of course, at one of the fanciest hotels in NYC, he orders a beer. He's such a boy. A boy when I want a man.

I watch as Kevin, our bartender, quickly makes our drinks. He's fast and efficient with his hands, and I find my mind immediately goes in the gutter. I immediately think of him using those hands to do naughty things to my body.

Kevin slides our drinks across to us on the bar, and I smile at him, despite the dirty things going on in my head.

I take a sip of my drink and immediately let go of those thoughts. I don't want Kevin. I glance over at Jake as he sits next to me, sipping on his beer. I don't want Jake. Instead, I want a man so dangerous that he basically tried to kill me the last time I was with him.

I shake my head as I take another sip. *How stupid am I?*

"So, how have you been since—"

"I don't want to talk about that night. I just want to have fun tonight," I say, not looking at Jake.

Out of the corner of my eye, I see Jake nod, and I watch as he takes another sip of his beer. I can tell he already has no idea what else he should say. And, honestly, I'm just as clueless.

Kevin, on the other hand, has plenty to say. "Are you two on a first date or something?"

"No, this isn't a first date. We used to date in college," Jake says.

"It just seems to me that, if I were on a date with a pretty girl like this, I would have a lot more to say. Or at least, if I had nothing to say, we wouldn't be wasting our time in a bar," Kevin says.

I watch Jake open his mouth and then close it. He really has no guts. He really sucks at confrontation.

I sigh. I guess I have to get this guy off our backs even though, honestly, I couldn't care less if he stayed here and talked to us all night. Kevin is already more interesting than Jake is.

"Maybe you need to mind your own business because you have no idea what we've been through. You have no idea that, this week, I was shot at. You have no idea that I almost died. You have no idea that my best friend's baby died before that. So, don't give me any crap about why my date and I aren't super chatty tonight. If you mess with us again, you'll regret it."

Kevin just smiles at us. I narrow my eyes at him, making it clear that I'm not in the mood to be messed with tonight.

A new customer walks up to the bar, and Kevin leaves us alone to go tend to the customer.

"I'm sorry. I should have been the one telling off the bartender, not you. I should be the one protecting you," Jake says.

I stare at my drink, not wanting to tell Jake that he's right. He should be the one protecting me even though he can't. I pick up my glass and move it to my lips. I tilt my head back, forcing the remainder of the liquid down my throat. I set the empty glass back on the bar.

"Let's get out of here," I say. I stand from the bar and grab my things, not waiting for Jake to answer me, just needing to get out of here. Needing to move on to step two of my plan because step one has failed miserably.

"Sure," Jake says.

Out of the corner of my eye, I watch Jake as he throws some bills down on the bar to pay for our bill. I start walking back to the lobby of the hotel, and Jake quickly follows. I feel him place his hand on the small of my back, but it's not strong or reassuring. He doesn't know where or how to guide me. He has no idea what to do to my body. If only he did, then maybe I might be more attracted to him instead of being attracted to a man who is likely to kill me.

"Where are we going?" Jake asks.

"We are going to my hotel room."

I walk toward the elevator bank with Jake trailing behind me a step or two, his hand falling quickly from the small of my back after a couple steps. I hate that I'm leading him on. *But am I really? If my plan fails, won't I want a man to make me forget about Nacio tonight? Even a man like Jake?*

A woman walks out of the elevator just as we arrive. We each step into the empty elevator, and I press the button for the top floor. The same floor that I went to that night with Nacio.

Jake and I stand on opposite sides of the elevator as it makes its way up to the top floor of the building. I bite my lip as I stare at Jake, hoping he'll do something, anything, to convince me that I should be with him. If he did, maybe I would change my mind and get over this ridiculous crush that I have on a monster.

But Jake doesn't do anything; he just stares at me. I'm afraid he can see that I'm turning into a monster for liking another monster.

The elevator doors open, and I step off first with Jake following me. I walk straight to the hotel room door, and this time, I don't hesitate. I just put the key card in the door and turn the handle. I step inside, and Jake follows me in.

"Want a drink?" I ask.

Jake doesn't answer me. He just walks further into the hotel room, running his hand across the expensive furniture, studying the room, studying me.

"Jake?" I wait for him to look at me in the eyes, and when he finally does, I ask again, "Do you want a drink?"

"Why am I here?"

"What?" I ask with a confused expression on my face. I thought I'd made it perfectly clear why he was here even if that wasn't the real truth.

I feel my phone buzz in my purse, and I quickly grab for it, but it's not Beast. It is just a message from one of my employees, asking for a meeting later this week. I frown and put the phone back in my purse.

"I don't think I'm here for what you're trying to make me think I'm here for."

I take a step toward Jake, trying to figure out how to play this. "Why would you think that?"

"For one, you're more worried about who's texting you or calling you than you are about me. You lit up when you grabbed for your phone."

I take another step. "It's only because I'm worried about Kinsley. If she calls me, I want to be there for her."

Jake frowns. "I don't believe you. You wouldn't be excited about getting a text message if you were afraid that it was Kinsley telling you more bad news. Your eyes wouldn't have lit up, your heartbeat wouldn't have sped up, and your cheeks wouldn't have flushed a bright shade of pink. What's going on?"

I freeze, trying to figure out my next move. I don't want Jake to know about Nacio. But I don't know how to get out of this. I never realized how observant Jake was. I never realized he knew my body that well.

I bite my lip, trying to figure out what to do when I realize there is only one thing I can do. I have to convince him that he's wrong.

I run toward him and grab ahold of his neck, pulling him into a deep kiss. He kisses me back, and we stumble backward until he has me pinned against a wall. His hand tangles in my hair, and I imagine Nacio doing the same thing but rougher. I feel Jake's cock press against my stomach, but I don't imagine it's his. I imagine it's Nacio's. Jake moans as he kisses me, and it's not quite as deep as Beast's.

Kissing isn't enough.

My Beast didn't come for me. I'd thought he would when he saw me with Jake. I'd thought he would when he saw me going to the same hotel room where he fucked me. I'd thought he wouldn't be able to stand the thought of me being with another man.

I was wrong though. Nacio might not have even been watching me. He probably doesn't even know I'm here.

So, kissing definitely isn't enough. I need Jake to make me forget. I need him to make me forget everything, so I won't do the stupid thing that keeps creeping up in my head. It's the only way I'm positive I would get Nacio's attention again, but by doing it, I could completely destroy my life.

I grab at Jake's shirt, trying to pull the buttons apart to get the shirt off. Needing to feel his hard chest and smooth muscles.

Jake growls as I do. And I lose it. I want him. Even if he isn't Beast, he'll do for tonight.

Jake's mouth goes to my neck, and I close my eyes, trying to get lost in his kiss. It's easy to because he's always been a good kisser. His hand travels down my right leg, pulling it up to his hip, and he pushes himself against me, telling me exactly what he wants.

"Fuck, Beast," I moan.

I move his head, intending for him to kiss me lower on my neck, near my cleavage, but he suddenly stops kissing me. His hand slowly lowers my leg. I open my eyes in confusion. We're both breathing hard as we just stare at one another.

"What did you just call me?"

I stare at him, trying to catch my breath. "I called you Beast because that's what I want you to be—a beast. I want you to attack me, to be a little rough with me, to control me."

Jake stares at me for a second longer, and then he starts taking steps backward. "I need to go."

I nod. I'm not gonna fight to convince him to stay. I was using him, and he knows it now. He somehow knows that, when I said Beast, I wasn't thinking of him; I was thinking of another man.

"Then, go."

Jake stares at me for a moment longer, and then he walks out the door of the hotel room, leaving me all alone.

I pick up my purse as I sit down on the couch, and I get my phone out of it. Still, no messages.

My plan failed. And I couldn't even convince a guy to stick around long enough to affect me and make me forget about Nacio for even a split second.

I need to talk to someone. I can't stand being alone right now. I could call Kinsley, but what good would that do? I still can't tell her the truth.

Preston.

I dial his number and wait. He answers quickly, which is surprising since it's so late at night.

"Scarlett? Are you okay?"

"No. I just need someone to talk to. I'm not handling being alone very well right now."

"You never have handled being alone very well. So, what wacky plan of yours failed?"

I begin nervously twisting my hair in my hand. "What makes you think I had a wacky plan?"

"Because you did."

I sigh. "Jake left. He figured out that I wasn't into him, and he left. And, now, I'm all alone."

"Good. You shouldn't be with Jake, even for one night, just to get over that Nacio guy."

I hesitate for a second because I want to tell him my next plan. I need to tell him because it'll greatly affect his life if I do it. But I'm also scared. Scared that he'll talk me out of it. Scared that he'll tell me to forget about Nacio. But more scared that he'll tell me to do it.

"I have another plan. A plan that's even crazier than this one."

"I don't want to hear your crazy plan."

I close my eyes and frown. My hand goes to my forehead, rubbing it, as I try to figure out what I'm going to do now if Preston won't even listen to me.

"Do you love him? Or do you want him back for some other reason? Is this just about sex? If it is, I can find a million other guys who will do whatever dirty things he did to you."

"It's not just about sex."

"Do you love him?"

"I don't know."

"Well, you might want to figure that out before you do something crazy that could destroy your life. If you do something crazy for love, that's one thing. If you do something crazy without a good reason, that's another."

"I'll think about it."

"Good. Now, because I know you well enough to know that you're going to do what you want to do, regardless if you love the guy or not, tell me why you really called. It wasn't for my brilliant advice, was it?"

"No, it wasn't. How would you feel if I took an extended vacation and you ran the company yourself for a couple of weeks?"

"I would feel terrified, but I would do anything for you, Scar, including running the company for you for a couple of weeks. So, don't worry about that. Go do whatever crazy thing you've planned to get him back. And know that I'll be here to help you pick up the pieces if he hurts you."

I take a deep breath and then another, trying to calm myself before I speak again. Preston doesn't know that, if Nacio decides to hurt me, there will be no pieces left to pick up. I'll be dead. And Preston will be left to run the company by himself.

"Thanks, Preston. You're the best."

"I know."

I'm about to end the call with him when I realize I have to tell him one more thing. "Oh, if something happens to me, like if you can't get ahold of me or if I disappear, I need you to promise me something."

"Anything."

I smile. "I need you to promise me that you won't come rescue me or send anyone else to rescue me. I need you to promise me that you'll give me time first to figure it out. Promise me?"

Preston laughs. "I promise, but only because I know you are hoping that Mr. Dangerous will come rescue you instead. I'll give him time to do that first, but only if I don't think your life is at risk. The second I think that you're in danger, I'll be coming after you myself."

"I'm not putting myself in any danger."

"I don't believe you. You love danger. That's why you did that stupid bungee-jumping thing the last time we were in Vegas. You love the thrill, the excitement, the danger. Just know, if he doesn't come rescue you, I will, but I'll give him a chance first."

I guess that's the best I'm going to get. "Thanks, Preston. I'll talk to you later."

"Good-bye, Scarlett."

I close my eyes as I hear him hang up the phone. *Why does that good-bye seem so final?*

I open my email and quickly type out an email to my lawyers. I need to make sure that Preston will get complete control of the company if anything happens to me. He's the only one I trust. I'm not sure if just sending an email will be enough to ensure that he'll get legal control of the company, but I hope that it is because I don't have time to wait to figure it out. I need to put the last part of my plan into motion before I lose my nerve and don't do it.

I consider the ways that I could make my plan work. *Steal something? DUI?*

No. Neither of those would work. I could easily make it out on bail for either one of those. I need something worse. I need something truthful.

I text a message to George, saying that I need him to come pick me up. He texts back, saying that he'll be here in five minutes. I take that time to do two shots of tequila to gather my nerves. And then I study the room one more time. The room that started it all and put me into this mess. The room where my heart beat fast and recklessly for the first time in a long time. And it continues to do so now.

I don't know if what I'm feeling is love. But, if it's not, it's got to be something close; otherwise, there'd be no way I'd be willing to do what I'm about to do. It's love—or something a lot like it.

I walk to the door and turn off the lights. I look at the room one more time in the darkness. My heartbeat immediately picks up, as I hope that he's somehow lurking in the darkness so that I won't have to do what I'm going to do next.

I open the door and head downstairs. I walk out of the hotel without looking back, and I go straight into George's waiting car.

"Where to?" George asks.

"The police station."

He quickly pulls out into the street, and I can tell from the frown on his face that he is assuming the worst. That I'm in danger. And not just from an outside threat. I'm in danger from myself.

"What happened? Are you okay?"

"Don't worry, George. Everything is fine. I just need to make a statement, and then we will be on our way."

George studies me in the rearview mirror as he drives, but I try to give nothing away. Slowly, we make our way to the closest police station.

"Do you want me to come in with you?" George asks.

"No. Thanks, George. I'll be fine now."

I climb out of the car without saying more to George. I don't want to let on that I will not be coming back to this car after I'm done with this conversation.

I walk quickly inside the police station and walk up to the desk. No one is sitting behind it, so I wait. And wait some more.

"Hello?" I shout into the room adjacent to the lobby.

But no one comes. Maybe I'm just not meant to be here. Maybe this is a sign that I should just leave and forget this whole plan.

But, now, I'm more determined than ever.

Finally, I see a young male officer approach the desk.

"How may I help you, ma'am?"

"I'm here to turn myself in."

7

SCARLETT

JAIL IS A HORRIBLE PLACE. It's even more horrible than I imagined. It's dirty. It's filthy. It's dangerous—and not in the exciting way. In the any-of-these-women-could-kill-me-at-any-second kind of way. I have no control over my day-to-day life. I don't get to choose what I wear or when I shower or when I eat.

And every second that passes makes me realize how stupid I was to turn myself in.

"Your lawyers are here," one of the officers says to me.

Thank God, I think silently to myself.

It's the second meeting I've had with my lawyers in the last forty-eight hours. The first meeting was to talk about bail and to ensure that Preston would have complete control over the company if I were gone. They wanted to get me out on bail, but that would defeat the purpose of the plan. I'm sure they're here to try to convince me otherwise now that I've been in jail for forty-eight hours, but I want to give Nacio another chance to get me out. To prove that he cares about me just like I care about him.

My lawyers walk in and take their seats across from me.

"We came up with a plan to get you off. We won't even have to worry about bail. We'll have you out of here by the end of the week.

You just have to testify against Nacio and tell them where he is, and then they'll make a deal with you that includes no jail time. They don't want you; they want him. They understand he blackmailed you into doing those horrible things with him. They understand he didn't give you a choice. They understand you had no choice but to tell him where you and your friend were going to be that night and that you didn't know he was going to try to kill your friend. All you need to do is testify, and they'll let you go," Tyler Lang, my head lawyer says.

I take a deep breath because I want freedom, but I don't want it at his expense. "I won't testify against him."

"Scarlett, you went with him after he attempted to shoot your friend. It's your only choice. You have to testify against him. If not, you could end up going away to prison for several years," he says.

"I need more time to think about it."

"Fine. Think about it, but I'm telling you, it's the only way," he says.

"You're not a very good lawyer if this is the only way to get me out of here," I say even though it's not fair of me.

These people are just doing their jobs. They don't understand. They don't understand that I turned myself in, hoping that Nacio would come and find a way to get me out and prove me right. They don't understand that. They don't understand love.

A week passes, and I'm no longer sure that Nacio cares about me. He's not coming for me. It's clear now.

I walk over to get in line for the phone to make my daily call to Preston, so I can see how the company is running. And I know, today, my time is up. Preston is going to find a way to get me out of here since Nacio hasn't. And it's what I want because I can't stand to be in here for another second.

I listen to the woman standing in front of me, talking on the phone. She's angry that whoever is on the other end of the phone hasn't gotten her out of jail yet. Every other word out of her mouth is *bitch, motherfucker*, or *shit*. I would hate to be the person on the other end of her call. But I don't blame this woman. She's fighting to get out of here while I'm the reason that I am in here.

But no more. I'm no longer going to sit and wait for Beast to come rescue me. I'm going to get out of here. Today.

The woman slams the phone down and storms off. She obviously didn't find anyone who could get her out of jail today. I take three steps forward to the phone and then pick it up. I begin dialing Preston's number. I wait as it rings multiple times before the collect call message tells Preston that he has a caller from jail.

"Hey, Scar," Preston finally answers.

I smile. It's the only time during the day when I smile.

"Hey, Preston. How are things going? The company hasn't gone up in smoke yet, has it?"

Preston hesitates before he answers me, and I know he wants to tell me to get my ass out of here and back to work. That he needs me.

He doesn't say any of those things though.

"Everything is great. I have everything under control. But I am going to ask for a raise after this. This time, I think I actually deserve it," he says.

My smile grows larger. "You're right. You do deserve it."

"How are you doing?"

"Great. I have everything under control," I say, repeating his words, lying just as much as he was.

"When are those sorry-ass lawyers of yours going to get you out of jail?" Preston asks.

I know he knows why I'm really in here. I know he knows that I'm in here because I want to see Beast again. But neither of us can talk about it on the phone. Our conversations are being recorded. So, instead, all we do on these calls is lie to each other and try to make each other laugh. It's all we can do.

"Soon. Very soon. Do you…" I stop talking though when my eyes are drawn to a woman.

She is walking slowly and deliberately toward another woman

who is sitting at a table in the center of the room, playing cards with some of the other women. I see something sharp in her hand, and I know how this is going to go down. A fight will ensue, followed by a lockdown for twenty-four hours. Basically ensuring that I won't get to talk with my lawyers today. That I'm going to be stuck in this hell for at least another twenty-four hours. I will do anything to keep that from happening.

I'm tired of the mush they call food.

I'm tired of being told when to sleep and when to wake.

I'm tired of wearing a jumpsuit.

I'm tired of being afraid that any woman in here could kill me with her bare hands.

I'm tired of being strip-searched for no reason.

I'm tired of waiting for Nacio. This was my last shot at getting him back in my life. It failed. It's time for me to take back my life.

"I have to go," I say to Preston before hanging up the phone without waiting for him to respond.

I'm not going to let this fight happen. I'm not going to let them throw us into our cells for the next twenty-four hours.

I walk slowly and deliberately toward the woman who has what looks like a knife in her hand. I don't know how I'm going to stop her without causing a fight. I have no idea how to do that. But I have to try.

The woman's eyes narrow in on her target, and I know I'm running out of time. My walk turns into a run as I try to cut the woman off. If I can just grab her before she attacks the woman, maybe I can put a stop to this. Or maybe I'll get shanked and die on the floor of the jail.

The woman begins running, and I run faster. Until my body is flying at hers. I hit her at her waist and try to tackle her to the ground, like I've watched football players do on TV. It's easier than I thought it would be. Probably because I had the element of surprise on my side.

We both crash to the ground, and I think I have her. I think it is over. I'm breathing hard and fast as I lie on top of this woman.

"You bitch." The woman raises the knife in her hand.

I grab for it, trying to stop her from stabbing me in the chest. I grab her arm with my hands, and even though she is stronger than me, I don't think her one arm can overpower both of mine. I'm so focused on the woman that I don't see the others until it's too late.

Women come at us from all angles. Two women jump onto of us. Someone slaps me hard across the face, and that's when I forget what I'm doing. The anger overtakes me, and I fight back. I dig my nails into the woman who is crushing my chest, and I am rewarded by her scream.

A woman behind me grabs my hair, pulling hard. I don't even register the pain. The adrenaline flowing through me must be covering up any of the pain. I grab her ankles and watch as she tumbles to the floor. I forget what I'm doing. I forget that I was supposed to be putting a stop to this ridiculous violence, not guaranteeing myself a cell in solitary confinement.

Right now, I don't care though. Right now, I want to get all this anger inside me out.

I forget until I'm being sprayed with something that immediately reminds me of what I'm doing and where I am. I think it's pepper spray because my eyes instantly burn. I close them tightly and stop everything. I move my hands to my eyes to try to protect them, but it doesn't help. I never want to open my eyes again. All I feel is pain and burning and more pain.

I hear the guards yelling at us to do something, but I can't comprehend what they are saying. I can't do anything but focus on my burning eyes that I'm sure I won't ever be able to use again. I'm certain that the chemical they sprayed did permanent damage.

I feel someone's hands on my arms.

"Stand up!"

I feel like crying, but I can't. My eyes burn too badly to even do that.

"Stand up!" the man yells again.

I try to move to my feet while keeping my hands over my eyes, but I can't.

I feel his hands tighten around my biceps when I'm pulled into a standing position. I feel the cold metal of handcuffs going around my wrists in front of my body, but I don't dare open my eyes to see who is doing it.

"Walk," the same voice says.

His hand is holding on firmly to my bicep, and he begins guiding me. I walk with my eyes closed. I already know where he is taking me anyway—solitary confinement.

I lose track of how far we've walked when I hear him open the door before leading me further.

"Sit," he says, forcing me down into a chair that is cold and rickety.

A wet cloth is thrown over my hands.

"Wipe your eyes," he says.

Then, I hear the door close, and I know I'm alone. I take the cloth to my eyes even though the handcuffs give me limited motion, and I begin crying as the cold cloth begins to soothe my burning eyes, mixing with my tears. I wipe quickly, trying to get what I now realize is pepper spray, out as quickly as possible. When I think I have it all, I finally open my eyes.

I was wrong. I'm not alone in the room. A man is sitting across from me at a table. The man I've been waiting for.

"What did you do, Beauty?" Beast asks.

8

BEAST

SCARLETT'S BIG, beautiful eyes stare at me in shock. She didn't expect me to be here. It was obvious from the way her eyes widened when they saw me. And, even though her eyes are red and swollen from the pepper spray the guards used on her, they are still beautiful.

I promised myself that I would be stern with her, so she would understand what kind of a mess she'd gotten us in. But I can't help but let a small smirk form on my lips. She fought someone.

Maybe she is ballsier than I thought? Maybe she could fit into my life better than I thought?

I immediately shake that thought out of my head. *No way.* No way does Beauty have enough strength to fit into my messed up life. No way. Once she sees what I really do, will she still want me? No way.

"What did you do, Beauty?" I ask again. Even though I already know the answer, I need to hear it from her.

"Nothing."

My smirk widens as I look at my scared Beauty, sitting across the table from me. She would be so easy to break if I wanted to.

"Don't lie to me, Beauty. Answer me."

"It doesn't matter what I did. It worked, so that's all that matters."

"Are you so sure that it worked? I came here, yes. But why are you so assured that I'm going to be able to get you out of here?"

She frowns, and I see the tiniest bit of fear in her eyes. She's afraid that I will send her back to the hell she's been living in for the past week. A hell that I know all too well.

"My plan wasn't to have you rescue me. I just wanted you to come, so I could talk to you, know where you were."

"Oh, so you had a plan. Because this looked like a suicide mission to me."

Her eyes narrow as she glares at me. "I don't need your help. I can have my lawyers get me out of here with one phone call."

I cross my arms and casually lean back in my chair. "No, you can't."

"Sure I can. I have the best lawyers in New York City. They already said they could get me out with no problem."

I nod slowly. "Yes, they probably could have. But that was before..."

"Before?" she asks, her voice shaky.

"Before you became a violent offender. Now, the officers won't let you go so easily."

She closes her eyes, trying to keep from crying or from showing me her fear. But, when she opens them again, I see neither. I see defiance.

"Fine. I'll stay in here longer. I got myself into this mess. Why would I think that a man I'd fucked a handful of times, one I'd fallen for and who I'd thought was falling for me, too, would want to do anything to help me? I was stupid to think that. You should just go, Beast."

I try not to react to her words. I try not to show her that I've already fallen. If I hadn't already fallen, I wouldn't be sitting here right now, jeopardizing everything.

The second I found out she was in jail, I wanted to run down here and get her out. The only reason I didn't was because I needed her to feel like she is feeling right now. Scared. Terrified. She needed to understand what she would be risking by coming with me. Because feeling terrified will never go away if she comes with me.

As much as I want to let her walk back into the jail, I can't—not because I want to protect her, but because I'm selfish. And, after seeing her sitting across from me again, I can't control myself for much longer. I can't keep my hands from pulling her to me. I can't keep my mouth from tasting every inch of her body. I can't keep my cock from punishing her body.

I stand from my chair and walk over to her. Her big, beautiful eyes follow me. I grab her wrists that are still handcuffed, and I pull her up until she is standing. I stare at her in her jumpsuit that has been washed a few too many times. Her hair is pulled back into a ponytail, and she isn't wearing any makeup. She probably thinks she looks like a mess, but I've never seen her look purer in my life.

"Beautiful," I say.

My lips find hers. I kiss her, telling her what I can't tell her with my words. I tell her that I've fallen. I don't know if it's love or something else. But whatever it is, I've fallen for her.

And her lips tell me that she knows. She knows that I've fallen for her, but she still needs me to say the words. But I can't say them. I don't know if I will ever be able to say the words.

Her wrists creep up my body as she attempts to put them around my neck while I kiss her. She can't though with the handcuffs. I grin as I kiss her. I could leave them on. Make her give up that control to me.

I won't though. I reach my hand into my pocket and pull out the key. I unlock the handcuffs on her wrists while my lips stay glued to hers. When I unlock the second handcuff, she slowly stops kissing me when she realizes her hands are free.

She takes a step back, then looks down at her freed wrists, and then back to me. "Why do you have a key? I thought you were here, just visiting. I thought..."

I shake my head. "It doesn't matter why I have a key. What matters is, you are free."

I hesitate to say the next words because, once I say them, I won't be able to take them back. Once I say them, I'll know she is coming with me. But maybe that's exactly what we both need. She needs to come with me to understand that this is not a life she wants and that she can't change me. And I need her to come with me, so I can get her out of my system.

I walk toward the door and hesitate with my hand on the door-knob. "So, are you coming with me or what?"

She stands, frozen. "I'm coming."

"Good. But, before you come, you need to be punished for what you've put me through this last week."

9

SCARLETT

I DON'T KNOW how he did it, but I'm free. Even though my plan all along was to let Nacio save me, rescue me, I wasn't sure if it was going to happen. I wasn't sure he cared about me enough to come rescue me. And, even if he did care about me, I wasn't sure he would let himself help me.

I take a deep breath for the first time in a week as we walk out of the jailhouse and into the warm afternoon sun.

I'm free.

Nacio walks fast, and I try to keep up even though I'm not sure I want to. He said he needed to punish me first. And I'm afraid of what that punishment could be.

It doesn't matter, I tell myself.

It doesn't matter because he's taking me with him this time. And I plan on going even if that means I won't sleep again to make sure that he won't run away from me at night.

"Where are we going?" I ask.

Nacio doesn't answer me. He doesn't turn around. He just keeps walking.

I speed up, trying to catch up to him. "Where are we going?" I ask more sternly.

He stops abruptly and looks to his left. "To serve you your punishment."

I freeze.

He turns to me and pushes me into an alleyway. He releases me after he's pushed me a few feet between the two massive buildings.

"Strip," he says.

My eyes widen. "Here?"

"Yes, here."

I look around at the dirty alleyway. *Is he really going to fuck me here?* I want him to, but I can at least wait until we get to his car. And...

"Anyone could see us though."

He frowns. "Strip."

I bite my lip, trying to decide what I'm going to do. I want to get out of this jumpsuit, but he doesn't have anything for me to change into. And I've been naked in plenty of magazine shoots before, so it's not that I'd have a problem if anyone saw us. I just know we are risking going back to the jail I just escaped from if anyone sees us.

I can see the anger flowing from his face as he says the words, "Scarlett, I won't ask you again. Strip."

I know if I don't do what he said, he won't let me come with him. And I know, with every second that I let pass without doing what he said, the anger is flaring up more and more inside him. His anger will make my punishment worse.

I move my hand to the zipper on the front of my jumpsuit and slowly begin unzipping it. Nacio's eyes stay glued on my hand as I move the zipper lower. His eyes are full of lust, need, and anger. I immediately forget that I'm standing in an alleyway just a couple of blocks from the jail. I forget that, at any moment, someone could see us and arrest us for indecent exposure. I forget that Nacio even said he would punish me.

I want him.

I shrug out of the jumpsuit like I have done with my dresses in the past, and I watch the oversize fabric fall to the ground in a heap. I'm not wearing the sexiest underwear. In fact, this is probably the unsexiest underwear I have ever worn. But I don't let it faze me. I know my body looks hot, no matter what I wear. And I can tell from the look on Nacio's face that he thinks so, too.

So, I rock the white granny panties and white sports bra like it is the nicest Victoria's Secret lingerie I have ever worn. I run my tongue across my lip as I let my hand trail down my body to the little bit of cleavage that is sticking out of the white bra. "I know you want me. So, take me. Neither of us can wait any longer."

Nacio's breathing picks up, but he doesn't move from where he is standing a few feet in front of me.

I hook my hand under the bra and slowly lift it over my head. The look Nacio gives me is a look I will never forget. I don't understand how he has enough self-control to stand where he is and not have his hands on me. His look, despite having all his clothes still on, is killing me.

I run my thumbs under the sides of my panties and lower them slowly and deliberately. I watch as Nacio sucks in a breath at the sight of me. He wants me. More than any man has wanted me before. I just don't know what he is waiting on.

I stand, trying my best to seduce him into giving in to his desires. At this point, getting to fuck him one more time would be worth going back to jail.

"What's wrong? You change your mind, Beast?" I ask.

He growls, and then I'm pushed, face-first, against the brick wall of the building.

"I told you to strip. Not to give me a tease and not to take your sweet time in doing it. Next time, listen to me, Beauty, or there won't be a next time."

I swallow as his hand firmly holds my neck against the wall. My cheek is pressed against the warm bricks, and my breasts have hardened against the rough wall.

"Answer me, Beauty. Will you do exactly what I say when I tell you to?"

"Yes."

"Good girl. Now, for your punishment..."

Everything inside me goes on high alert when he says the word *punishment*. I don't know what he has in mind, but I'm scared and turned on, all at the same time. Last time we fucked, he tried to convince me that he could kill me. This time, he's upset with me. Angry with me for what I did. This time is going to be worse. I can feel it.

His hand quickly and firmly comes down on my ass without any warning while his other hand holds me in place against the wall. My ass stings where he hit me, but it isn't as bad as I thought.

"You deserve so much worse than this, Beauty. I've never wished I had a whip or crop or any instrument to hit a woman with so badly in my life. But my hand will have to do."

He hits me again—this time, harder than the first. I whimper, but I notice that I also ache for him worse than I've ever ached for him before.

He hits me again—this time, spreading the pain to the other cheek.

"You risked my life by turning yourself into the police."

He hits me, but instead of pain, all I feel is pleasure forming between my legs. I know what is coming after the punishment, which no longer feels like punishment at all. It feels like lust and fear. Fear that he could have lost me.

"You risked your life by going to the police."

He hits again, and I moan in pleasure.

"Never again." He hits me again and then suddenly stops.

"I'm sorry. I won't do it again. I deserve the punishment."

Nacio leans forward, so his face is against my ear. "This isn't the punishment. This is preparing you for what I'm going to do next."

"I don't care what my punishment is. I just need you to fuck me. Now."

He laughs. "You will wish you hadn't said that."

I hear him unzipping his pants. I hear him tearing the wrapper from a condom. All the while, I wait. Naked, against a dirty wall, where anyone passing by could glance this way and see me.

It doesn't matter though. All I want is him.

"Last chance, Beauty. You can still run. You can still run and never look back."

"No."

"Then, I'm going to fuck you until I know that you will listen to whatever I tell you to do. I'm going to fuck you until you know to never put yourself in harm's way again."

I open my mouth to answer. To tell him I already promise that I won't do those things again. But I don't get a chance to tell him.

Instead, his cock thrusts inside me, and I scream.

His hand covers my mouth, preventing me from screaming again.

I don't know why I screamed. If it was the intensity of waiting mixed with the pain on my ass or if it was something else that made me do it. But I want to scream again as he pounds into me, punishing me with his cock. Every time he moves, I want to scream, and he knows it, so he keeps his hand over my lips.

He thrusts and slaps my ass again with his other hand, and the pain and need is too much. I need him to touch me. My lips, my breasts, my neck, my clit. Something. But he doesn't. All he is touching is my pussy with his cock, my ass with an occasional punishing slap, and my lips with his hand to keep me from scream-ing. I need more though.

He hits my ass again as he punishes me with his cock, and I do everything in my power to keep from screaming. I try to keep some semblance of control.

His hand loosens just the slightest around my lips.

"Touch me," I whimper beneath his hand.

"No, Beauty. Not until you understand." His cock punishes me again.

"I understand. Please. Please, Beast..."

"You have to learn to obey me first. It's the only way to keep you safe. I will not bring you with me if I don't think I can keep you safe."

He thrusts again, and every nerve in my body begs him to touch me. To make me feel good. To make me come.

"I will."

"I don't believe you," he says, mocking the words I told him the last time we were together.

"I promise. I will do whatever you say, just…"

His hand slaps my ass again, and I know I'm dripping with need. It wouldn't take much for me to come. To get some pleasure instead of the slow torture that he is giving me now.

My hands have been pressed against the wall, keeping my face from completely slamming against the bricks each time he slams into me. But, if I could just move one of them down between my legs, I could come before he even realized what I was doing. He's so lost in what he is doing—punishing me—that I doubt he would even notice.

I slowly move my left hand from the wall just the tiniest bit, and I get used to having just my right hand holding me up.

"You will obey me—whatever I say, when I say it."

"Yes."

I let my hand slowly move down to the side of my body.

"You won't hesitate. You won't ask questions."

"Mmhmm," I groan as he moves against me again.

My left hand is close. So close, resting against my thigh. I'm not even sure if my fingers need to touch my clit for me to come. Just need to be within the vicinity. Just need to touch myself somewhere, and I know I'll come.

"You will never put yourself in danger again."

"Never," I moan as I move my hand between my legs.

His hand grabs my wrist before I can touch myself. "Your pleasure is mine. And you just disobeyed me."

"I didn't! You never said I couldn't touch myself."

His hand comes down hard on my ass as his cock thrusts again, and I scream.

"Don't touch yourself, Beauty. Don't come without my permission. You hear me? Make me believe that you will do anything I tell you. Make me believe that I can trust you."

He releases my wrist, and suddenly, his hands are all over me. One at my breast, the other at my clit.

"Aw, Beast...I..."

"Don't come, Beauty. Not until I say. Make me believe that I can trust you."

"Fuck," I moan as his thumb rolls my clit while his cock thrusts inside me.

I need to come. That one motion would have been enough for me to come, but I'm too stubborn to come. Too stubborn to show him that I'm weak and that I can't do what he says.

I don't come.

He moves his lips to my neck.

My panting increases. I can't hold out for much longer, and I have no idea how long he is going to torture me. I have no idea how long he is going to make me wait until I can come.

I try thinking about other things. I try thinking about jail. I try thinking about work. About how sad I was when Kinsley lost the baby. I try thinking about anything, but nothing works. All I can feel is his lips sucking my neck, his fingers squeezing my nipple, his fingers flicking my clit, and his cock turning from punishing to trying everything in his power to milk an orgasm out of me.

He increases his speed and pressure, and I'm afraid I'm going to lose it.

"You like that, Beauty?"

"Yes," I get out, trying to focus on his words instead of what he's doing to me.

"You want to come?"

His cock pounds into me faster, and I have no idea how he hasn't come yet. How he is able to have so much control.

"Fuck," I moan.

He grabs my earlobe between his teeth, and I almost lose it. I almost come.

"I'll take that as a yes."

His tongue flicks my earlobe. "Not yet, Beauty. I get to come first."

His hands go to my hips, and he thrusts faster. I feel him building inside me. My body tries to build with him, but I won't let it. I try to focus on the pain stinging my ass as he moves, even though it's nothing compared to the pleasure I feel. I try to focus on the rough bricks that hit my face and breasts with each movement, but it's not enough either.

"Fuck, Beauty. I could do this all day."

I want to do something to make him come, and I know it wouldn't take much. A touch, a lick, a moan. I resist. I don't want him to think I did anything to make him come.

"You will obey me?"

"Yes, Beast," I moan, doing everything I can to keep myself from coming.

"Fuck, Beauty, I..."

I squeeze my eyes shut, trying to keep myself from coming, as Beast explodes inside me. His thrusts slow until he almost stops, but it doesn't keep me from being on edge. I could come with a single touch. A single thrust.

"You will obey me, no matter what?"

"Yes."

"You will never put yourself in harm's way again?"

"No."

"Come, Beauty."

I didn't realize that just two words would be enough to push me over the edge, but it is. It is more than enough. I come, and Beast rewards me by thrusting again, his fingers circling my clit, his lips sucking on my neck.

I scream again, but this time, it's for an entirely different reason. I scream because he finally let me come, and it is better than anything I've ever done in my life.

He might think he punished me, and he did. But he's also given me the greatest gift.

When he slowly pulls out and turns me to look at him, I realize I've given him a gift, too. I've given him the ability to trust that I will obey him, no matter what.

10

BEAST

I WATCH as Scarlett puts the jail jumpsuit back on. I have a bag with clothes for her to change into at the car along with anything else I thought she might need. I should have brought them to the jail and let her change there before we left, but I wanted her to feel vulnerable. I wanted her to understand that I was in control, not her. That the only reason she walked out of the jail was because of me. Now, watching her put the jumpsuit back on is torture for both of us. It's like watching her walk back into jail. I can see her going back to that place in her head as she begins to zip up the jumpsuit.

"I have a change of clothes for you in the car," I say.

She nods.

When she is finished getting dressed, I hold out my hand to her. "Come on, Beauty."

She grabs my hand, and I lead her out of the alleyway and down the street to where my car is parked. She lets me lead her, but I know it's a strange feeling for her. Even after she promised she would give up that control to me. Even after she promised she would obey me.

But I can feel her defiance already oozing out of her. It's in the way she walks and holds my hand. As we walk, she begins to pull in front of me, needing to be in control. And then she stops herself when she realizes what she has been doing, and she lets me lead her again.

Oh, Beauty, I think. *Is this really going to work?*

We get to my black Mercedes, and I release her hand to walk around to the driver's side of the car.

"Get in," I say.

Her eyes dart up to me and then back to the car. She doesn't argue with me or say anything. She just gets in the car, like I asked.

I start the car and then pull out onto the street. "Get dressed. There is a bag of clothes behind my seat."

She reaches back and pulls the bag to her lap. I glance over as I drive, and I can see her anger boiling. I can see that she wants to say something, but is trying to hold it in. She roughly unzips the bag and begins pulling clothes out, taking the anger out on the bag of clothes.

Finally, she stops. "I can't do this if you are just going to bark orders at me and expect me to obey you like I'm your dog."

I smirk. "You are not my dog, Beauty. My dog is better trained."

She glares at me, and it just makes me smile.

"I'm sorry. I'll try to stop barking orders at you. It's just my nature. It's what I've been doing my entire life. I don't know any other way."

"Well, find a better way. I'm not used to taking orders from others either. I promised I would obey you and stay out of harm's way. That doesn't mean you get to speak to me without any respect for my thoughts and opinions, like you already know that I'm going to obey."

"But I do already know that you are going to obey. So, why don't I get to act like I know you are going to obey me?"

She huffs and crosses her arms over her chest. "I can't take this! I will obey you on important things that are life and death. I can't obey every stupid little thing you say. I just can't!"

I shake my head as I laugh. "Well, that didn't last long, did it?"

She frowns, and I swear, I can see steam coming from her ears.

"Fine. I will try not to use my new power to order you around all day long—if you promise to try and just do what I ask." I run my hand through my hair.

This woman is going to be the death of me. I can feel it.

"Fine."

She begins unzipping the jumpsuit, and she shimmies out of it in the seat before pulling on the jeans and shirt I brought for her. When she is finished, I pull her cell phone out of my pocket and hand it to her.

"How do you have that?"

"It was with your belongings when you turned yourself in."

"Yes, but how do you have them? How did you get me out of jail? And, if you have my belongings, why wasn't I given my clothes?"

"Because I didn't want you to have your clothes."

She frowns.

"And I got you out legally, if you are wondering. They can't arrest you again. Unless you do something stupid, like turn yourself in again for a crime you didn't commit."

I narrow my eyes at her, studying her reaction to see if she plans on turning herself in again.

"Sorry."

I take a deep breath when I realize that I don't think she has any intentions of doing that ever again.

"Call your assistant, Preston, and let him know you are taking an extended vacation."

Scarlett gives me a dirty look.

I roll my eyes. "Please call," I add.

Not demanding her is going to take some getting used to. I want nothing more than to pull this car over and punish her again. But, if I do that, we will never make it to the house, and that would be putting her life at risk, which is something I promised her and myself I wouldn't do again.

Scarlett dials the number, and I listen to her speak.

"Preston, I'm out. I'm going on an extended vacation for a couple of weeks, and I'm leaving you in charge."

She smiles.

"Yes, it comes with a huge raise that you will actually deserve this time."

She pauses while Preston speaks.

Her eyes dart over to me, and I know she wishes I weren't listening to her conversation, which only makes me want to listen harder.

"Yes, with him. And, yes, the sex was better than last time."

I smirk.

"If anything comes up, call me; otherwise, I'll tell you all the dirty details when I get back. Good-bye." She ends the call and then stares at the phone for a second. "I need to make one more call," she says.

I nod.

"Kinsley's safe, right? I mean, we aren't leaving her, so you can have one of your goons come in and kill her, are we?"

"Goons? You think I have goons?"

She raises her eyebrow at me. "Don't you?"

I shake my head from side to side. "I guess you could call them that, but I just call them employees."

"Fine. Your employees aren't going to try and kill her while we are gone, are they?"

"No, they aren't. But that doesn't mean she is safe. Eventually..."

She takes a deep breath and frowns. "We can talk about *eventually* later. I just need to know that she will be safe while I'm gone."

I nod.

She dials Kinsley's number.

"Hey, Kins."

"Oh my God! You lied to me! You said you were on vacation when you were actually in jail!" I hear Kinsley scream on the phone.

Scarlett holds the phone away from her ear until Kinsley is done screaming.

"I'm sorry, Kinsley. I didn't want you to worry. It was all just a big misunderstanding. I'm out now, and now, I'm for real going on a vacation. I need a break after everything that happened."

I can't hear Kinsley's response, which I take as a good thing. Her friend has calmed down enough to talk rationally instead of just screaming at Scarlett.

Scarlett glances over at me again before she speaks, "I don't have an exact date yet, but a couple of weeks."

I nod.

She won't be gone for more than a couple of weeks. She might not be gone for more than a day or two after she sees what I really do. After she sees the family I come from, she might not want anything to do with me.

"No, there isn't a guy."

She waits again.

"Yes, I brought a bodyguard with me. Killian's keeping you safe, too, right?"

She pauses.

"When he's captured and it's safe again, we should go somewhere, just the two of us, and have a girls' weekend. We deserve that."

She bites her lip.

"Love you, too."

And then she ends the call. She stares at the phone that she is still grasping in her hand.

"I hate this," she says.

"Hate what?"

"I hate lying to her. She's my best friend."

"You don't have to lie to her. I can take you to her right now. You can tell her everything. The truth, if you want..."

"That just means, I would be giving you up."

I nod.

"No, that's not what I want. I want you both."

I shake my head because that will never happen.

She lets it go though. "Where are we going?"

"A house, about an hour away."

"Whose house?"

"Just someone I know."

She frowns. "You aren't going to be honest with me, are you?"

"I'll be honest with you about what I can."

Her frown deepens, and then it turns into a yawn.

"Sleep, Beauty," I say, not meaning to give her another command, but it comes out that way anyway.

She doesn't argue though. She leans her seat back. Then, she takes the jumpsuit, crumples it into a ball, and places it under her head before closing her eyes.

I continue to drive, trying to keep my eyes and thoughts on the road instead of on her, but I can't. I glance over at her at least a hundred times, watching her as she slowly drifts off to sleep. She must be tired. Jail is a hard place to get any sleep.

And my thoughts, they are all of her. How beautiful she is. How I want to fuck her again. How strong she is yet how she promised to obey me. How I'm ruining her life.

"Wake up, Beauty," I whisper in her ear.

"Mmm," she moans but doesn't wake.

I tuck a strand of her hair that fell on her face behind her ear. I could watch her sleep like this all day. And I have before. And I know, from the last time I moved her, that she is a hard sleeper and doesn't wake easily. I need her to wake now though. I need to feed her and make her comfortable in the house before I have to go do an unthinkable thing.

"Wake up, Beauty," I say again, gently shaking her this time.

Her eyes open suddenly, and she quickly sits up, causing her to hit our foreheads together.

"Ow," we both say at the same time as we each grab our own foreheads.

When she stops rubbing, she looks around. "Where are we?"

"Pennsylvania."

From the car, she studies the suburban neighborhood we've stopped in and then looks up at the large mansion-like house we are parked in front of. Her eyes widen. "Is this your house?"

I laugh. "No."

"Whose house is it then?"

"An acquaintance's. Come on, let's go inside."

I get out of the car, and she does the same. I grab my bag from the back, and she carries the bag I brought for her up the driveway. I walk up to the door and quickly pick the lock, trying not to let her see what I'm doing. She notices anyway.

When I open the door for her and she steps into the grand entryway, she stops and stares up before looking back at me. "You mean, it's the house of someone you plan on killing, right?"

I shake my head. "No, I don't plan on killing anyone in this house."

She narrows her eyes at me, trying to determine if I am telling the truth or not. She must decide that I am because she makes her way into the house. She makes it to the living room and then stops and stares at the family portrait of two young children and their parents.

"Please tell me the family is on vacation or something. Please say you aren't going to kill any of them."

I grab her shoulders and turn her to face me. I lift her chin. "I'm not lying to you. I'm not going to kill anyone in this family. I knew they were out of town for the weekend, so it would be free for us to stay here and lie low for a couple of days. And, yes, there is a job I have to do while we are here, but it has nothing to do with the two kids in the picture."

She nods and exhales slowly. "I'm sorry. This is just a lot for me to take in."

I release her. She can't handle my life. If she can't handle even the thought of me killing someone, she won't be able to handle it once she sees it happen.

"Well, well, you've brought a visitor."

I hear my brother's voice from behind me. I frown, and my face reddens with anger.

I turn slowly to face my brother. "What are you doing here, Santino?"

He smirks at me. "Just making sure you do the job we sent you here to do. It was supposed to be done two days ago, and Catherine was getting nervous."

"I still have plenty of time left in the window I was given. Tell Catherine, she has no need to worry. It will be done tomorrow."

"Catherine has plenty of reason to worry. We both know that, after you fucked up your last job, she couldn't trust you again."

"And she trusts you?" I ask, raising my eyebrows.

"I guess so. She sent me." Santino glances around me to look at Scarlett, who takes a step forward.

"I have no idea what the two of you are talking about, but I'm Scarlett," she says, holding out her hand to my brother.

Santino takes her hand in his and shakes it. "I'm Santino, the better-looking, funnier, and nicer of the Marlow brothers."

They smile at each other, and I lose it.

I break them apart. "Enough. Don't listen to a word my brother says."

It just makes them smile at each other more.

"Relax, Nacio. You don't think I would go to jail, deal with your neurotic tendencies, and come with you even though I knew you were a killer just to leave you for your charming brother, do you?" Scarlett says.

I frown at her. "Stay here," I tell her, making it clear that this is one of the times that she doesn't get to disobey me.

"And you," I say, grabbing Santino by the arm, "outside. Now."

"How do you put up with a man this controlling?" Santino asks Scarlett as I drag his ass outside.

Scarlett doesn't answer. Or, if she does, I don't hear her because I'm too busy with storming out of the house and onto the back patio. I slam the door shut and let go of Santino, who is laughing at me with his arms folded across his chest.

"I never thought I would see the day when you risked everything over some chick. And then you saved Kinsley and fucked everyone's lives up. I thought to myself, *You would never let that happen again.* Never let a chick destroy your life. And, now, there is a chick. Well, not exactly a chick because the girl standing in that living room is very much a woman. I never thought you would let another woman control you and destroy your life. Because that is what you are letting her do. Destroy you and everything that has happened these last ten years."

"Leave her out of this. She won't destroy anything. She's here because I want a woman to fuck at night, and she's the woman I happen to want. That's it."

Santino shakes his head as he looks at me. "She isn't just a woman you are fucking and letting tag along until you get bored and dispose of her. First of all, once you get bored of her, you are going to have to kill her. You can't just let her go. You know Catherine won't take that risk."

"Shut the hell up about Catherine. I don't give a fuck what she thinks. And, as for Scarlett, why she is here is none of your concern. She's here because I want her to be here. If you have a problem with that, then leave."

"I'm not the one who is going to have a problem with that, and you know it. I just don't think you can bring someone into this life without understanding that it comes with consequences. And I don't think you are ready to deal with those consequences."

"Don't worry about it. She won't last more than a day—two, at most—and then she will be running, wishing she'd never asked to be a part of my life. You won't have to deal with her for long."

Santino looks inside the house with a smile on his face. "I think you're wrong. I think she is stronger than you know, and this life might be exactly the kind of life she has been looking for."

"What makes you say that?"

"For one, you told her to stay, and I don't see her anywhere on the first floor of the house."

"Shit."

I run back into the house to find her. I thought I made it perfectly clear that she was supposed to do exactly what I said. She can't just run off like this. She can't just do whatever the fuck she wants. That's how people die.

"Scarlett?" I shout.

But, just like my brother said, I don't see her anywhere. I scan the living room to make sure she didn't fall asleep on one of the couches, but she isn't there. I go to the kitchen but don't find her there either.

There are three more rooms on the main floor, but I don't see her anywhere.

I run outside to my car to see if she left something there and went back for it. My heart pounds wildly as I go to see if she took the car and left. I still feel the car keys jingling in my pocket, so I'm not too worried, but just the thought that she could be gone freaks me out. I want her to be gone. I want her to be somewhere safe. But I also want her all to myself.

I get to the car and don't find her anywhere. I run back inside and see Santino searching the main level for her.

"Found her yet?"

"No," he answers.

I run upstairs and begin throwing doors open, searching for her.

"Scarlett!" I shout again.

I run down the hallway, and that's when the door at the end opens. Scarlett walks out and smiles at me as I approach her.

"What the hell? Didn't you hear me screaming for you? Did you not fucking hear me when I told you to stay? What part of *stay* don't you understand?"

She rolls her eyes at me. "Relax. I just went upstairs to check out the rest of the house. I wasn't going anywhere. And I assumed the reason you took your brother outside was because you wanted some privacy when you spoke to him. And I could hear everything you were saying to each other. So, I came up here to give you the privacy."

I can see the sadness in her eyes. She heard me. She heard the part where I said that I just brought her here to have someone to fuck until I got bored.

"It wasn't true."

Scarlett walks past me, and I know it's because she is about to cry. I grab her arm, but she quickly shakes me off.

"It wasn't true. I tell you the truth, but I don't always tell other people the truth."

She stops and shakes her head. "It's fine. Your words weren't meant for me, but I don't know if that makes them true or not. I guess I'll just have to wait and see how this turns out. Then, I'll know."

"There you are," Santino says as he makes his way up the stairs. "And it's perfect timing, too," he says when he finishes climbing the stairs.

"What's perfect timing?" Scarlett asks.

I already know what he's going to say because I got the text message, too.

"We found you just in time to take you with us."

"Take me with you where?"

"To go kill a guy."

11

SCARLETT

WITH NACIO in the driver's seat of his Mercedes, I climb into the passenger seat while Santino climbs in the back.

I just try to look calm. I try to act like I do this all the time. Like it's no big deal to get into a car and drive to a place and kill someone. Except it is a big fucking deal.

I didn't come with Nacio, so he could show me that he was a killer. I'd already known that about him. I came with him to see what was left of him that wasn't a killer.

What part of him wants to stop being a killer? What part of him wants something more with his life?

Nacio backs out of the driveway and begins driving us away from the nice house that belongs to random people who don't know we're staying there. I try to think of anything else, but all I can think about is that we are going to kill someone. And, this time, I won't be able to run from the fact that this is exactly who Nacio is—a killer. Even if I find the other parts of Nacio, he is still a horrible person who has killed people, and I don't know how to rectify that.

I bite my lip to try to calm my nerves as I glance over at Nacio, who seems much too calm, sitting in the driver's seat next to me. I glance behind me, and Santino is almost just as calm. The only difference is, he is buried in his phone while Nacio is driving.

I can't help myself. I can't stand the silence. "Where are we going?"

Nacio glances over at me, but doesn't answer.

"This restaurant that serves the best pizza and beer in town. Or so I've heard," Santino answers.

I glance back at Santino. "I'm guessing, we aren't going for the pizza?"

Santino grins. "Not really, but I still plan on grabbing a slice."

I take a deep breath. "So then, how are you going to..." I can't bring myself to say the word *kill*.

Santino's grin widens when he sees the stress in my eyes. "We aren't going to do anything. You are."

"What? I think you have the wrong person if you think I'm capable of killing anyone."

"We are all capable of killing. Some just get the chance and take it while others never get the chance," Nacio says, chiming into our conversation.

My eyes move slowly from Santino to Nacio. "I'm not capable," I say, my voice a little shaky.

"You are. Soon, you'll realize it for sure because, soon, you will want to kill me," Nacio says.

I frown. "I could never want to kill you."

Nacio just shakes his head in sadness, like he hopes I'm right but knows I'm wrong.

Nacio parks the car, and I see that we are parked outside of a pizza parlor. My hands shake a little, as I know that these men are planning on killing someone inside. Someone who might be eating their last meal or enjoying their last conversation with friends. Someone who I should warn to stay away from these people.

Nacio doesn't look at me. He just glances back at Santino, who takes over the conversation again.

"Relax, Beauty," Santino says.

I gasp when he says the nickname that Nacio calls me. Nacio

doesn't like it either because he turns and glares at Santino, who just smiles back at his brother.

"All right, all right, calm down. Don't get your panties in a bunch. I get it; she's yours." Santino looks back at me with a goofy grin on his face. "We aren't going to kill anyone in this pizza joint—at least, not yet. Right now, we just need to arrange for a time and place for him to meet us that is more convenient for us—if you get what I'm saying," Santino says.

I nod.

"And that's where you come in, Beauty," Santino says.

Nacio and I both glare at Santino again, but he isn't fazed.

He just continues talking, "We need you to convince the guy at the bar to take you out on a date tonight. Your only condition is that you want to drive."

My eyes widen. "You want me to convince some man in there to take me out on a date when, really, you are going to be waiting to kill him?"

"Yes," Santino says.

"I can't."

Santino shrugs and sits back in his seat. His arms outstretch over the back of the seat, like he knew that was going to be my answer and he couldn't really care less.

"Told you she wouldn't do it. Now, move on to Plan B," Nacio says.

Santino shakes his head. "She'll do it. The only way she gets to stay with you is if she becomes a part of this."

"What?" I ask nervously, glancing from Santino to Nacio, needing answers.

"That's not true," Nacio says.

From the sound of his voice, I don't believe him. That's when I realize, this is what he wants. He wants me to say no. He wants me to have to go back home without him where I'll be safe. He doesn't want me involved in his life.

"I'll do it," I say.

"I knew you'd come around, Beauty," Santino says. He pulls out his phone and then pulls something up on it before turning it toward me. "I need you to get this man to take you out on a date tonight where you will be the one picking him up. You think you can do that?"

Now, it's my turn to smile as I look at the picture of a good-looking man in his mid-thirties. "Of course. What's his name?"

Santino shakes his head. "You wouldn't know a stranger's name at a bar."

I narrow my eyes at Santino, trying to understand if he is playing me. If this—people's lives—is all just a game to him.

I reach for the handle to open the door when Nacio grabs my arm.

"You don't have to do this," he says.

I glance back at Santino. "Apparently, I do."

I climb out of the car without saying another word to either man and without looking back. I pull some lipstick out of my purse and put it on before I walk into the pizza joint. I glance down at my outfit of jeans, heels, and a tank top that they bought for me; I've seduced men in less flattering clothing.

I open the door to the restaurant and stand in the entrance, searching for the man in the picture that Santino showed me.

"Can I help you?" a hostess asks me.

I spot the man from the picture sitting at the bar, but he's not alone. A woman is sitting next to him.

"No. I'm just going to have a seat at the bar."

I begin walking toward the bar, trying to figure out what the hell I'm going to do. They didn't tell me he had a girlfriend or a wife. *Now what?*

I take a seat next to him at the bar and feel his eyes go to me. I don't glance back. Instead, I reach for my hair tie and pull it off my hair, letting it fall in long waves. I run my hand through my hair, loosening the waves. When I'm finished, I take a chance and glance over at the man, who is no longer looking at me but the woman on his left.

I frown. *Well, that didn't work.*

"Your martini, sir. And I'll be right back with that salad," the bartender says to the man.

I glance over at the man sitting next to me, my eyebrows raised. *What man orders a salad and a martini at a pizza place?*

The man touches the bartender's hand. "Thanks, Dominic," he says to the bartender.

A gay one.

The woman sitting next to him, I realize, misses the gesture and continues trying to push her fake boobs in his face. *That won't work*, I realize.

I have no idea if my plan will either, but judging from the expensive clothes he is wearing, he is into fashion, so I hope that name-dropping will work.

I text Preston to call the restaurant and ask for me, and then I wait.

The bartender comes back. "Can I get you anything to drink?"

"Gin and tonic."

A few moments later, he places the drink in front of me and gives a longing glance to the man sitting next to me.

"I'll be right back to take your order," he says.

"Is there a Scarlett Bell here?" I hear the hostess say from across the room.

I don't answer her though. Not until the man sitting next to me has a good opportunity to hear her and comprehend whom she is talking about.

"Scarlett Bell?" she asks again as she walks through the bar.

I still don't answer.

She walks up right behind me. "Scarlett Bell?"

I turn slowly in my chair. "That's me."

The hostess smiles and relaxes now that she has found me. "I have a call for you from your assistant. He said it was an emergency and to have you call him back right away, that Beautifully Bell would go under if you didn't."

I smile. Preston has always been good with dramatics.

"Thanks. I'll call him back," I say.

The hostess doesn't leave though.

I smile at her. "Is there more?"

She hesitates and then says, "You're that woman? The woman who runs Beautifully Bell, right?"

I nod and extend my hand to her.

She takes it and giddily shakes my hand. "I just love your new makeup line."

I smile. I don't get recognized often. Most people don't know the face running a large beauty corporation.

"Wait until you see the new eye shadows we have coming out. They are truly the best." I grab my purse and begin digging until I find what I was looking for. "I have some samples in here, I think." My hand finally grasps the eye shadows. "Here they are." I hand them to the woman.

"Oh, thank you!" she squeals.

I smile before turning back to the bar, and I begin sipping on my drink.

"You going to call your assistant back?" the man sitting next to me says, being nosy.

It worked, I think.

I turn to him. "No. He's always calling with some emergency or another whenever I'm away, and it never really is an emergency."

The man laughs. "I understand."

"You work in fashion and beauty, too?"

The man shakes his head. "I wish. No, I work in accounting. Very boring."

I smile. "I'm Scarlett," I say, holding out my hand to him.

"Marcel."

The bartender comes back to me. "So, what can I get you to eat?"

"What do you recommend?"

"New York-style pizza is our specialty."

I smile. "Thanks, but I think I'll take a salad. New York-style pizza outside of New York just seems wrong to me."

The bartender frowns, but Marcel smiles as the bartender walks away.

"I agree. Who would think New York-style pizza could be just as good as in New York? That's why I always order the salad myself."

"So, what's the deal with you and..." I nod in the direction of the bartender, who is typing my order into the computer.

Marcel sighs. "Nothing. That's the problem."

I smile.

The woman sitting on his other side doesn't seem to be happy that I'm getting all of the attention, and she strokes his arm. "Marcel, I want to go dancing tonight. Take me dancing?" she says.

When Marcel turns his attention from me to her, she flicks her hair. I can tell, he doesn't know how to turn her down and tell her that he is gay.

"He can't. Sorry. He's already got plans with me for tonight," I say, wrapping my arms around him and softly kissing him on the cheek.

The woman glares at me and then gets up from the bar, storming off.

I smile and let go of Marcel.

"Thanks for that."

"Of course. But I meant that sincerely. I'm staying in town for a couple of nights, and I could use a friend to just go out with tonight. We could get drinks and wash our sorrows away. I could forget about work for a little while, and you could tell me all about your problems with you know who," I say, careful not to say the bartender's name out loud.

Marcel thinks for a moment. "I guess I could do that."

I smile. "I have a driver, so I can pick you up around, say, eight tonight?"

Marcel nods, smiling. "I work across the street from here, so I'll just wait in here after work for you."

"Perfect."

Dominic brings my salad with a slice of pizza on the side. "You need to try the pizza. It's the best New York-style pizza out there."

I smile, but don't think that is possible. I pick up the pizza, fold it in half, and then take a bite. I chew slowly, trying to give the pizza a chance, but it's probably one of the worst slices of pizza I've ever had.

The crust is overcooked, the cheese is rubber, and there isn't enough grease.

"So, how is it?" Dominic asks.

"You own this place, don't you?" I ask.

Dominic nods.

I bite my lip, not wanting to hurt this man's feelings, but he needs to hear the truth.

"It was okay for a pizza. It's just not New York-style pizza. I think, if you advertise it differently, as something other than New York-style pizza, it will sell better."

Dominic frowns and then turns away.

"Don't fret. Somebody needed to tell him," Marcel says.

"And, now, he will need a shoulder to cry on about the mean lady who said his pizza was horrible," I say, winking at Marcel.

I dig into my salad while talking to Marcel about my company and his job. He's nice, and he reminds me a lot of Preston. He is somebody I could be friends with.

Marcel glances at his watch. "I'd better get back to work, or my boss will kill me."

I nod. "Me, too." I slap some twenties down on the bar.

"I thought you were your own boss?"

I smile. "I am, but I'm a tyrant."

Marcel smiles back. "I look forward to seeing you tonight."

"Me, too," I say as we both begin walking out of the restaurant.

I expect to see Nacio and Santino sitting outside the bar, still in the car, but I don't see them.

"My driver is parked around the corner. See you later," I say to Marcel.

He walks across the street, back to his work.

I begin walking, not sure of where I'm going, until I hear a car pulling up behind me. I stop walking because I already know it's them. I walk to the passenger side of the car and climb in.

Nacio begins driving.

"So?" Santino asks impatiently. "Are we on for tonight?"

"Yes. At eight. I'm supposed to pick him up from the restaurant."

"Wow, I'm impressed. I didn't think you had it in you," Santino says.

I turn around and glare at him. "I can seduce guys in my sleep, but you could have told me he was gay."

"Oops, must have slipped my memory," Santino says.

"Yeah, I bet." I sigh and turn back around.

Nacio grabs my hand, and I let him hold it.

"The important thing is, it's done," I say.

Nacio nods, but that's when I realize that this is far from done. This is far from over. All I have done is set everything into motion for this man to die at eight tonight. A man who is nice and friendly. A man who reminds me too much of Preston.

Can I really let them kill him tonight?

Like I have a choice.

But maybe I do. Maybe I can find a way to convince them not to kill him. That whatever they have against him is wrong.

Maybe I can find a way to save him, and in turn, save both of the men in this car.

12

BEAST

"I'm hungry. Can we get something for dinner?" Scarlett says.

"No," I say.

She frowns, crossing her arms, as she sits on the other end of the couch, away from me. She doesn't let my *no* faze her though. She leans forward, and as she bites her lip, she begins crawling toward me on the couch. When she reaches me, she grabs my chin and forces my lips to touch hers. Any other time, I would be happy to kiss her. Any other time, I would give her exactly what she wanted. Sex. Distraction. Passion.

Right now though, I can't give her any of those things. Because, right now, she's not asking for those things because she wants them. She's asking to try to distract me. She's asking because she thinks, if eight o'clock comes and goes, she can save Marcel. She thinks she'd be doing the world a favor by saving him, and in turn, she'd be saving me. But she can't do either. She can't save anyone. I'm not even sure if she can save herself at this point.

I push her back, stopping the kiss, and stand up. She frowns and huffs as her arms go back across her chest. She is frustrated, and I understand, but she chose to be in this life. She chose to be in my world, and my world involves doing a lot of things that you don't want to do to other people. In my world, sex and food and pleasure come after work.

"When are we going to have dinner? I'm starving," Scarlett says.

"Later," I say.

"I'm hungry now though." She gets up off the couch and heads over to the kitchen where her purse is sitting. She pulls out her phone and begins typing something in. "I'll order some pizzas," she says, lifting the phone to her ear.

I shake my head as I storm over to her and grab her phone out of her hand.

"Give it back," she says, reaching to grab the phone back out of my hand.

"No."

"Give it back; it's mine. And I'm hungry. I'm going to order a pizza."

She reaches for her phone again, and that's when I realize that she thinks she has any sort of control over the situation. She doesn't. She has no control. I thought I had taught her that. I thought I had taught her that she wasn't the one in control anymore. That I am. She still hasn't learned that yet though.

I drop her phone on the floor and immediately step on it, ensuring that it is shattered and unusable.

Her face drops as she looks at her shattered phone on the floor. She slowly brings her eyes back up to my face, and I see the pain and hatred in her eyes. Pain that isn't there because of a broken phone.

"I hate you."

I can't help but let my lips curl up into a smirk. She's acting like a teenager whose parents just took her phone and told her she couldn't go out tonight. She's not acting like the strong, sexy woman I know.

"This isn't funny. You just destroyed my phone without any reason. Give me your phone."

"No."

Her eyes narrow at me. She's trying to do her best to seem angry, but all I see is fear.

"I know what you're doing," I say.

"You don't have a clue as to what I'm doing."

I take a step toward her. "I know exactly what you're doing because I did it before. I stalled, trying to find anything else to do but the one thing I was supposed to be doing."

"No." She shakes her head.

"I did it when I was supposed to kill Kinsley. I stalled. I didn't want to kill her because I didn't want to hurt you. So, I stalled. But, in the end, I still had to go and try to kill her. Just like, right now, you're going to have to help me get Marcel into our car, so we can kill him. He needs to die."

"No. You're wrong. He doesn't deserve to die."

I sigh. I reach into my back pocket and pull out my phone. I pull up the images that I didn't want to show her, but she needs to know about them if she's going to be able to make it through tonight. I hand her the phone, and that's when she sees Marcel with boys. Boys too young to be doing what he's doing to them in the pictures. I watch the tears slide out of her eyes as she sees someone she thought was a good person doing some of the most horrible things.

"Marcel isn't a good person, Scarlett. He deserves to die, and I'm not going to wait any longer for you to get on board. You either do this with us, or you leave. This is my life. You are the one who chose to come. So, get on board, or go home."

Scarlett continues to stare at the pictures of Marcel. I don't include the part about why we are actually killing him. It has nothing to do with what he's doing to the boys in the pictures. In fact, the boys were probably supplied by my organization in the past. Marcel has to die because he's a snitch. He has to die because he's told too many things about our organization to other people. He has to die because he's no longer trustworthy. We no longer believe that he wouldn't turn us into the police at any chance he got.

Scarlett hands me back the phone with a look of disgust on her face. "I'm in."

I smile as I take the phone back and put it back into my back pocket. "Good. And, Scarlett, don't play games with me, trying to get me to do what you want me to do."

She nods although I'm not sure she will listen to me. I'm pretty sure she will do the opposite of listening to me at every step.

"Ready?" Santino says, walking into the living room.

I raise my eyebrows at Scarlett for her answer.

She just nods solemnly.

"We're ready," I say.

"Good. Let's go. We wouldn't want to be late. And I'm starving. I'll be hungry after this is over. We should pick up a pizza or something on the way home," Santino says.

Scarlett and I both nod.

Santino's eyes look from me to Scarlett, trying to understand what happened while he was napping upstairs. When he can't figure it out, he doesn't bother asking. He just walks outside, toward my car that is parked in the driveway.

I motion for Scarlett to follow. She grabs her purse and eyes her broken phone lying on the floor before she follows Santino outside. I pick up the broken cell phone and put it in my pocket. I follow behind, not bothering to lock the door to the house. We won't be coming back here anyway. It won't be safe after we kill Marcel. Santino already put our bags in the back of my car. There is nothing left of us here. Nothing to tie us to this house or this place.

Santino is in the driver's seat, and Scarlett is sitting in the backseat. I climb into the backseat, next to Scarlett, and watch her raise her eyebrows at me in surprise because I'm sitting next to her and not next to my brother in the front.

Santino begins driving in silence, heading toward the pizza joint where Scarlett is supposed to meet Marcel. I reach over and grab her hand, and she lets me. Her hand is shaking and sweaty with nerves. And there is nothing I can do to calm her. Nothing I can say or do will make her feel better. And I know, in a few minutes, she won't even let me hold her hand anymore. She won't let me touch her or comfort her. Not with hands that she has seen killing another person.

I've already ordered a car to be on standby and drive her back to her apartment because I don't think she will want anything to do with me after tonight. These next few minutes are the last time she will see me as anything other than a killer. After she sees what I'm about to do, she won't be able to get the vision of Marcel dying by my hands out of her head. Not when I'm talking to her or kissing her or fucking her. It will always be there. Just as clearly as she has been in my head when I saw her the first time. She doesn't know it, but she saved Kinsley from her grandfather. It wasn't me. It wasn't from the goodness of my heart that I put a bullet in Lee Felton, the man whom I had worked with for years, instead of Kinsley, a woman I barely knew. I protected Kinsley because, the second I saw Scarlett on the television in such pain over losing her best friend, I knew I couldn't make it real. I knew I couldn't take someone so loved away from this beautiful, courageous woman who was on the television, making sure that Kinsley would be remembered. Making sure that the police would go after the people who had supposedly killed Kinsley.

I will never get that beautiful image of Scarlett out of my head. When I looked at her on that television, I saw sex, fire, and love. I saw everything I wanted. I saw someone who might have a chance to save me, too.

Now, sitting here, next to her, I know that nobody can save me. I've sinned too many times. I can't be saved. I've already sealed my fate. I know how my story ends.

I glance at her. I watch her take a deep breath and then another, trying to calm herself. Trying to force herself to fit into my world. She doesn't and never will. And I already know how her story ends as well. Without me.

"Pull over here," I say to Santino when we are about two blocks from the pizza place.

I tuck a loose strand of Scarlett's hair behind her ear. This is the last time she will be able to look at me with any sort of innocence in her eyes. This is the last time she will look at me with any sort of love

319

in her eyes. So, I relish the moment and burn it into my memory forever.

"When we get there, all you have to do is get Marcel into the back of this car with you. We will take it from there. Understand?"

Scarlett nods.

"You can do this. Just keep the images I showed you earlier in your mind."

"You showed—" Santino starts to say.

But I glare at him, and he stops speaking. I know I shouldn't have shown her the images of Marcel, but it was necessary to get her to do what she had to do. If Santino is going to test her, I can at least make it easier on her by letting her see how horrible of a person Marcel is.

I turn my attention back to Scarlett. "You got this," I say, squeezing her hand.

She nods, but doesn't smile. Her hand is still a little shaky.

Santino begins driving us the final two blocks and then stops again in front of the pizza joint.

Scarlett reaches for the door and begins to climb out.

I slowly start to let go of her soft hand. When all I have left in my grasp are those fingers with the beautiful French-tipped manicured nails, I say, "I'm sorry."

Scarlett stops for a second and glances back at me. "I love you."

My heart rips at her words. Words I already knew she felt, but I don't deserve them. Words she will take back in just a few minutes from now.

I shake my head. "You don't. You just think you do because you don't know me yet. You'll realize you are wrong soon enough."

She shakes her head in disappointment. "I guess we will see."

I nod as I let go of her hand, and I watch the woman I love walk into the pizza place to bring back a man whom I will kill. And, with that, I'll destroy any chance of us being together.

13

SCARLETT

I TOLD him I loved him, and he said I didn't. That's all I think about as I walk toward the bar again. It should bother me more that he didn't say *I love you* back. If I had said that in a past relationship and the guy hadn't said it back, I would have been upset. I would have dumped his ass. Not that I have said *I love you* much in the past.

Nacio not saying it back doesn't bother me though. I know how he feels, and I know he says *I love you* even less than I do. If I had to guess, he might not have ever said that phrase to anyone. Not even his brother.

What bothers me is that he thinks I don't love him. After everything I have done to be with him, he still doesn't think it's possible. Yes, I don't know everything there is to know about him yet. But that doesn't change how I feel. And I don't think much could change how I feel. Even watching him kill a pedophile.

I scan the bar, looking for Marcel, trying not to think about Nacio. I need to focus if I'm going to be able to remain calm while I lead a man to his death. I don't see Marcel anywhere. I don't have a phone anymore, thanks to Nacio, and I don't wear a watch, so I have no idea what time it is or if Marcel is running late or not.

The bar is fuller than it was at lunch, but I find a seat at the end that has a good view of the door.

A different bartender comes over and asks if I want a drink. I order a gin and tonic because I know I'm going to need a strong drink to get me through tonight. The bartender quickly makes my drink, and then I wait. There is nothing else to do but wait. I don't have a phone. I don't have a way to contact Nacio. I don't have anything but my drink to entertain me while I wait.

So, I wait and drink and wait some more. I wait so long that I have finished two drinks. I wait long enough that I don't want to have another drink in this bar. I just want to go and get this over with. My glass is half full, but it doesn't stop me from finishing the drink in one shot. When I spot Marcel, I place the glass down and pull out some cash that more than covers my drinks.

I stand and walk over to Marcel before he can make his way to the bar.

"Sorry I'm a bit late. I had some work things I had to finish up."

I smile at him and notice that his fly is undone, his hair is much messier than before, and his face is flushed. He wasn't working. He was having sex...possibly with boys. I try to keep the smile on my face instead of the look of disgust I want to give him.

"It's not a problem. I got a couple of drinks while I was waiting. I'm ready to try a new bar though. My driver is waiting right outside if you are ready to go."

He smiles back. "Sure. Let's go hit up the town."

He holds out his arm for me, like a gentleman, and I take it. He's no gentleman though, even as much as he pretends to be. He is a disgusting, vile man who deserves to die. He deserves to be tortured and beaten first. I'm not sure what Nacio's plans are for killing this bastard, but I hope it is long and drawn-out. He doesn't deserve to have a quick, swift death.

He holds the door open for me, and I let go of his arm as I walk outside. I see Nacio's Mercedes parked on the corner in the same spot I left it in. When Santino sees me, he gets out of the car and makes his way over to the passenger side where he opens the back door for us.

"Good evening, Miss Bell," Santino says, like he is a professional driver who does this every night.

I smile at him. "This is my friend Marcel. He can tell you the best bar in town to get a drink from."

Santino nods and smiles. Then, he holds out his hand to me to help me climb into the car. My hand is no longer shaky as I take Santino's hand and climb in. Nacio is no longer sitting in the backseat. I glance in the front seat, but he's not there either. I try to glance around the block to look for him, but I don't see him anywhere.

Maybe he changed his mind about killing Marcel?

I try to figure out how I feel about that if it's the truth, but I can't figure it out. On one hand, I want Nacio to kill Marcel. Marcel deserves to die for what he did to those boys. On the other hand, I want Nacio to stop killing. I want him to find a different life. I never thought I would be so torn about Nacio killing someone.

"Sir," Santino says to Marcel.

Marcel climbs into the car, sitting next to me. "Nice ride," he says.

I smile. "Thanks. I like it. It serves its purpose."

I watch as Santino walks around to the driver's side while I sit in confusion. I have no idea what is going to happen now. I have no idea what the plan is.

Is Santino going to be the one who kills Marcel? Is he going to do a suicide mission and crash this car into a tree or something, killing all of us?

Thoughts like this keep racing through my head until, suddenly, the door next to Marcel is thrown open, and Nacio shoves Marcel into the middle of the seat before he climbs in next to him. Santino immediately steps on the gas.

"What the hell?" Marcel curses before he sees Nacio. "You bastard! What do you want?"

Nacio glares at Marcel as Santino continues driving, unfazed by what is happening in the backseat. "You didn't follow the rules, Marcel."

"Nobody follows the rules. That's why we are all in this business. None of us follow the fucking rules!" Marcel says.

Nacio shakes his head. "No, we all follow the rules. That's how we stay in this business without getting caught. When you don't follow the rules, there are consequences."

As Nacio says that, I don't see Marcel's eyes, but I can feel the panic oozing off him as he realizes that he fucked up.

Marcel turns to me. "You bitch."

He immediately begins climbing over me, trying to get out of the car. He elbows me in the boob as he tries to reach over me to grab the door.

"Ow," I say as I grab the tender spot he just hit. I don't try to stop him from climbing out of the car though. I don't want any more involvement now that he is in the car and about to die.

"You're not going anywhere," Nacio says calmly.

For some reason, Marcel freezes.

"Sit back down," Nacio says calmly.

I watch in surprise as Marcel sits back down, and that's when I see the gun that Nacio is holding in his hand, pressed against Marcel's temple.

"What do you want?" Marcel asks, his voice shaky.

"I want you to pay the consequences for your actions."

"Please...I'll do anything. I'll give you more money. I'll work for you. I'll do anything. I don't want to die."

I see a smirk form on Nacio's face.

"We don't need your money. And we sure as hell don't want a snitch like you working for us."

"Please," Marcel says, his voice shaky, with his eyes closed, like he is afraid Nacio is going to shoot his brains out at any second.

I freeze because, from the look of intensity in Nacio's eyes, I'm pretty sure he is going to shoot Marcel in the head and blow his brains out at any second. And I'm not sure how I feel about Nacio killing Marcel with me sitting in the next seat. I guess I thought Nacio would take him somewhere else before shooting him. I guess I thought I could be as far away as possible when Nacio killed him, not sitting in the seat next to him, watching the life drain from his eyes.

"I don't want to die..."

"Then, you should have thought of that before," Nacio says.

He looks at me, and I know this is it. It's happening now. He's warning me to brace myself, and then his eyes turn dark.

I try to close my eyes because I don't want to see it happen. I don't want to see Nacio shoot Marcel. I don't want to see the blood or Marcel going limp. But, for some reason, my eyes won't close. My body won't move to cover them either. I'm frozen. I'm not breathing. I'm not even sure my heart is beating.

Nacio doesn't fire the gun though. Instead, he grabs something else from his pocket with his other hand. Marcel doesn't see it though. His eyes are closed as his body shakes fiercely next to me. My instinct is to reach out and hold him. Calm him down. But he deserves this, and there is no way to calm a man who knows he's about to die.

I don't see what is in Nacio's hand until he uses it. Marcel yells out in pain from the sharp injection of a needle being thrust into the crook of his arm. I watch Nacio push the liquid into the arm as Marcel squirms, trying to get him off, but he can't. Nacio was too fast.

"What was that? What the fuck did you just do to me?" Marcel asks.

Nacio keeps the gun on Marcel. "I injected you with heroin. An amount that should invoke an overdose strong enough to kill you. But you never know. People have survived worse. Maybe you'll survive."

Marcel turns to me. "Call 911 now! Call right the fuck now! Tell them what this bastard did to me! Save me! Please!"

Frozen, I stare at Marcel. Somehow, I'm able to get the truthful words out of my mouth. "I don't have a phone."

Marcel begins digging in his pockets, trying to find his phone. Nacio doesn't seem to care about what he is doing. He just studies Marcel, watching the heroin slowly begin to take its hold on him.

Marcel's face slowly becomes pale. He tries to speak, but his words don't come out. Marcel's body slowly becomes calm, limp. Until all that is left is for his heart to stop beating or his lungs to stop breathing. I know, from the look on his face, it won't be longer than a few minutes.

Santino continues to drive, unfazed by what has been happening in the backseat.

I look back to Marcel. He won't survive this. The amount that Nacio gave him is too much for anyone to survive. Nacio made sure of that. Marcel is going to die, and if we don't get to wherever we are going soon, he's going to die with me sitting right next to him.

I try to force my eyes to look out the window, but I can't. I watch as Marcel slumps further back in his seat. I watch his chest slowly rise and fall. I have no idea how much time has passed. I have no idea if it's been seconds or minutes or hours. All I know is, Marcel's breath becomes further and further spaced out.

I'm able to slowly tear my eyes from his almost lifeless body until a gurgling sound forces my eyes back to him. It's a horrible sound. A sound I will never forget. It's a painful sound. A sound of death.

I don't know why, but I reach out and take Marcel's hand in mine. I hold it while he tries to take another breath that sounds worse than the first. It's his last breath. After that, he's gone.

14

BEAST

I WATCH Scarlett hold the bastard's hand, and I know I've lost her. I know that, the second she felt any sympathy for him, she wouldn't ever forgive me for what I'd done. She'll want to leave as soon as I tell her it's okay. I'll never see her again.

I try not to think about that yet. I still have a job to finish. And, until it's over, I can't deal with her.

Santino continues to drive without speaking to any of us. He doesn't even so much as glance in his rearview mirror. Not after he found out that I had told Scarlett what Marcel really was. He probably thinks I messed up by showing her too much. And that this isn't really a test to see if she is cut out for this life since she thinks he isn't innocent. He's right, of course. But I don't think she will be okay even with killing someone she thinks should die.

Scarlett doesn't look at me after Marcel is gone. She holds his hand for a moment longer and then lets go. She spends the rest of the drive staring out the window. I'm surprised she didn't throw up. Or cry. Or do something when she watched him die. I guess she was in shock. She probably still is, and that's why she hasn't done any of those things yet.

Santino pulls up to a car and parks right next to it, just like we planned. He hops out of the car and scans to see if anyone is watching us. I climb out of the car. I don't bother telling Scarlett what we are doing. She will figure it out soon enough.

Santino nods at me, signaling that the coast is clear. I dig through Marcel's pockets and find his car keys to his red Toyota Prius. I unlock the car, and Santino opens the door. I scoop Marcel up under his arms and drag his lifeless body out of the back of my Mercedes. I try to be careful not to damage his body in any way that might give away that someone else was involved. Not that it really matters. The police aren't going to catch us. Not for this.

His feet make a thud when I pull him out of the car.

Santino winces at the sound and then glares at me. "Careful with his body, man."

I roll my eyes. I've killed hundreds of times before. I know how not to get caught. We aren't going to get caught for killing a pedophile. Not after the police find out what he is.

Santino helps me get Marcel's body into the front seat of his car. I put the car key in the ignition and the syringe on his lap. From my pocket, I pull out the photos of him and the boys, and I scatter them in the front seat of the car, like he was looking at them when he shot up. The police will think it was an overdose, and after they see the pictures, they won't do any more investigation into how he died. They will instead turn their attention to finding the boys. Not that they will have any luck with that either, but that's not really my concern.

I close the door to his car and then climb back into the backseat of the Mercedes. Santino speeds off when I shut the door.

"So, you gonna tell her she can bail whenever, or do I have to do everything in this family?" Santino asks after a few minutes have passed and none of us have said a word.

"Bail?" Scarlett asks.

I take a deep breath and then let it out. "Yes. I've already arranged for a driver to take you wherever you want, no questions asked, if you want to leave. I promise, I won't follow you, if that's what you want. I won't talk to you again. You can just go."

"Why would I want to go?"

"Because I'm a monster, and you don't want anything to do with me. I just killed someone."

"Yes. I knew what I was getting into. I knew who he was. I knew he was a monster. He deserved to die. If I couldn't handle it, I wouldn't have come with you. I wouldn't be here. I would already be gone. I don't have to ask for permission to leave. I'd just be gone. I don't care that you killed Marcel or anyone else. I still love you, Nacio."

My eyes widen at her words, but I don't believe them. I don't believe her because, when she spoke, her voice shook just the slightest bit. Her cheeks are still pale, and her hands are fidgeting in her lap. She's still in shock. That's the only reason she's not running for the hills yet.

"You sure, Beauty? Because, once I get on the interstate, this car isn't stopping until we hit Chicago," Santino says.

"What? We aren't going back to the house?"

"No," I answer.

"Are we seriously not stopping until Chicago? Because that's, like, a million hours away," Scarlett asks.

"I guess I'll stop once for you, Beauty. But only because I'm in shock that you don't want to run for the hills after Nacio killed that guy. So, I guess we can spend the night in Ohio," Santino says.

I roll my eyes. "It was always the plan to spend the night in Ohio. No way were you going to drive for twelve hours straight."

"You're right. I was going to make you drive ten of them while Beauty and I slept in the backseat," Santino says.

I growl, "Stop calling her Beauty."

My idiot brother just smiles. He's going to regret it. At some point, he's going to have a woman he cares about, and I'm going to make him pay for teasing me about Scarlett. I'm not even going to be able to call her Beauty again without thinking about him. *Bastard.*

Scarlett yawns.

"But I think we are going to take your idea and nap until we get to

Ohio. If you get lost, Google it," I say as I stretch my arms and then lean back.

I want to grab Scarlett and wrap her in my arms. But I can't. I know she doesn't want my hands anywhere near her. Not after I killed Marcel.

I close my eyes and try to get my head comfortable on the headrest. I suck in a breath though when I feel her head lying down on my chest. My eyes open the tiniest bit as my hands go up in the air, not sure what to do.

How could she want to be near me right now? I don't even want to be near me right now.

Her hand immediately goes to my chest, and I feel her take some deep breaths of her own.

"I love you," she whispers. "You can believe me."

I don't answer her because, even if she does love me, I don't deserve it. No one should love me. Not even my own family.

I gently put my arms around her anyway. Later, I'll have to convince her that she doesn't love me. Because she can't. It's not possible. I haven't done anything to deserve love. I haven't done the things boyfriends are supposed to do. I haven't bought her flowers or candies or whatever shit women like men to bring them. I haven't taken her on a date. I haven't bought her jewelry or an expensive car. *How could she love me?*

In the rearview mirror, Santino makes eye contact with me. "Don't get attached. A beauty like her won't stick around for long," he says.

I don't argue with him. Because I agree.

We get to the hotel, and Santino gets us two rooms. The problem is, I have no idea what I should do now. Scarlett is asleep in the car, and I have no idea what she wants. *Does she want me to sleep with her tonight or not? Should I sleep in Santino's room?*

Santino grabs our bags, and I scoop Scarlett up in my arms. She doesn't stir. I follow Santino into the hotel and down the hallway to where our two rooms are. When we get to the first room, Santino opens the door and walks inside. I gently place Scarlett on the bed. Santino drops off two bags and then turns to leave. I begin to follow him.

"You aren't sleeping with me, man. Figure this shit out with her before we get to Chicago. If you don't, you know she is going to be pissed. So, figure out where the two of you stand before the morning. And, I swear, if I hear any sex coming from this room, I'm going to leave your ass here, and you can find your own way to Chicago," Santino says.

I smile and watch my brother leave.

He lets the door slam on his way out.

"Where are we?" Scarlett asks. She must have woken either from our conversation or the door being slammed.

"Ohio."

She nods and rubs her eyes, trying to wake up.

"Are you hungry?" I ask.

We stopped for dinner a couple of hours ago, but I don't know what else to ask.

"No."

I nod and place my hands in my pockets as I stand as far away from Scarlett as possible in the small hotel room.

She smirks at me. "What are you doing?"

"Standing."

"I can see that. Why aren't you being all bossy and controlling, like you usually are? Why aren't you telling me how you are going to do me and what I'm going to do? Why aren't you being my Beast?"

"I guess I'm not in the mood tonight."

Her smirk widens. "I think you're scared."

"What?"

She gets up off the bed and walks toward me. "You're scared shit-less that I'm going to leave. That's why you won't say you love me."

I shake my head.

"Admit it then. You love me."

"No."

"Admit that I love you then."

"No."

She walks closer until we are looking at each other, face-to-face.

"Admit that you are scared. That something happened in your past that made you feel unworthy of love. That made you think you can't love anyone else ever again. That love isn't worth it. Tell me what it is."

"No!"

"Admit that—"

I don't let her finish that sentence. She doesn't get to finish that sentence. She doesn't get to ask questions like that anymore. She doesn't get to ask about my past. She doesn't get to ask about my feelings. If she wants the Beast, she's going to get him. I'm done with giving her time to figure out how to deal with me being a killer. I'm done with waiting for her to get over her shock at watching a man die. I want her, so I will have her.

My lips devour her, shutting her up. She stumbles backward as I attack her with my lips, my hands. My hand goes to the small of her back, preventing her from falling backward, as her hands find the base of my neck, holding on for dear life. I push us backward, toward the hotel bed, until we are falling in a pile on the bed.

I haven't thought about how I want to take her. I haven't thought about what position I want her perfect body in or what I want her to do. I just know I need control, and I need it now. I just know I need her.

I kiss her hard and aggressively as I lie on top of her, crushing her body. Her hands crush around my neck as she tightly holds me to her body. Both of us are begging for control, and neither of us is willing to give it to the other.

My hand slides down her body. I need her clothes off. Need to feel her smooth skin against mine. I grab at her tank top, planning on ripping it in half, but when I try to move off her body so that I can rip her clothes off, her hands firmly hold me in place. Her lips keep me on her lips. I'm not able to let go long enough to get her clothes off. I could force her arms off of me. I could force her to do whatever I wanted to do. But that's not what I want. I want her to give up her control to me.

"Let go, Beauty," I say between kisses.

Her hands tangle in my hair. "I can't."

"I'm not asking. Let go."

I feel her grip on me tighten.

"Fine," I growl.

I flip us over so that she is on top, and I'm underneath her. My hands are now free to do as I please. I grab her shirt and rip it in half. I grin when I see her naked chest. She never wears a bra or underwear. I'm rewarded with an instant view of her plump breasts and hard nipples, showing me how much she wants me. I sit up so that she is sitting on my lap, and I take one of her nipples in my mouth. I bite harder than I was planning to, but this woman drives me mad. She deserves to feel a little of the pain I feel anytime I'm around her. Pain at knowing that, whatever the hell this is, it won't last. It can't.

She screams when I bite down on her nipple. I smirk. Santino definitely heard that.

She grabs my hair hard and rips my face from her breast. I lock in on her deviant eyes, so I don't even see it coming until I feel the sting on my face from her hand slapping me. My face turns from a smirk to an intense glare.

I grab her hand when she tries to hit me again.

"Don't," I say.

She stops as her chest rises up and down with each heavy breath.

"Don't hurt me," she says.

"I didn't. That wasn't pain. Not real pain. And I know, from the way your nipples hardened when I bit down, that you liked it, so don't act like you didn't."

"I didn't," she says, but her cheeks flush bright red.

She's lying. She just doesn't want to let me know that she enjoys the pain.

"Don't lie," I say. I grab her body and bite down on her other nipple equally as hard as I did the first.

She cries out again, but this time, she can't hide the pleasure. She loves it. And I want to show her more. More of everything. Pain. Pleasure. Everything.

When I let her go, she grabs my shirt and rips it in half. I growl. I need her hands where they can't touch me. I need her hands tied up and unusable, so she can't keep trying to take over. I quickly look around the room to find something to tie her hands together, but I can't find anything. Or my brain can't focus on anything but having her, so it can't come up with a simple solution to tie her up.

"On all fours," I say, knowing that it would at least make it more difficult for her to use her hands.

"No."

I want to flip her over and force her onto all fours. I resist the urge, only because I have eviler things in mind. If she thought the last time I fucked her was torture, she has another thing coming.

"I won't ask again. On all fours, Beauty, or be prepared to be tortured far worse than the last time I fucked you."

She bites her lip, and I can see her making the decision in her head. I can see her deciding if she should just give up control to me. How much easier it would be if she did and how much more pleasurable it would be for her. And then I see the spark in her eyes when she decides she won't do it. She won't give up control to me.

"Make love to me," she says.

I freeze. This is what this is about. This is why she won't give up control to me. She doesn't want to be fucked. She wants me to make love to her. I don't do that. I take control. I fuck. I punish. I don't make love.

"No."

She takes a deep breath, like she was expecting it, and grabs my chin, trying to get me to look into her eyes, like that will convince me to make love to her.

"No," I say again more firmly, more final.

Her eyes search mine, trying to figure out why I won't. Why I

334

won't give her what she wants. The last time we fucked, it felt like a lot more than just a fuck. If I'm being honest, every time with her feels like a lot more than just a fuck. But I can't consciously decide to do that. I can't give her that.

I let her go and get up from the bed.

"What are you doing?" she asks.

"I'm leaving."

"What? Why?"

I find my bag sitting on the floor next to the bed. I throw the bag open, searching for a shirt to wear since the one I'm wearing is ripped.

She gets up off the bed and walks over to me. "I'm sorry. I'll drop it. Just fuck me. Don't leave."

I can't stay though. If I fuck her, I know she will try to get me to make love to her. I know that's what she will be thinking in the back of her head. I can't. I can't make love to her. I can't love her. This whole thing was a mistake. All of it. I just have to get out of here.

I don't answer her. I just grab a T-shirt from my bag and walk out the door of the hotel room. I hear the door slam shut as I walk down the hallway, and I expect her to come running out. But she's not the type of woman to beg me to come back. She's the type to demand what she wants, and when she doesn't get it, she fights. I can expect a fight when I get back.

Right now, I don't care. I just have to get out of here. So, I keep walking until I get to my car, and then I climb in and drive as far away from her as possible.

15

SCARLETT

THIS IS why I don't date. This is why I sure as hell don't fall in love. Men are stupid. Idiots. They make you fall for them, and then they tear out your heart the next second because they can't figure out how to love you back.

The second Nacio walked out that door, I should have bought a flight out of here. I should have bought a flight to take me to a beach somewhere that could make me forget about him. I didn't though. Instead, I'm holding out hope that there is a chance he will come back.

I thought, if I pushed him, he would realize he loved me. That he would share something about his past that made him the way he was. That made him enjoy killing people. Because he does. He enjoys it. I saw it in his eyes when he thrust that needle into Marcel's arm. Nacio loves killing. And I think he loves me. He looks at me with the same intensity he did when he killed Marcel. He just won't admit it.

And, for some crazy reason, I want him to admit it. I should be running for the hills. I should be running from this life. From this dangerous man. Our lives will never fit together. I'm all about beauty, fashion, and superficial things that make others feel good. He's about ending others' lives.

How could we ever fit together?

Our nicknames for each other, those characters end up together in the fairy tales. Beauty and Beast end up together. They save each other.

But that doesn't happen in real life, does it?

I sigh. *What the hell am I doing here?* I love him, but it's not enough for Beauty to love the Beast if he can never love her back.

I wait all night for Nacio to come back, but he never does. So, when the sun comes up, I decide it's time to stop pretending that this could work. I fought for him. I went to jail to get him to be with me. I helped him kill a man. *What has he done for me? Nothing.*

I grab my bag that is lying on the floor and head to the bathroom. I don't bother showering. I just brush my hair into a ponytail and then brush my teeth. I hear a knock at the door, and I freeze. *Did he come back?* I'm not sure how I feel about that. I'm not sure what I'm supposed to do with that.

I spit out the toothpaste and rinse my toothbrush before setting it next to the sink. I walk to the door. I hesitate for a second and then open it without looking through the peephole first.

Santino is standing in the hallway with a smirk on his face. "I would ask how you slept, but from the screams I heard coming from the room last night, I would have to guess that you didn't sleep much."

I frown. "Nothing happened. Your idiot brother took off before he could fuck me. You wouldn't be able to help a girl out, would ya?" I ask. I don't know what I'm doing. I don't really want Nacio's brother to fuck me. I just want to get back at Nacio for leaving me high and dry last night. No, for leaving me wet and unsatisfied last night.

Santino smirks. "I know. Bastard took the car and took off. He's already in Chicago."

My eyes widen. He drove all night to Chicago. That's how badly he had to get away from me.

"Great. So, what the fuck are we supposed to do?"

Santino smiles. "We fly. Or I could get you a flight back to New

York, if you prefer? But then you'd miss out on me kicking Nacio's butt for leaving us, and you'd miss out on meeting our sister."

"You have a sister?" I ask, surprised.

I've read hundreds of articles about Nacio. No sister was ever mentioned. His parents are both dead. The only family I thought Nacio had is standing in front of me.

I smile. There is no way I'm missing out on talking to her and spending some time with Santino. Maybe, between the two of them, they can help me understand Nacio better. Maybe I can finally get some answers.

I thought the flight to Chicago would give me answers. All I've ended up with so far are more questions. From the limited time I have been around him, Santino seems like the more talkative, fun, outgoing of the two brothers. But get him on a plane, and I realize now why we were driving instead of flying in the first place.

"Santino, you have to calm down. How about I order you a drink? What do you want?"

Santino wipes the sweat from his brow for the hundredth time since we took off twenty minutes ago. He's breathing so hard and loud that everyone on the plane is looking at us, trying to figure out what is wrong with him. I'm still trying to figure it out as well. A grown man is holding my hand so firmly, I'm afraid he's broken some bones. I've never seen someone so terrified of flying.

The flight attendant begins walking down the aisle, and I stop her. I don't care if it's not time to serve drinks yet. One or each of us needs a drink now if we are going to survive this flight.

"Ma'am, I'm sorry. My friend here is very nervous about flying. Would you mind getting him a whiskey or something to try and calm his nerves?"

The woman smiles like she probably does to children who are flying for the first time.

"Of course. It doesn't matter when the first flight happens; it is always a bit scary. Can I get you anything?"

"A gin and tonic would be great. And an ice pack for my hand."

The woman laughs and nods before leaving to get our drinks, but I wasn't joking about the ice pack. My hand is in a lot of pain from the way Santino is squeezing it.

"How about you talk to me about something to distract yourself? Where did you and Nacio grow up?"

Santino shakes his head back and forth. "Can't..." He huffs air in and out. "Talk..." More air is forced in and out of his body.

We hit a bump of turbulence, and Santino's grip on my hand becomes unbearable.

"Fuck," I let out, despite children being near us. This time, I heard some bones crushing when he squeezed my hand.

The plane levels off, and Santino only slightly loosens his grip on my hand.

Sorry, I mouth to the woman across the aisle who has a young child sitting next to her.

She just smiles at me and laughs at my situation.

"How about I tell you about myself and see if that distracts you?"

Santino doesn't say anything, so I just start talking. If anything, maybe it will distract myself from the pain in my hand.

"I grew up in Las Vegas. My parents didn't give two shits about me. Um...I went to Yale for college. I'm an only child, so I didn't have the pleasure of having a sibling. Since grade school, Kinsley has been my best friend. She went to Yale with me. We both majored in theater although I realized acting wasn't really what I wanted to do. I've done a lot of modeling. After I graduated and after everything that happened to Kinsley, I realized I wanted to start my own company. Life is too short, you know."

I look over at Santino. He is nodding along even though his grip hasn't loosened any, and his face is still pale and sweaty.

"So, I started my own company. Yes, I used my parents' money to start the company, but still, I'm the one who built it from the ground up. I paid them back all the money I'd borrowed and then some. I haven't spoken to them since."

I try to think of more interesting things about my life, but it's hard when all I'm thinking about is the pain caused by Santino's grip on me. Nacio must have really wanted to torture me if he put me on a plane with his brother, knowing that he would act like this.

"Um...I love to travel. I hate doing my hair and makeup, despite having my own beauty line. I hate mac and cheese. I know it's a weird thing to hate, but I do. I think it's because that was the only dish my mother ever made for me."

I take a deep breath when I see the flight attendant coming back with our drinks.

"I made you each a double," she says, winking at me.

"Oh my God! Thank you," I say, taking my drink from her. I take a long gulp that immediately makes me feel better.

The flight attendant hands Santino his drink, which he grabs ahold of with shaky hands. He takes a sip, but it doesn't have the same immediate calming effect that my drink gave me.

I sigh. "How much longer is the flight?"

"An hour," the flight attendant says. She smiles at me with an apology in her eyes.

"Thanks. Keep the drinks coming then, please," I say, holding up my drink.

"Of course," she says, smiling.

I sip on my drink for a while.

"How about you tell me something about you now, Santino? A funny story from your childhood? Your favorite food? Make fun of your brother? I bet you have lots of stories about Nacio."

"Can't...breathe..." Santino says.

I frown. He's not going to talk to me—at least, not on this flight. I finish the rest of my drink and then close my eyes, trying to get through the rest of the flight without crying.

341

When Santino and I walk out of the airport and onto the curb, Nacio is leaning against his Mercedes, like nothing happened.

"Why do you have an ice pack on your hand?" Nacio asks.

Santino and I both frown at Nacio, who looks at me with concern in his eyes.

"You can go to hell," I say.

I walk past Nacio and around to the back passenger door, and I climb in. I don't want to talk or see Nacio right now. I press the ice more firmly on my hand that is "just bruised," according to the EMT who checked it out at the airport. I'm getting a second opinion because, from the color and swelling and pain, I swear it has to be broken from Santino squeezing it so hard.

Nacio doesn't climb into the driver's seat, like I expected. Instead, he climbs in next to me.

"What happened? I need to know if you are okay. Answer me," Nacio says. His eyes are filled with frustration and concern at the same time.

"No, you don't get to ask that. You abandoned me last night instead of talking to me. You left me with your brother, who, I'm sure you know, is scared to death of flying. You left me when I told you I loved you. You don't get to demand that I answer any of your questions right now. Honestly, I don't even know why I'm here right now. I should be on a flight home instead of coming here to see you."

"Why are you here?" he asks solemnly.

I glance over at him. He looks like such a child, sitting there, like that. He looks so scared. I don't know what happened in his past to make him this way. But I plan on finding out. Then, I will convince him that he can love and deserves to be loved.

"Because I love you."

He shakes his head, like it can't be true.

I glance at the front where Santino is about to climb into the driver's seat.

"I wouldn't let him drive if I were you. I think his nerves are too shot."

Nacio frowns and stares at me for a second longer before he

climbs out of the backseat and walks around to the driver's seat. He climbs in while Santino climbs into the backseat, next to me.

"How long of a drive is it?" I ask Santino.

"An hour," Santino answers.

I yawn. Enough time to get a nap in.

"Come here," Santino says to me, holding out his arms. "It's the least I can do after the hell I just put you through."

I smile at Santino. At least one of the brothers is nice to me. I scoot to the middle of the seat and lean my head on Santino's chest. I keep the ice pack on my hand as his large hands go around me. One of his hands begins gently rubbing my back. I close my eyes. I could get used to this.

If only his brother were this considerate. If only he knew how to love.

Whatever screwed up Nacio didn't do the same to Santino. Although I do wonder if Santino's humor is his way of dealing with whatever happened in their past.

I push thoughts of whatever happened to them out of my head.

Instead, I dream of Nacio. I dream of him telling me he loved me. I dream of a white dress and getting married to him. I dream of having kids with him. Somehow, the images come quickly, but the man in the dream is a blur. As much as I want the man to be Nacio, it isn't. It's not clear who the man is.

All that is clear is, these are still things I want. Someone to love me. Someone to marry. And someone to have kids with.

I'm just not sure if Nacio can give me any of those things.

But, if he could just do the love part, would that be enough?

16

BEAST

I HATE WATCHING Scarlett out of my rearview mirror. I hate how easily she went to my brother when he invited her into his arms. I hate that she is okay with lying in anyone's arms other than mine. She's mine, but right now, watching her drift off to sleep in his arms, that statement couldn't feel less true.

"What happened to her hand?" I hiss through clenched teeth at Santino when I think she has drifted off to sleep enough that I won't wake her.

"Dude, you need to chill," Santino answers.

"Just answer me, goddamn it! What happened to her hand?"

Santino looks down at Scarlett. He strokes her long hair, and I about run the car off the road.

He looks back up at me with sadness in his eyes. "I hurt her."

I swerve, not expecting that answer. But I quickly realize how wrong that statement is and calm down. When I regain my control on the vehicle, I ask, "How? She wouldn't be lying in your lap like that if she thought you were to blame for hurting her."

"You know how horrible I am to fly with since my accident last year?"

"Yes," I say, needing him to get to the point quicker.

How could I forget how horrible he is to fly with? Ever since he was on a flight that crashed last year, he's been horrible to fly with. It's one of the reasons I took the car and hoped they would fly. I knew she wouldn't be able to get any answers out of him like she could if they had driven.

"She was holding my hand to try and keep me calm on the flight, and I guess I squeezed a little too hard..."

I clench my teeth together and tighten my grip on the wheel to try and prevent myself from climbing into the backseat and strangling him. This isn't his fault. This is my fault. I was the one who made them fly in the first place. I just didn't think he was bad enough that he would actually hurt her.

"How bad?"

"The EMT guy said it was just bruised, but..."

I glance at her hand that is lying across his stomach with an ice pack still strewed across it. It looks bad. Even from here, I can tell that it is swollen, red, and bruised. Thank God my sister is just as masterful with medical issues as she is with running a company. Otherwise, I would be headed straight for a hospital instead of to her place.

"Can you at least keep your hands off of her until we get there?"

Santino smirks. "No. Even though I hurt her hand, she still likes me a hell of a lot more than she likes you. I didn't abandon her after she told me she loved me."

I can feel my face burn a bright shade of red. "Mind your own fucking business, Santino."

His smirk widens. "She is my business. The second you decided to go after her, you made her part of our whole family's business. You brought her into our world. You can't just kick her out because you're bored with her."

"You think I'm bored with her?" I growl a little too loudly. I glance back in the rearview mirror again, but it seems that Scarlett is still asleep in his lap.

"No. I don't know how any man could get bored with her. I couldn't," Santino says, stroking her face again.

Fuck. I leave her alone with him for a few hours, and he has already fallen for her. I understand. She's easy to fall for. But she's mine, not his. And I really don't want to have to fight with my brother right now. Not when I have a lot more important shit to deal with at the moment.

I want to say more. I want to yell and scream and dump him out of the car on the side of the road for touching her. I don't though. Instead, I drop it.

Santino is easier to love than me. If she wants to be with him, then she should. I won't stop her, and I won't get mad at him for loving her when I can't. Someone should, and it might as well be my brother.

I pull up to my sister's house. It's not as nice as some of the other houses my family owns. But it still has its own charms that make it an impressive home. It's a large brick and stone house that has half a dozen or more bedrooms and even more bathrooms. It's an old Tudor-type house with green vines that climb up the side of the building, and a large old oak tree sits in front. The inside is even more impressive than the outside, and I can't wait for Scarlett to see it. If she loved the last house we stayed in, she's going to die when she sees the inside of this one. The only problem is, she is going to choose Santino to share her excitement about staying in such a gorgeous house, not me.

I frown. "We're here," I say as I slam on the brakes, parking in the long curved driveway.

It jolts Scarlett awake in the backseat. Santino pats her back, comforting her a bit, as she gets used to her new surroundings.

I can't stand to watch it anymore. I get out of my car, slamming the door. I can't watch her fall for him, and I know she will. Santino is the only one in my family who isn't completely broken. He's the only one who hasn't suffered real pain like the rest of us. I guess that's why he has a harder time with killing than the rest of us. It's probably why he still has a sense of humor. She'll fall for him if I give her the chance. And I will if that's what she wants. I just can't be around to watch it happen.

I walk into my sister's house, not bothering to wait to walk in with them. When I open the front door, I stop and stare for just a second at the entrance that always takes my breath away whenever I see it. It's got a split grand staircase and old-style chandelier that makes this room perfect. I don't stay long though, just long enough to take in its beauty again.

I walk quickly to the back patio where I know my sister is. It's her favorite spot in the house. It's where she drinks her afternoon coffee and prepares for the evening of work ahead. She's always been a night owl, so she prefers to work more in the evening than during the day.

I find her in her favorite chair, just where I expected her to be.

"Good afternoon, Reina," I say as I walk over to her and kiss her on the cheek.

She frowns at me as I take a seat in the chair next to her.

"Why didn't you tell me that you were bringing her here?" she asks, not bothering with hellos and getting straight to the point.

"I didn't think it was any of your business if I brought her here or not. It was my decision to make."

"No, it wasn't your decision to make. It was *my* decision. This is my company now. Not yours. You fucked it up when you didn't kill that girl like you were supposed to—again. You don't get to make decisions anymore without consulting me." She raises her eyebrows at me.

Reina drives me mad. I hate giving up control to anyone, but she's the only one I will accept giving up control to, and she knows it. She knows I will do whatever she wants if she asks. She knows I will do whatever I can to protect her.

I nod. "She won't stay long. Trust me, Reina. She's not meant for this life." I lean back in my chair, happy to be around my sister again. It's been too long since I've seen her.

Reina shakes her head. "We will see. In the meantime, I have another job for you while you're here. This one is going to take some planning. I'll discuss it with you later. Dinner tonight though?"

I hear the door to the patio open, and I know it's Scarlett and Santino. I can't stay and watch them together.

I stand and kiss my sister on the cheek again. "Yep, just the two of us, as always, Reina."

She smiles.

"Take a look at her hand, please," I say. Then, I leave. I can't stay.

17

SCARLETT

NACIO WON'T LOOK at me as he leaves the patio. He just walks away, and I won't keep going after him. If he wants to be a stubborn ass, then I'll let him be one. Instead, I turn my focus to the woman sitting on the patio.

She's striking. Beautiful. She has long almost jet-black hair, dark brown piercing eyes, and olive skin. She looks close to my age, but if I had to guess, she's a few years older. Her eyes give away at least the illusion of her being older. I don't have to ask who this woman is. It is clear she is Nacio and Santino's sister. They look too much alike not to be family.

"You must be the tramp Nacio decided to bring home. Or do you prefer my other brother?" she says with a wicked grin on her face.

"I'm here with Nacio. I didn't think a sister would be cruel enough to pin her two brothers against each other in a fight over a girl."

Her grin widens as she glances from me to Santino. "She's feisty. But, from the looks of her, I don't think she is cut out for a job here. You both know the rules. No one stays unless they work for us. I don't care who Nacio is fucking," she says.

"Reina, relax. She's already involved enough that she won't cause any trouble. And, if she can't stay here, she can stay at my house. You don't have control over every part of the world, as much as you think you do," Santino says.

Reina—the bitch has a name, I think.

I walk over and take a seat next to her. "I'll do whatever job you want me to do. I don't mind working for a strong woman who runs her own company," I say.

Reina studies me. "You that desperate for a job? From the looks of your expensive clothes and designer shoes, I would think you made plenty of money without needing a job here."

I smile. I like this woman, despite how she is treating me. I know she is just trying to protect her company. I would do the same thing if I were in her position.

"I would answer your question, but I'm sure you already know the answer. I'm sure you have already looked me up and know more about me than even Nacio does."

Reina smiles. "I do."

"Then, you know that I respect women who run their own companies. And you know the only reason I'm here is for Nacio. But I'll do whatever job you need me to do, so I can stay here."

"I don't know that you are here just for Nacio. You could also be here to get revenge for your friend. Kinsley, is it? After what my family did to her, I wouldn't be surprised if you were here for payback."

I narrow my eyes. "I guess I'll just have to prove that's not why I'm here then."

"I guess so. Let me see your hand."

I hold out my hand to her, and she studies it. She takes it in her hand and begins pushing on it.

"Ow," I say as I pull my hand back out of her grasp when she presses too hard.

"Nothing's broken. You'll be fine." She lowers the sunglasses that she had on the top of her head and then sits back in her chair.

The conversation is over.

I gently rub my hand, trying to get rid of the pain. It's going to take a lot more work than I thought to get this woman to open up to me about why Nacio is the way that he is. But I'm willing to try.

"Where did Nacio go?" I ask Santino, who is still standing, watching us.

He shrugs.

"Will you help me find him?"

Santino thinks for a moment. "How about I show you around the house instead? I can show you a much better time than that fool of a brother of mine can anyway."

I smile, but it's fake. I get up off the padded patio chair. "Show me the way."

Santino smiles. "As you can see, here is the backyard. Not much to look at. We have more expansive properties in other parts of the world, but for the location, this is a pretty big yard. I'll show you back inside where the house has its real charm."

I nod and follow Santino from the yard that looks plenty big enough to me. It is filled with large trees, paths, and a large patio. I agree that inside is much nicer though.

The inside of the house is beautiful. Crown molding, high ceilings, dark wood flooring. I can see a lot of custom work has obviously been done on the house as Santino walks me through the main floor that includes a kitchen, living room, formal dining room, a couple of great rooms, and half a dozen bathrooms. It's impressive, but my favorite room so far is the entryway. The grand split staircase is beautiful. If the house were mine, I would put a comfy chair in the center at the top of the two staircases and just sit there all day.

"Whose house is it?" I ask.

Santino stops at the base of the stairs. I can see him trying to figure out how to answer.

I raise my eyebrows with a smile on my face, trying to lighten the mood, so he'll give me an honest answer.

"It's an easy question. Shouldn't be that hard to answer." I walk past him, making sure to brush his shoulder. "I know you're attracted to me, but it shouldn't be this hard to answer a simple question, Santino. Don't turn into Nacio on me. He won't give me any answers."

I immediately regret flirting with Santino to get any answers out of him. The look he gives me is dangerous. I shouldn't flirt with someone who is into me when there is no chance of me wanting him back. I can't help it though. It's what I'm good at, and I need answers even if Nacio isn't the one who will give them to me.

"It belongs to Reina now."

"Now?" I take a step down the stairs, moving closer to him. I'm on the step just in front of him. Just out of reach but close enough that I could lean down and kiss him if I wanted.

"It used to belong to Nacio."

I narrow my eyes. "Did he sell it to her?"

"Not exactly." Santino darts his eyes from me to the ground.

I reach my hand out to his chin and lift it, so he's looking at me. I hate myself the entire time I do it. Santino has been nothing but nice to me. He doesn't deserve to be led on when there is no chance of more happening.

"What happened?" I ask, batting my eyelashes at him.

I watch him gulp as he looks at me.

"Nacio used to run the company. He took it over from our father and ran it with Kinsley's family. When Nacio fucked up and ended up in jail, he turned the company over to Reina. She's been running it since then, and she turned it into what it is now."

"Which is?"

"A company of hitmen. She got rid of the smuggling and all that shit. The number of people we employ is much smaller now. Only a few people need to be involved when we can get huge amounts of money to kill people."

"Why do you get paid so much?"

Santino shrugs. "Because Nacio is the best. Not only can he kill, but he can also make it seem like the person died in any fashion you want by any person you want. And Reina is good with people. She demands the highest price for Nacio or any of the other team member's services."

"And Nacio doesn't want to run the company again himself?"

"Beats me." Santino shakes his head. "Come on, you've gotten more answers out of me than you should have. Let's go do something more fun."

I see the hunger and need in Santino's eyes as he runs up the stairs.

Shit. I'm not fucking him, I think.

But I might have just done something really stupid to get answers that I probably would have eventually gotten anyway. I head up the stairs after Santino at a much more leisurely pace.

"This is your room," Santino says, pointing to a room. He doesn't stop though; he just keeps walking down the hallway. "I'll bring up your bag later."

"Thanks," I say as I peek my head in the room. I just get a glimpse, but it is a gorgeous large room, just like everything else in the house. I want to ask if it is also Nacio's room, but I don't. I'll find out later.

Santino continues to walk, so I continue to follow, despite the lump in my throat.

I don't know what I'm going to do. I can't have anyone else not speaking with me. Nacio won't talk to me. And it's clear Reina doesn't like or trust me yet. I can't handle Santino not being on my side as well.

Santino turns into a room, and I freeze just before the entrance, trying to figure out what the fuck I'm going to say or do to get out of this.

I could play sick? Pretend my hand hurts too much? Or just tell him the truth?

I take a deep breath and then step into the room that I assume is Santino's bedroom. I smile though when I see the room. There is a large pool table in the center. Along the walls are several other games —pinball, shuffleboard, air hockey.

"I told you that you'd have more fun with me than you would with my brother. I don't know what he's doing to you, but from the screams I heard coming from your hotel room the other night, he's not doing it right," Santino says, leaning on a pool stick.

I laugh. "You're probably right. You need to give him some tips, so he doesn't make me scream like that anymore."

"Will do. Now, come whip my ass at pool," he says.

I laugh again. "You suck at pool?"

"No. I just know better than to beat a woman at pool. You're always supposed to let them win."

I walk over and pick up a pool stick. "I do happen to be very good at pool. I've beaten many a men at too many bars to count. You're telling me, they all let me win, huh?"

"Yep. If they wanted to get laid, they let you win."

"Well, since you won't be getting laid either way, how about you play your best and try and beat me? Then, we will see who is the best."

Santino grins mischievously. "Deal."

18

BEAST

"READY TO GO?" I ask, knocking on Reina's office door.

She looks up from her desk. "Sure." She closes her computer and grabs her purse off the rack in the corner of her office.

I smile at the changes she has made to the office since it was mine. One is something so simple—a coat and purse rack. Not something I thought much about as a man, but it is something that Reina thought about. The same with the fresh flowers on the table and the curtains next to the windows. They are all things that she thought about.

"Where are you taking me?" she asks.

"Oh, I'm not paying. You're the boss. You're the one who makes all the money. I thought you were taking me to dinner," I say, teasing her.

She smiles. "I also know how much I pay you, and I pay you more than I make."

I grin widely. I know that's not the truth, but it's close enough. "Can't help it that I'm the best and I deserve the best."

"I don't know about the best, but you're goddamn expensive. I need to find some more young men who will do it for the love of it instead of the money."

"I don't think you are hurting too much for money, sis. But I'll take you to dinner. I was thinking Harry Caray's. That used to be one of your favorite steakhouses here, right? There is one within walking distance."

Her eyes light up, and I know I've picked right.

We walk to the front door, and I open it for her. She glances up the staircase where I can hear Scarlett and Santino yelling playfully with one another.

"Sure you don't want to invite her?" she asks.

"I'm sure."

She just nods and walks out the door. I pause for a second as the sound of them laughing together pierces my heart. It hurts that Scarlett enjoys spending time with him, but tonight isn't about her. Tonight is about reconnecting with my sister, whom I haven't seen in months.

We walk the couple of blocks to the restaurant in silence. That's the one thing I like about my sister. Neither of us has to say anything. We just get one another. We understand each other. Unlike if I were walking with Santino down the street right now, he would have already made a dozen or so jokes. He always needs to talk. Not Reina and me. We are both content to just be in the silence.

We get to the restaurant, and I hold the door open for Reina to walk in. The restaurant immediately feels comforting. It's a nice restaurant, but it's not over-the-top fancy, like a lot of other steak restaurants in Chicago. We are seated immediately, and I order Reina's favorite bottle of wine to share.

After the waiter has poured our wine and we each have ordered, Reina finally asks me the question that I know she's been wanting to ask since I came here, "Why her?"

I sigh and sit back in my chair. "I don't have an answer for you, Reina. At least not one that will satisfy you."

"Try," she says. She sips on her wine.

"I don't know. From the second I saw her, my whole world changed. What I wanted changed. For the first time in a long time, I wanted a future that involved more than just my job."

"You fell in love," she says, smiling at me.

"No."

"Yes, you did."

"No, I didn't."

She takes another sip of her wine. "You're an idiot, Nacio. You fell in love, and that girl is equally as crazy about you."

"I might have fallen for her, but it's not love. You already know I'm not capable of love. And she doesn't love me, despite what she thinks. She can't love a monster like me."

Reina rolls her eyes at me. "You're not a monster. None of us are."

"How has running the company been going?" I ask, trying to change the subject. "Don't want to relinquish the control and power to someone else, do you?"

She smiles. "Having all the control is what I've always wanted. It's what I've needed. You know that. I didn't think it was possible though until you fucked up and gave it to me." She pauses for a second, studying me. "You're not regretting giving it to me, are you? You want the control back, don't you?"

"I like the control as much as you do. But I still get plenty of control when I kill. It's enough for now."

She nods. "You know you still have to do the job. You still have to kill Kinsley. We are being paid too much to just let that one go. And our reputation is on the line."

I nod. "I know. But we still have time. The contract said I have till the end of the year."

She shakes her head. "If you are still going to do the job, then you just need to hurry up and do it already. If you want Scarlett out of your life, the best way to do it is by killing her best friend. That's unforgivable."

She studies me and then laughs. "You still haven't decided if you are going to kill Kinsley or not. This Scarlett girl really has you wrapped around her finger if you are considering giving up your family and everything you've ever worked for." She sighs. "Just tell me what you decide soon, so I can hire someone else to do the job if you aren't going to do it."

I don't answer her as our steaks are being placed in front of us.

"I have another job for you in the meantime. It's high profile, and it will have to be done right."

"How much?"

She smiles. "Two billion."

I raise my eyebrows. That is a lot compared to what we usually get paid.

"So, who is this guy?"

"Roderick Burrows."

I frown. "The good-looking senator, who is also the city's favorite bachelor? The most well-known man in politics who will be vying for a presidency campaign in the next election? That Roderick Burrows?"

She smiles. "Yes."

"I hope you fucking told them no. Even I can't pull that shit off, and you know it. We will get caught and end up in jail for this. This will be the one that breaks us."

"No, it won't. You're the best, and now, you have the girl who can help you pull this off."

"No. Scarlett won't be involved in this."

"Sure she will. You already involved her in Marcel's death. Why not Roderick's?"

I frown, shooting daggers at her with my eyes. "How do you know that?"

"Santino told me. That was his job, remember? To keep you on track and make sure shit got done like it was supposed to. You've been too much of a loose cannon lately."

"I'm not involving her in this. This is on a different level."

She shakes her head. "I disagree. You are going to do this with her. You want to find out if she is cut out for this life? You want to find out if you love each other? This is how you do it. If you aren't going to test her with Kinsley, then test her with this man."

She digs into her steak, but suddenly, I've lost my appetite. I can't eat anymore. I've dragged Scarlett into my world, and I'm afraid my sister is going to make sure she stays locked here. And my world is not the place I want Scarlett to be stuck in.

19

SCARLETT

I SPENT my entire evening with Santino and then found out that the room I was staying in was nothing more than a guest room. It wasn't Nacio's room. I didn't see Nacio again last night, and I didn't go looking. I'm tired of running after him. He's going to have to figure some things out himself.

But, still, last night, I didn't get much sleep. It was hard to get much sleep, knowing that Nacio was somewhere in the house but not next to me in the bed. I wanted nothing more than to get out of my comfy king-size bed that is even nicer than my bed at home and go find him. I wanted nothing more than to have his hands all over me, his lips pressed against mine, and three words to slip from his lips. That didn't happen though. Instead, I slept alone. I showered alone. I got dressed alone. I ate breakfast alone.

At least I was until Reina came downstairs.

"Good morning," I say to her.

When I look at her, I realize it isn't a good morning. Reina clearly isn't a morning person. She's wearing a robe, and her hair is a frazzled mess. She walks over and pours herself a cup of coffee without saying anything to me.

"We have a meeting in five minutes in my office to discuss our next mark," Reina says. Then, she walks out of the kitchen.

I stare at her in confusion. I'm not sure if I'm supposed to follow her or not. I'm not even sure if I'm invited to this meeting or not. I don't have a clue. I don't know what I'm supposed to do. I take another bite of the banana I got out of the pantry.

I hear Santino laughing behind me. I turn around and face him.

"That was meant to be an order. Reina meant for you to follow her now."

"Oh," I say in surprise. "I guess I didn't understand that from her words."

Santino walks over to me. He snatches a piece of toast off my plate and takes a bite. "You'll learn to understand Reina's language. She's not a morning person, so she will use the fewest words possible to make her point, which is usually an order."

"Then, why are we having a meeting this early?"

Santino just shrugs.

I stand and snatch the toast back out of his hand. He pouts as I do, and it's adorable.

"Sorry, I'm hungry, and I know I'm going to need my strength to handle Reina. Get your own toast."

"No time. Let's go," he says, walking toward Reina's office.

I follow behind. When we get to her office, Santino doesn't bother knocking. He just walks in and takes a seat on one of the couches in the room. I do, too, before I see Nacio is already seated in the chair next to Reina.

"Finally. I don't have time to wait for you two," Reina says.

Santino gets up from the couch next to me and walks over to Reina. He picks her up and squeezes her. "Relax, sis. No one wants to work for a bitch." He places an angry Reina back down in her chair and then takes a seat back next to me. He slings his arm around the back of the couch, causing his arm to be right behind me.

I lean over and whisper in his ear, "I think you've just angered her instead of making it better."

Santino laughs. It's a loud belly laugh that only makes Reina angrier. I laugh, too, until I see the look on Nacio's face. I don't understand the look. He looks jealous. I look to Santino next to me, and he's grinning at Nacio as he puts his arm around me tighter.

I sigh. Men.

"Enough. We need to get this meeting over with. I have to head back upstairs soon to shower and get ready. I have a meeting in LA this afternoon," Reina says.

All eyes immediately go to Reina, and we give her our full attention.

"Our mark is Roderick Burrows—"

I gasp when I hear the name.

Reina glares at me.

"I'm sorry. You don't mean *the* Roderick Burrows, the politician?"

"Yes, that's exactly who I mean." She eyes me, and I shut up.

I realize now is not the time to argue with her, and questioning her is not winning me any points at the moment. I glance over at Santino, who is unfazed by the announcement. I chance a glance at Nacio though, and it's clear he isn't even listening to his sister. Instead, his eyes are locked on me. I nervously tuck a loose strand of hair behind my ear as he looks at me. I wish he would just talk to me instead of giving me intense looks and then running away whenever I enter a room.

"Our timeline is short on this one. We have only a week to get it done, or we won't get paid. Nacio is running point on the operation, and the two of you will do whatever he needs to get the job done." She turns to me. "Whatever he needs. Do you understand?"

I nod. "I'll do whatever you need."

"Good. Because my thought is to have you seduce Roderick. It seems you are good at that since you did it with both of my brothers and even a gay man. Your vagina must be made of—"

"Reina!" both Nacio and Santino say at the same time, cutting her off.

She grins.

I stand though. I've had enough of this woman. "You're right; I do know how to seduce men. If I were you though, I would just be a little nicer to me. I didn't come here to be walked all over. I run a company that employs hundreds of employees and makes billions of dollars a year. I know plenty of powerful people and could easily destroy you if I had to. You don't have anything on me. So, unless you are planning on having one of your two brothers kill me, then you need to start treating me with some respect."

I turn to storm out, but she smiles brighter.

"I knew I liked you," she says.

I pause. I'm so confused.

"Sit back down, Scarlett, if you would please. I don't like weak women, but you seem more than capable of handling yourself. I'm not used to women like you in our lives. Most of the women that my idiot brothers bring around are weak and can't do much more than bat their eyes at men and expect to be taken care of. You're different. I can see that, but I won't give you the respect you feel you deserve until you earn it, just like the rest of us. Do this job, and you'll have earned my trust."

She glances at her phone. "I need to go, so I can catch my flight. I want the plan sent to my phone before I board the plane in three hours, so I can review it on my flight."

"You'll have it," Nacio answers.

"Good." Reina leaves her office, leaving me, Nacio, and Santino.

"So, what's the masterful plan, bro? I know Reina already told you all the details last night at the little dinner you two had without us," Santino says.

Nacio runs his hand through his hair as he glares at his brother. "Yes, I already have the plan. It's none of your concern though. She'll be where I ask, when I ask."

Santino shrugs and then stands. "Sounds good to me. Less work I have to do. As long as I'm not the one who has to pull the trigger on this one, I don't care."

"Don't worry. You're never the one who has to pull the trigger," Nacio says.

I'm not sure if it was meant to be a jab or not.

"Whatever, dude. I'm out of here," Santino says, walking out of the office.

"Are you going to tell me what the plan is?" I ask.

Nacio stands, so I do, too. I want him to walk over to me. I beg him to with my eyes. I beg him to come wrap me in his arms. He doesn't.

"No. Just wear something slutty, and be ready to leave around six," Nacio says as he walks out of the office.

I run after him before I realize what I'm doing, and I stop just outside the office. I am not going to run after him. I will not be that girl. I do not chase men. He can either come to me, or after this is over, I'm gone.

I see Santino rummaging through the fridge in the kitchen, and I walk over to him. "Can I borrow your phone?"

"What happened to yours, Beauty?"

"Nacio destroyed it."

Santino frowns. "I'll get you a new one after I eat something. But, yeah, you can borrow my phone until then." He pulls his cell out of his pocket and tosses it to me.

I catch it. "Thanks."

He nods, and I take the phone back upstairs to my room. I text Kinsley first to let her know that I lost my phone, but I'm getting a new one soon and will text her the number when I get it. And then I call Preston.

"Hello, this is Preston of Beautifully Bell Enterprises. How may I help you?"

"Preston, it's Scarlett. I lost my phone. I just wanted to see how things were going."

"Oh, Scarlett. Thank God! Please tell me you are calling to tell me you are on your way home?"

"Um...no, I'm not on my way home. Should I be?"

Preston pauses, trying to decide what to say.

"Preston? Should I be on my way back?"

"No. Everything is fine. I'm just a little overwhelmed."

"I'm sorry. I think I will be away for another week, max. And then I'm coming home."

"Is a hot stranger coming home with you?"

I sigh. "I honestly have no idea."

"I'm sorry."

"I fell for him, Preston. He just didn't fall back, or if he did, he won't admit it."

"I'm sorry, baby. Give him a little more time to figure his shit out, but if he doesn't express his undivided love for you soon, then I would drop his ass. You can do better than him. You deserve to be loved back."

I nod even though he can't see me. "I just don't know how to get my heart back if he doesn't love me."

"It will be hard, but you'll recover. Most likely, by getting your ass back to work and losing yourself in your work."

I smile. "Thanks, Preston."

"Anytime," he says before we end the call.

I dig through my bag, but I'm not sure if I have anything slutty enough to wear tonight, as Nacio requested. I want to wear something slutty enough that it will make Nacio regret saying that to me. Enough that even he won't be able to keep his hands off me.

I walk into the hallway and look for Santino. I don't see him, so I head back downstairs and find him finishing up his breakfast. "Can I borrow a car to go shopping? I can get a phone then and an outfit for tonight."

Santino reaches into his pocket and pulls out car keys before tossing them to me. "It's for the Ford truck."

I hand him his phone back. "Thanks."

"You know how to drive a stick, or do you need some help?"

I smile at him. "I know how to drive a stick, but I would love some company, if you want to join me."

Santino nods, and we walk to his truck. He lets me drive, so I can go pick out a slutty outfit to wear for his brother.

20

BEAST

"Scarlett, we need to leave now!" I holler up the stairs as I pace.

I hate this as it is, but we are on a very strict timeline. If we are going to do this, we need to leave in the next five minutes, or this isn't going to work, and I don't have a Plan B.

"Scarlett!" I shout again.

"One minute," she shouts back down the stairs.

I haven't been around her enough to know how long she takes to get ready. I don't know if she is the kind of girl who takes hours or five minutes to get ready. I don't know how she likes her coffee. I don't know her favorite sex position.

I just know that she spent the entire damn day with Santino. They were gone all day long, and the second she got back, she went up to her room, and she has been getting ready ever since. And I've been down here, pacing. I tried waiting in my room, which is right next to hers—not that she's noticed—but it was impossible. She was too close for me not to be able to touch her.

I need to touch her. I need to kiss her. I need to have her.

I haven't been able to get anything done today because all I've been thinking of is her.

I can't fucking do this. She's either mine, or she needs to leave. I can't handle her being with Santino. That might not be fair, but I don't care. I'll end up killing myself if they stay together. I don't want to know what they did today. I don't want to know where he took her. I don't want to know what he did to her.

Did he kiss her? Fuck her? Take her on a date?

I have no fucking idea what they did because Santino didn't come inside, so I couldn't beat it out of him.

I finally hear the door open and close to her bedroom. *Finally.*

I wait at the base of the stairs for her to come down. I glance up, and my mouth drops when I look at her. Her hair is curled in long waves down the side of her head. Her makeup is striking, making her eyes pop larger than I've ever seen. But that isn't what leaves me speechless. Her body is what does it. She's wearing a very see-through dress. I can see her hard nipples piercing through the thin black lace fabric. I can see her black underwear beneath the fabric. I can see everything.

My cock instantly hardens. If the thought of not having her all day was hard enough, then seeing her almost-naked body is enough to drive me mad.

She can't wear that. She just fucking can't. I will lose my goddamn mind, or I will take her in the backseat of my car, like a horny teenager.

"Is this slutty enough for you?" she asks, smiling, as she approaches the bottom of the stairs.

I nod, my mouth still hanging open.

Her smile brightens. "Good. I was worried it wasn't slutty enough, but from the looks on your and Santino's faces, I think it's perfect."

I frown when she says my brother's name. "It will do. Let's go."

I walk out the front door to my waiting Mercedes. I hear her following me in her heels. I try to force myself to not turn around. I try to force my legs to move in the opposite direction of her, so I won't take her upstairs and punish her like I want for wearing that thing she calls a dress or for doing whatever she did with my brother all fucking day.

I stomp to my car and unlock it. I climb in while I wait for her.

She follows a second later and climbs into the passenger seat. I put the car in reverse as soon as her door is closed. I don't bother waiting to see if she's buckled her seat belt or not. I just stomp on the gas, and we zip out of the driveway.

As I drive, I try not to think about her. I try not to look at her, but of course, all I see are her bare nipples beneath the fabric. I see her toned stomach. I see her black underwear.

"Are you going to talk to me, or are you planning on ignoring me the rest of the time I'm here?"

"I saw you with Santino."

"What are you talking about?"

When I pull to a stop at a stoplight, I turn and look at her. "I saw you with my brother. Why the fuck would I want you after my brother had you?"

I stomp on the gas too hard as the light turns green, and we both fling forward in our seats.

She laughs. "Are you serious? You think something happened between me and your brother?" She looks at me, and then her smile drops. "You're serious? You think that Santino and I are fucking?" She shakes her head. "What do you not understand about the words *I love you*? Those words typically come with an exclusivity clause. Sorry I didn't spell it out for you, but I'm not sleeping with anyone else. I won't sleep with anyone else as long as I love you. I know we haven't defined our relationship, and I have no idea what the hell we are doing together, but when I'm in love with someone, that person is usually it for me. So, get off your high horse, and listen to me. I love you. I love you, Nacio, Beast, Killer, Brother. Whatever you want to call yourself, I love you. And I'm going to prove to you that you deserve it and that you love me, too. If you didn't love me, you wouldn't be so pissed at the thought of me and Santino possibly being together."

I try to comprehend what she said, but it just doesn't compute. I don't believe her words. I don't believe that a beautiful, intelligent, confident woman who runs a billion-dollar company would be interested in me. I don't believe her.

"You can try, but I still think you might fall in love with my brother first."

She moans. "You are such an insufferable, ridiculous, and frustrating man. Ah! What do I have to do?"

She grabs my head and pulls it to her. I feel her soft lips land on mine, and I forget what I'm doing. I just kiss her. Our tongues find each other. Our lips lock together. My hand tangles in her perfectly curled hair, messing it up.

A horn sounds, bringing me back to reality. I'm kissing her instead of paying attention to where I'm driving. I grab ahold of the wheel again, and we swerve just in time to avoid a head-on collision with the car speeding past us.

"Sorry," I mumble.

I glance over to her, and she is running her thumb across the bottom of her lip.

"You're right. You don't love me. There was nothing behind that kiss, except for lust. I'll stop trying," she says, smirking.

I tightly grip the wheel. I will not give in to her games. I will not show her how badly I want her because it's embarrassingly bad. It's I-would-come-within-one-second bad.

"So, since you don't love me and all, what's the plan for tonight with this Roderick guy? Or do I not get to know, and I have to just walk in blind to this situation?"

I let out a long deep breath to try and keep myself from losing it with this woman next to me. "The plan is, Roderick goes to the same bar every Thursday night after work. He's known for picking up ladies there. He is never caught leaving the bar with a woman; it is rumored that he later meets up with the woman he meets at the bar. So, it is usually swarming with women who are hoping that the famous Roderick will pick them to take home for the night, so they can hopefully trick him into marrying them."

"So, why pick tonight if the bar is going to be swarming with women? I know I'm good at picking up men, but I'm not so good that I can guarantee he'll choose me over all the rest."

I shake my head. "First of all, you are that good. Trust me. If you walk into that room, any other woman in there won't stand a chance. And, second, you don't necessarily have to get him to ask you out tonight. You just need to get him interested. We can work it from there. But, with a large crowd of women interested in him, no one should be able to single you out as the woman he went home with, so they couldn't possibly tie you to his murder later. This way, he will be equally tied to all the women in the bar. You will just be another woman in the bar."

"Are you coming in with me?"

"No."

I watch the frown slip over her face as her shoulders slump back just a little in disappointment.

"You know, you've never taken me on a date. With each day that passes, you are going to have to up your game when you do finally take me on a date. I won't just accept dinner and a movie or going to a bar. You're going to have to plan something amazing now since you've waited so long."

"No, I don't because we aren't dating. We aren't together."

She smiles, and I see a hint of a dimple I didn't notice before on her cheek.

"Sure we are. You just don't understand what being together means yet. Just like you don't understand the phrase *I love you*. Don't worry; you will," she says, winking at me.

I pull over in front of the bar where Roderick is. "Go work your charms on Roderick," I say, nodding toward the bar. "Just don't fuck him."

I grab her neck and pull her lips back to mine. After the kiss from earlier, I need to kiss her. I need her to understand that she is mine.

When she pulls away, she says, "Don't worry; I know I'm yours." She winks and then gets out of the car.

I have to grip the wheel until my knuckles turn white to keep myself from following her inside as I watch her ass sway back and forth before she walks inside the bar.

This woman is going to be the death of me.

21

SCARLETT

I WALK into the bar and immediately regret what I'm wearing. I thought I would be by far the sluttiest-dressed woman in the bar. I was wrong. I look tame compared to some of these women. And I look just as desperate as all of the other women in the bar who are vying for Roderick's attention.

I'm going to have to try a different route to even have a chance at talking with Roderick tonight or even getting him to look in my direction. I just don't know what that direction is yet. He probably isn't a man who would be impressed that I own a beauty empire. He's the type of guy who is only impressed by smart, intelligent women. Or very flexible, dirty women, from the looks of the bar.

I begin to make my way through the crowded room and head up to the bar when someone crashes into my hand, and I feel the sting again. I hold it in my other hand. It's still swollen, and it has turned a dark purply color. It looks awful and feels just as bad. I don't trust the EMT's or Reina's judgment that it isn't broken. When I get home, I'm going to see my doctor.

I finally make my way up to the bar, still holding my hand to keep it from hurting, when the idea strikes me. The damsel-in-distress thing always works. It could work for me. The only problem is, I'm about ten people away from Roderick, who is sitting at the other end of the bar, talking with other women.

So, I'm going to have to try something else. I see the bartender begin to make his way down the bar toward me. I could flirt with the bartender. Try to get Roderick's attention that way by making him jealous and then act like I'm uninterested. Or, at the very least, get friendly enough with the bartender to see if he'll slip Roderick my number.

As the bartender approaches, I continue to hold my hand, displaying it on the counter and in easy view of anyone nearby.

"Can I get you anything? Wow, that's some bruise."

I look up and smile at the bartender, whose name tag says *Cory*.

"Yeah, it's flaring up again. I should get it looked at, but I just don't have time."

"Let me get you some ice to put on that and a drink. I'm guessing you are a gin or whiskey girl." He pauses, reading me. "I'm guessing gin and tonic. Am I right?"

I smile. "Good guess. It's like you do this to hit on girls or something."

Cory shakes his head. "I save it for the most beautiful women in the bar. I'm Cory, by the way, in case you were wondering."

He holds out his hand, and I shake it with my left hand instead of my right swollen one. It's awkward and uncomfortable but somehow still sweet.

"I'm Scarlett."

"Nice to meet you, Scarlett. I'll be right back."

I smile at him as he moves away from me to grab me ice and make my gin and tonic. I watch as several other women try to get Cory's attention, but he ignores them as he continues to focus on getting me my drink and ice. Probably all have the same plan I do. If you can't get Roderick, might as well settle for second place with the hot bartender for the night.

I glance down the bar to Roderick, who raises a hand in the air to flag down Cory. Cory notices him right away. After all, it's his job, and if Roderick comes in as often as they say, then Cory would treat him like a regular.

Cory walks over to him and says something to the effect of, "I need a minute."

Roderick doesn't seem used to being told to wait and says something that looks like, "I'm your best customer. Why should I have to wait?"

Cory holds the ice up in his hand and motions to me, saying something about my hand to Roderick, who is now looking at me. I smile but make sure to keep my focus on Cory, not Roderick. I need to keep playing hard to get, like I'm not here for Roderick. But I can feel his eyes noticing me. I can feel his eyes taking in my hand. I can feel his eyes staring at my breasts beneath the fabric that might as well not be there for as well as it's covering me.

Cory stops talking to Roderick and makes his way down to me. He sets my drink in front of me and then says, "Here, let me."

He tenderly holds my hand as he applies the ice, and I wince.

"Thanks."

"So, how did you mess your hand up anyway? Bar fight?" he asks, smiling.

I smile back. "No. Are you sure you have time? It seems like that man down there isn't too happy that you aren't giving him your full attention."

"Rod can get over it. He comes in here every Thursday and expects the star treatment. He can chill a little. Although it makes me happy to know that you don't know who he is. That's why all the women are in this bar tonight."

"Hmm." I glance his way again and see his eyes are still locked on my body. "He seems familiar, but I can't place him. He doesn't matter though." I sip on my drink. "If you can believe it, on my flight here, my friend was afraid of flying and squeezed my hand so hard that he caused the bruising."

"Wow. I didn't know that was possible."

He leans forward on the bar, and I know I have this man. I just don't know if I have the one down the bar from me.

"Yep, it's possible." I take another sip of my drink.

"Are you from Chicago or..."

"Nope. I live in New York City."

"And what do you do there when you're not flying with your friend who squeezes your hand so hard that he causes bruises? And please don't say your friend is really a boyfriend."

I laugh. "Nope, not a boyfriend. I own a company. You might have heard of it—Beautifully Bell."

His eyebrows raise. "Oh my God. You're, like, a billionaire. I'll just leave now. I don't have a chance in hell with a woman like you, do I? Be honest."

I laugh. He's got the funny thing going for him. It's probably what makes him a good bartender.

"Hmm...I don't know," I say, smiling.

"Oh, jeez. I'll just go then," he says, putting on a pouty face that makes me laugh again.

I reach out and touch his hand. "No, don't go! You totally have a chance with me."

"Good," he says, eyeing Roderick down the bar from us. "But I do seriously need to serve my other customers and all. I'm not made of money, like some people. I actually need to get paid in order to buy things, like food and all."

I smile. "I'll be here, waiting."

He nods and then makes his way down to Roderick. I try my best not to stare at them, despite how badly I want to. The music in the bar has increased, which makes it harder for me to hear what they are saying, so my only chance is to read their lips now.

I take another sip and then glance their way. Roderick is in a deep conversation with Cory, who is frowning deeply and seems to be arguing back. Not a good sign.

Roderick scribbles something down, and I assume he's paying his tab. Then, he gets up from the bar and walks out the back.

Shit. Well, there goes tonight. I should be relieved though. If we fail, it means Roderick gets to live. Although I wonder if Roderick is involved in some bad shit, like Marcel was, and deserves to die. I should ask Nacio that later. It will make me feel better to know.

Cory paces back and forth behind the bar, and I wonder what Roderick said to him. Several women try to get Cory's attention to make them drinks, but he ignores them all.

He slowly walks over to me.

"What was that about?" I ask.

He frowns. "This."

He places the piece of paper Roderick gave him in front of me. I pick up the paper and glance at it in confusion.

I raise my eyebrows. "What is it?"

"He chose you."

"Who did?" I ask.

"Roderick."

I shake my head in confusion even though I know exactly what this is.

"He chose you of all the women in this bar to spend the evening with him. That number is the code you will need to get into his suite that he has above the bar. It means I'm fucked because you will choose him over me. No woman turns down Roderick."

I smile. "Well, I am."

I stand from the bar.

"What?" Cory asks.

"I'm turning this Roderick guy down." I pull some cash out of my purse and put it down on the bar.

"Did you not just hear me? Nobody turns Roderick Burrows down."

"There is a first time for everything then," I say, slinging my purse over my shoulder.

"You can't just leave," he says.

"I am."

"What am I supposed to tell him?"

"Tell him that, if he wants to get to know me first, he can come find me and talk to me like a normal human being."

"Do you want to write your number down for him?"

"No. Just tell him my name is Scarlett Bell, but he would have known that if he'd come over to talk to me. He'll figure out anything else he needs to know about me if he has the guts. Otherwise, he's not worth it."

Cory's jaw has dropped completely open. He doesn't know what to say, and I'm afraid, whenever he talks to Roderick, he is going to get yelled at for not delivering me to him. But I don't feel too sorry for a guy who evidently finds Roderick girls on a weekly basis.

"I'll see you around, Cory. Thanks for the ice and drink."

I turn and walk out of the bar. I begin walking down the street, looking for Nacio, but I don't see his car anywhere, and I don't have his number in my new phone yet. I walk two blocks before his car pulls up beside me. I climb in the passenger seat. He begins driving without saying a word to me.

When we are back on the interstate, he says, "So?"

I shake my head. I do all the work, and I get a one-worded question.

"We got him."

Nacio takes a deep breath and then lets it out.

I laugh. "So, you didn't think I would be able to do this?"

"No. I thought you would be able to. I just thought you would be up in his suite right now."

"Unbelievable. He asked me up, but I said no—you know, that word you say to me all the fucking time now."

"You did well. Thank you."

"Just get me back. I want to get out of this dress and into a warm bath."

22

BEAST

"Heel," I say to my two large mutt dogs as we turn the corner.

They don't listen very well anymore. They used to listen perfectly to my every command. That was before they became couch potatoes that stayed home with Reina every day instead of running with me. But, with as often as I travel, it makes more sense for them to stay here than travel with me. Although I miss them, so they might need to go with me this week.

I pick up speed a little as we run the last mile back to Reina's house. The dogs pick up with me, right on cue. I smile, happy that they will at least run full speed with me when I want them to.

I need this run. I need to clear my head and forget about Scarlett. I need to give my dick a break from all the masturbating that happened most of the night because, true to her word, she went back yesterday, took a bath, and spent the rest of the night in her room, and I didn't have the balls to talk to her. No, that's not true. I have the balls. I just don't know what I fucking want anymore. I don't know if I want her to stay or go. I don't know if I want her to love me or not.

I'm clueless as to what I want. And, for the first time ever, I'm conflicted about if I should kill or not. I don't believe my sister. There is more to killing Roderick than she is telling me. And I need to find out what that reason is before I decide if I'm going to kill him. And, for that matter, what I'm going to do about Kinsley.

I run faster the last couple of blocks to Reina's house until I'm completely out of breath. I stop abruptly when I reach the house and pass out on the front lawn. The dogs come lie down next to me, licking my face first, of course, for good measure.

"Wow, so you'll let dogs love you, just not me. That makes sense," Scarlett says as she stands over me.

I squint in the sunlight to look up at her. "The dogs don't love me. They respect me and obey me and think of me as their leader. There is a difference."

Scarlett smiles and shakes her head with her hands on her hips. "Sure there is a difference."

She squats down and begins petting the dogs that, of course, go over and begin licking her immediately while excitedly wagging their tails.

"So, what are their names?" she asks.

"Coco and Lady."

"And who do these gorgeous dogs belong to?"

"Me."

She slowly nods her head as the dogs turn their attention back to me when I stand up, looking to see what I'm going to do—if we are running some more or if I'm going to give them a treat.

Scarlett stands, too, and looks me in the eye. I can't understand the look on her face, but I know I don't like it. I don't like how she looks at me, like something I'm doing with the dogs somehow makes me a better person.

"Just because I own dogs, it doesn't make me a better person, Beauty."

Her face lights up. "You called me Beauty. Maybe my Beast is coming back a little."

"Don't count on it."

"And owning dogs does make you a better person. Especially rescue dogs, as these clearly aren't purebreds. Dogs won't obey people they fear or who are dangerous."

I shake my head. "Dogs will listen to anyone they see as the leader of the pack or who has food."

She rolls her eyes, like I'm ridiculous.

The front door of the house opens and draws our attention away from the dogs. Santino comes out in only a pair of shorts. Not that I can say anything since I'm not wearing a shirt either.

"So, you must have made Romeo fall for you hard last night. He's been calling nonstop, asking for you. Nice work," Santino says, raising his hand to give her a high five.

"Thanks. Is it Cory or Roderick calling?"

"Who is Cory?" Santino and I both ask at the same time.

Scarlett bites her lip, like she messed up. "He was the bartender I hit on to get Roderick to ask me out."

I raise my eyebrows. Great. Now, I have to worry about this Cory guy, too. There are too many men for me to keep up with.

"So, what do you want me to do?" Santino asks, looking from Scarlett to me.

"Set up a date. Tonight," I say.

Santino nods and then heads back inside to make it happen.

I look at Scarlett. "You up for this?"

She nods. "Of course. I'll go work on figuring out what I'm wearing tonight."

Scarlett pets the dogs on their heads one more time and then heads back inside. Leaving me alone. And, somehow, even though she's here and made it clear that she is mine, I have never felt more alone in my life.

23

SCARLETT

Nacio rented a house for me to pretend like it's mine for when Roderick comes to pick me up for the date tonight. I've spent the afternoon finding the perfect outfit and going over the plan. Nacio isn't ready to kill him—yet. I'm not supposed to bring him back to the house tonight. I'm just supposed to flirt and get one final date where I can bring him back here.

I apply my red lipstick that matches the red dress I'm wearing. I decided to wear something a little less slutty tonight. I'm not competing against hundreds of women for Roderick's attention tonight. And, honestly, the only reason I wore the dress last night was to get Nacio riled up. It worked. But, tonight, I need something classier, something that I would be more likely to wear. Something that leaves more to the imagination.

I fluff my hair as I look at myself one last time in the full-length mirror in the master bedroom.

This house is amazing. Almost as nice as Reina's house, just slightly smaller—but only slightly. It must have cost a fortune to rent this house for the week. And I'm afraid to see whose name Nacio rented it in. If he rented it in my name, it will mean I have no way of escaping this world. Even if I'm not the one who pulls the trigger, the police will always have something that ties me to Roderick's murder.

I need to ask Nacio what the plan is. I need to ask who he is going to frame for Roderick's murder because I don't see a way out of this for me. *If I'm the last person to see him and if he dies here, then how am I not going to become the prime suspect?*

I walk out of the bedroom and down the stairs to go find Nacio. I'm ready much earlier than I'm supposed to be, so he isn't pacing downstairs, waiting for me, like he was last time. I walk through the large house, looking for him, when I spot him sitting at the kitchen counter with his laptop open. He's typing furiously, to the point that he doesn't even notice me coming up behind him.

I wrap my arms around him, and he freezes, which makes me smile. It's such a normal thing, something that I would do to a boyfriend, but for Nacio, it is anything but normal. For Nacio, it is something that means love and pain and hurt. I hold on to him a second longer, trying to get him used to the affectionate embrace without pushing him too far. I know the physical contact doesn't bother him. It's the physical contact without sex that bothers him. It's the intimacy.

I release him and walk around to the other side of the kitchen island, so he can see me. I feel his eyes burning into me as I walk, which just makes me sway my hips harder, until I turn to face him.

He has a grin on his face as he looks at me, and I can tell he doesn't even know it's there. His eyes drink in my toned legs and curve-hugging dress before he realizes that he is smiling at me like an idiot, and then he wipes the smile from his face.

"Will this do for tonight?"

He nods as his eyes memorize every curve. Every exposed piece of skin. I do the same back. I study how his muscles move beneath his tight shirt as he breathes. I study the intensity in his eyes that are hiding something I might never find out the truth about. And I study his lips that I want nothing more than to kiss or, at the very least, see forming his sexy smile.

"So, are you going to tell me how I won't end up in jail for murdering Roderick when this is all said and done? Or is that the plan? Make me go down for this?"

He narrows his eyes and closes his laptop. "You think I would let you go to prison for this?"

I shrug. "I don't know what you would do."

He stands and walks over to me until our bodies are pressed closely together. His hand goes up to a loose strand of hair, and he tucks it behind my ear. "Just like you tell me you will love me, no matter what, and that I need to realize that, you need to realize something. I might not know how to love, but I know how to protect. And, for the rest of my life, I will do everything I can to protect you. You can count on that."

His hand releases my face, and I let out a deep breath I didn't realize I had been holding. He takes a step backward and then leans against the counter, looking at me.

"Don't worry about it, Beauty. You're safe. I wouldn't let you do anything that could risk your safety. Understand?"

I nod and don't ask any further questions because, for some stupid reason, I trust him. I trust he will protect me because he always has. I might not understand him or understand what he wants out of our relationship, but I do trust he will protect me even if it means he is putting his own life at risk.

I hear the doorbell, and I close my eyes to keep from crying. I don't know why, but after Nacio opened up to me like that, I don't want to leave him. I want to further our connection. I want to see if I can grow closer to him. I don't want to go on a date with a stranger. I want to be with Nacio.

I open my eyes, and Nacio is standing right in front of me again. His hands tenderly go up to my cheeks, and his lips softly touch mine for just a second. Our eyes stay open as we kiss, making the moment more intimate than I could have imagined a kiss being.

When he releases me, he says, "Pretend it's me. Pretend I'm taking you on that first date you imagined. You got this."

I smile and nod before walking to answer the door.

"Just don't fuck him!" he shouts to me.

It makes my smile brighter just as I open the door to see Roderick standing there.

"You sure know how to make a man work for what he wants," Roderick says as he stands in front of me in a three-piece gray suit.

"Sorry, if you wanted easy, you picked the wrong woman. I'm anything but easy, and if you think that was work, you have another thing coming before anything more happens."

He cocks his head to the side as he looks at me. "I look forward to becoming that man for you."

"If you're not that man already, then we really should cancel this date because I want a man who is already a hard worker and someone who, once he starts dating me, steps up his game about a thousand percent. If you're not that man already, we are probably wasting our time."

Roderick laughs and pulls out, from behind him, the largest bouquet of flowers I have ever seen, filled with mostly roses.

I smile as I take them from him. "It's a good start."

He smiles. "Good. I'm Roderick, by the way. You can call me Rod if you want, all my friends do." He leans forward and softly kisses me on the cheek. "And you look beautiful, by the way."

"Thank you. I'm Scarlett. My friends call me Scar, but since you aren't my friend, I wouldn't want you to call me Scar. And, since I hope we will be something more, I think you can come up with a better nickname for me."

He laughs. "I got myself a feisty one."

I shake my head as I place the vase of flowers on the table in the entryway behind me and then walk out the door. "You haven't gotten yourself anything yet."

I feel his eyes studying my ass as I walk, and I know I've picked the perfect dress to seduce two different men. He runs to catch up and opens the door to his black BMW. I climb in, and he moves around to the driver's side and climbs in.

"So, where are we going?"

He leans over and softly kisses me on the cheek. "It's a surprise, beautiful."

I frown a little when he says *beautiful*. I don't like him calling me anything that reminds me of Nacio because, as much as Nacio said I should pretend that I was on a date with him, I don't want to pretend. I'm still holding out hope that there will be a first date with Nacio. And it sure as hell had better be better than whatever Mr. Money-bags next to me has planned.

Okay, maybe I was wrong. Nacio has a lot to live up to when he takes me on our first date because tonight was amazing. Roderick had a perfect night planned, and just with the amount of work he put into the date, even if we didn't connect, I would have gone on a second date with him. He took me to a steak dinner. A bar with amazing music. And a carriage ride through a park. And he had my favorite drink of gin and tonic ready for me at each stop. It was a perfect night.

Too perfect is what I would be thinking if this were a real date.

As our date is ending, Roderick walks me up the drive to the house that I'm pretending is mine.

I get to the door, and then I pause on the porch. "So, this was a little too perfect. What's the catch? There has to be a catch."

He tucks his hands in his pockets, and it's adorable—the look he gives me like I caught him, and there is no point in denying it.

"Fine, you caught me. I do have one secret that not even the media knows. But I know a good thing when I see it. You're special."

He reaches up and tucks a loose strand of my hair, in a similar manner that Nacio did. I try not to react, but I want to swat his hand away. Even though he has been nothing but nice to me all night, he isn't Nacio.

"Yeah? What's that?" I ask with a smile on my face.

"I can trust you, right, Scarlett? I shouldn't be telling you this. I've never told a woman this, but after tonight, I think I've found the woman I want to spend the rest of my life with. I know it's too soon to propose or talk seriously about any future together, but you are what I've been looking for all these years. You are the one I want beside me when I make a run for the White House. Can I trust you?"

"Of course," I say.

"Good. I do have a secret that makes me less than perfect." He pulls his phone out of a pocket and hands it to me. When I look at the screen, I see an image of a young girl. I look up at him in confusion.

"That's my daughter, Jane."

His lips crash down on me after that. It's a nice kiss. It's everything a kiss should be, but it's not Nacio.

And all I can think about the entire time he's kissing me is, *We can't kill him. We can't kill him. He has a daughter.*

"Good night, Scarlett," he says when he lets go of my lips. "I'll call you tomorrow."

I nod. "Good night, Roderick."

He walks back to his car, and I burst into the house, looking for Nacio, but instead, all I find is a note that I can sleep here tonight or take the car in the garage back to Reina's. I can't fucking sleep tonight until I talk with someone, so I go with Option B.

I run to the Prius that is parked in the garage and drive as fast as I can to Reina's. The whole time, I'm doing everything I can not to cry because I don't know what to do if I can't get them to listen to me.

Do I go to the police to try and stop them? If I do, I'll lose the man I love.

But he doesn't love you back, that voice in my head says.

But he does. He just won't admit it to himself or me.

I drive faster until I get to her house, and the wheels squeal as I turn into the driveway. I'm not even sure if I've turned the ignition off as I run into the house.

"Nacio!" I yell as I run through the house. But I don't get an answer. "Nacio!" I yell again.

"He's not here," Reina says as she appears, standing in the entryway to her office.

"Where is he?"

She shakes her head. "Doesn't matter."

"It does. I need to talk to him."

She motions for me to come into her office. "Talk to me."

I sigh, but follow her anyway. I don't want a lecture, not tonight. And I think I'll have a better chance at convincing Nacio not to kill Roderick than Reina, but I guess I'll have to start with her anyway.

She walks all businesslike into her office and takes a seat behind her desk. She motions for me to take a seat in the chair opposite her, and I do.

"Now, what do you need to talk about?" she asks, raising her eyebrows at me.

"We can't kill Roderick."

She smiles. "Really? And why not?"

"He has a kid. He's a father. We can't..."

I see her face, and I realize this isn't a shock. She already knows. Nacio already knows.

"You already know."

She nods.

"And you were still okay with killing him?"

She nods.

"You're a monster."

"No, I'm not a monster." Reina runs a hand through her hair. "You need to understand a few things, Scarlett, about Nacio and me. We have been through some tough shit. Seen things as kids that no kid should see. It messed us up. That's why we kill. Sometimes, people need to die, and the justice system isn't always able to provide that type of justice, so we do it for a large fee."

"Roderick doesn't deserve to die though. His child doesn't deserve to grow up fatherless."

She smiles. "And how are you so sure that he doesn't deserve to die? You've spent all of a couple of hours with him, and now, you think you know that he shouldn't die. What makes you so sure that he is any better than Marcel was? What makes you God? What makes your judgment of who should and shouldn't die any better than mine? Since you're obviously such a good judge of character and all, you think you can judge him? You don't think I haven't thoroughly researched him? You don't think I know a lot more about him than you do?"

"Have you met him? Have you been face-to-face with him before? Have you looked into his eyes? Because I have. And, if you haven't, you need to, and then you won't be so sure if you should kill him or not. No matter what evidence you have."

Reina laughs. "If you judge someone by how they make you feel, you won't judge them correctly. You can't have any emotions in this business."

"That explains why Nacio is the way he is."

Reina nods. "Nacio knows this business better than anyone, even me. He can't mix emotions and his job. This is his life."

I take a deep breath. It means that he can either live the life he has always lived, or he can love me. He can't do both.

"Why do you think Roderick should die?"

Reina smiles. "Because he's killed before."

24

BEAST

I WATCH Scarlett leave Reina's office. She's been crying. I can see it from the look on her face.

She's come to the same conclusion that I have. That Roderick shouldn't die. I've killed plenty of people before who didn't deserve to die. But, this time, it's different. A child is involved. And Scarlett is involved. It doesn't feel right.

This time, everything is going to be more personal than with Marcel. She's kissed this man. Spent more time with him than Marcel, and Roderick obviously trusted her enough to tell her that he had a daughter.

I can't let her be involved in killing an innocent man. It's just different. It will destroy her. And she doesn't deserve to be destroyed, like Reina and me.

Scarlett looks at me, but doesn't say anything. We just stare at each other in the darkness. Trading thoughts without saying a word. Scarlett looks away first and walks upstairs. It's obvious that she isn't satisfied with whatever Reina has told her.

I enter Reina's office without knocking. "What did you tell her?" I ask.

"The truth."

"Which is?"

Reina crosses her arms and leans back in her chair. "I don't really like your tone of voice. You could be a little nicer to your sister."

I glare at Reina. "Don't play games with me, Reina. I don't believe your story about Roderick. *You* are the one paying me billions to kill him. There is no client. There is no outside money. And I don't believe you have any good reason for me to kill Roderick. I think you are playing us. So, tell me the fucking truth. What did you tell her?"

"I told her that Roderick has killed before."

I sink into the chair. I didn't expect her answer. "Who?"

"An ex-girlfriend."

"That's what you told Scarlett?"

She nods.

"Is it true?"

She shrugs and gets up from her chair. She walks around the desk until she's leaning against it in front of me. "Who cares if it is true or not? You've never cared before if they deserved to die or not. You love killing; it is all about the excitement and money with you. This one is definitely exciting, and it's more than the amount of money you deserve."

"You know why it's not okay for me to just kill for no reason anymore."

She smiles. "I guess you will just have to trust me then. You owe me."

I glare at Reina as I get up, but I've made my decision. I know what I have to do because I do owe Reina, and this is the only way to pay her back.

I storm upstairs and knock on Scarlett's door. She comes to the door a moment later and looks at me with big eyes.

"I'm going to kill him. I have a plan. It will happen tomorrow. You ready?"

She hesitates for just a second and then answers, "Yes. I trust you."

25

SCARLETT

I NERVOUSLY TAP my fingers against the table while Nacio sits next to me. We haven't talked. Not one word since he came to my room last night. There has been no reason to talk. Santino told me the plan this morning because Nacio was already busy with setting everything in motion.

The plan is simple. Roderick will be picking me up at my place again. I'll lure him inside. And then Nacio will kill him. Simple.

Except it is anything but simple. Even though I said I trusted Nacio, I'm having doubts. Regrets.

I try to remember what Reina said. That Roderick is a killer. He's killed before, and he deserves to be punished for that. But, by that reasoning, Nacio and Reina and their whole family deserve to die, too. They deserve to die for killing others.

It doesn't bring me any comfort to know that Roderick has killed.

I wish Roderick hadn't shown me that damn picture of his daughter. *Why did he have to trust me like that?* I would have rather not known. But even not knowing that he had a child wouldn't be enough to make this easy.

This time just feels different than Marcel. I know what to expect, and I'm deliberately agreeing to take part in it. I am one hundred percent complicit in this murder. I could go to jail for this. I could go to hell for this.

I glance over at Nacio, who is sitting calmly at the table, just staring at me. He doesn't say anything. He doesn't show any emotion. He just stares.

I trust him. That is why I'm doing this. I trust him. And I love him. And love makes you do crazy things.

The doorbell rings, but neither of us moves. We just stare, refusing to move and give up this moment together. A moment when life isn't perfect, far from it, but a moment of peace before the storm that is about to happen. A moment that I would have liked to stay in forever with Nacio.

"You got this?" Nacio asks.

I nod. I get up from the table, and Nacio does the same. I walk toward the door as the doorbell rings again. I feel Nacio behind me, but when I get to the door, I glance behind me, and I don't see him. I know he's there though, ready to kill.

I open the door with a frazzled look on my face. I grab at the robe I'm wearing, tying it together more tightly. "I'm so sorry. I'm not quite ready yet."

Roderick smiles as he looks at me, and I can't help but think it will be his last smile.

"Come in. You can have a drink while you wait for me to get dressed," I say. To my surprise, my voice is steady. *I trust him.*

"I would love to."

I open the door wider, welcoming him in. *I love the Beast.*

Roderick steps inside, and I shut the door.

"What can I make you?" I ask as I lead him toward the kitchen. "I have beer, wine, and most hard liquors."

"I'll have—"

He never answers me though.

I turn around and see Nacio has tackled him to the ground, and he has a wire in his hand.

I stare, frozen. I thought it would be over quickly. I thought Nacio would shoot him in the back of the head before he even realized what was happening.

This is why Nacio didn't want me in this life. This is dirty. It's personal. It's terrifying.

It's also the most electrifying thing I've ever been a part of.

I watch the men roll on the ground. Both are fighting for the upper hand. Roderick is bigger than Nacio, but Nacio is more experienced and knows how to manipulate Roderick to his advantage. I watch them grunt and shove and push each other until Nacio has Roderick pinned to the ground beneath him. He takes the wire and begins twisting it in his hands.

"Scarlett, help me!" Roderick screams.

I stand firm, looking at him. "I can't."

Roderick moves beneath Nacio, trying to break free, but Nacio has the wire, and he's pressing it against Roderick's neck.

Roderick doesn't beg, like Marcel did. He just looks death square in the face as Nacio begins tightening the wire around Roderick's neck.

I don't know why, but I'm drawn to them as I watch Nacio kill Roderick. I'm drawn forward, needing to see the life leave Roderick's eyes. Needing to see the look that is on Nacio's face as he takes a life.

I step close, and I can see the look in Roderick's eyes. It's not fear or terror, like I expected. It's defiance.

I open my mouth to speak. Nacio needs to know that Roderick isn't done fighting. Despite the cuts digging into his neck from the wire and the oxygen he isn't getting, he hasn't given up. He's just waiting for something.

"Naci—"

I don't get anything else out because Roderick has kicked me hard in the shin, and I tumble to the floor from the unexpected kick. It's the distraction Roderick was looking for because, instead of Nacio focusing on finishing the job, he is now focused on me. On making sure I'm okay.

"Nacio, look out!" I scream as Roderick punches Nacio square in the side of the head, knocking him down to the ground.

Nacio grabs his head and is slow to move after Roderick punched him. Roderick is ready. He jumps on top of Nacio and grabs his neck with his bare hands. He doesn't bother to use the wire.

I stand quickly and run over to them. "Get off of him!" I scream as I grab at Roderick, trying to get him off Nacio.

When I see the look on Nacio's face, I about lose it. He doesn't have a look of terror or fear either. But he doesn't have a look of defiance. He has a look of acceptance. Like this is the way it should be. This is the way things should happen.

I won't accept that though.

Roderick removes one hand from Nacio's throat long enough to shove me hard back to the ground. "I'll deal with you after I deal with your boyfriend here," he says.

"Like hell you will!" I quickly get up, not accepting that this is how Nacio is going to die. Not accepting that this is how I'm going to die because I know that is Roderick's plan as soon as he is done with Nacio.

I see Nacio fight with Roderick for a second.

Then, Nacio says, "Run, Scarlett! Get out of here."

I freeze, trying to decide what to do.

"You promised," he says.

I take a deep breath. He's right. I promised I would obey him when it really mattered. That I would do what he said, no matter what. I know this is why he told me that. To protect me. To keep me out of harm's way.

But he should have known better than to think that I would obey that promise if it meant him dying while trying to protect me. That's why he's not fighting. He's giving me time to run. To escape.

I won't leave him though.

I break my promise. I run toward them, scooping the discarded wire off the floor. I don't have a clue as to what to do with the wire. I don't know if I have the strength to do what needs to be done. But I just need to get Roderick off Nacio long enough so that it doesn't matter. That Nacio realizes I'm not leaving, so the only way he can protect me is by fighting back.

I run up behind Roderick, and I throw the wire around his neck. I pull like I've never pulled before.

"Scarlett, I told you to leave!" His air is closed off again by Roderick's hands. A few seconds later, he gets enough air again to whisper, "Run."

His words just make me tighten the wire harder until it forces Roderick to remove one of his hands from Nacio's neck to protect his own.

"Get off of me, bitch," Roderick says, trying to grab the wire but failing.

His hand grabs my wrist, and it's the one that I know is broken. I scream from the pain of him digging his fingers into me.

I can't hold on to the wire much longer. I'm in too much pain. But I won't let go. Not until Nacio starts fighting.

I don't have to wait long. Suddenly, we are both being pushed backward as Nacio pushes Roderick off of him.

I grab my hand as I fall to the ground, my head bouncing gently on the hardwood floor. Roderick somehow doesn't land on me but next to me, and Nacio grabs the wire. This time, he doesn't mess around. He pulls it tight, and I watch as Roderick struggles to get it off his neck.

I watch him gasp for air. I watch his face turn to pain, then fear, and then terror. I watch him try to suck in oxygen, but he can't get enough. I watch his body go limp. I watch Nacio take his life.

When Roderick is dead, Nacio falls back to the ground and then looks at me. I can see it in his eyes. He didn't want to kill Roderick, but he had to, to protect someone. I can see the anger in his eyes because I disobeyed him. I can also see something else there, and I'm not sure what it is.

I, on the other hand, know exactly what I look at him with.

"Why did you stay?" he asks. He pants hard, trying to catch his breath.

"Because I love you, and I couldn't live with myself if you died."

Nacio shakes his head and then smirks. "You will never learn to trust me, will you? I was never in any danger. I could have gotten out of that at any second. I was just trying to protect you."

"Uh-huh," I say. But I don't care about his words. I'm tired of waiting for him to come to me. I will run after this man to the ends of the earth because I love him.

I launch myself at him and tackle him to the ground, next to Roderick's body. And then I kiss Nacio with everything I have.

26

BEAST

SCARLETT KISSES ME. I don't understand this woman at all.

She kisses me after she just watched me murder a man.

I pull away from her, trying to get her to stop. She can't kiss me. She can't want this.

"What are you doing?" I ask, afraid that she has lost her damn mind.

She is kissing a killer. She's seen me kill twice, and there is no denying it this time. There is no denying that I'm a monster.

"I'm kissing you."

I let her kiss me again because I want her. God, I want her. I've never wanted anything more in my life than her right now. And I can't resist her kisses. Her soft lips are just as desperate for me as I am for her.

But I force her away again because she has to be in fucking shock. She can't want this.

"What are you doing? I want to kiss you. I want to do a hell of a lot more than kiss you. So, stop tearing me away from you because I need you more than I need air right now," she says.

"You just watched me kill a man."

"I watched you protect me."

"That wasn't self-defense. We attacked a man, and he acted in self-defense."

She nods. "I know. But we both protected each other, and that's all I care about right now. I love you, and I need you to fucking make love to me right now."

She kisses me again on the lips, and I give in. I don't care that a man we both killed is lying on the floor next to us. I don't care that we most likely have no future together. All I care about is her.

Taking her. Pleasing her. Loving her.

For the first time in my life, I want to make love to a woman because I know, without a doubt, she loves me.

I kiss her back, and she moans, happy that I'm finally on board with her.

She wouldn't have stayed if she didn't love me.

I rip her robe open, exposing her body that is completely naked beneath it. I growl. I wasn't expecting that.

"You're such a naughty girl," I say as I kiss down her neck.

She smiles and rips my shirt open. "You have no idea how naughty."

"Oh, I know exactly how naughty you are, Beauty."

I kiss down her neck to her breasts.

"I'm not nearly as naughty as you," she sighs.

"Maybe not. But you're close enough."

She wouldn't have faced jail time.

She screams as I nip at her breasts, and it's the most beautiful sound I've ever heard.

I need to kiss every inch of her body. That's what I need. And it seems she needs to kiss every inch of mine. She battles my kisses with her own. I kiss her breasts. She kisses my chest. I kiss her stomach. She kisses my abs. It goes back and forth in slow, torturous kisses until I can't handle it anymore.

She wouldn't have faced absolute death.

I stand, scooping her up in my arms. If I'm going to have her for the first time in days, I'm going to have her in a proper bed that doesn't have a dead body right next to it. I lift her up, and she puts her arms around me, like we have done this a million times before. Like she was expecting me to do this.

She kisses my lips, my neck, my chest. Every part of my body that she can get her lips on, she kisses. And I kiss any part that I can kiss. I carry her up the stairs to the bed, but instead of tossing her, I gently lay her down, unable to let her leave my arms for even a second. I need her close too much to do anything else. To even let her go for a second.

She, on the other hand, is no longer patient. She lowers my pants as I stand next to the bed with her still in my arms. She pushes my pants down until my cock is free.

I need to feel every inch of her. I need to love her. I climb on top of the bed, and then I realize my fucking mistake, but I don't know how to fucking stop.

"I don't have a condom."

She laughs. "You think I'm worried about getting pregnant or getting an STD after we just killed someone? I'm on birth control, and if you have an STD, you'd just better not give it to me."

I push my cock against her entrance because I can't stand it if she is playing with me.

I need this. I need her. I need to love her. I need that feeling that I've never experienced, proving to me why I went after her. Why I've lived the last ten years of my life for her, since the moment I saw her. To prove that, for once in my goddamn life, I did the right thing.

"You sure?" I ask.

"Yes," she breathes.

I enter her, and it's like entering heaven. She's perfect for me. She's what I've been searching for my entire life, even when I didn't realize I'd been searching for anything. She's everything.

I move, and she moves with me. I groan, and she groans. I kiss, and she kisses. We are in perfect synchrony as we move.

My eyes stay locked on hers, and hers are on mine. We tell each other everything.

That what we did was okay.

That this is perfect.

That this is what it's like to make love to someone.

Each time she says something, we thrust and move together, getting closer but needing more from each other. Each needing something that has to be spoken and not just felt. Each needing confirmation that, in this moment, what we are feeling is real and not something that will disappear after we've left this room.

I keep thrusting until the emotions are all I feel. Until I can't help but feel anything else. Until I know that what I'm feeling is for real. Because I couldn't bear telling her how I feel and it not being the absolute truth. Because I know it is. I can see it in her eyes. I can feel in the way she makes love to me. I know it's true from the way she tried to protect me from Roderick earlier.

I open my mouth, and for the first time in my life, I say words that I never thought I would say to anyone, "I love you, Beauty."

She gasps, as I know I'm pushing her slowly over the edge. "I love you, too."

We both come, and it's the most beautiful, peaceful thing I've ever experienced. It's also the most electrifying thing I've ever experienced. None of the killing I've done can even compare. None of the other women I have been with make the radar. Only her. Only my Beauty.

I collapse on top of her and then roll over so that she is on top of me, but I don't exit. I need to stay inside her forever. I can't leave. Not after that. I need to feel connected to her forever. I'm afraid that, once I leave her, this thing we have going right now will be over. And that can't happen. I need her. Need her with me forever.

We both breathe hard with me still inside her. With us still connected. We just made love for the first time, and I don't know what to do about it now.

"We still have to figure out what to do with Roderick's body."

I laugh. "That's what you are thinking about right now? I just gave you my heart and soul, and that's all you can think about?"

"No. I just don't want to make a big deal about what you said. I already knew you loved me. I don't need to rub it in your face."

I tangle my hand in her hair. "You're right. Don't worry about

Roderick. We are going to make it look like his ex-girlfriend and her boyfriend were the ones that killed him."

"Am I supposed to be the ex-girlfriend?"

"No. This house isn't in your name, and I'll make sure none of your DNA is in the house. You're safe. I'll protect you."

"And I'll protect you," she says.

I smile. "I know."

"What do we do now? Do we need to do anything with—"

"No. I'll have Santino do it. You don't need to worry about anything."

"What about us? What are we going to do about us?"

I take a deep breath. "I don't know. All I know is, I love you," I say.

She smiles and snuggles into my chest. "That's good enough for me."

27

SCARLETT

I DON'T KNOW what just happened, and I don't care. I don't think about what we did to Roderick. I don't think about what he did to us. I don't think about how Nacio's and my DNA is probably everywhere in that house and that it's going to be impossible to get it all out and frame someone else. I don't think about how horrible it is that we would frame someone else.

All I think about are three simple words that I finally heard Nacio say. *"I love you."*

He loves me. Not that I didn't already know that, but he finally admitted it. It means, there is a chance. A chance at more than just this week.

I don't know what it means for our future. I don't know if it means he will give this up and come back with me. I don't know if it means I'll give up my job and join his world. I don't know if it means we will support each other's jobs and live in this fantasy world between the two.

But it means he will work as hard as I will to make something happen.

I walk into Reina's house, blissfully happy. I shouldn't be happy after killing someone. It's wrong. It's the worst thing. But it's the truth.

I'm happy. For the first time in a long time. I'm happy and in love and loved. And, for now, that's enough.

Nacio doesn't walk in with me. He gives me another kiss and says he's going to go help Santino. He doesn't say with what, but I already know what he's talking about. He's going to help Santino fix the crime scene to look like someone else did it.

I have no idea how I ended up in this world. A world where it is okay to kill people. But I don't care because I found my Beast. A man whom I still don't fully understand. I know he still has demons lurking that he hasn't told me about, but don't we all? And we can get past them. Together.

I skip into the house. I skip past the kitchen and living room. I skip past Reina's office until I hear her fucking voice, "We need to talk."

"I don't think we do."

"We do."

"Why?"

"Because I need to tell you the truth."

I freeze. I don't want to talk to her. I don't want to hear that she didn't tell me the truth. She doesn't have to. I already know the truth.

"I already know the truth."

"No, you don't."

I watch as Reina walks into her office. I pause, trying to decide what I should do. *Do I follow her?*

I know I'm going to regret my next decision, but I follow her into her office.

I stand at the entrance with my arms crossed across my chest. "What do you want to tell me? And make it quick; you're killing my buzz."

She smiles. "Good. Most people are a wreck after the first time they have been involved in killing someone."

"It wasn't my first time."

She nods. "You're right. Still, your demeanor is unusual." She shakes her head. "Anyway, my point is, I lied to you, and I just wanted to apologize."

"You lied to me about what?"

She sighs. "Everything."

I don't know why I trust this woman, but I walk toward the seat and sink into it, hanging on to her every word. Needing to know whatever truth she is going to tell me because the truth I thought I knew might not be the whole truth.

"I lied to you about Roderick. He isn't a bad person. Well, he wasn't."

"What do you mean?"

She sighs, like it was just a silly mistake she made about what color to paint her office or something. "I got a little mixed up, but Roderick didn't kill anyone."

My whole world shatters. "You're lying."

"I'm afraid I'm not. It's the truth. I told Nacio last night, but he insisted on doing the job anyway, something about testing you. I should probably explain more about Nacio's past now that it seems the two of you are an item."

I hear her speak, but I don't register anything. I haven't known this woman long enough to know if she is telling the truth or not. I'll have to wait until Nacio gets back.

"So, you asked me a while back about why Nacio is the way that he is. Well, I've decided, you've earned the right to know about his past."

I laugh. "You sure this isn't all a part of a scheme you have?"

"And what scheme would that be?"

"I'm not sure, but I plan on finding out."

"You do that. Anyway, I just thought you should know why Nacio is the way he is."

"I would rather find that out from him."

She nods. "Of course. I'm just afraid he will never tell you. You see, it involves me, too, and he thinks he can protect me by not sharing it."

I suck in a breath. I don't trust this woman, but somehow, I'm hanging on to her every word.

"You see, Nacio messed me up when I was a kid. He did some

unspeakable things to me. Our father did it first, but then Nacio joined in. He didn't protect me when he should have."

To hear her story, I need more air than this room is holding. I study her, trying to decide if she is telling the truth or not. *But why would she lie when a simple question to Nacio or Santino would get me the truth?*

"He helped my father rape me. Nacio abused me. He hurt me."
No. No. No.

"I almost died because of him."
She's lying. He didn't.

"So, you see now, he will do anything to protect me."
She's wrong.

"Including killing an innocent man because I asked him to. He owes me that much. He owes me my life back."

"You're lying," is all I say.

"Ask him yourself." She smiles as she points to the doorway where Nacio is standing.

I don't know why he's standing there. He couldn't have made it to the house where Roderick's body is and back so soon. Reina told him to come back, is the only answer I can come up with.

I don't have enough strength to ask multiple questions. I don't know how long he has been standing there. I just need to know if what she said is the truth. And, if it's not, then I can take him upstairs and make love to him again and again. And, if it is...then I'm not sure what I will do.

"Is it true? Is what she said true?" I ask him.

"Yes."

28

BEAST

THE PAIN I feel when I tell Scarlett yes is worse than anything I've ever felt, and I went through a lot of shit as a kid. I was spanked harder than most kids ever have been. I watched and participated in my sister's abuse. I've watched people die in front of me since I was three. But nothing compares to the look Scarlett is giving me. I thought she loved me. I thought I had finally found someone who loved me. I was wrong. She doesn't love me, or she would be giving me a chance right now. Instead, she is giving me no chance. None.

"Reina, can you give us a minute?"

"Sure." Reina gets up, smirking at me, like she was right.

She's never right. I watch her leave, and then I shut the door behind her.

"Is it true? Is it all true?" Scarlett asks, looking at me like she's never looked at me before.

"Yes," I whisper.

She looks down at her lap and then back up at me, and I see the tears in her eyes.

"I trusted you. I protected you. I killed for you. And you lied to me!"

I stand, frozen, not denying it because it's the truth. "I told you I was a monster. I told you not to fall in love with me, that you were wrong."

Scarlett stands suddenly, and I don't know what to do. She paces back and forth in the office, occasionally grabbing her hair or falling to her knees in tears.

"I need to go," she says suddenly.

"Where?"

"I need to go home."

I nod. "I'll get you a flight."

She nods and then walks toward me, tears staining her cheeks. "Come with me."

"What?"

"Come with me. Give up this life. Try again. Start over. You can be whoever you want to be. You can be a better man," she pleads.

I look at my Beauty standing in front of me, and it's exactly what I want to do. I want to come with her. I want to give up this life for her. But there are things she simply doesn't understand. There are things she doesn't understand, and I can't tell her yet, despite how I feel about her.

"I can't."

Her face drops, and I see more tears falling from her eyes.

I begin wiping them. "Please stop. Just wait. We can figure this out. Just give me a day or two, and I can come up with something that will work for both of us."

"I can't."

I freeze because I don't know where we go from here. Two people who love one another, but are unwilling to yield. That only leads to one place. Being apart.

"I need to go. I can't stay here," she says as she tries to brush past me.

I can't let her leave like this. I grab her arm, keeping her with me.

"Do you still love me? Despite everything you know? Despite everything I've done?" I ask.

If she says yes, I will do whatever she wants me to. I'll leave everything behind. I'll give my whole world up for her. I'll do anything for her, if she just says yes. If she just says she loves me, I will make her my whole world. After what I experienced this afternoon, it will be worth it.

"Do you still love me?" I ask again when she doesn't answer me.

Her eyes find mine, and we just stare at each other. Trying to understand what the other is saying, but not understanding because the connection is gone. The love is gone.

"Do you still love me?"

"No."

And then she's gone. The only good thing left with just a single word.

29

SCARLETT

I LEFT.

I just fucking left the only man I ever truly loved, standing there, after I let his sister tell me the truth. I didn't even wait for him to tell me the rest. I just fucking left.

And, since I made it back to NYC, I've done everything possible to forget.

To forget about Nacio.

To forget about his siblings.

To forget about two men who are now dead because of me.

To forget about Beast.

He hasn't reached out to me since that day. He hasn't called. He hasn't texted. He hasn't shown up in NYC.

Nothing.

It's all I want. For him to text me, like he used to for a late-night booty call. To do something so simple.

He doesn't though. He hasn't contacted me at all.

And it's been six months. Too long for him to come tell me I'm wrong. Too long to come offer an apology. Too long for me to go to him and tell him I still love him.

Because I do. I don't understand it, but despite everything, I still love him. I still want him.

I've done everything I can to move past him.

At first, it was burying myself in my work with Preston.

Then, it was hanging out with Kinsley every evening.

Then, it was taking a different man home to my bed every night.

Because that's what I do when I'm lonely and alone and broken. I fuck strange men. I try to forget about Beast. I try to forget about everything, but he doesn't let me forget. He haunts my memories. He haunts my dreams. My thoughts. My everything.

Even knowing how bad he truly is.

Even though he made me just as bad as him. A killer.

I still think of him.

I still want him.

I still love him.

I don't know how to let him go. I just know, I need to do something to redeem myself. I need something to make me whole again that doesn't involve Nacio. I need something to bring life into the world when I've taken so much from it.

And I know exactly what that is.

30

BEAST

IT'S BEEN six months without Scarlett. And I hate my life. I hate it. I hate every fucking second of it.

I hate that my life is meaningless now.

I hate that I kill for a living.

I hate that I'm nothing but a puppy to Reina.

I hate that I fucking messed up.

I hate that I still love Scarlett.

"Nacio!" Reina hollers at me from her office.

I walk in, waiting to hear about the next man that she wants me to kill. I've killed too many men since Scarlett left. I've killed men just because I can't have her and I need her. I've killed because Reina asked me to. I've killed, and I hate the person I've become.

I walk into Reina's office. "What?"

"I have another one for you," she says.

I look at the picture of a young man who can't be more than twenty before I take a seat. "I need a break, Reina."

She freezes and looks at me. "We don't take breaks."

"I don't care. I need one."

"Fine. Just promise me, when you come back, you'll handle Kinsley."

I freeze. I've been waiting for Reina to ask me about her since Scarlett left. Reina thinks that, just because Scarlett left, it will make it easier for me to kill Kinsley now. It doesn't. It's still just as hard for me.

"I'll think about it."

She shakes her head. "I need an answer. Today."

"Then, my answer is no."

She frowns. "Why? She left you. She doesn't love you anymore. You should just let it go."

"I can't."

"Why?"

"Because I still love her."

Reina's smile drops. "But what if she doesn't love you back?"

"What if she doesn't love me because I didn't fight hard enough for her?"

She sighs. "You need to fight then."

"What?" I ask in confusion. That wasn't what I was expecting from her. "I thought you hated Scarlett."

She smiles. "I like Scarlett. I just want the absolute best for my brother. So, I'll do anything to make sure that happens."

"What did you do?"

Reina walks over and sits next to me. "I didn't do anything. I just told her the same lie that our father and I have been telling you for years. It's not the truth though."

I glare at Reina. "What's the truth?"

"That you weren't involved in my abuse. That you were just as innocent as I was."

"No, that's not true. I abused you, just like our father did."

Reina grabs my head and forces me to look at her. "No, you didn't, Nacio. I hoped you would remember on your own. I wanted you to realize on your own that you deserve to be loved. You just haven't. I thought Scarlett would help you with that, and she did, but I realize now that I hold the other part of it. That you can't fully love her and let her love you without me telling you the complete truth."

I soften my eyes as I look at her. "And what is the truth?"

418

"Our father forced you to do everything you remember doing to me. He videotaped it. He sold it to the highest bidder to make the most amount of money."

"That's not true. I remember what I did to you. It was horrible."

She shakes her head as tears stain her eyes. "You remember what happened after he brainwashed you."

I fall to my knees at the realization that my entire life has been based on a lie. All of it is a lie. An untruth. All of my life has been based on the fact that I knowingly fucked my sister. That is the worst crime I committed. And it was all a lie.

"Why didn't you tell me before?"

"Because I didn't realize what the truth was until recently, and even then, I didn't think you would believe me."

"So, you hid it from me."

"Yes."

I grab my head, just trying to get over the pain at realizing I could have done better. I should have protected her. I shouldn't have given in. But I also feel too much anger at what my sister did.

"Do you realize what I've done for you? You don't even realize how I've protected you these last few years. You have no fucking clue what you've done, do you?"

"No. But I'm so sorry, Nacio. I want to make it right. I need to make it right."

I shake my head. "You can't."

She looks at me and smiles. "Yes, I can. Go see Scarlett."

31

SCARLETT

I GET HOME from another miserable day at work. Not miserable because work is miserable. Just miserable because it was another day without Nacio.

I flick the light switch and freeze, standing in my apartment, when the lights don't come on.

"Hello?" I shout into my apartment.

But no one answers.

I reach into my purse to pull out my phone to call the damn super to get my lights fixed. When I reach into my purse, I feel a hand on mine. A hand I instantly recognize, despite not having seen him for over six months.

"What are you doing here?" I ask.

He doesn't answer.

Instead, I feel his hands go around me. "I'm here to kiss you in the dark."

His lips land on my neck, and I moan softly.

I've dreamed of this every night for months. I've thought of nothing else but what it would be like to reconnect. I've dreamed that this day might actually happen.

But, now that it is, I have no idea what to do. I have no idea what to say. I have no idea how to feel. So, I concentrate on figuring out how I feel as his hands move over my body, as his lips touch my neck.

"And after?" I ask with a shaky voice.

"After, I will do anything you want."

I suck in a breath. "Anything?"

He spins me around, and his lips crash with mine. He kisses me, and the world stops. All that matters is this kiss.

I forget why I was mad at him. I forget why I left him in the first place. All I care about is kissing him and letting him kiss me back.

I tangle my hand in his hair and pull him hard, toward me. Desperate to have him. Desperate to forget that he hurt me.

He pulls away though after a few more moments pass, and I immediately feel empty, needing more of his kisses. Needing more of him.

"I will do anything for you."

Suddenly, I come to my senses.

The last six months flash through my head. Those six months were some of the hardest months in my life, and he wasn't there for me. And, now, he's walking back into my life, like nothing fucking happened. Like it was a silly mistake that he can easily fix. He doesn't understand what happened during these last six months. He doesn't understand that I've changed.

"It doesn't matter now. You left, and I've moved on. It's too late," I say.

I turn and begin to walk farther into my apartment, hoping to escape him, but he won't let me. He pulls me to him.

"Beauty, I love you. I'm so sorry for hurting you. I will do anything to make this better."

I shake my head as I feel the tears coming after hearing words that I've dreamed of hearing every day for six months. Words that are so perfect but too late.

"I don't want to hear it now. It's too late."

He grabs my cheeks and kisses me again. The kiss is hard, passionate, and desperate. I cling on to his desperation because it is the same feeling I have. But I break away as tears sting my eyes and flow down my cheeks.

"I can't do this. I won't just take you back because you came back and said some nice things to me. You still fucked up. You still killed an innocent man. You still messed up your sister. You're a monster, Beast."

I can't see him, but I can feel his sadness at my words. My words needed to be said though. I feel him move closer to me, and then I feel his thumb wipe a tear from my cheek.

"I'm sorry. I am a beast, a monster. And you don't have to love me again so easily. You don't have to take me back right now, but I'm going to spend the rest of my life making you fall in love with me again."

I suck in a breath at his words. I love his words, but I don't love him.

But I could fall so easily in love with him again. *How long would it take? A year? A month? A week? A day? A second?*

None of those times are long enough. Because I can't fall in love with him again. I can't. It will destroy me, just like last time. He's not good for me. And I need him to go. I need him to stay out of my life before he makes me fall in love with him again. I have no doubt that he could do that.

So, instead, I say the only thing I can think of to get him to leave. I tell him a truth, "I'm pregnant. That's why you can't stay, Beast. You're a monster. I can't have you around this baby."

There is a long pause between us. I know he has comprehended what I just said. He's trying to figure out the timing of it all. Trying to understand if it is possibly his.

I wait. I wait for him to ask the question that I know he wants to ask, but doesn't at the same time. I wait because, for these few moments when he's not asking, our world isn't completely shattered, and there is a chance we can be together again.

But I won't let that happen. And I already know that my answer to his question is going to shatter him.

I hear him suck in a breath, and I'm pretty sure he has sucked in all the oxygen from the room because there is none left for me.

"Is the baby mine?"

"No."

The End

Keep reading for Definitely Forever...

DEFINITELY FOREVER

1

BEAST

"Is it mine?" I ask.

"No."

That word kills me, destroys me. It was absolutely the last thing I expected when I came here today. I expected Scarlett would be upset with me. I expected she would yell. I expected she would kick me out.

But I also expected I could eventually convince her that I loved her. I thought I could convince her that I'd changed, that I could continue to change for her. I thought I could convince her to let me protect her with some work on my part.

But that one little word has changed all those thoughts. That one little word has destroyed any chance of any of that ever happening. That one little word has destroyed me.

I've been frozen since that word fell from her lips. I could hear the anger in her voice as she said that word. She had known what that word would do to me. But I also felt the tiniest bit of sadness. On some level, that means she still cares about me.

I take a deep breath for the first time in minutes after she told me my world was over. I close my eyes as I breathe. I can already feel the pain sinking into my chest. I can already feel it spreading throughout my body.

I take another deep breath and open my eyes. I look across the darkness at Beauty, who is standing frozen as well, staring at me. I don't know what is going through her mind right now. I don't know what she is thinking. But I can feel her pain with every breath. And I have to know why she is putting herself through so much pain. *For whom?*

"Whose is it?"

"We aren't doing this, Beast."

I wince when she says the word *Beast*. It no longer feels like an endearment. It feels like a knife being shoved into my heart.

I watch her turn to walk away from me, heading toward the door to get me to leave, but I can't leave yet. Not without answers. I have to know why she's destroyed everything that could have been.

I run toward her and step between her and the door. "Stop."

She does.

"Whose baby is it? You owe me that, don't you think?"

She shakes her head. "I don't owe you anything. You lied to me. You tested me. You hurt me. I moved on. That's all you need to know."

She tries to push by me, but I grab her arm, quickly stopping her in her tracks.

"Please."

I can hear her swallow as she contemplates my request. It's pathetic—my begging, my *pleading*. I'm not used to such words falling from my lips. I'm used to hearing that word falling from her lips when my cock is buried deep inside her.

She takes a deep breath, and I watch her chest rise and fall. I know she's in pain, just like I am.

She shakes her head, but doesn't say a word. She doesn't answer me.

I run a hand through my hair, trying not to let the defeat overwhelm me, like it so easily could. If I let it, I'll do something crazy, like go out and kill whomever I think the father is. I can't do that. I have to think straight. At least, I can't kill someone until I'm sure who the motherfucker is.

"I need to know who destroyed us, Scarlett. I need to know who took away the only good thing in my life, Scar," I say. I don't know why I called her Scar. I never have before, but it feels like I'm pleading with a best friend instead of a lover. Instead of the woman I want to spend all my life with. If I don't have her, I'm not sure what's the point of continuing my life.

To protect her.

"You're the reason we aren't together. You're the reason we can never be together. Don't blame the guy who knocked me up. Long before he came around, you made it clear we could never be together."

She brushes past me this time, and I watch in horror as she walks to the door. There is nothing left to do short of throwing her over my shoulder, tying her up, and torturing her until she tells me who did this to her. But her words ring in my ear. It was me. This is my fault. I did this. I'm the monster here, not anyone else.

I just need to get out of her life before I destroy anything else. Before I cause her any more pain.

I walk toward the door that Scarlett has her hand on, ready to throw me out the second she can't handle talking to me anymore, which I know is only seconds away from happening. I know she is seconds away from tears staining her cheeks, and I know she won't let me see her cry. Not today. Not after what I did to her.

I stop a foot away from her, but it doesn't stop me from asking again because I have to know. I have to know that she and the baby are going to be taken care of. I need to know.

"Just tell me. Please."

She opens the door, and the light from the hallway pours into her apartment.

"No, Nacio. You don't get to know the answer to that. I don't want to go to bed, worried that you are going to kill the father. We are through. And, if you do anything to change that, if you do anything to hurt me, my child, or the father..." Her voice trembles.

I involuntarily reach out to try to hold her. She lets me for a second, obviously just needing comfort from wherever she can get it. I hold her until she stops shaking. I smell the fresh, flowery scent in her hair from her shampoo. I study every curve of her body as she is pressed against me. I memorize the sound of her breathing, so I can take it with me forever to recall while I try to sleep.

I let her go without waiting for her to ask me to. Letting her go is the hardest thing I will ever do. And I'm not sure I will survive it. I'm not sure I'm strong enough.

"I love you, Beauty. I'm sorry it took me so long to figure it out, but I do. I never meant to hurt you. I just hope that the father takes care of you like you deserve."

I watch her drop her head. I see a tear sneak out from her eye and roll gently down her cheek. With one finger under her chin, I lift her head so that she is looking at me. And, looking at her, I know who the father is. There is only one other man it could be. Her ex. Jake.

I drove her back to him. I drove her to do something stupid. I drove her to a lifetime of being stuck with that jerk. This is my fault.

"I'm sorry," I say with my own tears burning my eyes as I see how broken she is by what I've done to her.

"Me, too."

I close my eyes and lean my forehead against hers, wishing that things were different. If one or two things had been different, if I had just done things differently, she would have been mine right now. The baby would have been mine.

My heart speeds up at that thought. I'm not even scared at the thought of having a baby anymore. Not if a woman like Scarlett were there to take care of the baby with me. That will never happen now though.

I lean back. "I'm not going anywhere. If you need me, just call. No matter if it's just for a shoulder to cry on. No matter if that is all I can be for you."

She doesn't say anything. She just stares at me with her arms crossed over her chest, holding herself, trying to bring herself some comfort now that she is no longer in my arms and probably never will be again.

"I'm going to protect you. No matter what. You don't have to worry. I can at least give you that."

I turn my head to the brightly lit hallway and then look back at her one more time. I look at her in the darkness that she fits into so well. A darkness that I brought her into and taught her about. A darkness that welcomed her with open arms.

But she doesn't really belong in the darkness. She doesn't really belong with me. It was only meant to be a chapter of her life. A dark, dangerous chapter that she would tell her kids about when they were teenagers to explain the dangers of the world. It wasn't meant to be forever.

Now, it's my turn to step into the light. Not because the light will take me to her. Because I know it won't. It will just allow me to protect her in the way she deserves.

I take a step out into the lit hallway and don't look back.

"I'll protect you, Beauty. I love you, Beauty. No matter what."

2

SCARLETT

My phone buzzes with the alarm, startling me from a nightmare. The same nightmare I have every night. The nightmare that has become my reality.

The man I love is gone. He came to see me, and I just let him leave. No, I pushed him away and told him there was no chance of us being together. That we were over.

I told him the exact opposite of what I wanted to happen, but it was what had to happen. I can't be with him. Not now that a baby is involved. Not when so many people need my protection.

I roll over to grab my phone and turn off the alarm. I'm not getting out of bed today. I can't handle another day where he isn't in it. I don't see the point of getting out of bed. I roll back over, throwing the covers over my head to block out any light and the chill of the early morning.

I don't know why I set my alarm last night. It wasn't like I was actually going to go into work today. Last night, I felt defiant though. I felt like I could do anything. But, in the morning light, everything has changed because I didn't sleep for more than a couple of hours last night.

I take a couple of deep breaths, trying to get back to sleep, when my phone begins buzzing again.

I sigh. I must have hit the Snooze button instead of the Off button. I throw the covers off my head and grab my annoying phone off my nightstand, prepared to break it to get it to stop because I can't handle the shrill sound any longer.

I grab the phone and realize that the alarm isn't going off. Instead, Preston is calling me. I narrow my eyes at the phone as I read his name. I hit the Ignore button and then flop back down onto my bed. The phone rings again a second later.

I grab my forehead that is now pounding in pain with a headache.

On the third ring, I grab the phone and answer it with my eyes closed. "What?" I bark.

"Good morning, Scarlett. Just wanted to call and make sure you were up. I didn't want you to miss work again for the third time this week."

"I'm sick. I'm not coming in."

Preston laughs. "You don't get sick. I don't think, in the almost ten years I've worked for you, that you've ever called in sick, except this week. Even when you were nearly dying from the flu three years ago, you still came in until I convinced you to go see the doctor. And, even then, you didn't leave until after lunch. You're not sick. You sound fine."

"Well, I am sick. So, get over it, and just handle things, Preston."

"You're not sick. You're just depressed about that stupid guy. And you still haven't told me what happened with him."

"I'm sick. I'm not depressed about him. And don't expect me to talk about him when you still haven't told me why you broke up with your girlfriend."

He pauses, and I think that maybe I've won. That he is going to let me sleep in. It's a Friday. No point in going in for one day and then not working all weekend. I would just have to start all over again on Monday. It'd be much better to just go in on Monday instead of starting off on Friday.

"You are coming in, Scarlett. Even if I have to come to your apartment and carry you into work myself. And I have a wedding I'm going to in California, so I would really like not to be sore or suffering from any broken bones because you know I'm not strong enough to carry even your light ass. So, don't make me come over there and do that because I will."

I sigh. Nothing he says is convincing me, but I am afraid that he is going to come here and drive me crazy until I come into work. I look around my messy bedroom. Clothes, pregnancy books, and leftover food are scattered throughout the room. I haven't told him yet that I'm pregnant, and I'm not ready to tell him today.

"Fine, I'm coming in. Don't get your panties in a bunch." I end the call just as a wave of nausea sets in.

I jump out of bed and run to my bathroom that is just off my bedroom. I make it just in time to empty my stomach into the toilet.

When my stomach finally seems to settle, I lean back against the wall, trying to catch my breath. I hate throwing up. It's the worst feeling. My doctor says it's a good sign. It means I will have a healthy baby, but it still isn't very reassuring. Not when I'll be dealing with my pregnancy symptoms alone—at least, for a little while longer. And it doesn't reassure me that I will have a healthy baby, not after my best friend lost her baby.

I go to the sink and wipe my face. I brush my teeth before I go back to my bedroom to find some clothes to wear. My phone buzzes, and I see a text message from Preston. He already let George, my driver, know to be ready to pick me up in half an hour.

I pull up George's number and ask him to pick me up some ginger ale and saltines. I'm going to need it to get through the day if I don't want to spend the whole day in the bathroom instead of working.

"You look like hell," Preston says with surprise as I walk into my office.

I run my hand through my hair that I washed, but didn't bother blow-drying or straightening. I know it's only a matter of time before it turns into a frizzy mess. I don't really care though. If I have any important meetings where I'll have to look better than this, I can have one of our stylists fix my messy hair.

"You didn't even put on any makeup," Preston says as he follows me into my office.

"Nope. I'm going for the fresh-faced look. Isn't that the style these days?"

"Well, yes, but in order to pull off the fresh, clean face, most women still wear some makeup. They just wear it in such a way so that it looks like they aren't wearing any makeup. You look like..."

"Death."

He nods.

"I told you, I'm sick. I don't feel well. So, can you please stop discussing how horrible I look and tell me what I absolutely have to do today so that I can get out of here as soon as possible?"

Preston nods and then places my latte on my desk. I pick up the drink, lifting it to my lips, but I know I can't drink it. I haven't drunk coffee in weeks—and not because caffeine isn't the best thing for the baby. I would love to drink some caffeine if it helped me get out of bed in the morning. For some reason, the baby—who I will question a lot in the future about torturing me so much while I was pregnant —doesn't like coffee and won't let me drink any without getting sick.

For the last couple of weeks when I have been in the office, I've waited until Preston has left before I pour the latte out, so he won't grow suspicious because, all of a sudden, after ten years, I no longer drink lattes.

My nose scrunches up at the smell, and I know I'm not going to be able to wait until he leaves. The smell alone is going to make me—

I run to the trash can in the corner of the room and dry-heave into it since nothing is left in my stomach. To my surprise, Preston runs over to me and rubs my back as I attempt to vomit.

It takes a moment for my stomach to settle before I sink onto the small couch in my office. Preston runs out of the room and returns with some ginger ale. It's the second one I've had today after George got me one this morning.

I take a sip. "Thanks."

Preston takes a seat next to me as I lean my head back against the headrest.

"I'm sorry. I didn't realize you were really sick. I thought you were just moping around because of that guy. And we have a meeting with Madeline, so I just thought—"

I sit up and look at Preston. "Wait, today is the meeting with Madeline, the amazing designer from France?"

Preston nods. "Yes, she flew in this morning and is in town for only a couple of hours. I know you wanted to meet with her and see if she would be interested in working with you on a children's line. I knew you wouldn't want to miss it, but I can see now that we will have to find a way to reschedule."

"No."

Preston narrows his eyes at me. "No? But you are sick, Scarlett. You can't possibly get through a meeting with her when you are likely to vomit all over her if she decides to bring in a coffee or any other food, which is likely since the meeting is supposed to be over lunch."

I glare at Preston. He's the one who called me into work today when I told him I couldn't make it, and now, he's trying to convince me that I shouldn't actually work after I dragged myself out of bed to come here. That's not happening. I'm taking the meeting, no matter what he says.

"I'm taking the meeting."

"No, you aren't. You're sick, Scarlett. I'm taking you to see a doctor. Then, I'm taking your butt to the nearest bed, and I'm not letting you leave until you feel a lot better."

I shake my head. "I'm not going to the doctor. I already know what I have. And I'm going to be fine."

I stand up to walk back to my desk. Preston stands as well, stepping between me and my desk. He pushes me back into a seated position.

"You are going to sit your ass down right there until I can make sure you have an appointment with your doctor, and then I'll get ahold of George to come pick you up."

I get a whiff of something. I think it is peanut butter on his breath, and I reach for the trash can, scared that I'm going to vomit again. I feel the uneasiness in my stomach grow as I try to deal with the offensive smell, but since nothing is left in my stomach, I don't actually throw up.

"See? You can't even sit here for a couple of minutes without getting sick."

"I didn't get sick," I say, glaring at Preston.

He rolls his eyes at me. "Close enough. Now, let's get you to the doctor," Preston says, standing in front of me with his hands outstretched to help me off the couch.

"Oh, for Christ's sake! I'm pregnant, Preston!"

Preston's eyes grow large, and he falls back onto the couch next to me.

"Whose baby is it?"

The question doesn't come from Preston sitting next to me. The voice comes from the male standing in my doorway. A man I know all too well.

I run my hand through my hair that is now more frizz than wet ringlets. I try to force a smile onto my lips, but it's no use. *How can I smile when I just told an ex I was pregnant after I'd planned on not telling anyone yet? Not even Preston.*

"Hi, Jake," I say, getting up from the couch. I walk over to my desk like I'm his boss and not his ex-girlfriend. "What can I help you with?" I ask, trying to shift the conversation from my pregnant belly that Jake is now staring at, despite it not changing shape yet, to work, the only thing I'm willing to talk about with Jake.

Jake takes a step into my office. I glance to the door. I don't remember if Preston closed it or not when we entered. I don't know if Jake just pushed into my office without knocking or if he just happened to be standing outside of my open door when I shouted out to the world that I was pregnant. I watch as Jake turns around and shuts the door, like that is going to help now.

Jake turns back to me. "Whose baby is it, Scarlett?"

I narrow my eyes at him. I can't believe he just asked me that again. I take a seat behind my desk without removing my eyes from his. "What do you need, Jake?"

He briskly walks forward and places his hands on my desk as he leans over, looking me square in the face. He's not happy. His cheeks are red, and his eyes darken as he looks at me. But he has no reason not to be happy with me. He's not my boyfriend anymore, not even my friend. He's just an employee that I can't wait to get rid of.

"I need to know who is responsible for knocking you up. I need to know so that I can make sure he is properly taking care of you."

I shake my head. "I can't believe you. You have no right to ask me that. It's none of your business. None." I take a deep breath, trying to remain calm. I don't know much, but I'm sure getting angry won't help the baby at all. "Now, if you don't have any work-related things to talk about, I think you should leave."

"Scarlett, just tell me. I want to help," Jake says.

"I don't need your help. All I need you to do is keep your mouth shut. I mean it. Not one word to anyone in this office. If I find out that people know, I'll blame you, and I will fire you so fast that you won't be able to get another job anywhere in the city. As far as you are concerned, I'm not pregnant. I'm not anything."

I can see the anger steaming off of Jake. His cheeks are redder than I've ever seen them, and his eyes are piercing through me, begging me to tell him the truth. But he doesn't get to know the truth yet. No one does.

Jake slowly removes his hands from my desk and stands up straight. "I'm here if you need me." He turns around and walks out the door.

I get up from my desk and quickly shut and lock my office door behind him. I don't need anyone else overhearing my conversation with Preston.

Preston—who has been quietly sitting on the couch, watching my exchange with Jake—gets up and walks over to me. He puts his arms around me and pulls me into a hug. A hug I didn't realize how much I desperately needed.

The hug doesn't last nearly long enough. Not long enough to wash away all the pain and despair I've been feeling. Just long enough to bring me enough comfort to get through the rest of my day.

"Congrats, Scarlett! I don't know how you feel about the baby, and it seems you aren't ready to share who the father is, but I know you'll be happy once the baby is here," Preston says as he lets go of me.

I smile and wipe a tear that found its way onto my cheek. "Thanks, Preston. I am excited about this baby. I know it's the best thing that has ever happened to me. And, no, I'm not ready to talk about whose baby it is yet. But thank you for being so supportive."

"And don't worry; I'll help keep your secret quiet, and I'll make sure Jake does the same."

I nod. "Thank you. That includes Kinsley, too, though. I'm not ready to tell her yet."

"Why?"

"After what she went through, I'm just not ready to tell her. I know she will be happy for me, but I don't want to cause her any pain."

Preston studies me for a second and then nods his understanding. "Of course. Whatever you want. Just know, I'm always here for you. Always."

I feel the tears coming again, but I can't handle any more crying today. "Good. Now, go get me some saltines and a ginger ale. Then, get someone to come up and do my hair and makeup so that I'm prepared for my meeting with Madeline."

Preston nods and then leaves.

I sigh, staring at the pile of work lying on my desk. I don't know how I ever managed to take a few days off to be with Nacio. There is just always too much work.

My stomach grumbles, and I place my hand over it. I still can't believe there is a baby inside me.

Albeit it is a teeny, tiny baby that is only a few weeks old, it's still a baby.

A baby that will be the redemption I need after all the horrible things I have done. A baby that will save me.

3

BEAST

"I'M PICKING YOU UP," Santino says on the other end of the line.

"No," I say.

"I'm picking you up," Santino says again.

"No, I'm done. I don't want to have anything to do with the business anymore. Tell Reina I'm done."

Santino laughs. "I'm picking you up. Now. After all the shit you've put me through, you owe me."

He ends the call, and I toss my cell onto the couch cushion of my new black leather couch. A couch I bought along with all the other furniture in this expansive penthouse apartment that I recently bought after deciding to move here permanently. As long as Scarlett is in New York, this is my home. I can't stand being away from her. I can't stand being in a different city or state or country. I have to be here. So, I've finally settled down in an apartment after years of living in hotels. I finally have a permanent home that has nothing to do with my family or the business. Or my life before prison. Before I saw her. Before my whole life changed.

Except this apartment is anything but a home. It feels more like a prison. A cage where I am trapped and can't escape to go to her. Despite that being all I want to do.

But I don't want to leave and deal with Reina's or Santino's crap. I just want to sulk. I don't want to work. Because even working isn't going to bring me out of the darkness that has overcome me while I've been without her. And the only way to protect her is to stay away from everything in my past.

I hear three loud pounds against my front door. I know it's Santino, but I don't want to face him. I don't want to work, not today. Today, I want to finish the scotch that I poured for myself before Santino called. I want to drown my sorrows away until the pain from finding out that Scarlett is pregnant by another man is gone.

I hear Santino knock again, but I don't go to the door. Instead, I grab my glass of scotch and plop down on the couch. Nope, I'm not going anywhere today. I don't plan on going anywhere unless it is to see Scarlett or spy on her and make sure she is okay.

I take a sip of the scotch and enjoy the numbness that follows each sip of the amber-colored liquid. The pounding on the door stops, and I assume that Santino has given up. That he will leave me the fuck alone now. Something that I was very used to until Scarlett came into my life and showed me that being alone sucks. It's lonely and empty. It's not what I want.

I hear someone messing with the lock to my apartment. *Shit.* I run my hand through my hair, and then I take another sip of my scotch, knowing that this will be my last moment of peace and quiet before Santino breaks into my apartment.

I glance over at the door just as Santino breaks into my apartment.

"I told you, you are coming with me," Santino says.

"I told you, no," I say.

"And I told you, you don't get to tell me no," he says.

Santino storms over to me and snatches the scotch out of my hand. "Enough drinking. It's time to get to work," he says.

"No. I'm done working for her."

"You don't get to decide that. Only Reina decides when you can quit."

Santino carries the glass to my kitchen and sets it down on the counter next to the sink.

I get up off my ass, angry that he took away my scotch, the only thing that was holding me together these last couple of days. "Can't you handle the job on your own? Or are you really not capable of handling anything on your own?"

Santino frowns at me. "This is a two-man job."

"Sure it is."

I snatch the scotch off the kitchen counter and down the whole thing before he can protest. If I'm going to do this, I'm at least going to enjoy myself. Because I know he's not going to leave me alone until I agree to go with him. I slam the glass back down on the counter, sad that I wasted twenty-five-year-old scotch by downing it in one gulp.

"Let's go then. I want to get this over with, so I can get back to sulking, like I want."

Santino shakes his head at me and then begins walking toward the door of my apartment. I follow him out, and we take the elevator down to the garage level where my car is parked.

I climb into the driver's seat of my Mercedes, and Santino climbs into the seat next to me. I begin driving without asking him where I'm going. It doesn't matter. Every job is the same. Every job ends with death, suffering, and pain.

"So, what's the job anyway?" I ask.

Santino looks at his hands before he answers, "It's an easy job really. The guy's already dead. We just have to dispose of the body in such a way that it sets up his boss—some Callum guy."

I watch Santino out of the corner of my eye as I continue driving, still not having a clue as to where I'm going. He looks nervous, anxious. His hands are fidgeting in his lap, and he won't make eye contact with me. His normal joking manner is gone. Something is up, and it has nothing to do with this job that he brought me to help out with for God knows why. Because this job is simple, just like he said. Setting up a guy for killing another is easy. We've done it hundreds of times before. And, honestly, Santino is better at this kind of job than

I am. So, there's another reason I'm involved in this. There's something he's not telling me.

"What the hell is going on?" I ask.

Santino abruptly looks up at me. "Nothing. Just wanted to get you out of your funk."

"I don't believe you. Something else is going on here. Why would Reina care so much if I helped you do this job or not?"

Santino sighs and grips the back of his neck, rubbing hard. "We are worried about you. We know Scarlett's pregnant, and from the amount of scotch on your breath, I'm guessing the baby is not yours."

"How the hell do you know that Scarlett's pregnant? Have you been spying on me?"

"Of course we have, Nacio! That's my second job, man—to make sure you are okay. I know I am supposed to be equal to you in the company, another man who Reina hires to do her jobs. Let's get real though; that's not really my job. My job is to make sure that you, the perfect one, are okay, so you can do your job. Because everyone knows you're better at this than I am. You were born to do this, bred to do this, while I am just supposed to make sure you stay alive."

I feel my anger boiling inside me. I hate that Reina thinks she has to send Santino to watch out for me. And I hate that Santino doesn't think that he is just as capable of doing this job as I am. Because he is. The only difference is, what I've been through versus what he's been through. I'm messed up; he's not. That's why I'm better at this job than he is. If he'd experienced what I had been through, he would have been just as much of a killer as me.

I don't want to talk about this anymore. Despite the anger pulsing through my veins, I don't want to talk about Scarlett or Santino. I don't want to think about any of it because, if I'm distracted while doing this job, despite how easy it is, I'll fuck up and get caught. And I really can't take that chance right now. Not when I need to do everything in my power to protect the people I love.

"Where are we going?"

Santino curiously looks over at me, wondering about the sudden change in topic. But he doesn't question me about it.

"Long Island," he says.

I turn a hard right onto the next street to head in that direction. I don't stop driving until we've reached our destination.

I slam the ax down and watch as the left arm separates from the body. I watch the blood splatter onto the dirt ground. I've seen worse. Things that would make most men's stomachs churn. Not mine. Not my brother's. This is just daily life for us.

I drop the ax and begin putting the body parts into the garbage bags that Santino brought with us. Then, I make sure to place the hairs from Callum—the man we are setting up for the body I just dismembered—into the bags along with the parts. I scatter Callum's blood into the bags and on the ground to mix with the man's blood. I still don't know the man's name or why he died. And I don't care about either. Just like I don't care that I could be sending Callum, an innocent man, away to jail for a very long time. Although I doubt he is truly innocent. He might be innocent of this man's death, but everyone is guilty of something.

We leave nothing to chance as we plant the evidence for the police to find. We tie up the plastic bags and then toss them into the back of my car until the entire body is resting in the trunk. We gather up our things, the leftover trash bags and the ax. I wrap up the ax in a garbage bag before placing it next to the body parts in the trunk—things we will have to dispose of later—before climbing in the front seat.

I don't have to ask Santino where we are going to dump the body. I know we will dump the body anywhere along the shoreline to ensure that it washes up. This isn't one of the times when we want to kill someone and make them disappear. This is one of the times when we want to make sure that they are found. I drive a little ways from the warehouse where this man's body was originally dumped.

I park once I find a beach that isn't currently crowded, but where

I know the body will be quickly found come morning. Santino and I climb out, and I pop the trunk. From the shore, we make quick work of the body, tossing all the pieces into the water, not caring that his body won't even make it out to sea. We don't bother to stand and contemplate what we just did. Neither of us is affected by it. We just do our jobs and then quickly climb back into the car without so much as a glance in the rearview mirror.

I begin driving back to my apartment, and that's when I feel the anger coming back. Because doing the work without thinking or talking gave me time to realize why Reina had sent Santino to have me help him do this job. And it has everything to do with Scarlett.

"Reina sent you here to convince me to kill Kinsley, didn't she?"

Santino doesn't look at me, but he answers, "Yes."

My grip on the steering wheel is so hard that my knuckles begin turning white. "How could she think that I'd be able to kill Kinsley when I'm in love with Scarlett? How could she ask me to do that?"

Santino solemnly looks at me. "Because she still thinks you want revenge. For Kinsley sending you to jail and..."

I raise my eyebrows at him.

"And she thinks you want to hurt Scarlett now that she's hurt you."

"No way in hell! No way in hell am I going to do that! I don't want to hurt her. I want to protect her."

"Calm down! That's what I told her. I told her that you wouldn't want to do it. But she wouldn't listen to me. She never listens to me. She only ever listens to you."

"Well, tell her anyway. Tell her, no fucking way."

Santino nods. But I'm not satisfied with a nod. Not satisfied that Reina still wants me to kill Kinsley. That can't happen.

"You have to tell me what Reina is planning. I know she wants me to be the one to kill Kinsley. It sends a better message to our competition if one of the Marlows takes her out in revenge. But it's not going to be me. And it sure as hell is not going to be you."

Santino nods in agreement.

So, I continue, "But it can't be anyone else. No one touches her.

Find out what Reina's plans are. I need you to find out who's going to do it and when it's going to happen, so I can stop it. Can you do that?"

Santino nods again.

"That's not good enough. I need to hear you say it."

"I can do that. Although I'm pretty sure, if Reina has anything planned, she'll tell you first."

That might have been true in the past, but it's no longer true now. Since Reina told me the truth, we are no longer the brother and sister we once were. She knows she no longer has me in her corner. So, she won't tell me anything.

4

SCARLETT

I TAKE a sip of my water as I sit in the booth of the Italian restaurant where Kinsley agreed to meet me. She's a little late, which I usually don't mind, except I'm starving today. After I've been sick for most of the morning, the baby has finally decided it's time to eat something. I'm thankful for that. I'm just not thankful that Kinsley is late. She's never really late. I'm the one who's always late.

The waitress comes back over with a smile on her face. "Can I get you anything else to drink or an appetizer to start? Or would you prefer to wait until your friend shows up?"

"How about you bring me some breadsticks? I'll just stick with water for now."

The waitress nods. "I'll be right back."

I pull out my phone to check and see if Kinsley texted me. However, when I check, there are no new messages. None. None from Kinsley. None from Nacio. Not even any messages from Preston about work.

I sigh and then sip on my water, but it does nothing to quench my hunger or thirst. I stare at the door of the cute little Italian restaurant we chose to meet for dinner. Killian is working tonight, and I haven't seen Kinsley in a couple of weeks. And I know she's anxious to see me.

My fingers drum along the table as I wait for Kinsley—or at least for my breadsticks to appear. Finally, after what seems like hours, the waitress finally brings me a basket of three breadsticks. I pull the first one out of the basket and quickly eat it without setting it down. And then I pull the second one out of the basket and make quick work of it before Kinsley finally arrives.

"I'm so sorry, Scar! Traffic was a nightmare, and Killian decided to sneak home for an hour before he had to go back in for some meetings," Kinsley says, winking at me. She leans over to give me a quick hug and then takes a seat in the booth opposite me.

I smile at my friend across the booth. "It's not a problem at all. I figured something like that happened."

Our waitress quickly finds her way back to our booth and says, "Can I get you anything to drink?"

"Yes! I'm in desperate need of wine. Scar, will you share a bottle of white wine with me?"

"Oh, I don't think so. I drank too much last night, and I'm still a bit hungover. You go ahead though."

"Since when do you not drink?" She turns her attention to the waitress. "Bring us a bottle of your best white wine. Something sweet."

"Certainly. I'll be right back with the wine and to take your order," the waitress says before leaving.

"Kinsley, I'm really not in the mood for any alcohol. I've still got a splitting headache and a queasy stomach."

"Exactly why you need a little bit of alcohol. It will do you good."

I sigh and take another sip of water, trying to figure out how I can get out of not drinking without telling her I'm pregnant. I want to tell her. I'm dying to tell her, but I'm just not ready yet.

I snatch up the third breadstick from the basket and start absentmindedly eating it, not even thinking about how it might look.

Suddenly, Kinsley squeals, "Oh my God! You're pregnant!"

I slowly swallow the breadstick in my mouth as I try to figure out what I'm going to say. I open my mouth, but no words come out.

"I knew that was why you wanted to have dinner with me tonight. I knew it!"

"I'm not pregnant," I say nonchalantly while rolling my eyes, like she's crazy.

"Yes, you are."

"No, I'm not," I lie through my teeth.

The waitress comes back with our bottle of wine, temporarily halting our conversation. Kinsley tastes the wine that was chosen, and after she approves, the waitress pours us each a glass of white wine.

"Are you guys ready to order?"

"Yes, I'll have the lasagna," I say.

"And I'll have the spaghetti," Kinsley says.

"Anything else? Soup or salad or another appetizer to begin with?"

I take my time thinking, trying to come up with something else to order, something else to keep Kinsley from asking me more questions, like if I am pregnant or not. I'm not ready to tell her that I am. I don't want to hurt her. I don't want to get her hopes up and then have to go through the pain with me if I lose this baby like she lost hers. Better to keep it to myself until I'm farther along.

Kinsley smiles, like she's somehow read my thoughts. "No. Just the pasta will be fine."

The waitress walks away.

"So, you're not pregnant?" Kinsley asks with a smug smile on her face.

"Nope, not pregnant. Just like I told you before."

"Then, prove it." Kinsley nods in the direction of the wine sitting in front of me.

I lift the glass of wine to my lips and take a drink as nonchalantly as I can. And then I swallow. I know one sip of wine isn't going to do anything to harm the baby. In fact, my doctor even said it was okay to have an occasional glass of wine. Although I have never had a drop of alcohol since finding out I was pregnant.

"Satisfied now?" I ask.

Kinsley takes a drink of her own wine as she stares intensely at me. "No, but it will do for now."

"So, how are you and Killian doing? Anything new?"

"Not really. We are planning on going to Mexico next week just to give ourselves a little bit of a getaway."

"That'll be fun," I say.

Kinsley takes another sip of her wine, thinking deeply. "Yeah, it will be. I'm just not sure if a vacation is going to be enough to bring me out of my depression over losing Wesley. I know it's been months since we lost him, but it's still hard. For me, it still feels like yesterday."

"I understand. You guys just need to do whatever you can to try to heal. It's not going to be easy, but you will get there eventually."

Kinsley smiles and nods as she lifts her glass of wine to her lips again, drinking until her glass is only half-full. Her eyes go to my wine glass that is still completely full.

Damn it! How am I going to get out of this?

I lift my own glass of wine to my lips and pour some of the liquid into my mouth. I don't want to swallow any more of the alcohol. I know it's not great for the baby, and if I drink more alcohol, I'm sure I'm going to be sick. I put the wine glass back down, still holding the liquid in my mouth, when I remember my water glass. I pick up the water and touch the glass to my lips, slowly letting the liquid pour into my water glass. The glass is opaque, so it's hard to see exactly how much liquid is in it. I'm thankful that Kinsley ordered white wine instead of red.

"Work is going well. Nothing new to report really," I say.

Kinsley sips on her wine again, so I do the same, forcing the sweet liquid into my mouth and then out again into my water glass.

"Have you met any new guys lately?" Kinsley asks, wiggling her eyebrows at me.

"No. I haven't really been thinking about guys lately. Just focusing on my work, you know."

Kinsley nods, but from the smile on her face, I can tell that she doesn't believe me. *I don't care. Let her think what she wants about me.*

The waitress brings our food, and I dig in right away, not caring that the boiling hot cheese is burning my tongue as I eat my lasagna. I'm starving.

We continue our meal together, going back and forth about how our jobs are going and things we want to do. We continue eating. I'm laughing and talking and drinking until we are each on our last glass of wine. Mine has mostly been used to refill my water glass although I will admit that I drank an occasional sip or two.

"I'm going to use the restroom," Kinsley says, getting up from the booth.

I nod and watch as she walks to the restroom. Then, I quickly flag down our waitress.

She walks over and then asks casually, "Can I get you anything?"

"Yes. Can you get me a new glass of water?" I hand her my glass filled with wine.

She takes that away and quickly comes back with my glass of water. As soon as she brings it, I drink half of the glass of water, thankful to finally be able to drink something to get the taste of white wine out of my mouth.

Kinsley returns from the restroom, takes a seat in the booth, and we each leave some cash on the table to pay for our bill.

"Are you ready to go?" I ask.

"Almost," she says with a sly smile on her face.

I quizzically look at her. "Almost?"

Before I realize what Kinsley is doing, she grabs my glass of water and takes a sip.

I stand, watching her, with my arms folded over my chest. After she finally determines that my glass of water is in fact water, she sets it down on the table with a frown on her face. She quickly gets up from the booth.

I follow her and stop her before she makes it to the door of the restaurant. "What was that about?"

"Sorry. I just thought you were pregnant and that you were slipping the wine into your water glass. I guess I was wrong."

I grab my friend and wrap her in a tight hug. "It will happen. One of these days, it will happen for one of us. And, when it does, it will be amazing. Because that child is going to have love from both of us, no matter whose it biologically is."

And, even though that day is now, I can't tell her. It would break her heart if something happened to this baby. She wouldn't survive. And, if she didn't, I wouldn't either.

5

SCARLETT

I CLIMB into the car as George, my driver, holds the door open for me. He shuts the door after I get in, and he quickly makes his way to the driver's seat.

As he begins driving me back to my apartment, I sulk in the fact that I just lied to my best friend. I hated doing it, but it was necessary at this point. I need to wait until the pregnancy is much further along and I know I'm as safe as I can be before I tell her. If I lose the baby after she lost hers only months ago, it will destroy her. I don't think she will survive that kind of heartbreak. And I don't think I'm strong enough to do that to her or to get her through the heartbreak. I'm not sure if even Killian would be strong enough to get her through that.

I go through my messages on my phone, trying to distract myself, but I have no text messages again. I go through my emails, all one hundred seven of them, and begin typing out quick responses. I get through about twenty before George pulls up in front of my apartment. I sigh. Looks like I'll be spending the rest of my night answering emails.

George opens my door, and I climb out.

"Thanks," I say, trying to keep a smile on my face so that George doesn't grow suspicious.

I'm pretty sure though that George already knows I'm pregnant. After the doctor visits and the late-night runs to get me crackers, Sprite, or ice cream, he must at least have his suspicions. George is a good man though. I'm not at all concerned that he will mention this to anybody.

"Have a good night, Miss Bell. I'll be on call. If you need anything tonight, just let me know."

I smile. "You're the best, George."

He nods and watches me walk into my apartment building, like he always does.

"You didn't tell her," a voice says next to me.

It's a voice that I recognize all too well.

"What are you doing?" I ask as I stand frozen with my hand on the door that leads into my apartment building.

"Why didn't you tell her?" Nacio asks against my ear, ignoring my question.

I turn and face him as my heart stops. He's gorgeous, standing next to me, in his jeans and T-shirt that fit his muscles all too well. Every bit of him begs me to take him back, to just forget about everything and start over with him.

Somehow, I gather the strength to ignore him. I push the door open and walk into my apartment building. I don't wait to see if he is following me or not. I want him to stay the hell away. Stay away so that my life is safe and happy and makes sense. But, on the other hand, I want him to follow me, to come up to my apartment, to not take no for an answer. And the second feeling is the one I'm worried about. It's the one that might get me in trouble.

I climb onto the elevator and push the button to my floor. I watch as the elevator doors close without Nacio. He didn't follow me. I breathe a sigh of relief, but I also feel my anxiety growing. My heart is beating fast. I ready myself for the pain that is about to come, knowing that I'm not going to get to spend time with him today, that I'm not going to get to spend time with him ever. And that kills me.

The elevator seems to be moving in slow motion as it rises higher and higher until it reaches my floor. I step off the elevator, and I walk toward my apartment door. Then, I can't help myself as I grin when I see Nacio leaning against my door. I don't know how in the hell he beat me up here, but right now, I don't care. I'm happy to see him. Way too happy to see him.

"I'm surprised you haven't already broken into my apartment," I say.

He grins. "I'm trying to be good."

I walk to the door and feel my hand brush against his for just a split second before I insert the key into the lock. "You call this being good?"

He nods slowly.

"You call following me to the restaurant and then spying on a private conversation good? Because I call it stalking." I push the door open and hope that he's going to follow me inside without being invited.

I walk straight to my kitchen and grab the gin from my bar. I begin pouring myself a glass before I realize that I can't drink. "Shit," I curse when I run my hand through my hair. I take the glass and pour it down the drain.

I glance up and see him watching me with the same eyes that Kinsley was watching me with before. Trying to decide what the truth is or not. To see if I'm just pretending like I can't drink or if I really can't because I'm pregnant.

But, unlike Kinsley, I can't tell if he believes me or not. His face is too hard for me to read. Despite knowing every line on his chiseled face, every muscle, every face this man makes, I don't know him well enough to know if he believes me or not.

"Why didn't you tell her that you are pregnant?" Nacio asks.

He takes a step forward and then another until we are standing face-to-face. He reaches out and tucks a strand of hair behind my ear. "If you're really pregnant, then why didn't you tell your best friend?"

"Because I don't want to break her heart if something happens and I lose this baby," I answer honestly, not really sure why I'm telling him the truth. Not sure why I can lie to my best friend but not to this man.

"And Kinsley finding out that you lost your baby would break her heart?"

I nod. "Yes, it would. I know most people wouldn't understand that, but Kinsley and I are close. We are connected in ways that most people don't understand."

Nacio studies me again with his piercing eyes and unreadable expression.

I have a hard time breathing as he stares at me. I hate how easily he can affect me. I hate that, despite knowing all he's done—the killings, the abuse, the lies—I would still let him flip me over and take me right here on my kitchen counter if he wanted to. And, from the way he's looking at me now, it makes me think that is exactly what he wants to do. I let him know that is what I want, as I bite my lip, waiting to see what he will do.

I'm quickly disappointed when he takes a step back instead of kissing me like I want him to do. Instead of throwing me over the counter and doing dirty, nasty things to me to make me forget all the reasons we can't be together.

"I didn't come here to just ask you that question. I need to talk to you," he says, turning away from me and walking toward my living room.

I take a second to catch my breath, and then I follow Nacio into my living room. He takes a seat on the couch, and I take a seat next to him, waiting for him to tell me whatever he came here to tell me. Whatever he came here to tell me doesn't come easily for him. I try to be patient as I wait for Nacio to talk. And I don't know if it's because I'm tired, just tired of dealing with all the lies, or if it's the pregnancy hormones, but I lose all my patience.

"Just tell me already. Whatever it is, it can't be worse than what I already know about you."

Nacio looks at me with such sadness in his eyes, and I'm afraid that it might be much worse than what I thought.

He instantly gets up from the couch and begins pacing the room. He walks back and forth, and I try to remain calm by counting his steps.

One, two, three, four...

And so on and so forth until I lose count somewhere around two hundred.

He runs his hand through his hair and then grabs his neck before he finally stops and looks at me.

"Everything Reina told you was a lie," Nacio slowly says, staring at me with such intensity, such hope, that I realize he must be telling the truth. There is no way someone could say words like that with such meaning behind them if they weren't true.

"How...how is that possible? So, you lied to me earlier when you told me that her words were true?"

"No."

I stand, trying to understand his confusing words, and I find myself pacing just as he was before as I try to make sense of what he's saying or not really saying.

Nacio stares at me in silence as I pace back and forth, and I assume he's counting my steps just like I was earlier. *What else could be going through his head?*

I finally stop and look at him. "Explain."

"At the time, I thought everything that Reina told you was true. I thought that I had abused her when we were younger. I thought I had destroyed her life. I thought I was a monster and born to be a killer. But it's not true."

I watch as he takes a deep breath in and out, as if he is still trying to come to terms with it himself.

"But what I didn't realize was that, even though I had done all those things, I had been abused, just like Reina. My father was the one who had made me do those things. I'd only abused her because my father forced me to."

I can see the pain and the demons that haunt him in his eyes. His entire life, he thought that he'd hurt his sister. That he was the one who had destroyed her life. In reality, he was only a child who had been just as abused as she was.

I move to him and wrap him in my arms. I hold him while I try to take the pain away. I feel his body shake, and I know he's crying. I hold him tighter, letting him know it's okay to cry, to feel the pain, to feel everything. And, to my surprise, he opens up and cries harder.

I don't know how long we stand there, just holding each other, but it's long enough that I cry, too. I cry for the boy who was abused and, in turn, forced to appease another. I cry for the young man who thought he was a monster. I cry for the man I'm holding in my arms who is forced to relive everything.

When I know we can't cry any longer, I pull his buried face from my shoulder and look at him.

I see him for the first time. Not as a killer. Not as Nacio. Not even as Beast.

Just as a man.

A man who has feelings and dreams and desires, just like all the rest of us. A man who deserves love. Love that I want to give him.

I don't know how it happens, but my lips slowly lower to his. It's a slow, gentle kiss. I rationalize it as a sweet, innocent kiss and nothing more. But my sweet kiss soon turns to fire as Nacio grabs the sides of my face with his hands. He firmly holds me to him as his tongue slips forcefully between my lips.

I moan; I can't help myself. I've denied myself this feeling for months now.

And what will a couple of innocent kisses hurt?

I kiss him back as my hands go around his neck, needing him to be closer to me, needing more, but there is no way our bodies can get any closer. Our tongues are already buried inside each other's mouths, our lips are locked so tightly that both of us can barely breathe, and our hands are grasping on to each other as our bodies are pressed tightly together.

At the same time, we each realize that the only way to get closer together is to remove the clothing separating us. We start undressing each other. I grab for the hem of his black T-shirt and pull it off over his head. He grabs for the hem of my halter top and pulls it over my head. For that split second, our lips part, and clarity forms in my head. His mouth moves to cover mine again, but I put a hand up to stop him.

"I can't." I can't look at him as I say it because I know the pain I'll see there, and if I see it, I'll give in. I'll give in to letting him kiss me again. If I give in, I know, soon, we will be completely undressed and having sex before my mind clears again.

"I understand."

I look up because I wasn't expecting that response from him. "You do?"

"Yes," he says with such sadness in his eyes. "I understand that you still see me as a killer, a monster, as Beast. I know it will take some time for you to truly believe me."

I reach out and touch this broken man. "That's not why. I believe you. I believe that you're not a killer, a monster, or Beast."

"Then, why?"

"Because I realized, since coming back to my life, that we aren't right for each other, good for each other. Despite not being a killer or a monster, you will still want to kill for a living. And, despite me being more than just Beauty, I will still want to run a fashion empire and do more good in the world. How can those two worlds ever coexist?"

"They can't," he says.

I nod as a tear escapes, but he can't leave, just feeling pain. We have to feel *more*. We have to feel some tiny bit of happiness before I can let him leave again.

I kiss him. It's tentative, as I'm not sure that I should really be doing this, but I'm doing it all the same. And then, within a matter of seconds, it becomes so much more. It becomes what we both need in this moment. Comfort, happiness, love.

And then the kiss turns desperate. Desperate for more than we can give each other.

We kiss like it could be our last kiss with each other, desperately clinging on to one another. I grab ahold of his hair, desperately holding on to him. He grabs my waist, promising never to let me go. We know that promise he silently gives me with his body is a lie. We know that, despite how much we need to be together in this moment, it can never last. It can never be more than just a moment.

Nacio accepts this reality before I do. Gently, tentatively, he pulls away, and the pain I see left in his eyes equally matches my own.

"You won't let me fuck you like I want to. You won't let me take your pain away or let me show you how much I love you, but..." He pauses for a second and then gives me a dirty smile. "Will you let me watch you pleasure yourself while I do the same?"

I know his words are meant to be a question, but it's not; it's a command.

I bite my lip for a second as I consider his request. "Yes. That's exactly what I want."

He grins, and I about come just from the sexy smirk on his face, which only makes him grin wider.

"Undress for me, Beauty. Or would you prefer I do that for you?"

I watch as his eyes land on my bra and the jeans I'm still wearing. I know letting him undress me might be tempting us too far, but I don't care. I need his hands on me at least one more time.

"You," is all I can get out.

His grin turns serious now as he walks back to me and then steps behind me. A serious look for a serious task. If he lets himself lose control, we will wind up doing something that, although we will enjoy it in the moment, will destroy us in the end.

I feel his hands on my hips, and then they slowly slide around to the front. I close my eyes and ball my hands into fists to keep myself in control, to stop myself from turning around and throwing my body against his. His hands move to the button on my jeans, and he slowly undoes it, followed by lowering the zipper. Then, his hands are back at my hips, slowly moving the material down over my ass and then further down my body until my jeans are lying in a heap on the floor around my ankles. He kneels in front of me before he slowly lifts one of my ankles to remove one of my black pumps, followed by one side of my jeans. He is careful with where he places his hands, making sure not to tempt us any further by touching me anywhere but where he has to, to remove my clothing. He does the same to my other leg. As much as I want him to kiss my smooth, toned legs, he doesn't.

I feel his hands move back up my body to my bra. He undoes the clasp and then removes the straps from my shoulders until the bra falls on the floor, releasing my breasts. I suck in air as the cold air hits my nipples. I wait for his hands to go to my breasts, to touch me, but they don't.

"Touch them," he commands in my ear.

I suck in a second breath, but don't do as he said.

"Touch your breasts like I would. I know you want to."

I can't resist. I move my hands from my sides to my breasts. Keeping my eyes closed, I massage them like he would. I grab them and then run my thumbs across my nipples that are beyond hard. As I do so, I lose track of where his hands are, and I soon find that he is slipping my panties to the floor. I step out of them.

And then his hands are off me.

I open my eyes, searching for him, for some sort of connection now that his hands are no longer on my body. I find him staring at me with the same serious expression as before. My eyes trail over his body, from his naked torso to his jeans. Then, I come to a stop at his bulge.

I glance back up to his eyes, silently asking him the same question that he asked me, *Do you want me to undress you?*

He nods.

I walk over to him, and instead of standing in front of him, I kneel. He doesn't close his eyes like I did. Instead, he watches me. I take my hands and run them up the sides of his body until I reach the top of his jeans. My hand slides over to find the button. I slowly unbutton it, followed by lowering the zipper. He kicks off his shoes, and then I slide his jeans as I stare at him from where I'm still kneeling on the floor. My hands move back up to the waistband of his briefs, and I begin pulling slowly until I release the hard bulge hiding beneath. I don't watch as his underwear falls to the floor. Instead, my eyes are locked on his cock that has just sprung free.

"Like what you see?" he asks with a smug grin.

I bite my lip since no words can come out. Then, I look up at him with my big eyes, showing him how much I want to take it into my mouth but can't.

"Touch yourself," he says.

I respond automatically as I throb, needing to be touched. I slide my hand between my legs, between the folds, and rub slowly, spreading my juices over my pussy. The whole time, I never take my eyes off of his. I watch as he struggles to keep his hands off my body as I touch myself. I can see him beginning to lose control. I see the desire and lust in his eyes. His hands are shaking, begging to touch me, to fist my hair, to stroke me, anything.

But, instead, he grabs ahold of his cock and begins pumping as he watches me.

I struggle with deciding if I should keep my eyes on him or his cock. My eyes keep going back and forth, up and down, trying not to miss a moment of how his hand is wrapped around his cock or his expression as he looks at me while I pleasure myself.

As we touch ourselves, we struggle to breathe or move at the same time, and I know we are both close. I can't take it much longer when he looks at me with such intensity. I come about a second before him and then watch as he comes all over my breasts.

When we have each finished, we collapse onto the rug on the floor. Neither of us says a word. Neither of us has to because we know what the other is thinking—how that was exactly what we needed, but we will never get enough.

I drift in and out of sleep, lying on the floor for a long time, until I finally decide to get up. "I'm going to go take a shower." I head upstairs toward my bedroom without waiting for an answer, a good-bye, or a word.

And, after my shower, when I make my way back downstairs in a tank top and pajama pants, he's gone.

6

BEAST

I STEP out of the shower in my own apartment, feeling emptier than ever.

I went to see Scarlett. I thought, if I told her the truth, she would want to be with me, despite everything that was going on. I was wrong.

Instead, she told me that I couldn't change. She told me that, although she didn't think of me as a killer or monster or Beast, it was still what I would always want to do for a living, that there would always be this desire in me to do just that.

I look at myself in the mirror. Maybe she's right. Because all I see when I look at myself is a killer. And that's not good enough for her. I don't deserve her love or to be around for her baby if that's all I am.

I need to change. I need to be someone else. I just don't know who that is yet.

All I've ever known is how to be a killer.

I walk back into my bedroom and get dressed, not having a clue what to do. I have plenty of money, so that's not a concern. If I know Scarlett, she doesn't care if I ever work another day in my life because, between the two of us, we have more money than we would ever need.

But I need to find some purpose in life, something to show her that I've truly changed my path, but it's not going to be volunteering or doing some job that saves the world and all that crap. That's not me.

I just don't know who I am beyond a killer.

My phone vibrates on my nightstand, and I walk over and pick it up. The number on the screen is unknown. But I know exactly who it is—my other employers, who are more demanding than Reina. They are bigger monsters than us all. I wouldn't put up with their crap, but the pay is better than what Reina can offer.

I answer the phone, "Hello?"

"Do you have anything for us?" Elliot, my boss, asks.

"Not yet, but I'm on it. You'll know soon enough."

"That's not good enough! We need that info now. You are losing our trust, and you need to get it back before we rescind your deal."

I pace back and forth as I speak, "Not going to happen. That wasn't part of the deal. I don't have any new info for you. And, if you keep pressuring me, I'll quit, and then you'll have nothing."

"Calm down, calm down. Let's all play nice here. Neither of us wants that to happen, but you have to work with us a little bit, give us some information. The more defensive you get, the more we think you're lying. We are all on the same side here."

"You need to learn to trust me." I hang up the phone before he can argue back.

I'm tired of being everybody's puppet. I've always been Reina's and Santino's, and now, I'm Elliot's. I'm done. I should quit both jobs.

All I care about is keeping Scarlett safe. That's who I am—a protector. I'll make damn sure that no one hurts her or my family or anyone else.

I don't know how to show that to Scarlett or if she would even believe that's what I am. But I do know, from our conversation earlier today, that she is beginning to lose all control when it comes to saying no to me. And it won't take much for her to start saying yes a whole lot more.

So, that's what I have to do—prove to her that I'm more than just a killer. That I can be a nice guy, a caring guy, a loving guy. Prove to her that I can be her protector.

Because that's exactly what she needs—to be protected.

7

SCARLETT

I HEAR a knock on the door just as I finish blow-drying my hair. I run down the stairs to the door, hoping it is Nacio. But I already know it's not him. As I approach the door, I don't feel the spark of excitement that I usually do whenever he is close. When I open it, a doorman is standing there with the largest bouquet of roses I've ever seen.

"These are for you," he says with a smile on his face.

I look at him in confusion. "Are you sure? I don't have a boyfriend or husband or anything."

The doorman smiles wide. "I'm pretty sure. Are you Miss Scarlett Bell?"

I nod.

"Then, these are for you. Where would you like them?"

"I'll just take them from you," I say, reaching out my arms to take the large vase.

The doorman just smiles. "It's not just these flowers, ma'am. There are also at least a dozen more right behind me."

I pop my head outside my door and see half a dozen men, each one holding two vases in their hands. My jaw drops as I look at them. "Just bring them inside and put them in the kitchen or living room or wherever you can find a place for them."

I move out of the way and hold the door as the men begin carrying flowers inside before setting them all around my apartment. I watch as the men slowly leave, and then I go over to one and pick up an envelope. I open it and read.

Dear Beauty,

I haven't given up on us yet. I know that Beauty and the Beast get together, but that's just a fantasy, just a movie, a story. It's not real life. But I want to make it real life. And I don't want anything to stand in the way of that.

I'm slowly figuring out who I am and how we can fit together. I don't have it all figured out yet, but in the meantime, I thought I could do something to at least bring a smile to your face. You've done the same to me from the second I saw you when I went away to jail ten years ago.

These flowers aren't enough, but they're a start.

Love,
Beast

I walk into my office at Beautifully Bell and stop dead in my tracks. My office is covered with flowers—roses, daisies, and several exotic flowers that I don't know the names of. Every flower imaginable is covering every surface in my office. I can't even see my desk because it's covered with large bouquets. I can't see the floor because rose petals are everywhere. Even my couch has flowers draped across it.

I tiptoe into my office, careful not to disturb any of the flowers or petals on the floor, as if it would cause a bomb to explode. I finally make it to my desk and carefully sit down in my chair as I look around the room, trying to understand what Nacio thinks he's doing with sending me all these flowers. I've been sent flowers before but nothing like this. Nothing this extravagant or over the top.

I jump when Preston enters my office without knocking.

"These from him?"

I look at Preston with confusion, as I'm not sure whom he's referring to. *Nacio? Jake? Or the baby's father?*

"It depends on what you mean by *him*. If you're referring to Nacio, then yes."

I begin trying to move the vases of flowers around on my desk so that I can get to my computer, but I soon realize it's no use. Once I pick up the first vase, I can't find another place for it on my desk. I guess they're all going on the floor, which is a shame since they are so beautiful. But it has to be done. So, I lift the first vase again and place it on the floor, followed by another.

"Here, let me help," Preston says, walking over to my desk.

"Thanks," I say.

"Nacio really sent you all these flowers?" Preston asks with a knowing smile on his face. "He doesn't happen to be..."

I roll my eyes. "I already told you. I'm not ready to tell you who the father is yet."

He shrugs. "Had to try."

"Just help me get all these flowers arranged somewhere, so I can actually get some work done today."

"And, if anyone asks, who am I supposed to say all these flowers are from?"

"Just say they are from you."

Preston raises his eyebrows at me. "Nobody's going to believe that I sent you these flowers."

"Sure they will. Just tell them you've noticed I've been feeling down lately, so you wanted to do something to cheer me up."

"I still don't think anyone's going to believe me, but I'll spread the lie around anyway."

"Thanks," I say as I place the last vase of flowers onto the floor. I'm not sure if it'll really work either, but it's the only option I have.

And it's not like Nacio's going to send me anything else. It's just for today.

Except it wasn't just for one day. It was for an entire week.

Every day this week, Nacio sent me something to my apartment, followed by more things to my office. He sent enough chocolate for everyone in my office to have a piece, cupcakes in the shape of a heart, and art pieces that are now covering my office walls. Today, the theme must be jewelry.

When I walk into my office, not as many items are covering my desk as there have been the last few days. Instead, only five boxes are sitting on my desk. And, without looking inside any of the boxes, I know he spent a lot more money today than he did on any of the items this past week. Because the jewelry that he sent to my house was nice, nicer than anything I'd ever bought for myself—and I like diamonds and have money. I wouldn't be surprised if all these diamonds and jewelry combined cost him at least a million dollars. And I don't want to know how he earned the money to afford all these things.

At least this time, I will be able to hide his gifts. I quickly grab all the boxes and shove them into my desk drawer. I take my key from my purse, prepared to lock them away before anyone else gets the chance to see what he sent me. Before anyone gets a chance to question who the gifts are from and who my new boyfriend is.

After the first day, no one believed the story that Preston had sent me all the items. I spent the rest of the week dodging questions from everyone in my office and rumors about who my new mystery boyfriend could be. Jake is the obvious conclusion that most people have come to. That we are back together. Although there are even rumors that Preston and I have been hooking up. That would never happen.

I put the key in the lock on my desk, ready to lock them all away, but I freeze. I can't lock them all away without at least peeking. I glance at what Nacio bought me. Now, I'm regretting not wearing at least one of the pieces of jewelry that he sent to my apartment into work today. I knew that wearing something like that would incite more rumors, so I didn't, but it still didn't prevent me from wanting to.

Here's my second chance. I pull the drawer back open and take the last box back out of the desk. I hold it in my hands, but I don't open it. The second that I do, I'll want to wear it, and I'll fall even more in love with him for giving it to me.

But I can't stand just holding it in my hands. I open the box and see the most beautiful ruby ring that I've ever seen. It's a large oval-shaped ruby with tiny diamonds that go all the way around the band. It's perfect for me. *If this man has such good taste in jewelry, I wonder what an engagement ring from him would look like.*

I shake my head. That can never happen.

I take the ring out of the box to get a closer look and then somehow find it on the ring finger of my right hand. I don't know how he knew what size ring to get me, but he did.

I hear a knock at the door, and I startle, slamming the box shut and tossing it into the open drawer. Closing it quickly, I flick the lock on the desk before I finally look at who's standing in my doorway.

Jake.

I can't even muster a fake smile as I look at him.

Once the rumors started to spread, he made it his mission to find a reason to stop by my office every day this week. Every time, he made up an excuse. It's always been work-related, but I know that's not why he is here. He is here to try to figure out who his competition is.

"What do you want, Jake?"

He smiles and takes a seat in front of me. "It must be a good sign if you are already locking my gifts away so that no one can steal them."

Fear takes over at his words. I try to think if I saw a note attached to the boxes, anything that would indicate who the jewelry was from. I don't remember a note being attached. I don't remember any indication that the jewelry was from Nacio and not Jake. I just assumed it was from Nacio since he was the one who had been sending me gifts all week. I never thought the gifts could be from anyone else.

"Good. I thought you would like it," he says with a smug smile as he studies the ring on my right hand.

My panic rises as I realize Jake got me this gorgeous ring. This ring that I had such a connection with and instantly felt a connection for the man who had given it to me, but now, I feel torn. I didn't fall in love with Nacio because he bought me this beautiful ring or any of the other gifts.

It doesn't matter anyway. I can't be with either of these men for the same reasons as before. Jake is a douche bag. And Nacio is Beast. Neither of them can give me what I truly want.

"Is that all?" I fold my arms across my chest and then lean back in my chair, hiding the ring from his view.

Whether it was from him or not, he doesn't need to know how I feel about it.

"I want to do more for you than just buy you nice jewelry. I want to help you. If he would quit sending you stupid gifts, like flowers and chocolate, then I could help. None of that shit is worthy of you. Let me help you. I would make a great father to your baby. Just give me a chance."

"No."

Jake ignores my no and begins walking around to the other side of my desk so that he is standing inches from me. I turn in my chair to glare at him, trying to get him to leave, to understand that he and I will never be an item. And, if he's not careful, I'll fire his ass right now instead of waiting until his contract is over.

He doesn't take the hint.

"Let me take you out tonight. Prove that you're wrong. Prove that

I'm the man for you, that you need me to help you take care of this baby, Scarlett. You can't do this alone, not after how you were with my niece and nephew. You don't know how to handle children. Let me help you."

I thought this man had made me mad before, but I was wrong. I've never felt so much anger in all my life as I do right now.

"Get out of my office!" I scream at him, not even bothering to talk reasonably with him after he just said I would make a terrible mother. That I wouldn't be able to do this on my own.

Jake doesn't budge. He just stares at me, like he can't believe that I have any reason to kick him out.

So, I say firmly, "Get out of my office now."

He slightly steps back but still doesn't get out of my office like I asked. I pick up my phone and begin dialing Preston, prepared to call security or the police if I have to. Anything to get this man out of my office and my life forever.

"I want you out now, and if you don't leave, I'll call my security team. I also recommend that you start looking for other employment."

I am almost finished dialing when I hear Nacio say, "Are you ready for our date? If we don't leave now, we will be late for our dinner reservation."

I glance up and meet Nacio's eyes. I smile at him, thankful that he is standing in my doorway, even though I have no idea why he is here. "Yes. I was just finishing up a meeting."

I slip on my shoes and sling my purse over my shoulder as I brush past Jake. Nacio meets me halfway and takes me into a deep, passionate kiss, like he just came back from war or something. My mind is blank of everything but the kiss until Nacio lets me back up for air with a wide smirk on his face. It takes a second for enough air to return to my lungs. Then, I realize that Jake is still in the room, staring intently at us, and that Nacio just kissed me to mark his territory. Although, right now, I'm happy he did.

Nacio gets a handle on the situation long before I do. He says, "If you need anything else, just leave a message with her assistant."

He takes my hand and pulls me out of my office before Jake or I can protest. I let him lead me out of my office as people stare at us with smiles on their faces, obviously happy to have a new suspect to add to their growing list of guys I might be dating.

Once we get outside, I expect to find his black Mercedes. Instead, I see George standing outside of his car with a smile, like he was expecting me. He holds the door open until I climb in, followed by Nacio. The door shuts, and before I even realize it, George has begun driving.

Nacio still has ahold of my hand, and I feel his thumb rub over the ring that I'm not sure if Jake or he was the one who bought it.

"This one is my favorite. I thought this would be the one you chose to wear," he says, smiling.

I sigh. "You are the one who bought the jewelry for me?"

He stares at me for a moment. "You think Jake got you the jewelry?" He raises an eyebrow at me.

"No...I just wasn't sure. Well, Jake said..."

He shakes his head. "There is no way that scumbag is capable of picking out anything half as nice as this."

I glance back down at my ring as Nacio is still holding my hand.

"He did get you something though." He begins rummaging in his pocket. He pulls out a skinny rectangular box and hands it to me.

I curiously look at him. "Did you forget to give me one of the pieces of jewelry?"

Nacio shakes his head. "No. This is from Jake."

"And how did you get it?" I say as my eyes widen.

"Jake left it for you this morning, but I didn't want you to confuse it with the gifts I got you."

I slowly open the box, curious as to what Jake bought me. I see a tiny bracelet covered in jewels. I can tell from looking at them that they are fake diamonds and rubies, not like the jewelry Nacio got me. This bracelet probably cost no more than a hundred dollars, while Nacio easily spent thousands, possibly totaling a million. And I know a million to him isn't much money.

But I can see now why Jake was pleased with himself. The red from the bracelet matches the color of the ring that Nacio gave me. Jake must've thought that he had done well in picking it out since it matched a ring he thought I'd bought for myself. He didn't realize that Nacio had given me that ring only today.

I glance over at Nacio, who's looking at the ring. He's clearly not happy that Jake also decided to get me jewelry on the same day that he decided to.

The car suddenly comes to a stop, and I glance around, looking for the restaurant that Nacio might be taking me to. But I don't see any restaurants. All I see are condo and apartment buildings.

"Where are you taking me?"

"I'm not taking you anywhere. This is my apartment building. I asked George if he wouldn't mind dropping me off here before he took you to wherever you wanted to go."

He leans over and softly kisses me on the cheek, gentler than he's ever been before. I watch him climb out of the car without so much as a good-bye, and then he begins walking toward what I assume is his apartment building, leaving me behind in the car.

I stare down at the bracelet that Jake got me. A bracelet that does nothing to make me want him back. And, while jewelry and materialistic things aren't what makes me want to be with Nacio, it does show me that he's willing to at least try. Try to do something nice for me to show me that he cares.

And, right now, I don't care about my damn promise to myself to stay away from Nacio. Right now, all I care about is getting the date he promised.

I toss the cheap bracelet onto the seat next to me and then holler to George, "I'll be right back."

I can practically feel George smiling at me in approval. He wouldn't have gone along with Nacio's plan, or any man's plan, if he didn't approve of them in the first place. I climb out of the car and run after Nacio, getting to him just as he begins walking inside.

"Wait!" I reach out and grab his shoulder.

Nacio stops and slowly turns around to face me. I can see the hope slowly filling his eyes as he looks at me, slowly erasing the tiny drops of fear that I saw there.

"What about our date?" I ask.

He sucks in a breath. "What about it?"

"Why aren't you taking me on a date, like you promised?"

"Because you told me that we couldn't do this, that we couldn't be together, and I'm trying to respect that while still protecting you."

"I don't buy it. What were all those gifts for all week if you weren't trying to win me back?"

"I guess I was hoping that I could still win you back. And, if not, then you could at least find some pleasure in the gifts every night, knowing that somebody loved you...even if"—he glances down at my stomach and then back at me—"the father doesn't. I just want you to know that I love you and that you aren't alone, not that you need any help."

When I don't say anything, he continues, "Even if you don't still love me, I'll always be here."

I glance up at him. "I still love you."

"I know."

"So, how about that date? I'm starving."

I watch as his grin slowly appears on his face.

"Sure."

"Just as friends though. You have to promise me that we won't end up back here at your apartment at the end of the night. Promise?"

He flashes me his sexy grin, and his eyes change from fear to lust. "Promise."

8

SCARLETT

MY ALARM SOUNDS on my phone, and I roll over. I barely open my eyes, just far enough so that I can find my phone on the nightstand next to my bed. I hit the alarm off. I rub my eyes, still feeling exhausted. My alarm goes off every Saturday at seven, no matter what I did the night before. No matter if I was out drinking or partying or simply just working late. I know I'd feel worse if I slept in.

My body feels tired, but I slowly climb out of bed. I am immediately hit with queasiness in my stomach. Since I got pregnant, it's hit me every morning and often throughout the day. I know I need to quickly head to the kitchen to make myself some toast and eggs before the queasiness becomes too much. Usually, just getting a little bit of bland food in my stomach is enough to settle it.

I rub my eyes again, trying to force myself to wake up. I wake up enough to begin walking to my kitchen, but I stop in my tracks when I see a large flat screen TV on the wall across from my bed, which is odd since I don't have a TV in my room. I glance back at my bed, except it isn't my bed. Instead, a large black bed sits in the place where my white bed frame is supposed to be. A man is sleeping in the bed where no man should be.

I'm not at my apartment. I'm in Nacio's.

I don't have time to think about how I got here. All I have time to deal with is getting food into my stomach and fast. I sneak out of Nacio's bedroom, careful not to wake him. It takes me too long to find his kitchen. This apartment is massive, and it makes me wonder if he's living here with someone else because there is far too much space in this apartment for just him. I don't have time to think about that now though.

Instead, I search for food. Any food, anything, to make the nausea go away. I throw open the pantry and find it completely empty. Not one thing sits inside. Not crackers or junk food, not even stale bread. I try the fridge next and come up almost just as empty. I only find a couple of beers and a bottle of ketchup. I start opening the rest of the cabinets in the kitchen, hoping that maybe he stores some food in one of the other cabinets.

But, after searching almost all of them, I come up empty. I don't find any food. I hardly find any other items in the cabinets other than a couple of plates and glasses but no pots or pans or cooking utensils really of any kind.

I move to open the last cabinet when I feel my stomach decide that enough is enough. I glance around the kitchen for a trash can but don't see one. It must be one of those pullout-type cabinets. Despite opening most of the cabinets, I haven't seen the trash can though.

So, instead, I run to the sink just as I begin vomiting. I hate the feeling. As a kid, I would do everything possible not to get sick. I hate being sick, and I'm a terrible patient to take care of. I always think I know how to take care of myself better than anyone else. When I think my stomach is finally finished, I turn on the faucet and rinse out my mouth in the sink.

"Are you sick?" Nacio asks, standing at the entrance to the kitchen.

I wipe my mouth with a paper towel I found next to the sink. I shake my head. "Just need to get something in my stomach."

"There's a little café that has breakfast around the corner. I can go pick something up for you. I don't want to leave you alone though if you're sick. I can call Santino and have him pick us up something, or I can see if they deliver, but I don't think they do."

I shake my head. "I'm not sick. Just give me a second to get dressed and brush my teeth, and I can go with you. I'm not sick, just pregnant," I blurt out without thinking.

Realization at what I let happen last night slowly takes over my mind again. I destroyed everything I'd been working so hard to protect these last few months. One stupid mistake last night has ruined everything. And, in doing so, I've put everyone's lives at risk—Kinsley's, my baby's, Nacio's, and my own life.

In an instant, I remember. My memories come flooding back.

I remember going to a nice steak house with Nacio. I remember talking about nothing, yet talking about nothing was everything because we didn't talk about all the shit we were dealing with. We didn't talk about what Nacio did for a living or his family or my job or my family. We didn't even talk about my baby or who the father was.

Instead, we talked about our favorite music, movies, food. Instead, we told silly stories from our childhoods. Instead, we talked about things that people typically considered unimportant but always were important.

And, last night, I learned that we had virtually nothing in common.

I had been brought up as a beauty, and he had been brought up as a beast.

I like all things beautiful and pretty. I like making the world a better place. I have hope in the good of the world.

Nacio had been brought up to be a killer, to destroy the world, to see only the bad in people.

And those upbringings affected everything, including what food, music, and movies we liked. The experiences in our pasts affected our futures.

Still, it was an enjoyable night. I loved having a normal conversation with him even if we had nothing in common. Somehow, that made everything that much more exciting.

After dinner, I climbed into the back of the car with him, and

George began driving us toward Nacio's apartment to drop him off. I remember every second that passed by as I sat next to Nacio in the back of that car. I remember wanting nothing more than for him to rip off the dress I was wearing and to take me right there on the backseat even though George could see us.

But Nacio did nothing. He stayed silent and honored my earlier request not to let me come up to his apartment. To just stay friends and be nothing more.

So, when George pulled up at Nacio's apartment, I said, "I need to pee. Mind if I use your bathroom?"

Nacio opens the door to his apartment and flicks on the lights while I stand behind him at the entryway.

This has to be one of the nicest apartments in New York City. It's the penthouse, and it has large, expansive windows, just like my apartment does. The only difference is that these are at least twice the size as mine with a much more spectacular view of downtown.

"The bathroom is down the hall, to the left," Nacio says, breaking me from my spell.

I nod and make my way toward the bathroom. I get inside and close the door even though I don't need to use the bathroom. I just used the restroom at the restaurant before we left. But I guess being a pregnant woman and having to pee every five minutes sometimes has its advantages. Really, it was just an excuse to come up to his apartment.

I spend my time in the bathroom, trying to decide if I should really risk everything.

Is he really worth it?

Yes, he's worth it.

I don't know if it's how horny I've been these last few months without a man to keep me satisfied or the fact that my vibrator simply isn't cutting it anymore or if my pregnancy hormones are finally catching up to me, but I'm desperate for him.

All through dinner, I could barely concentrate because all I could think about was how I needed his hands on me. I needed his mouth pulling and tugging and kissing on my lips. I needed him buried inside me, making me scream. I needed him.

And, now, no matter how much my brain is telling me not to because, in the morning, I will realize how much of a mistake this is, I have to.

I flush the toilet and wash my hands in the sink. Then, I open the door to the bathroom and slowly find my way back to the living room where Nacio has made himself comfortable on his dark leather couch with a couple of fingers of scotch that he's sipping slowly.

I walk over and take a seat next to him on the couch. "You have a nice apartment. Does anyone else live here with you?" I ask, wondering if Santino or Reina live here at least part-time. Or if he uses it as an apartment for his employees when they have work to do here in New York. Or if there is a girl living here with him.

"No. I live here by myself."

I let out a breath I didn't know I had been holding.

"I just recently bought this apartment when I realized I'd be spending a lot more time in New York."

I don't know why it makes me feel relieved to know that no one else lives here with him, not even family. But it obviously would have bothered me. And, as for the part about him spending a lot more time in New York, I know the reason—me.

"Can I get you anything to drink? Some wine maybe? Or I think I have some gin somewhere, or you can have some scotch if you're up for it?" he asks, and then he frowns when he realizes his mistake. "I'm sorry. I wasn't thinking."

"It's okay." I don't want him to think about my pregnancy. I don't want him to hesitate to fuck me.

I begin slowly sliding on the couch toward him, my black dress inching up higher and higher as I do.

Nacio raises his eyebrows at me but doesn't say anything. Instead, he takes another sip of his scotch. I inch closer again, and my dress goes up even higher, now barely covering my underwear. I watch his eyes stay glued on my bare legs. And I'm happy that I wore this curve-hugging dress, despite wishing I had worn sweatpants into work today. I'm not showing yet, but I feel plenty bloated enough to already want to trade in my dress for something more comfortable.

I slide a little closer and watch Nacio squirm a little as he takes another sip of his scotch, trying to be good. Trying not to give in to his desires.

"I think you should go home now. I can call George and tell him you're ready for him to take you."

"You're not going to take me home?"

"No. I don't think that's a good idea."

He takes another sip of his scotch even though there isn't much left at this point. He's trying to avoid my gaze and my body, but the scotch isn't going to help him for much longer. My hand finds its way onto his chest and then moves up his body to his neck. I grab the nape of his neck and pull him toward me until his lips are hovering over mine.

"Kiss me," I whisper over his lips.

He doesn't hesitate to ask me if I'm sure that's what I want. His lips just devour mine, not allowing me to hesitate either or think or do anything but kiss him back. He takes all my air, my thoughts, with the kiss.

He pushes me back, moving quickly to keep both of us from thinking this through. He pushes me until I'm flat on my back on the couch, our mouths locked together. And, despite how much I know we shouldn't be doing this, it's the best feeling in the whole world.

His kisses demand more and more with each one. His hand tangles in my hair, and I feel his erection pressing against my stomach. I know I have only seconds left to stop this, to say no, before we both get so lost in each other that we won't be able to stop.

I don't want to say no though. Instead, I say yes.

I grab the hem of his shirt, and I begin tugging upward, needing to see his chiseled hard body above me, on me. Needing this to go further than a junior high make-out session on my parents' living room couch.

He doesn't get the hint though because he keeps kissing and devouring me, not letting our lips leave one another, and I slowly let myself get lost back in his kisses. I forget about everything, even what I want, except to kiss this man whom I'm madly in love with. But, with each kiss, I come closer and closer to destroying his life.

Beast finally comes up for air, and as he does, he pulls his shirt off over his head. "God, I missed this."

I bite my lip. "Me, too." I grab the hair on the base of his neck and pull him back to me, not able to go another second without his lips on mine.

I've never felt this way before. I've never needed a man in my life as much as I do right now. Before, I only needed sex, which is what I could get with any one-night stand. But, now, I need so much more, and he's the one I want more with. Right now, what I need is lots and lots of sex.

Nacio finally gets on the same page as me when my moans turn desperate beneath his lips. His weight shifts off me just slightly, and his hands disappear underneath my dress. I feel my panties being pulled down my body, replaced with his skilled fingers. His fingers move slowly around me, teasing me, taunting me, but never giving me what I really want. But I'm not a patient woman, and I don't plan on waiting a second longer to get what I want.

I bite his bottom lip and firmly put it into my mouth to grab his attention. "I want you now. I can't wait, Beast."

I release his lip and lap at his wound with my tongue. Then, I grab his hand and help him push his fingers inside me, showing him that I'm not willing to wait. I scream out from how good it feels to have him touching me there again after so long.

His eyes watch me come undone with just his fingers. "You have to be patient, Beauty."

"I can't," I moan as he expertly slides in and out of me, making me moan, crazy with need.

My panting grows so hard that I can barely breathe, let alone talk or command him to do what I want him to do. I want him to take me, but he's taking his sweet time. I begin to try to focus on my breathing, to slow it down so that I can tell him what I need between kisses, while his fingers glide back and forth inside me. But, every time I get close, his fingers take me further away, and I'm close to losing my mind instead of growing closer to him being inside me.

This time, when his fingers slide back out, his cock slides in, and I finally get what I really want. Somehow, in the midst of everything, I close my eyes and push everything out, but when I do, all my feelings come rushing in.

"Open your eyes, baby."

I do. I look at him even though I know it's a mistake. His eyes have so much love that I could cry. And then I do. I cry as he fucks me. I cry as he slides in and out, and for some stupid reason, every time he moves, I cry harder. I've never been a huge crier to begin with. I cry during the normal times, like at sad movies, the loss of someone, or after a tiring day. But I've never cried in the middle of sex.

Right now, I don't care what Nacio's thinking as he watches me cry. Instead, I just enjoy it. He doesn't move fast. Instead, we find our own slow rhythm together as I figure out what I need from him —love.

We move together in unison until I come with him buried inside me, and he comes just after with our eyes locked together. He doesn't collapse on top of me like he usually does after he comes.

Instead, he looks deep into my eyes and says, "I love you, Beauty, and don't ever forget that." He wipes the tears from my cheeks before kissing away the remaining ones on each cheek.

I lie on the couch, exhausted, and watch as Nacio stands next to me before lifting me into his arms.

"Where are we going?" I ask tiredly, practically falling asleep in his arms.

"I want you in my bed."

I yawn and stretch my arms over my head, but the second our bodies hit that bed, I know I'll be ready for round two. But we both know after a good night's sleep comes clarity, and that clarity will remind me that we can't be together.

And just like I thought last night, the clarity sets in this morning. But with the clarity comes confusion because I'm just as torn as I was before. "I need to go."

Nacio runs over to me as I begin searching for my things around his apartment. I spot my purse slung over the arm of his couch in the living room, and I make my way over there.

Nacio stops me though, grabbing ahold of my shoulders and forcing me to look up at him. "You're not going anywhere until I get you some breakfast and make sure that you're okay."

"I'm fine. I need to go home." I brush past him and am able to snatch up my purse before he gets to me again.

"Please, just let me take care of you. It doesn't mean that we have to start dating again or be together in any real capacity. Just let me take care of you. Please."

I look down at what I'm wearing—his T-shirt and shorts. It'll have to do because there's no way I'm squeezing back into the dress that I wore over here. I just need to get George to take me home, and then all I have to do is walk into my apartment. I don't care what I'm wearing for that.

"I need to go now. I need to get some things sorted out in my head. I'll call you later." This time, it's my turn to reach up and kiss him on the cheek and then walk away without a good-bye.

I walk out the door of his apartment, and I'm gone before he has a chance to come after me.

9

SCARLETT

I SPENT the entire weekend on my couch in my apartment. Thinking. Trying to come up with any way possible that what I just did last night with Nacio didn't just ruin everything I'd worked so hard to protect. At the same time, I was also trying to find a way to get Nacio to fuck me again and again and again. Because, after Friday night, I know now more than ever what it means to give up Nacio. And it's not how I want to live the rest of my life. I want to live my life experiencing that over and over and over again.

By the time I get to work on Monday morning, I'm even more clueless than I was before. Preston is sitting at my desk, waiting for me, as I get into work. I'm a little disappointed when I notice that no gifts are covering my desk like usual.

Preston notices my disappointment and says, "He left you a note."

I watch him hold up the note in his hand. I reach out to take it, but he pulls it back out of my reach.

"So, where have you been all weekend?" he asks.

"I've been at home, alone, lying on my couch and watching Netflix."

"Sure you have. You haven't been sucking face with Mr. Nacio Marlow, have you?"

I walk around to the back of my desk and snatch the note out of his hand. "No, I haven't."

Preston gets up from my chair, and I take a seat as I begin opening the note from Nacio.

"Then, why does the note say that he's sorry if he fucked up the other night but that it was one of the best nights of his life, and if you let him, he'll repeat it every night forever and ever?"

In frustration, I hit Preston's arm with the note. "You read my note? Don't you know that's an invasion of my privacy?"

"Not according to you. I'm one of your best friends. You share everything with me, remember?"

I roll my eyes but don't argue with him any further. "What's on my schedule for today?" I ask.

Preston looks at me, and I know he has something really important to tell me, but he doesn't want to tell me.

"What is it?" I ask, getting frustrated.

I see the determination in Preston's eyes as he prepares to tell me whatever he has to say.

"You need to start telling people about the baby, Scarlett. You can't keep waiting."

"He already knows about the baby," I say, exacerbated.

"The whole truth?" he says, raising his eyebrows at me.

"Enough."

Preston shakes his head. "You have to tell him everything. You need to talk to Kinsley, too."

"I'll tell them all everything when I'm ready. I'm not ready yet."

"And why not?"

"For lots of reasons that I don't have to explain to you."

With every second that passes, I get more and more frustrated with this conversation. Preston walks over to me.

I stand because I can tell from the look on his face that he needs a hug, and honestly, so do I. I know he's just pressuring me because he is looking out for me. We hug.

I don't know how everything got so messed up. But it did. I used to have a simple life. The only thing I worried about was what was going on with the company, but lately, I haven't so much as thought about what's going on with the company. It's been the last thing on my mind.

When he steps back, he asks, "Have you told Kinsley about Nacio?"

"Has she told me about what with Nacio?" Kinsley asks as she stands in the doorway to my office.

I look at Preston, and he's giving me an I'm-sorry-but-not-really-that-sorry look on his face. I turn from Preston to Kinsley. "Just that I'm less worried about him coming after us again. It's been a long time since it happened, and I just don't want to live in fear every day."

Preston motions to me that he's going to go, and I nod. Then, I'm left alone in my office with Kinsley.

"So, what are you doing here today? Not that I mind you stopping by anytime. I just have a lot of work to catch up on today. You'll have to ask Preston if I can do lunch or something later."

Kinsley narrows her eyes at me, not concerned at all with my words. "Now that he's gone, are you still going to lie to me?" she asks.

"Am I going to lie to you about what?"

"Don't play dumb with me, Scarlett Bell. You know exactly what you're lying to me about. I want you to tell me the truth right now!"

My eyes widen as I look at my best friend who thinks I've deceived her in some way. I have, but I just don't know in which way she's talking about. Although she shouldn't be this mad at me if she understood why I lied to her and deceived her. Every time I deceived her, it was to protect her, to keep her safe. But I haven't seen Kinsley this mad at me in a long time, not since I stole her Barbie doll and cut off all her hair before giving it back to her in the second grade.

But I'm not going to start admitting to things until she tells me what she's upset about. I've protected her for too long to stop doing it now.

"I don't know what you're so upset about. Just tell me. I'm sure I have a reasonable explanation for it."

Kinsley crosses her arms over her chest as her eyes bulge, big and wide. "I saw you with him."

"Who?" I ask, still playing dumb. But I know who she's talking about.

On Friday night, I was afraid, when Nacio took me to the restaurant near where Kinsley and Killian live, that we were taking a chance in getting caught. But that was half of the fun and excitement of it. And I didn't actually think we would get caught.

I plead with God, *Please, God, no, no, no, no, no, this can't be happening. I couldn't have ruined everything in one moment.*

Except it is happening.

"Nacio."

I nod. Not sure of what else to say.

"How? Why? How is this possible?"

"I..." I open and close my mouth, trying to figure out what I can say to help her understand. But I don't think anything I say will help.

If I can't explain my relationship with Nacio to my best friend, how in the world will I ever have a chance at explaining it to the world?

But I have to try.

"I fell in love with him before I even knew who he was. And, now, I'm not sure I can let him go. Kins, I've tried letting him go. I thought it was the only way to protect him and you. But I've failed."

I watch as the fear in her eyes turns to anger.

Her face tightens, and her cheeks flush bright red as her eyes narrow on me. "I just don't understand. How could you not know who he was?"

"I don't know. I just didn't."

"How could you?" Kinsley asks as her voice trembles. "After all the horrible things he did. After what he did to me. He's killed who knows how many people. You're just okay with that?"

I guide her over to the couch, afraid she is going to pass out if she doesn't sit down.

I don't know how to look her in the face when I answer. I know I need to tell her the truth, but the only way to help her understand would be to lie. That option isn't great, so I go with the truth. "Yes, I'm okay with it."

Kinsley runs her hand through her blonde hair and then stands from the couch, unable to even sit next to me. "You're okay with the fact that he's a smuggler? That he trafficked women and children? That he killed them when they didn't behave? That he is a killer?"

My tears sting my eyes. Today, I am going to have to give up someone I love. Either Kinsley or Nacio. They can't coexist together.

"Yes."

"You're okay that he tried to kill me twice? You still love him, even after that?"

"But he didn't try to kill you. He saved you."

Kinsley glares at me with her gorgeous eyes that have turned cold. "He didn't try to kill me? Are you fucking kidding me? So, I just saw bullets flying past my head twice, but neither of those times, he was trying to kill me? He was trying to protect me?"

I nod even though I realize that now is not the time to argue the point with her. I can't even really prove that he was saving her those times. I just know it to be true. She's already decided that Nacio is a monster, and right now, there's no point in trying to convince her otherwise.

She sits back down on the couch, and I take her hands in mine.

I plead, "I wish I didn't love him. Everyone's lives would be easier if I didn't. If I hadn't fallen for him. But I did, and now, I can't take it back. I can't make it go away, no matter how hard I wish I could."

Kinsley's eyes soften a little but not enough.

I know she can't understand, but I try to make her understand anyway.

"When you first met Killian, was he the guy you thought he was? Was he the perfect man with no flaws?"

"Don't you dare. Don't you dare compare Killian to Nacio. They're not even in the same stratosphere."

I try a new approach. "What if Killian had been a killer? What if he had killed dozens of people? Would you still love him? If you'd already fallen in love before you found out, would you still have married him?"

"That's not fair. Killian isn't a killer. Nacio is. I would've never been so stupid to fall in love with a man who was a monster."

Her words hurt more than she knows. Because I was stupid enough to fall in love with Beast. And I'm not certain that a beauty can turn him back into a man.

I take a deep breath to keep the tears from falling. I don't want her to see me cry, to see how badly she's hurt me. "Maybe I am stupid for falling for him. But there's nothing I can do about it now."

Kinsley raises her eyebrows at me. "There's plenty you can do now. For me, you can stop seeing him and turn him into the police."

"I can't."

"Sure you can. I'll go with you. You just go to the police and tell them you didn't realize who he was, and as soon as you found out, you turned him in. It's that simple."

"I can't."

"Why not?"

"Because I love him."

"What about me? What about my feelings? Do you even care about me?"

"Of course I do, Kins. I just love him, too, and it's not as simple as just giving him up."

Kinsley stares at me in disbelief. "Fine. If you won't, I will."

She turns to leave, but I run to the door, blocking her exit.

"Please, Kins, you don't have to do this. We can figure something else out. Please just give me a little bit more time to figure it out."

"I can't," Kinsley says.

I move away from the door and watch as my best friend walks through it, leaving me all alone and ending our friendship that I'm not sure can ever be healed again.

10

BEAST

SCARLETT'S GONE. Again.

I got her back, and I lost her, all in a stretch of a few hours.

I'd never expected to get her back so soon. I hadn't thought that, once I got her back, I'd ever lose her again.

But, now that I have, it sucks even worse than before.

I hear a knock at the door, and I can't help but let a little bit of hope back in at the thought that it could be her. Or it could be about a million other people. I try not to get my hopes up, but it's too late. If Scarlett isn't standing on the other side of my door, I'm going to be devastated.

I run to my door, hoping to God that Scarlett is standing on the other side, but as I get closer, I can feel it in my gut that it's not her. She just left this morning. There is no way she would come back so soon. She wanted time to think, to figure out if she still wanted to be with me.

Unlike her, I don't need time. I already know we are supposed to be together. I just don't think we will ever end up together. I don't think I deserve a happily ever after. I don't deserve her.

I reach for the doorknob and turn it before throwing the door open. Santino is standing in the doorway with a smug look on his face.

"What do you want, asshole?" I ask, walking back to my kitchen to pour myself a scotch. I know it's too early to start drinking, but I need the alcohol if I'm going to survive today without her.

I pull a glass out of the cabinet and then pour myself a glass. Santino reaches into the cabinet and pulls out another glass. I frown but pour some of the scotch into his glass as well. Maybe I won't have to deal with much of his crap if he's drunk.

He takes a drink as he stares at me, studying me, like he will be able to tell what I'm thinking just by looking at me. He probably can. It's clear to see that I'm not thinking about anything other than Scarlett.

I walk from my kitchen to the living room, collapsing on the couch where I fucked Scarlett just last night. A couch that I should replace if I want any chance at keeping my sanity. Not that I could ever part with anything that Scarlett touched.

I watch as Santino takes a seat on the love seat, kitty-corner to me. His eyes are still studying me.

"Reina send you?"

He nods.

I frown and take another sip of my drink.

I always thought that Santino would be on my side. I thought he would always be loyal to me, but I'm not so sure anymore if he's loyal to me or Reina. Or maybe he thinks he can be loyal to both of us. He can't. Not anymore. He has to choose, just like we all do.

"What does she want?"

"For me to convince you to kill them."

My eyes widen. "Them?"

His eyes fill with sadness. "Yes. Kinsley and...Scarlett."

I stand as I throw my drink down on the ground. I watch the glass shatter, and the liquid covers my hardwood floor. I never thought that Reina would stoop so low as to have a woman I loved killed. I thought we were closer than that.

Now, I realize what she really wants—to control me.

"That's not going to fucking happen."

"I know. I told her as much."

"Then, why are you here?" I ask, staring him down. I have to know if he is on my side or hers.

"To let you know, so you can protect them and keep them safe."

I growl. I don't know if I believe him or not. Right now, my concern though is keeping Scarlett and Kinsley safe. Keeping them alive. If something happens to either of them, I'll die.

I pace the room, trying to figure out a plan on how to keep them safe. My mind is racing though, so it makes it hard to think straight. To think of any sort of plan.

"Talk to me. Let me help you. I want to protect them, just like you. There is no way we are going to let Reina do this."

I turn and glare at him. Then, I let my anger and fear get the best of me. I rip him up from where he is sitting and shove his body against a wall. My arm holds him, pinning him against the wall.

But, unlike all the other times when I've pulled something like this on him, he doesn't fight me. He just lets me hold him against the wall, like he deserves it. I ease off just a little, confused by his behavior.

"I want the same thing that you do," he says calmly.

"I can't trust you."

He narrows his eyes. "You don't have a choice."

I let him go and walk away because he's wrong. I always have a choice. And my choice is not to trust anyone right now.

I hear a knock at the door, and I stop and look back at Santino, who is still standing against the wall.

"Who is that?" I ask.

He shrugs and then walks back to where his scotch is sitting next to the couch. He picks it up without looking at me.

I sigh and then make my way toward the door. I swear, if it is Reina or someone else she sent to convince me to kill Scarlett, I'll kill them right now. I reach for my gun in the back of my jeans as my other hand goes to the door. I glance back at Santino to see what he is doing, but he seems unfazed by whoever is at the door.

I turn my attention back to the door, ready to shoot if I need to, and then I open the door.

"Scarlett?" I ask, like I'm not sure it's really her standing in front of my doorway.

She glances down at the gun in my hand, hardly seeming fazed that I'm pointing a gun at her.

"I'm sorry," I say nervously before I holster my gun in the back of my jeans.

She shakes her head as she walks into my apartment, like she's at home. I wish this were her home. I wish we could move in together, like any other normal couple.

"Don't be sorry. You should be ready to protect yourself," she says.

She walks into the living room and drops her purse on the floor while I curiously look at her, wondering why she is okay with me pulling a gun on her.

She notices my stare and continues, "Kinsley knows."

I cock my head, not understanding what Kinsley knows. "You told her about your pregnancy? About who the father is?"

She shakes her head. "No. She saw us together."

I smile. "Okay."

She runs her hand through her long brown locks with curls that have come loose, hanging down past her shoulders. "Okay? That's all you have to say? You're in danger."

I smile and reach up to tuck her strands of hair behind her ear. I get lost in the smell of her hair as I touch her. I'm just so happy that she's here, that I can touch her again. Hold her, be with her.

"Nacio," she says sternly, trying to break me from my dream.

I glance back at her, trying to focus. "Yes?"

"You aren't taking me seriously. This is serious. Your life is in danger. You could end up back in jail, or Killian could hunt you down and kill you before the police have a chance to take you to prison. I can't...that can't happen."

I smile and touch her cheek, trying to calm her. It works. She closes her eyes and just feels my hand pressed against her cheek. When she opens her eyes, I see tears.

"I can't lose you," she says in a whisper.

"You won't."

I move my hand to her chin and lift her mouth up to meet mine in a gentle kiss. She purrs a little in her throat as I kiss her. And my cock takes it as an invitation. I ignore it, knowing now isn't the time or place, even as much as I want it to be. I need her desperately, and I think she needs me, too. To show her that I'm still hers and that no one is going to take me away from her. But, first, I have to talk to calm her nerves.

"You don't need to worry about losing me. All you need to worry about is keeping yourself and your baby healthy. Let me worry about the rest."

She stares at me, and then she notices Santino sitting on the couch, watching us. She smiles for the first time since she stepped foot inside my apartment.

"I missed you, Santino," she says, walking over to him.

He stands, and they hug. "I missed you, too."

I glare at Santino as his hands tighten around Scarlett. He meets my glare but doesn't taunt me with the fact that he is touching her and I'm not. I don't see jealousy in his eyes. In fact, I think I see...

I shake my head. Santino doesn't care about anyone but himself. He's loyal to his family. That's it. He doesn't care about her.

Scarlett pulls away. "He's not going to listen to me, is he? He's not going to protect himself?" she asks Santino.

Santino looks from her to me. I stand frozen with my hands in my pockets.

Santino turns back to Scarlett. "No."

Her face drops.

Santino lifts her chin. I want to attack him again until he says, "Don't worry though, Beauty. That's why I'm here. To protect him and you. I'll make sure nothing happens to him even if he won't listen to you."

Santino looks at me, and it's the first time I start to believe him. Not enough to trust him to protect Scarlett yet, but I do believe he cares about her.

He gently kisses Scarlett on the cheek. "I'm glad you're back, Beauty. He's been a mess without you," Santino says. He turns and begins walking down the hallway. "I'll see myself to one of your dozens of bedrooms."

I smile and watch Santino leave before I walk over to Scarlett. "Listen to him. You don't have to worry about me."

She shakes her head. "That's all I do. Worry. About you, the baby, Kinsley. I'm not going to just stop now."

I touch her cheek again, needing to touch and comfort her, to stop her from worrying about something that is not worth worrying about. "You don't need to worry about me going to jail. They don't have anything on me, and as far as Killian is concerned, I can take care of myself."

"What do you mean, you don't have to worry about going back to jail? They have you on camera, attempting to kill Kinsley." She pauses for a second, thinking. "How did you get out of prison in the first place?"

"Don't worry. I got out legally, despite what Killian or the media might have reported. I got out for good behavior. I was on probation for a while. I'm not anymore. And they don't have me on camera. I'm a pro, remember? I made sure that the security cameras didn't record anything that night."

"But they have Kinsley's testimony. Her word is a lot more believable than yours."

I sigh. "Maybe so, but it would never get that far."

"Why? What do you know?"

"Just trust me. I'm not in any danger." I don't add that Kinsley and she are the real ones in danger. I don't want to cause her any anxiety that could affect the baby. I'll only tell her if she needs to know to stay safe, and right now, she doesn't need to know.

"I'm sorry," she says, twisting her hair in her hand.

"You have nothing to be sorry for."

"I do. I should have made sure that Kinsley never found out. I know that I've sent you mixed signals about what I want when it comes to us, but I can't lose you. You can't go back to prison."

I take her hands in mine, loving the feeling of her smooth skin. "What if I deserve to go to jail? What if everyone will be better with me gone?"

"I won't be better. I need you."

She might as well be promising me forever because that's how I take her words.

"Promise me, you'll do everything you can to keep yourself safe?" she asks.

"Only if you promise to do the same."

I can see the hesitation in her eyes. She doesn't want to promise. She thinks she needs to protect me. That my life or Kinsley's might be more important than her own.

I raise my eyebrows at her, waiting for a response that I never get. Instead, her lips claim mine. This kiss is mind-numbing. And I feel her promise with her lips, signifying that she will do whatever she can to protect herself.

Because she is mine. Forever.

And, this time, after I'm done with her, I'm not letting her go. No matter what excuse she gives me.

I need to show her that she is mine.

My hands run over her body and lift her as she wraps her legs around me. I fist her mane of hair, holding her tight to my body, as I kiss her everywhere that I can get my lips. On her lips, her neck, her chest. I'm desperate to have her, to claim her, like I really want. I should have done this the first time I saw her. I should have claimed that she was mine. I was stupid to ever let her think that she was anything but mine.

I carry her to my bed, not believing that she just left my bed this morning. I thought she was gone again, and I never imagined I would have her back in it so soon, but if I have my way, she won't be leaving my bed for the rest of the week.

I lay her down on my bed and kiss her soft lips before I stand up.

She whimpers when I stop kissing her. "Please, I need you."

I kiss her, and her whimpers stop.

"Don't worry, Beauty. I'll give you everything you need and more."

I grab the hem of her shirt and lift it over her head before removing my own shirt. I remove my jeans and briefs, needing to feel her skin against mine as soon as possible. She watches me as I do, studying my every movement. I undress her until she is completely naked, and then I climb on top of her, kissing my way down her body.

"This is mine," I say as I kiss her neck.

She moans her agreement.

"And these, these are mine," I growl as I kiss each of her breasts.

I continue kissing until I get to her still perfectly smooth stomach. A stomach that contains a baby, despite not showing any outward signs to indicate her secret. I know it's there. Taunting me that she slept with another man so quickly after she left me. Right now, she's not all mine. She's still his, whoever he is.

I kiss her stomach, over every inch. "And this..."

She grabs my hair, trying to pull me back to her lips so that she can silence me.

I don't let her. I kiss over her stomach again. "I don't care whose sperm created the baby." I slowly and deliberately kiss her stomach as I keep my eyes locked on hers. "This is mine."

She sucks in a breath as I lower my kisses until I'm kissing her pussy. She jumps from the unexpected touch, and then she moans as my tongue swirls around her folds.

"This is mine."

"I'm yours," she says, looking at me.

I lower my mouth to her pussy again, making sure she's good and wet, before I take her the way I want. And then I claim her again and again in every way.

"You're mine, Beauty." I insert a finger into her pussy. "Mine."

She bites her lip to keep from screaming.

I place another finger at her ass. I slowly insert it, filling all of her. "Mine."

She bites her lip harder to keep from moaning louder.

I remove my fingers and then place my cock at her entrance. I forgot to grab a condom, and I begin to reach down to grab my pants off the floor to search for the condom that I know is in the pocket, but Scarlett stops me.

"You don't need a condom."

My eyes widen.

She trusts me, and I trust her.

I've never fucked a woman without a condom.

I slide into her, and the feeling is different. I can feel all of her against me. Every drop of her liquid covering me. The tightness of her pussy. I can feel it all.

My lips move to hers as I rock slowly in and out of her, getting used to the new feeling of her. She keeps my lips on hers, trying to muffle her screams.

"Moan for me, Beauty. Let it all out."

She shakes her head. "Your brother is in the next room," she whispers.

I laugh. "I don't care about him. You're mine, and I need you to tell the whole world that you're mine."

I thrust again, making sure to rub against her clit, as I kiss her neck. She moans but still tries to stifle it by digging her mouth into my shoulder.

I'm not going to let her keep quiet. I need the whole apartment building—no, the whole world to know that she's taken.

I lower my lips to her nipple and nip at it while I thrust, driving her wild. I hold her hands over her head to keep her from using them to cover her mouth, her screams. She tries biting her lip again to keep herself from screaming, but I bite down as I pull an orgasm from her.

"Nacio!" she screams.

I growl as I shoot my cum inside her. And then I collapse, holding on to her, needing to feel that she is mine.

"You're mine, Beauty."

"Forever," she whispers back.

I hold on to her tighter as our breathing gets slower, deeper, and I know that we will soon let sleep take over us. I'll have to wait to claim her again until after we've both slept. I just hope, when we do, clarity won't change how she feels again. That she will understand that she's mine.

11

SCARLETT

I STIR out of my zombie-like sleep. I don't know how long I was out, but it was long enough to dream of what my life could be if everything were different. If Nacio and I could just move in together and do normal couple things, like going to dinner, watching movies, and sleeping in. How I long for the simple things like that in our relationship instead of worrying if he's going to end up in jail or dead.

I slide out of bed, careful not to wake Nacio. As much as I wish that we had a life where we didn't have to worry about someone killing us or ripping us apart, that is exactly what I have to worry about. I get dressed and sneak out of Nacio's bedroom.

I need to go see Killian. I need to find out what the police or FBI is planning. I need to know how to keep Nacio safe because he clearly has no concern for his own safety. I grab my purse and then leave Nacio's apartment without waking him.

I don't call my driver, George. I don't want to let Nacio or anyone else know where I'm going. I need to talk to Killian without worrying if Nacio is going to try to find me and get himself thrown in jail.

I flag down a cab, and once I climb in, I give the driver Killian's work address. I try not to think as the driver pulls into traffic, but all I can do is think.

I touch my stomach as I think about what Nacio did. How he kissed my stomach. How he called the baby his even though he knows full well it isn't.

It made me fall more in love with him. It also made me that much more desperate to save him.

I wanted to tell him who the father is, so he could understand that the baby would never be his.

And, because of this baby, I could never be his. Not really.

Because I have to choose between him and this baby, and as much as I love him, it's not even a decision. I have to choose this baby.

A tear drops, and I wipe it away. I just wish it were that easy to wipe Nacio away. I wish I had never met him. I was just fine with being alone.

The cab driver pulls up in front of Killian's work. I pay him and climb out without a word. I don't see anyone as I walk into the hotel where Killian works. Not because they aren't there, but because I can't see them since I'm too focused on finding Killian.

"Scarlett?" Killian asks as he pauses in front of me, finding me before I found him.

"Hey, Kill. Can we talk?"

He reluctantly nods and then pulls out his cell phone. He types something in before he looks back at me. "I can spare a few minutes. Come on, let's go to my office."

"Thanks."

Killian walks me to his office and then takes a seat behind his desk while he motions for me to take a seat opposite him. I do, dropping my purse to the floor, feeling strange about sitting on this side of a desk. It makes me feel less in control.

"Why are you here, Scarlett?" Killian asks as he stares at me with anger in his eyes.

"How is she?"

He stares at me, trying to read me. "Kinsley doesn't want to speak to you right now."

"And you?"

He narrows his eyes. "I'm talking to you because she can't."

I suck in a breath, trying to keep from crying again. I lost Kinsley, I'm going to have to give Nacio up, and I'm going to lose...

I can't even think about it.

"I'm sorry," I whisper.

Killian looks away for a moment and then back to me. "She hasn't gone to the police yet. She's torn up about what to do."

I nod.

"I haven't gone to the police yet either," he says.

"Thank you."

"Don't thank me," he says, angrily getting up from his chair.

I watch as it slides backward and slams against the wall.

"I haven't told them because of her. I don't want to go against her wishes. But I'm not going to let her get killed. I'm not going to let that man anywhere near her ever again. We've increased security." He pauses and then looks at me with tears in his eyes. "Do the right thing, Scarlett. Turn him in. End this."

"I can't do that," I whisper.

"She needs you, Scar. She needs you."

I get up from my chair and hug him because that's what we both need.

I slowly let go. "Just give me some time to figure this out. He won't hurt Kinsley. I promise you that."

He sighs. "I'm going to the police with this first thing next week if you don't."

"Thank you."

He shakes his head, and I know I've disappointed him.

I walk back to where I dropped my purse on the floor, and I dig through it until I find the envelope that I've been carrying around for a while now. Kinsley needs to see it. I hold out the envelope to Killian.

He curiously looks at it but takes it. "What's this?"

"It's for Kinsley."

He narrows his eyes at it.

"Just have her open it with you when you see her next. It doesn't have anything to do with Nacio."

He stares at it as he holds it in his hand. "I don't think she is going to want to read any notes from you. She's really not in a good place right now, Scar."

I swallow hard. "I know, and I'm sorry. But she needs to see what's in the envelope. Just promise me that you will make sure she opens it."

He nods.

I hate that he doesn't promise, but I didn't promise him that I would turn Nacio in.

There's nothing left to do. The envelope is my only hope at restoring my relationship with Kinsley. Now, I just have to figure out how to protect Nacio.

12

BEAST

I STARE DOWN at my phone as Scarlett walks out of the hotel where Killian works. I pull out my wallet and throw some bills down to pay for the coffee I ordered while I waited for Scarlett to get done talking to Killian.

I get up and follow her at a safe distance. I want to see what she is going to do. *Is she going to go to the police?*

I don't care if she does. I just want her safe.

I followed her here shortly after she left my apartment. When I'd woken up, she was just gone. But I'd put a GPS tracker on her phone the first time I was with her. I won't let her out of my sight, especially not now that Reina wants her dead.

I should kill Reina for threatening to take Scarlett's life. I should, but I can't. I can't kill Reina any more than I can kill Scarlett or Santino. She's family.

And I understand why she wants me to kill Scarlett, too. To protect herself and her family. In Reina's mind, Scarlett knows too much to stay alive. If she's not with us, then she's against us. And anyone against us must die, so we can protect ourselves.

I watch as Scarlett climbs into another cab instead of having George drive her. I shake my head. She thinks I can't track her if she isn't with George. She doesn't understand that nothing will stop me from tracking her. From being with her.

I climb into my car that is parked down the street and follow her cab. Her cab turns toward her apartment, and I sigh because I know I can protect her at her apartment. I've set up enough cameras and alarms to ensure that I can watch her and keep her safe.

I park at the end of her block and watch her walk inside her apartment. I pull out my phone and pull up the cameras that are hooked up in her apartment just in time to see Scarlett entering her apartment.

She looks tired and worn down as she drops her purse the second she gets inside her apartment. She walks to her fridge and pulls out some Chinese takeout. Then, she begins eating from the box without bothering to heat it up.

As much as I want to, I resist the urge to pick up some real food for her and run it up to her apartment. She doesn't want to be with me right now. I won't go up unless she isn't safe. And, although I could make a good argument for cold Chinese food not being safe, I don't think she would see it that way.

She carries the box of food with her as she goes upstairs to her bedroom and then to her bathroom. She turns the faucet to her bathtub on, and she begins to undress. I've watched her many times on the security cameras, but I never watch her undress. I never invade her privacy like this. But I can't keep my eyes off of her as she undresses.

I watch her slowly remove her shirt, and I can see the lace of her bra hugging the top of her breasts. She cracks her neck from side to side, trying to get the tension to leave her body. Then, she slips out of her pants until she is standing in just her underwear.

My cock twitches as I remember the feeling of taking her without a condom, of claiming her. I want to do it again right now. I growl instead, forcing those thoughts from my head.

When I look back at the screen, she's completely undressed and climbing into the tub. She stretches before she lies down in the tub. She grabs the carton of Chinese food and begins eating again. She takes a while to finish eating and then places the carton on the edge of the tub. She leans her head back and closes her eyes, trying to relax, but I can see her tension, even from here.

I want her to relax. I need her to relax.

I pull her number up on my phone and dial before putting it on speakerphone so that I can still watch the security cameras. I watch her look to the floor when her phone buzzes. She sighs as she reaches down to grab her jeans and pull out her phone.

"Hello?"

"Hi, Beauty. I miss you. I wish you hadn't run out on me."

She smiles, happy to hear my voice. "I miss you, too. Sorry I ran out on you earlier. I just had some errands to run, and I didn't want to wake you."

"You sound tired. Can I come take care of you and help you feel better?" I ask seductively.

She smiles. "I wish you could. I have a couple of more errands to run, and then I can stop by."

I frown. I don't want her to go anywhere else. I want her to stay with me where it's safe. I also want her to feel better. To relax after whatever that fucker Killian told her.

"That's too bad. I was just about to take a bath, and I was hoping your naked ass could join me. I wanted you wrapped around my cock while the jets and my hands massaged you."

She sighs, and I can see my words affecting her as she adjusts herself in the tub. Her cheeks flush from her just thinking about it.

"God, that sounds nice."

"It's not too late to join me."

She bites her lip. "It's too late. I'm already in my tub at my apartment."

I growl into the phone. "It's not too late."

I hear a tiny gasp.

"I can still please you from here."

I watch as her hand goes to her chest, and I know her heart is beating quickly.

"How?"

"By getting you off with just my voice."

I hear her swallow hard on the other end of the phone.

I grin. *This is going to be fun.* "Lay your head back on the back of the tub."

I watch on the screen, but she doesn't do it.

"Is your head lying back yet?"

"Yes."

"You're lying. Trust me. Lay your head back against the side of the tub."

She glances around the room, wondering if I'm there, but then she does as I said.

"I am."

"Good girl. Now, I want you to touch your finger against your gorgeous lips and suck it like it's my cock. Get it nice and wet for me. Imagine it's my cock."

She does exactly as I said, and my cock hardens. I reach my hand down, needing the release, but I stop. This isn't about me. This is about her.

So, instead, I watch her suck her finger.

"Now, I want you to rub your nipple, swirl your finger around it."

She does, and from just watching her, I think I might come in my pants like a teenager, not an experienced man who has been with too many girls.

"How does it feel when you touch yourself?"

She purrs. "So good. God, I wish you were here, touching me."

"Close your eyes. I'm there. I'm touching your nipples, squeezing them hard."

She does exactly as I said, and I watch her chest rise and fall as she does.

"I'm lowering my hand from your breast, over your smooth stomach, and between your legs."

I watch her do just as I said.

"I'm rubbing your pussy in slow, torturous circles."

Her hand slips between her legs under the water, but I know what she is doing—rubbing herself.

"Yes, Nacio," she moans.

"I find your clit as I slip a finger inside."

"Yes."

"And then I fuck you with my fingers."

She does just that. "Fuck, Nacio, I'm going to…"

"Come for me, Beauty."

I watch her explode on the screen, not feeling anything but bliss.

A rap on the window makes me jump out of my seat. I glance over and see Santino climbing into the passenger seat next to me.

"What the fuck are you doing?" I ask.

"Scaring the shit out of you." He glances at the phone that I have been holding in my lap, and then he smiles. "Did I interrupt something?"

"Yes! Now, get the hell out!" I turn the phone away, so he can't see Scarlett. "I said, get out!"

"Reina is tired of waiting. She put out a hit on them."

"Both of them?"

He nods.

"Fuck."

I jump out of the car and begin running toward Scarlett's apartment building. There is no telling how long Reina has had the hit out or which one of her killers has been assigned to the job. My security cameras won't do anything to protect Scarlett. I need to protect her. Now.

I burst through the door of her apartment building with Santino on my heels. He's just as concerned as I am. And, to protect Scarlett, I also have to protect Kinsley.

"Go get Kinsley!"

Santino freezes. "Where do you want me to take her?"

"I'll let you know."

I keep running and then stop again. I shout back to Santino, who has already begun running in the opposite direction, back out of the building, "And don't kill anyone!"

He freezes and smirks.

"Well, don't kill anyone that Scarlett would hate us for killing."

515

"Don't worry, Nacio; I'm not the killer in the family."

I run toward the elevator, not even registering what Santino said. I just keep running. I get to the elevator, and over and over, I press the button to go up, waiting, as the elevator takes its sweet-ass time getting down to the ground floor. A man steps out, and I shove him as I climb in, needing him to get out faster so that I can make it up to Scarlett.

I press the button for her floor and then the button for the doors to close, begging them to close faster so that I can make it upstairs faster. They finally close, but then I'm stuck in this cage, unable to move or do anything to protect her. I'm helpless.

The fear sinks in that, in these few moments I'm not with Scarlett, Reina could have her killed. Scarlett could be dead. I pull the gun from the waistband of my jeans. If she is, I'll kill everyone who even so much as thought about killing her.

The doors open, and I rush out, not stopping until I reach her door. I don't bother knocking. Instead, I pull the key that I have to her apartment and unlock the door with my gun drawn. I step inside, looking for any signs that anyone has broken in, for any signs that anyone is here to kill her.

I keep moving, quickly scanning her apartment, until I get to her bathroom. I throw the door open without thinking, just needing to know that she is okay.

She screams, still in the tub, and she starts scrambling, trying to grab a towel, her phone, or anything that might protect her.

"Shh...it's okay. Scarlett, it's just me. I'm not going to hurt you."

She wraps the towel around her body. Then, she finally sighs. "Then, why are you aiming a gun at me?"

I realize that I still have my gun out, pointed right at her. I lower it but don't put it away. I haven't checked every room in her apartment. She might not be safe.

"What are you doing here?" Her face turns red. "I thought you were at your apartment? That's at least a twenty-minute drive, a lot longer in traffic. We weren't even on the phone for five minutes. How did you get here so fast?"

I swallow. "I've been sitting outside your apartment the whole time."

She tightens her grip on the towel around her. "What were you doing?"

"Protecting you."

She glances around the room and then spots something in the corner. She runs over to it, looking up, staring at the tiny camera. "You've been watching me! Haven't you?"

"Scarlett, this really isn't the time. I need to get you out of here. You're not safe here."

She stares at me with wide eyes, frozen. "You've been watching me!"

"Scarlett, stop. I need you to come with me. Now. I'll tell you anything you want later."

"I'm not going anywhere with you. I thought you were done with lying to me. I guess I was wrong."

I don't have time to deal with her, to explain. I need her safe, and I need her safe now.

I walk over to her and scoop her up. Then, I begin carrying her out of her bathroom while she begins hitting me, trying to get me to let her go.

"Let me go."

"No."

I feel her towel slipping off her body, but I'm not letting her go. Not for a second.

I begin walking toward the front door of her apartment.

"Where are we going?"

"Somewhere safe."

Her eyes grow wide as she studies me. "What's going on?"

"I don't have time to explain. We just have to get out of here now."

She grabs my chin to force my eyes to look at her, and I pause for a second, letting her know how serious I am.

"I will carry you out with nothing but a towel on, Beauty. I have to protect you."

She takes a deep breath. "Just let me put something on."

I study her eyes, afraid it's a trick. If I put her down, she might make a run for it.

"Trust me," she says.

I slowly lower her to the ground. "Fine, but I'm not letting you out of my sight, and it has to be quick. We can get you new clothes later."

She nods and runs back upstairs to her bedroom. I follow with my gun in my hand, scanning to make sure that no one is going to touch her.

She moves to her closet and pulls out some sweatpants and a T-shirt. I don't think I've seen her in anything this casual before, but she looks just as beautiful as always.

She freezes as she ties the sweatpants so that they will stay up around her waist. "What about Kinsley? Is she in danger?"

"Santino is making sure she's safe."

"I need my phone. I need to call her. I need to warn her and Killian."

I shake my head and grab her arm. "We don't have time. We have to go now. Santino is on it. He will protect her."

"I have to call her—"

"Think about your baby, Scarlett. You have to protect your baby. Kinsley will be fine. Trust me."

She hesitates for just a second longer, and then she takes my hand. "Okay."

13

SCARLETT

I TRUST NACIO. I do. More than I even think he realizes. If I didn't trust him, there would be no way I would go with him after I found out that he'd put cameras all over my apartment. He says they are for my protection, but then why would he need to put a camera in my bathroom? I trust him though. So, instead of refusing to leave with him, I'm riding in the passenger seat next to Nacio as we drive to who knows where.

I glance over at Nacio, who is focused. More focused than I have ever seen him. I have questions. So many questions. But I don't ask any of them. I trust him to keep me safe, just like he trusted me to keep him safe. He shouldn't have. I can't keep him safe any more than he can keep me safe.

I close my eyes as the images of the men I helped kill flash in front of my face. Neither of us deserves to be safe. We both deserve to die for killing.

The only one who doesn't is this baby, I think as I touch my stomach. *This baby is innocent. This baby deserves to live.*

"Where are we running to?"

"Somewhere safe."

I sigh. Nacio is terrible at communicating with me, at being honest with me.

"Whom are we running from?"

Nacio briefly closes his eyes and then opens them, and I see the pain.

Reina.

We are running from his sister. And it's killing him that he is protecting me from someone he used to spend all his time protecting.

I want to ask if Kinsley is okay, if Santino found her safe and sound. I wonder what he is doing to protect her. Is Santino dragging Kinsley out of her home right now, forcing her into a car, and driving her here? Because I know that Kinsley won't go willingly if that is their plan.

Nacio doesn't know anything about Kinsley though. His phone hasn't rung once since I've been with him. He knows nothing more than I do, so there is no point in asking. There is no point in worrying. I can't do anything to protect her right now. I just have to hope that Santino got to her in time. I trust him almost as much as I trust Nacio. Santino will do everything he can to keep her safe.

"How long have the cameras been in my apartment?" I ask instead.

"Since the first time I fucked you."

"So, you have been watching me on the little cameras. Watching personal things. Watching me undress and bathe and, and, and...pee."

His lips curl up into a tiny smile, and it makes me smile.

"You're worried that I watched you pee? What kind of a creep do you think I am?"

We smile at each other.

"I never watched you get naked or pee or do anything like that. I put the cameras up strictly as a way to protect you. The only time I ever watched you while you were naked was today."

I shouldn't believe him. I mean, what man wouldn't watch a

woman he was attracted to while she was naked on a video any chance he got? But, for some stupid reason, I do.

"Okay, I believe you. But you still haven't said you're sorry yet." I raise my eyebrows at him.

"That's because I'm not sorry."

"You're not sorry? How can you not be sorry? You invaded my privacy. You stalked me."

He smiles. "I'm. Not. Sorry. Everything I did was to protect you. You would have never allowed me to put those cameras up if I had asked permission and told you that your life was in danger. That, just by being involved with me, your life would always be at risk. Always be in danger. I have to protect you from that, and that means not telling you everything."

"No."

His eyes widen as he glances from the road to me. "I will protect you without worrying you. You don't deserve to live your life in fear because of me."

"No. If I'm going to be with you, we'll do this together."

"No," he growls.

I ball my hands into fists to keep from strangling him. "Nacio, this is never going to work," I say, trying to keep my voice calm. "We are in this together. I have to be a partner. We can't—"

"Get down!" Nacio screams at me.

"What?" I cock my head at him, not understanding what he's talking about.

"Scarlett, get down!" Nacio pushes my head down between my legs.

"Nacio, what—"

Nacio swerves the car as a pop and crack make me jump. I try to peek up to figure out what the unfamiliar sound was, but Nacio pushes my head back down.

"I swear to God, Scarlett, if you don't stay down, I'll—" He never finishes that sentence. Instead, he swerves again as the loud popping comes at us, this time louder and longer than the first.

Gunshots.

Someone is firing at us, I finally realize, as a bullet hits my window.

I scream, expecting the glass to break, but somehow, it doesn't. Instead, when I glance back up, there is a spot where the glass is cracked, but it didn't shatter on top of me. I don't know how that's possible, but I don't ask. There are more important things to worry about, like figuring how we can both stay alive.

I turn my head to Nacio, who has sped up and is now holding a gun in one hand with the other on the steering wheel.

"Who's after us?"

"Reina's men."

Nacio glances in the rearview mirror and then speeds up as he swerves the car. I grab ahold of my legs, the only thing I can hold on to, as he makes a hard right. I can feel my stomach rumbling, telling me it's not happy with the car ride. It needs to empty itself, but I push that away. I can't vomit. It would distract Nacio, and what he needs right now is to focus to keep us both safe.

He swerves the car again and then stops suddenly before speeding up again. The movement almost does it. I feel liquid sloshing in my stomach, but I don't vomit.

"Is there anything I can do?"

"No, just stay down, Scarlett."

Nacio doesn't even glance my way as he drives. I hear more shots firing at us, breaking glass.

I scream again and keep my eyes on Nacio, praying that he doesn't get hit. He doesn't. The glass next to his head has cracked but hasn't broken. The car is bulletproof, I realize. I don't know much about how bulletproof cars work, but I do know that we aren't completely safe. A bullet can still get through; it's just harder.

I don't know what to do as more shots ring in my ears. I feel completely helpless. My heart is racing as I hope that we all stay alive —Nacio, the baby, and me.

We have to stay alive.

I don't know how many people are chasing us. I don't know how many cars surround us. But, when I look at Nacio, I see a calmness that shouldn't be there. He's been in this situation before. This is where he thrives.

I, on the other hand, feel useless. I can't help him as much as I want to. I can't save him or protect him. I'm helpless.

The only thing I can do is try to keep myself alive. So, that's what I do. I stay bent over while Nacio protects us.

He drives faster and faster, and I'm afraid we are going to crash. I don't know how he is going to get us out of this situation. But I know that he will. I have faith that he will save us, and in his eyes, I can see that he believes he will, too. There is no other option.

"Stay down, and brace yourself," Nacio says.

I do.

And, for a split second, he glances at me out of the corner of his eye. It's just long enough for us to see the love in each other's eyes, and that could be the last thing we take with us if we die. It's a moment that I will take with me forever, and it'll probably be the last thing that goes through my head before I die, no matter if it's in the next few seconds or years from now.

And then his eyes aren't on me anymore, but my eyes are on him.

He stomps on the brakes.

My heart and world stop.

The car spins deliberately.

The window on his side goes down, leaving him vulnerable but allowing him to aim the gun out of the window.

He gets off a shot, and I hear loud popping sounds that make me want to squeeze my eyes shut to shut out the world and pretend this isn't happening.

I don't though. My eyes stay on Nacio. I watch him squeeze the trigger again.

But the car keeps spinning faster and faster until my vision goes blurry.

I can't see anything.

I can't see Nacio.

I can't feel my heart beating.

I can't tell if I'm breathing.

I can't tell if either of us is even alive.

I feel the car move again, so I must be. We must be.

We begin moving faster again, and the sound of bullets hitting the car becomes fainter and fainter.

I feel my heart beat. Once. Twice.

Then, it beats quickly, so fast that I can no longer keep track.

I breathe again, and the fog begins to clear.

Nacio.

He's still alive. He's driving the car fast but nowhere near as fast as we were going before.

I touch my stomach, and I know the baby is still alive.

I'm still alive.

I don't have to ask Nacio if I can sit back up. I know it's safe.

The threat is gone. For now.

I feel it in the air around us.

I slowly sit up, wincing a little as I do.

"Easy," Nacio says, putting his hand on the back of my head as I ease up. "Easy. I think you hit your head on the dash."

I feel my forehead, and I don't feel any blood, but it's sore, so I must have hit it against something even though I don't remember it.

"How do you feel?" he asks.

"A bit dizzy."

He holds the back of my neck, rubbing harder than what feels nice, but I don't dare tell him to stop rubbing. I need him to touch me, reassuring me that we are both alive.

I take a couple of deep breaths as the fog and dizziness continue to clear out of my head.

I look at Nacio clearly for the first time. "Are you okay?" I ask.

"Yes. You're alive."

I smile and lean into his hand that is now on my cheek. I close my eyes and then open them again.

I don't ask if we are safe. I already know that we aren't. There is just no immediate threat right now.

I reach out to touch his face, but we hit a bump, and my hand lands on his arm. He winces when I touch him.

My hand automatically jerks back, and then I see why he winced, as blood stains my hand. I see blood trickling out of his bicep. It doesn't look like that much blood, considering a bullet is in his arm.

"We need to get you to a hospital."

"No."

My eyes widen, but this time, I'm not taking no for an answer. "Damn it, Nacio! You are going to a hospital even if I have to call an ambulance to chase us all over the state. You can't protect me if you're dead."

He smiles. "Glad you have finally realized that I am the one who needs to worry about protecting you."

I frown. "This isn't funny, Nacio. You could die from this."

He laughs. "I'm not going to die. I was hit by one bullet. I'm barely bleeding. It just hurts like a motherfucker."

I lean over toward him and take a closer look at his injury. It doesn't look too bad, but I'm not a doctor. I know nothing about injuries like this. For all I know, he could die from this.

"It could get infected."

"It won't."

"You could bleed out."

"Unlikely."

"You could—"

Nacio traps my lips with his, shutting me up. He kisses me like a man who is very much alive, not like a man who is in danger of dying.

"Where are we going then? You can't just leave the bullet in your arm. You need medical treatment."

"We are going somewhere that Reina thinks I would never go—to one of our childhood homes in the Hamptons." He grins. "And, as far as medical treatment goes, I think it's your turn to save me."

14

BEAST

I TURN onto the street of the house where I spent so many summers. A house I vowed I would never go back to. And never, ever voluntarily. Yet here I am, driving toward the monstrous house, the only one on this street. I glance out my window to the grass that belongs to my family, despite still being a couple of miles away.

I try to keep my focus on Scarlett and why I'm doing this—to keep her safe. But it kills me.

The second that I said where we were going, Scarlett understood what it meant. How hard it would be for me to drive here after what happened here. After I hurt my sister here and, in turn, destroyed myself.

I glance over at Scarlett, and she is staring out the window at the water flowing by next to us because, of course, our house has one of the best views in the Hamptons.

It's worth it though to know that she is alive. That she will be safe here.

I will never forget the terror I felt when I saw them pull up behind us. I'd been in similar situations before. I'd felt the adrenaline that comes with being in that situation, but I never felt the fear. I'd never cared if I lived or died. I still don't.

But, the second I saw the cars behind us, I wasn't sure if I could save her. I wasn't sure I was strong enough. I had no idea what to do. I just reacted.

I don't know how we got out of there alive. We're lucky that all that happened was a bullet to my arm. It should have been so much worse.

They had three cars. We had one.

They had guns, too many guns. I had one.

The only difference was, for the first time in my life, I had something to live for. Someone to save.

I'd never driven so fast once I realized that she had to live.

I'd never had my mind be so focused.

I'd never known exactly what to do before I even did it.

I'd never shot so perfectly.

I'd never been so thankful in all my life.

I drive to the end of the street where our house stands proudly on the hill. A house we should have bulldozed a long time ago. Instead, it's still here. My father's dead, long gone. He was the only person who gave a shit if this house was still here. The second he died, Reina and I should have destroyed the house. Instead, we chose to never think about it again, but it was always there, in the backs of our minds, just like the memories that always haunt us.

I park the car and take a deep breath as I look at the overgrown yard filled with weeds. It's been a long time since anyone came here to take care of the house. But the house still stands proudly behind the weeds, taunting me.

Scarlett takes my hand and gently rubs it. "Come on, let's go inside. The sooner we go inside, the sooner you will find out that I have no idea how to fix your arm, and the sooner we will get out of here and go to a hospital, like I wanted you to."

I chuckle. She does that to me when I need it the most.

I nod and then let go of her hand so that I can get out of the car. I walk to the back and pop the trunk to retrieve my bag that is always there with extra guns, ammo, and medical equipment for situations just like this.

I walk around to Scarlett's door that she tried to open but can't, from the looks of it. I try the handle, but it doesn't budge. I pull on it again, using my whole body, and I feel the pain in my shoulder. When I finally get the door open, I hold my hand out to her to help her out. She takes it, staring at the cracked glass. If it wasn't bullet-proof, one or both of us would have died.

I pull her to me and kiss her, as much for me as for her. We both need something to wipe away what happened and to remind us that we are alive.

The kiss is perfect, but it can't take away the pain in my arm. It just helps her to understand the pain as well, and she pulls away. I try to pull her to me, but the pain is too much.

I've been shot before, and I know what's coming next. The adrenaline is leaving my body, and with it gone comes the pain that I barely felt before.

She takes my hand again. "Come on, let's get you inside."

With the bag in one hand and Scarlett's hand in the other, I walk us to the door of the house. I drop the bag and grab the handle, praying that it's unlocked because I don't have the strength or energy to deal with breaking in. It turns, and I push the door open before picking the bag back up and leading Scarlett into the house.

We step inside, and Scarlett coughs as we both breathe in the layers of dust covering the house. It's clear that no one has been here in years. I walk over to the light switch, flipping it up without thinking, but no lights come on. There isn't any electricity, just like there won't be any air-conditioning or water. Maybe this wasn't my smartest idea.

I guide Scarlett into the kitchen. I don't have to think or guess where to go. I just walk automatically, as if I were here yesterday. I stop when I get to the faucet, flipping it on but no water comes out.

We will have to make a run for supplies later. Right now, I have to deal with my shoulder.

I walk over to the kitchen table, drop my bag on top, and then pull two chairs out. I motion for Scarlett to take a seat in one. She does, and I take a seat in the other, trying not to move my right arm that is now all I can think about.

With my left hand, I pull my bag to me and start to unzip it with the help of Scarlett, who holds the bag while I pull the zipper. I begin digging around in the bag to find everything that we are going to need. I find the painkillers and antibiotics. I pop the bottles open and take some of each without water. Scarlett watches me as I do.

I reach back into the bag and pull out the medical bag that contains the rest of the things Scarlett is going to need. With a terrified look on her face, Scarlett watches me as I pull each item out of the bag.

"You can do this," I say, trying to reassure her.

She gives me a tight smile, but I can tell she doesn't believe me.

I take the water bottle and hand it to her. She takes it, curiously looking at me.

I lift the sleeve of my shirt up so that she can easily see the wound.

"I need you to flush out the wound with the water."

She nods and slowly begins moving toward my arm. I know, if she can't even do this step, this is going to be a long process. She unscrews the top and then holds my arm with one hand as the other slowly moves closer with the water bottle. Her scared eyes focus on the wound, like the bullet is going to jump out and attack her, too.

"You need to flush out the wound with the water. Understand?"

She nods and then begins to flush my wound with the water. It burns, but I don't move.

She swallows hard when blood along with the water pours down my arm.

"That's good," I say.

She stops, and I see her chest slowly rise and fall. Despite being scared to death, she's calm. She can do this.

"I need you to look at the wound. There is a bullet in there, correct?"

She looks up at me and then puts her hands back on my arm as she moves in closer to study my wound. "I think so. Yes, there is a bullet."

"Okay, if you think you can do it easily, you need to try to remove the bullet without injuring anything."

She nods.

"Good."

I begin arranging all the items she will need on the table.

"You need to slowly open all the instruments, careful not to touch them. Then, put on the sterile gloves, and pick up the tweezers."

She takes a deep breath but begins doing as I said. When she has the gloves on with the tweezers in her hand, she freezes.

I grab her chin and force her to look at me. "You can do this, Scarlett. Use the tweezers and pull the bullet out of my arm."

"It's going to hurt. I can't hurt you."

"It's going to hurt worse if you don't remove it."

She nods.

"Good girl."

She takes ahold of my arm with one hand, and then with her other hand, she begins to insert the sterile tweezers. I bite down, trying to keep from making a sound or moving, as she digs into my wound.

Fuck, it hurts.

I growl through my clenched teeth.

She doesn't look at me when I growl. She ignores me and stays focused on her task at hand.

I bite down, trying to keep from yelling or cursing, as she digs the tool deeper into my arm, but I can't keep from cursing.

"Fuck, that hurts. Hurry." I clench my teeth again as I feel her pulling the bullet out.

When the bullet is out, she applies pressure with the gauze, and I can finally breathe again. As she watches the blood soaking the gauze, I can't take my eyes off of her. I'm in awe of how strong she is.

She applies new gauze, tightly holding it to my arm that still hurts.

"I think the bleeding has slowed enough. Now what?"

"Clean the wound with some water again."

She does so as I contemplate how she should close the wound. It's too big to heal on its own or with medical tape. It will have to be closed with either stitches or staples. I decide on staples since it will be faster.

When she's done cleaning it out, she looks at me with big eyes because she knows what she needs to do next but not how. She's worried, but pulling the bullet out was the hard and risky part. This part will be easy, and then all we have to worry about is infection. The antibiotics should help with that. And Santino is good in a medical crisis. He will be able to help once he gets here.

I pick up another pack of sterile gloves and put one on my left hand. I pick up one of the sterile tweezers.

"Pick up the other tweezers and the staple gun."

She does so, holding one item in each hand. This would be easier with two people and four hands, but we don't have that luxury, and I don't want to take the time to show her how to stitch up my arm.

I look down at my arm and grab ahold of one side of my wound with the tweezers. "Grab the other side until it is touching mine."

She takes a deep breath and then pulls the wound together with her tweezers. She pushes a staple into my arm without asking or telling me she's going to do it. The pain from the staple is nothing. I barely wince when she does it.

I move the tweezers over to the next stop, and she does the same. We repeat the process over and over until the wound is closed.

She drops the tweezers and staple gun onto the table and then takes off her gloves while I do the same.

We both stand at the same time, our hands grabbing each other's faces, and we lock our lips together.

We've survived.

We keep kissing, tangling our tongues together, our bodies together, as we cling on to the lives that we shouldn't still have.

We kiss anywhere we can get our lips. We take turns kissing each other's lips, necks, ears, cheeks, chests. Anything that is visible, we lay our lips on it.

Scarlett needs more though. She drops to her knees and pulls at my pants, undoing the buckle and zipper and pulling down until she finds my cock. Her lips wrap around it, needing more and more.

When she touches me, I growl, feeling my fire finally returning to me. Finally truly feeling alive again since that moment in the car when I thought our lives were over.

She sucks and licks and pumps my dick like no woman ever has.

I fist her hair in my left hand as her eyes smile up at me. I want to fuck her when she's done, but first, I need to shoot cum down her throat. I need to—

Thoughts stop as the wicked woman takes me all the way into her throat.

She does it once, twice...

And then—

"Fuck, Scarlett," I growl as I tighten my grip on her hair and shoot my cum down her throat.

She smiles when I finish and takes her time with licking me until I'm clean.

She begins to tuck me back into my pants, but I'm not done with her. I reach down to lift her up to me.

She shakes her head. "I have something I need to tell you first."

"It can wait."

I begin pulling her up again.

"Really, Nacio? You couldn't wait until you found a bedroom?" Santino says, standing in the kitchen with an angry Kinsley next to him.

15

SCARLETT

I DON'T GET a chance to tell Nacio about what I need to tell him. I can't hide secrets from him anymore. It's burning inside me, and I need to tell him. But, just as I tried to tell him, Santino and Kinsley walked into the house.

I don't know how we didn't hear them earlier, but here they are.

I look at Kinsley standing next to Santino and notice his hand gripping her bicep. He forced her to come here. She didn't come willingly, like I had hoped.

"Kinsley," I say weakly, trying to smile at my best friend, who I know hates me right now.

I don't notice what Nacio or Santino are doing.

I walk toward Kinsley.

"You let him kidnap me!" Kinsley screams.

It makes me pause for a second. She's pissed, and she has every reason to be. But she is safe—or as safe as she can be—so she can be pissed all she wants, but I'm relieved. I should say I'm sorry, but I'm not, and I'm done lying to people I love.

"Let go of me," she says, trying to shake Santino off of her.

"Can't do that, sweetheart. You'll run," Santino says.

"Then, kill me already. That's why I'm here, right? You're going to kill us. Just fucking get it over with."

Kinsley jerks, trying to break out of Santino's grasp, but he holds on to her arm tighter.

"Kinsley, they aren't going to kill you or me. They are trying to protect us."

"You're wrong, Scarlett! They want to kill us. They've done this to me before. They haven't changed. They are going to kill us, and it's all your fault!" Kinsley screams, looking straight at me.

I take deep breaths in and out, trying to find a way to fix this. I will do whatever it takes to protect my best friend and keep her safe, including having Santino tie her up.

"Kinsley, they are protecting us. Their sister is the one after us, not them."

She shakes her head. "They don't have a sister."

I nod. "They do. Her name is Reina. I've met her. She's the one who sent men after us. They are protecting us from her men."

"No."

I see the tears in her eyes, and it kills me.

"We were shot at on the way here. We almost died. Nacio was shot." I point to him and his newly stapled arm, blood running down his side and onto the floor.

Kinsley shakes her head. "I don't believe you. If you were shot at, it's because he has too many enemies. Someone was just coming to seek revenge. That was all it was."

She's never going to trust me or believe me again until I can show her that I'm worth trusting. And it has to have nothing to do with Nacio or Santino or this situation.

"Killian didn't give you the envelope, did he?"

"No, he didn't get the chance. This scumbag kidnapped me before he had the chance."

Killian.

Why isn't he here with Kinsley and Santino?

I don't know if he's safe or not. I need to ask Nacio about that soon but not in front of Kinsley and not until I'm sure that she trusts me again.

Only one thing will convince her to trust me again. To love me.

I walk slowly toward Kinsley as I watch more tears glisten in her eyes.

When I get to her, I glance to Santino. "Let her go."

To my surprise, he does without a fight. I pull Kinsley to me and hug her. She lets me but doesn't hug me back.

And then I whisper into her ear, telling her everything...things that I can't tell Nacio yet. I need him to protect me and the baby and Kinsley, and I'm not sure he will if he finds out the truth.

16

BEAST

"Do you think I would risk my baby if I didn't think they would protect us? No matter how I feel about him, no matter that I love him, I would never risk this baby," I hear Scarlett say.

She was quiet before, just whispering to Kinsley. But, now she's speaking so softly I can't make out what she is saying. My eyes stay on Scarlett; that's all my eyes ever do anymore. They consume Scarlett, everything about her. Every movement, every look on her face, every curve of her body, everything. I know it all.

"Fine," Kinsley says.

Her word gets my attention enough to look from Scarlett to Kinsley. I try to tell if she's lying or not, but despite my time with Kinsley, I don't have a clue about her. I haven't studied her face like I have with Scarlett. I don't know if Kinsley is telling the truth or just saying what we need to hear in order to trust her.

So, I look to Scarlett instead. She knows Kinsley. She knows if Kinsley is lying or telling the truth. And she believes Kinsley, so I have no choice but to do the same. I don't know exactly what Scarlett told Kinsley to convince her that I can be trusted, but I have a hunch it had something to do with Scarlett's baby.

Scarlett hugs Kinsley again. Both have tears in their eyes.

I walk over to them, needing to get this off my chest so that I can let them have the space they clearly need. "I'm sorry," I say to Kinsley.

She wipes her tears and lets go of Scarlett so that she can face me, strong and defiantly. "Sorry is not good enough. You shouldn't have taken me—again. The FBI could protect me from your sister. Killian could protect me." She pauses. "Killian. Is he okay? Does he know I'm okay?"

"The FBI couldn't protect you. Reina has people who have infiltrated the FBI. The FBI isn't safe. And, as far as Killian, he's safe. Reina doesn't give a shit about him. She doesn't kill unnecessarily. He's a smart man. He knows how to stay alive. The FBI will be able to protect him."

"Does Killian know where she is?" Scarlett asks.

"No."

I motion toward Santino to follow me out, so we can give them some privacy and figure out some sort of plan.

But Kinsley steps in front of me, stopping me. "Scarlett tells me you love her. Is that true?"

I glance over at Scarlett. "I love her."

"So, this is all to protect her from your sister? To protect me so that she doesn't have to suffer from the pain of losing me?"

"Yes, I'm doing this to protect her. I'm not a good man, you know that, but I love her. I'll do anything for her."

"Even kill your sister?"

My mouth drops a little at her question. "I don't think it will come to that."

I step around her to find Santino, but she pushes her way back in front of me.

"That's not good enough. If we are going to rely on you for protection, if I'm going to trust you, I need to know that you are putting us first. Will you kill Reina if you have to, to protect Scarlett?"

I take a deep breath in and out, trying to think about what I would do. Reina is my sister. I've protected her my whole life. She was the only woman I ever loved before Scarlett came into my life.

I see Santino standing behind Kinsley. He awkwardly shifts his weight, waiting for my answer.

If I killed Reina, it would destroy him and me.

If I let Reina hurt Scarlett, it would destroy Kinsley and me.

Neither option is a good one. That's why I will do everything in my power to avoid having to choose one or the other.

I turn and look over my shoulder to Scarlett. "I'll do anything it takes to protect Scarlett, including killing my sister if it comes to it."

Scarlett sucks in a breath as I promise to put her first.

I look back to Kinsley. "Satisfied?"

"For now," she says, frowning at me.

I've had enough of being questioned about where my loyalties lie. I brush past Kinsley and motion for Santino to follow me.

"Are you sure?" he asks, glancing back at the girls with obvious worry that they might run away.

I roll my eyes at his ridiculousness. "They are fine. Scarlett isn't going to go anywhere without me, and Kinsley won't go anywhere without Scarlett. We are all safe."

I keep walking, not waiting for Santino's response.

I walk back outside of the house where I can think. I can't think about anything in that damn house. I don't hear if Santino followed me out, but I assume he did, like the good younger brother that he is. I close my eyes and rub my forehead, trying to make the pain go away, as I think.

"There is no electricity. No running water. No food. I need you to go to the store and pick up everything we will need," I say.

"I can do that," Santino says from behind me.

I blow out air through my pursed lips, trying to push the pain out. "I'm going to need more painkillers, too. I'm almost out, and between my arm and head, no one is going to want to be around me if I'm in this much pain."

Santino chuckles. "No one is going to want to be around you either way."

I turn and look at Santino, and he stops chuckling.

"So, what's the plan since you are going to be all serious? Wouldn't this be one of the first places Reina looks?"

I glance at the house behind Santino. I can hear our father's voice telling me to be a man. To destroy my sister. I can hear my sister's screams. I can feel my own pain.

"No. This is the last place she would think that I would go."

Santino looks at me and then understands. "Are you going to be able to stay here?"

"Yes. I wasn't lying when I said I would do anything to protect Scarlett."

He nods. "So, what is the plan?"

"Right now, we stay here, and we wait Reina out and keep them safe."

17

SCARLETT

I STARE at my phone as the morning light peeks in through the windows. I didn't sleep, not one second. No one else did either.

I flick my phone on and off, staring at the clock that shows it's six thirty a.m. It's about the only thing I can do on my phone other than play a few offline games due to not having any reception here.

I roll over and look at Kinsley, who is picking at the threads on the blanket, pulling them apart and then braiding them back together. We are both lying on the floor in the living room, something we haven't done since we were kids. But we wanted to be together last night, and Nacio wouldn't leave us to a room on our own. Said it wasn't safe. That's how we all ended up sleeping in the living room, despite there being dozens of beds in this house.

I glance over at Santino, who is lying on one of the couches. He's snoring. He must have fallen asleep recently because, the last time I looked, he was awake, like the rest of us.

Nacio sits up on the couch next to me, watching us. But he's not really watching us. He's reliving what happened to him here. I can see it in his eyes.

I chose to sleep next to Kinsley because I thought she was the one who needed me the most last night. Now, I'm not so sure.

Is this going to be my life from now on? Always having to choose between the two of them, never getting to choose them both?

Yes.

I get up off the floor because I'm not doing Kinsley any good by just lying next to her. Despite telling her about my pregnancy and doing my best to convince her that Nacio is a good man, she's still mad at me.

I don't blame her. I just don't know how to change anything. And I don't regret falling in love with Nacio.

I walk over to the couch and take a seat next to Nacio. "Stop thinking."

I pull his chin to mine, and I kiss him. He's hesitant at first, still letting his ghosts haunt him. He slowly, tentatively tries to let them go as he pushes his tongue into my mouth, but I can tell he's not really here. He's still being haunted. Still thinking, not really kissing me.

I grab the nape of his neck, digging my nails in harder than usual, trying to draw him to me. It doesn't work.

I try moaning as I kiss him, despite there being two other people in the room.

It doesn't work.

I try moving my hand over his cock over his shorts.

Nothing.

I pull away. "Nacio?"

"Huh?" he asks after a few seconds pass.

I frown. "Is there anything I can do to help you?"

"Just stay alive."

I nod my head. I don't know how long we are all going to last here in this house.

"I'm going to go make us some breakfast." I get up from the couch and head to the kitchen where Santino stored the supplies of food he brought back yesterday. I didn't see what he'd gotten, but hopefully, it's something good because I know Nacio isn't going to let me leave this house if we need anything.

I dig through the bags on the counter and find some protein bars, fruit, peanut butter, and bread. I sigh. I guess Santino could really only get nonperishable foods. I pull out a banana and a protein bar. I guess this will have to do. I hope we aren't going to be here long.

Kinsley walks up behind me. "What do we have for breakfast?"

I hold up the protein bar and banana.

"Yum, yum. Did he get any coffee?"

I shake my head. "Good thing, too. Just the smell of coffee has been making me sick lately."

She smiles. "Coffee used to give me morning sickness, too."

"You okay? I mean, I know this is tough, seeing me pregnant after..." I can't finish my sentence. I can't say, *after you lost Wesley.*

She nods. "This is a happy time, not sad. This is how it's supposed to be."

She reaches in and pulls out a bar and banana as well. "Do you think Mr. Safety would care if we ate our breakfast outside? I need some fresh air after breathing in all of this dust all night."

I bite my lip, knowing that Nacio isn't going to be happy about us being anyplace that isn't within his eyesight.

Kinsley rolls her eyes. "Hey, Nacio, Scar and I are going to eat our breakfast outside. If you have a problem with it, get your ass outside to ward off whatever snipers are out there, waiting to shoot us."

I frown at Kinsley.

She huffs and then walks outside. I wait for Nacio to walk over to the kitchen.

"I'll give you some time alone. You should be just as safe in the backyard as in the house. The fence surrounding the property isn't climbable. I have an errand I need to run anyway," he says.

I frown. "Want some company?"

"No, Kinsley needs you more right now."

"What errand are you going on?" I ask, trying not to sound worried. But I'm afraid he's going to do something dangerous.

"It's nothing you need to worry about. Just going to get some security equipment, so I feel safer with us sleeping in actual bedrooms and moving about the house without having to stay right on top of each other. I'm afraid, if we stay in this house together for too long, we will be more of a threat to each other than Reina's men."

I smile, but it soon fades when I see something oozing from his wound.

"It's fine."

"It doesn't look fine. It looks infected."

"It's not infected. The oozing is good. The wound is cleaning itself out."

I frown. "It's infected."

He kisses me on the forehead, like I'm a child. "I'm taking my antibiotics. I'm fine. Don't worry about it."

I watch him dig through the bag and pull out a protein bar before he leaves. When he leaves my view, I walk out onto the deck where I find Kinsley lying on one of the couches, eating her protein bar.

I take a seat on a chair next to the couch and begin unwrapping my own protein bar.

"So, explain to me again why you're so in love with that monster?"

"He's good to me."

"You mean, good in bed."

I blush. "He's good in bed, but there is more to him. We just...connect."

Kinsley sits up and narrows her eyes at me. "And there is nothing I can do to change your mind? Nothing I can say about what I've been through with him to show you that you shouldn't be with him?"

I shake my head. "I've seen him at his worst, trust me."

"You've seen him torture and kill people?"

"Yes."

Kinsley leans back. "I always knew you were the wild one between the two of us. I just never expected you would fall for a criminal."

"It wasn't like I planned it. I just don't see him as a criminal."

"That's because he's never pointed a gun at your head."

I swallow, trying to avoid her gaze.

"He's pointed a gun at your head before?"

I bite my lip, trying to figure out how to paint Nacio in a better light for Kinsley instead of bringing up worse things about him. "Not exactly. We've just done some exciting sexual things," I say with a grin on my face.

Kinsley blushes. "I really don't think I can handle hearing about your sexcapades."

"Why not? I have had to hear about your boring married sex acts for the last ten years."

She frowns. "I miss him."

I get up off my chair and sit next to her on the couch. "I know, but he's safe, and you're safe."

"I just wish I could text him or talk to him and let him know that everything is okay."

I nod. I hate that we don't have cell phone reception here. "I'll talk to Nacio when he gets back and tell him we need to do that ASAP."

"You think he would really be okay with me doing that?"

I smile. "He will be if that's what I tell him we are doing."

She chuckles. "Glad you have him under your spell at least."

We each work on eating our protein bars for a while as we enjoy the nice morning weather outside. It's been a long time since I've had nothing to do. Work always consumes me, and when I'm not working, Nacio or Kinsley consume the rest of my time.

"So, how far along are you?"

I think for a moment. "I think thirteen, maybe fourteen weeks."

She frowns. "So, not early enough that you know the sex of the baby yet?"

I shake my head. "No. I'm supposed to go in for a eighteen-week ultrasound. They said they might be able to tell then."

She nods. "Well, we can still have fun coming up with baby names."

I smile and try to think of names. "How about Mason?"

"Not bad. Lily?"

"That's pretty. Caden?"

She wrinkles her nose, which makes me laugh. "Sophia?"

I shake my head. "Benjamin?"

"Nah. Catherine?"

I laugh. "Based on the names we are throwing out, you think this baby is a girl, and I think it is a boy."

She laughs, too. "I guess so."

I grab her head and pull her toward my lap so that her head is resting on my stomach.

"I can't believe you're pregnant. You're not even showing. You just look like you ate for once. I knew it that day at the Italian restaurant, but you tricked me."

"I know. I'm sorry about that. I just didn't want to cause you pain."

She's silent.

I stroke her hair as she lies on my stomach, and I feel her quickly falling asleep. I lean my head back on the couch and close my eyes. I know I'll be asleep as well soon. We might as well sleep. There is nothing else that we are going to be doing today.

18

BEAST

BORING AFTER BORING day passes until we no longer have to count in days but in weeks. It's been two weeks of living in this nightmare. Two weeks of restless nights, followed by grumpy mornings, where we all just annoy each other until the boredom sets back in.

Despite how big this house is, there isn't much to do here, not when you don't have power or TV or any real sort of entertainment. We have a chessboard and a pool table, but after a few rounds of each, those both become boring. We all smell, as we shower only every few days.

I bought battery operated security cameras to monitor the property twenty-four/seven. That's where I spend most of my day, monitoring the cameras and tweaking where they point, even though all I ever see on them is the occasional bunny or squirrel.

I also make excuses to go into town to pick up supplies and check messages on my phone. Each time I do, I hope that Reina has called and is ready to put an end to this. Instead, the messages are always from them. They think they can solve this, but they can't.

After the first day, I brought Scarlett and Kinsley into town, so they could call Killian and Preston and let them know that they are safe but not coming home for a while. Now, they want to go into town with me every chance they get. I do the best to keep them at home where it is safer. They don't realize that what I'm really hoping is that Reina will show herself to me here, and then I can put a stop to this. That never happens though.

Instead of coming with me, Scarlett and Kinsley spend most of their days talking with each other about the baby. Baby clothes, baby cribs, baby things that I didn't even know existed.

I've barely even spent time with Scarlett these past two weeks. And, with each day that passes, I feel Scarlett slipping further and further away.

Scarlett wants Kinsley in her life, not me. Kinsley would be better with the baby than me. And Scarlett knows that we both can't be in her life. Despite being cordial to each other, Kinsley and I haven't exactly grown closer.

That's partially why I'm so annoyed that I haven't figured out a plan to stop Reina. To put an end to this, so we can figure out what our lives are going to be like after this.

"She's slipping away, you know," Santino says from behind me.

I pull the staple remover from my bag. I should have removed the staples a few days ago, but it didn't even cross my mind. My arm has healed as good as can be expected, and now that the pain is gone, I barely think about it anymore.

"Is that meant to be a motivational speech or something?" I begin pulling the staples out of my arm. It burns a little as I rip out a few arm hairs and skin that has begun to grow over the staples since I left them in for too long.

Santino chuckles. "I can see why Scarlett likes you, you being so pleasant and all."

I pull out a staple and toss it on the table, ignoring him.

"We can't keep doing this forever, you know. At some point, we are going to have to go on the offensive or at least talk to Reina. We can't keep hiding forever."

I nod. I agree with him. I'm just trying to come up with a plan that doesn't involve me having to put a bullet between Reina's eyes.

"I know," Santino says even though I didn't say anything. He knows what I was going to say. He feels the same way. "I'm going to go pester Kinsley. She's always fun to annoy."

"We are supposed to be trying to get Kinsley to like us."

Santino laughs. "No. You are supposed to be trying to get Kinsley to like you. I'm not the one trying to fuck her best friend."

"Fucking," I correct him.

He stops at the door to the patio. "Uh-huh. I haven't noticed any of that going on since we got here."

"It's not exactly what's on my mind when I'm trying to protect us all."

"Sure, whatever you say, Nacio. Just know that I meant what I said. We can't keep doing this forever. Our time here is coming to an end, and you need to remind Scarlett why she fell for you in the first place."

"Which is?"

He laughs. "I assume the fucking." He opens the door and then shouts, "I think Nacio needs help with his staples, Beauty!"

I glare at him when he calls her Beauty for the millionth time even though I've asked him to stop the same number of times. He enjoys getting to me, which I allow him to do every time he uses my name for her.

Scarlett walks into the kitchen, and when she sees all the staples are out, she glances down at my arm in confusion. "Santino said you needed help with the staples?"

"Santino thought wrong."

"Oh, okay." Scarlett bites her lip. She glances back at Kinsley and Santino out on the deck and then turns back to me as a slow smile curls up. "Fuck me," she says.

I raise an eyebrow at her, not sure I heard her right.

She laughs at my expression. "Fuck me."

She walks toward me, and my eyes grow heavy, needing to see her naked body that can no longer hide the baby in her stomach. Her breasts have swelled, and she's never looked more beautiful. Despite the sweatpants and tank top that she is wearing, she's beautiful.

I swallow the thought down though. I let her suck me off in this house before, but now, all I can think about is keeping her safe and trying to keep the memories of this house that haunt me at bay. I'm too afraid to fuck her for real in this house.

"I need to check a camera out front again. I think a cord came loose." I get up and begin walking toward the door.

Scarlett grabs my arm, and I stop and look at her, my eyes showing the demons that haunt me. I show her that we can't do this. I can't do this.

She doesn't take no for an answer though. She kisses me. But I can't even focus on the kiss. Instead, I grab her wrists and slowly push her away from me.

"I can't."

Scarlett narrows her eyes as her hand touches my face.

I glance away, but every time I do, another memory haunts me—Reina's screams, my father's voice. I can't let my mind go any darker. If I do, I'll never recover.

She sees it all though. "Fuck me."

I don't answer her. She already knows that I can't. I can't fuck her. I'm too afraid that the past memories in this house would mix with current memories and ruin any chance of us staying together.

She takes my hand. "Fine, let's just eat then."

I let her guide me back to the kitchen even though I don't understand why she's okay with going from wanting to fuck to wanting to eat, but she's pregnant, so I'm not going to question her.

"What do you want to eat?" I ask.

"I want to eat some of the cake Santino bought to satisfy my sweet-tooth cravings."

I nod and get the cake out of the pantry. I search for a knife to cut the cake, but Scarlett doesn't bother with a knife. Instead, she sticks her finger into the icing and then slowly brings it to her lips, slowly sucking on it.

I freeze, watching her tongue lick her bottom lip that is still covered in icing. She repeats the motion of licking her finger clean of the frosting, but this time, she lets out the softest moan possible. I'm not even sure I heard it.

"I know what you are doing," I say.

She cocks her head to the side as she runs her finger across her bottom lip. "I'm not doing anything, just eating." She sticks her finger back in the frosting and then holds it up to my lips. "Want some?"

I suck in a breath.

But then she doesn't give me a choice as her finger moves to my lips. I take her finger into my mouth, sucking gently until all the frosting is gone. She closes her eyes and moans.

When I release her finger, she scoops up more frosting, and I watch as some of it falls from her hand to the peak of her breast.

I lose it.

My lips suck the frosting from her breast as I push her backward, needing our bodies pressed together. I keep pushing backward until one of the windows behind her stops us.

I suck on her breast long after the frosting is gone.

"Fuck me," she whispers in my ear. "Fuck me here, against the drapes on this window."

God, I love my dirty girl. The white drapes are thin, basically see-through, and Santino and Kinsley are sitting out on the deck where they could glance over at this window at any second. That's what she wants though. She seeks the danger, just like I do.

"My pleasure, Beauty."

I lift her hands high above her head, holding them in one hand. My other hand reaches under her tank and moves it higher until it covers her eyes. I watch her mouth part and pant. She needs me as desperately as I need her.

I rip the shirt off her body and toss it on the floor. I unhook her bra and toss it next. Still holding her hands above her head, I have to take a step back to get a good look at her body.

"You're beautiful, Beauty."

She drinks in my words, and for a second, our eyes connect like we haven't done in days.

I hear furniture being scooted on the patio outside, and it reminds me that there is a time limit. We can't take our time if we don't want Santino or Kinsley to catch us. Not that I'd give a fuck if they did. I want them to catch us. I want them to see how I love this woman. Maybe then Kinsley would realize that I would do anything to protect Scarlett.

I spin her around, pressing her against the thin veil of fabric and glass that is doing nothing to hide her naked breasts from Santino's or Kinsley's sight.

My hand tangles in her hair as I press myself against her body, and my lips kiss her ear. "They could see you." I grab ahold of one of her swollen breasts. "They could see your perfect breasts." I rub her nipple between my fingers and am rewarded with a gasp. "Or your face when you come."

"I don't care. I need you to fuck me."

That's all I need to hear.

I pull my cock out as fast as I can while I kiss her neck and rub her breast. Thank God I don't need to wear a condom anymore because I don't think I'd have time to stop and put one on. She has me so wound up that I can't wait another second to have her and remind her that she's still mine.

Mine to protect, to love.

I slip her pants down, revealing her perfect ass, as I push my cock against it.

I feel her melt a little against my touch, begging me to get inside her.

"I will, Beauty. Patience."

She growls. "I need you now, Beast."

My cock pushes at her entrance, and I feel her wetness covering me, showing me how ready she is.

I glance up and see that Santino and Kinsley aren't paying us any attention. Scarlett turns her head and I kiss her again to show her that I'm still here with her instead of lost in my haunted memories. All I see and feel is her.

I quickly push inside her without warning and listen to her gasp.

I continue to fuck her against the drapes and glass.

It's a feeling I will never get enough of. I will never get enough of her, and guessing from the sounds leaving her mouth and throat, she can't get enough of me either.

Scarlett screams louder than she should, and I place my hand over her mouth to quiet her. I watch as Kinsley turns her head a little toward us.

"Don't move, Beauty. Don't make a sound. She'll see you if you do." While telling her that she has to be silent so that Kinsley doesn't see us, I reach down between her legs, rubbing her clit hard and fast, torturing her by bringing her so close to coming.

I feel her about to come, so I meet her there until we are both silently coming as our mouths connect to keep us both silent. Her eyes are closed, but my eyes are open, watching her. Then, I glance past her. Kinsley peeks over at us for just a second, and I see the flush of pink on her cheeks.

Good, maybe now she'll realize that I love Scarlett.

I frown. *Or she'll think I'm just using her friend for sex.*

Scarlett collapses in my arms, clearly exhausted. I scoop her up along with her clothes and carry her to the couch. I dress her as she smiles at me.

"Did I get rid of your demons?" she asks.

I nod. "When I'm with you, I can't think of anything else but you."

"Good."

She holds out her arms, and I pull her tank top down over her body before grabbing a throw blanket and covering her.

"Stay," she says when I stand back up.

I grin. "One second."

I walk back to the dining room to put the cake away, but I stop in my tracks when I see a man standing in the hallway. I immediately reach for my gun because I'm sure he's here to kill me. There is no other reason he would be here but to get his wife back and he'll kill me to do that. But I'm not going to be the one who fires the first shot. I'm not going to kill Killian if I don't have to.

19

SCARLETT

"Where's my wife?" I hear a man say from the hallway.

I quickly get up off the couch because I know that voice.

But I still can't believe it when I make it to the hallway and see Killian standing there.

"What are you doing here?" I ask even though I know it's a stupid question.

The more important question is, *How did he find us?*

Because, if he could find us, that means that Reina can, too.

He doesn't answer my first question, and I don't get to ask my second. Instead, I hear the can't-believe-it scream from Kinsley behind me before she rushes into Killian's arms.

I glance over at Nacio, who has his hand on his gun in the back of his pants. I'm surprised he doesn't have it out.

If I thought the display that Nacio and I just did against the window was embarrassing, Kinsley and Killian's display of affection is almost just as bad. They kiss as their hands go all over each other's bodies. Grabbing things that I don't want to see grabbed. Making sounds that I don't want to hear coming from my best friend and her husband.

I clear my throat, trying to remind them that we are all still standing here, but they don't acknowledge that they heard me at all. They just keep kissing and feeling each other up.

Santino laughs from behind me. "You don't have much room to talk. Don't think we didn't see you two going at it against the window."

My hand goes up to cover my gaping mouth. "You saw what?"

This just makes Santino laugh harder.

I turn my shocked expression to Nacio, who is just shaking his head like it doesn't matter. He knew. He knew that they could see us, and he didn't stop. He didn't pull me away from the window. He just let them watch. They probably heard my screams, too.

I cross my arms over my chest, annoyed with Nacio and Santino for embarrassing me. Not that I'm that embarrassed, but it's still not something I wanted them to see. I just liked the idea of possibly getting caught.

Kinsley and Killian finally stop kissing and turn to look at us. Nacio slowly lets go of his gun when he sees that Killian is holding on to Kinsley with a smile on his face.

"You might not want to let go of your gun. If I can find you, then Reina can, too. What sort of protection do you have set up here?" Killian says to Nacio.

Nacio looks to Killian in surprise. "I have security cameras set up on every inch to warn us if Reina sends any more men after us along with plenty of weapons to protect us."

Killian nods and smiles. "Good."

Kinsley looks up at her husband in confusion, just like I'm looking at them. "Why aren't you trying to rip Nacio's head off right now?"

Killian quickly kisses his wife on the lips. "Because he's one of the good guys."

Kinsley's mouth drops as she looks from her husband to Nacio to me. I shake my head. I have no idea what he is talking about.

I look at Nacio, who is frozen, not letting on about anything either.

"What do you mean, he's one of the good guys?" I ask Killian because I don't trust Nacio to give me a straight answer.

Killian cocks his head to the side, like he can't believe that Nacio hasn't shared the one good thing about himself with me. "He works for the FBI."

Kinsley looks at Nacio. "How is that possible?"

Nacio just stares at her but doesn't answer, so she turns back to her husband.

"He was given an opportunity to work for the FBI in exchange for his freedom from prison. In fact, since he's gotten out, he's had a hand in helping the FBI take down several career criminals."

I turn to look at Nacio. I'm trying to understand how he works for the FBI, knowing the things he's done.

Out of the corner of my eye, I see Santino, and he looks just as shocked as the rest of us.

"So, you've turned to the good side." Kinsley glances at me then back to Nacio. "Maybe I can accept your relationship with my friend after all."

Nacio still hasn't said anything, not one word since Killian began speaking. I try to read Nacio's face, but I can't. I try to understand why he hasn't spoken, but I can't.

The first movement Nacio finally makes is to shake his head, and then he screams in terror as he reaches back to pull his gun.

A loud popping sound rings out. A sound that I have learned to associate with gunfire.

I hear screaming, but I can't make out what anyone is saying. I crouch down, protecting my head, as bullets fly overhead.

Killian might not have meant to, but he brought Reina's men with him. He showed her our location, and now, the house is under attack by who knows how many people.

I search the room, trying to decide on what to do or where to go. But all I see is chaos.

Hands wrap around me, and I jump and let out a scream until I realize it's Nacio.

"We have to go," he says, pushing me forward, as he fires a shot over my head.

I scream again. I can't help it.

"Now, Scarlett." He pushes me forward, and then we are running, but I have no idea where.

He pushes me toward what I think is the garage, and I scream as I see a gun is pointed at us from around the corner. Nacio pushes me behind him as he fires his gun. I watch every bullet that flies by our heads, afraid that any single one could end either of our lives.

The gunshots don't stop, so I pull Nacio back, trying to get him to retreat away from the gun in front of us, hoping that if we move away we will be safe. He holds me firmly while firing another shot that ends the gunshots raining down on us.

He grabs my arm and then marches us forward with his gun in his hand. This time, instead of running, we walk slowly and carefully, assuming someone else is going to run out and attack. I don't know whether to keep my eyes on Nacio or on what's ahead of us. But, if I'm going to die by a bullet, I would rather keep my eyes on Nacio. I do but realize that keeping my eyes on him doesn't ensure his protection. I must do something to help protect him, and watching him is doing nothing.

"I need a gun," I say.

He glances at me like I'm crazy but then realizes that giving me a gun is the only thing he can do. While we've been here, he should have spent time teaching me how to shoot. Instead, he hoped that he would be able to fight them off without me.

He reaches down by his ankle and produces another gun that he hands to me. I take the gun. It feels strange in my hand. It's the first time I've ever held a gun.

Nacio places his hands over mine, quickly showing me how to hold the gun. "Just keep your eyes open and only shoot if you have to."

I nod.

We keep moving forward, passing the body of the man who was

firing at us. I don't look down as we step over him. I don't want to give this man the satisfaction of haunting my dreams.

We make our way to the garage. Nacio opens the door and then quickly looks around, holding out his gun, before he allows me to enter. We move quickly to the car as Nacio digs out a key and presses a button that turns on the remote start.

But the car doesn't start.

"Damn it!" Nacio runs to the hood of the car and pops it open. "They've taken the battery."

He grabs me and pulls me back toward the door that leads back into the house.

"Stay close behind me. I'm going to get you out of here safely."

"What about everyone else?"

"Killian is more than capable of watching out for Kinsley, and Santino will do fine by himself. They might have already put an end to this by the time we make our way back into the house."

I take a deep breath, hoping his words are true.

But in case they aren't...

I kiss him without thinking. He kisses me back, letting the kiss go on for far too long. Neither of us cares though. This could be our last kiss, and we are going to make it memorable if it is.

Nacio finally forces our lips apart and tightly grabs my hand before he quietly leads me back into the house. We slink silently down the halls, but as we grow closer to the main living area, we can hear it. Gunshots are ringing in every direction.

Nacio looks into my eyes, and I can see the indecisiveness there. He's trying to decide if I would be safer with him or staying out of the line of fire.

"I'm coming with you."

He doesn't agree or disagree. He just moves again, and I follow. I firmly hold my gun, despite my shaking hands. And I keep my eyes glued on what is in front of us, knowing that I can no longer think about Nacio. I have to focus on keeping us both alive.

I move with Nacio as he stealthily makes his way, following the shadows, without being seen. He sees a man around the corner and fires multiple shots at him. I didn't see him until it was already too late. The man falls to the ground before he even gets a shot off.

We creep forward to the edge of the hallway.

"Stay here," he whispers without looking at me.

He takes a step out into the line of fire and begins quickly shooting in multiple directions while I cower against the wall, petrified. I think I see Kinsley and Killian taking cover behind some cabinets in the kitchen. Otherwise, all I see is Nacio and bullets flying.

I hold my gun up, prepared to shoot, but I have no idea what I'm doing. I can't see anyone but Nacio. So, I just stay frozen where I am with my eyes locked on his body.

I see it happen. I see him get hit in maybe his chest or his stomach. I can't tell from where I am, but wherever he was hit, it's not good.

I don't think. I just react.

I run forward, needing to make sure that he is okay. I keep my gun up, trying my best to scan from side to side to keep myself out of danger, while all I'm thinking about is how he can't die.

I reach him, wrapping my arms around him, trying to protect him from any more harm, while searching for where he was hit. I can't find it though, and he is trying to drag me away to somewhere he can keep me safe.

I won't let him go though because I can tell in the way that he is moving me that he isn't safe. He's hurting worse than when the shot hit him in the arm. And I will not leave him alone to suffer in pain and likely die.

I glance up behind him, and I see a man. His gun is aimed at Nacio's head. He'll never turn around in time. He'll never move in time to get out of the way of the bullet.

I squeeze the trigger of my gun that is already aimed in his direction. I fire over and over again as I scream, begging the world to not let him die.

The man drops in a similar fashion to the one Nacio shot. And then the room is silent.

Nacio gently pulls me away from his body so that he can look at me, making sure I'm not hurt. He then quickly glances around the room and makes a motion to Santino, who nods in agreement.

We are safe—at least at the moment.

I touch Nacio's chest and find the wound. I exhale all my air when I realize that the wound is superficial, even less so than the one on his arm. It must have just knocked the wind out of him.

"Damn it, Scarlett. I should punish you for being so stupid. You could have died."

"You could have, too."

He kisses me again, sucking all the air from my lungs, making me dizzy with each kiss but not caring in the slightest.

We are all alive.

Even though this will not be the last battle we have to fight, it is the last battle for the moment.

Pain shoots through my head. The room spins so much that I can't even see Nacio standing right in front of me. I don't even know if I'm in his arms anymore.

I hear him and others shouting my name.

I hear, "Scarlett," and, "Scar," and, "Beauty," all ringing in the air.

But I can't answer any of them.

20

BEAST

I LET Scarlett go for just one second. Just one fucking second.

And, because I let her go, she's gone.

She fell to the floor before I could grab her. The memory will haunt me forever and be far worse than the demons of my past. Everything moved in slow motion when she fell, but even still, I couldn't do anything to stop her from falling. I couldn't save her.

"Beauty!" I scream. I drop to my knees to protect her from whoever is shooting, but I don't hear the sound of a gun firing, and I didn't before.

I hear Kinsley scream as she runs over along with Killian and Santino. We all surround Scarlett, searching for the wound that caused her to fall. But I can't find it.

"Scarlett! Beauty! Wake up!"

She doesn't move.

I place my head on her chest and find her breathing. She's alive.

"I don't know what's wrong with her!" I shout to the others.

Kinsley is already kneeling next to me and is searching Scarlett's body. She looks at me, and she doesn't know what's wrong either. "We need to get her to a hospital."

I nod even though I hate hospitals. There are too many questions in hospitals. People in hospitals just get sicker; they don't get better. But I don't know how to make Scarlett better. I don't know what's wrong.

I scoop her up, and Kinsley screams as she grabs at Scarlett's head. I see the blood on Kinsley's hands from the wound on Scarlett's head, and then I'm afraid.

"Santino, get the gauze!" I shout.

He does and quickly comes back. Kinsley grabs it and applies it to Scarlett's head.

Then, we both run toward the front door without saying a word to each other. We don't argue or fight. We just help save a woman we both love.

We run through the door with me holding Scarlett's body and Kinsley applying pressure to her head. I spot what I hope is Killian's black SUV. We get to the doors that are unlocked and climb in the backseat.

"Go!" Kinsley and I both shout to Killian at the same time as he jumps in the driver's seat.

Santino gets in on the passenger side.

Killian steps on it and quickly makes his way down the drive. Santino already has the address of the nearest hospital pulled up on his phone.

I squeeze Scarlett's hand. "Just hold on, Beauty. We are going to get you some help. Just stay alive, like you promised. You and your baby both, please just stay alive."

Kinsley looks at me with tears in her eyes and then back to Scarlett's head. I can see the blood soaking through the gauze.

"Head wounds always look like there is more blood than there actually is."

Kinsley nods.

"Keep applying pressure."

I glance up to Santino. "Did you bring more gauze?"

"Sorry, that's all we had."

I pull my shirt off and hand it to Kinsley. "Put the shirt on top of the gauze to soak up the remaining blood. Don't remove the gauze. Just apply the shirt on top of it."

She does, and I keep looking until I'm satisfied that she is applying enough pressure. I realize that she is looking at me, staring at my body, and then she glances up to meet Killian's eyes in the rearview mirror. I watch the exchange in confusion.

"I can see why Scarlett likes you," Kinsley says.

I cock my head to look at her. "Why?"

"For one, you are far more loving and caring than I thought possible."

I nod, squeezing Scarlett's hand harder, willing her to wake up.

"And, two, you are one sexy beast."

I can't help but smile at her words. I don't know if Scarlett has told Kinsley her nickname for me or what, but I finally feel like I have her approval to date her best friend. I just hope it's not too late.

I know Killian is driving as fast as he can, but I just need him to drive faster. Every second that goes by is another second that I risk losing her.

I finally see a hospital coming into view.

"Just hold on, Beauty. We are almost there. Just a couple of more minutes."

Killian pulls over to the emergency side of the hospital, and Santino pops out before we have even stopped. He opens my door, and I begin to slide out with Scarlett still in my lap. Kinsley slides with me, still applying pressure to her head.

I'm finally out of the car with Scarlett in my hands, and I wait just a second for Kinsley to get out while holding her head. Then, we both race inside to the counter of the emergency room.

The nurse behind the desk doesn't ask us any silly insurance questions. She just presses a button on her pager and calls for a doctor immediately. "What happened?"

"I don't know. She just collapsed, and I think she hit her head," I say.

Doctors and nurses rush in with a gurney that they instruct me to put her on. I do, and Kinsley reluctantly lets go of her head as a nurse takes over.

"She's pregnant!" I shout over the noise.

"How far along?"

"I don't fucking know."

"I think sixteen, maybe seventeen weeks," Kinsley says.

The nurse nods.

And then I see them start to take Scarlett back into the ER, away from me. When I brought her here, I knew that was what would happen, that they wouldn't let me back to be by her side. Still, it kills me to see her leave. I walk behind her as they push her back behind the doors until one of them puts a hand up to stop me, and I stop.

"I love you. You're going to be okay!" I shout as the door shuts in my face.

I turn to see Kinsley standing right next to me, doing the same thing. She's just as helpless as I am. Neither of us has any idea of what could be wrong with Scarlett. Neither of us knows if she is going to live or die. Neither of us has any control over what is going to happen to her next, despite that we'd both be willing to give our own lives to protect hers and her baby's.

Instead, all we have left of her in the moment is each other. To my surprise, Kinsley steps toward me, and I'm afraid she's going to lecture me, tell me that this is exactly why I can't date Scarlett. That I'm putting her life in danger every day that I'm with her.

Instead, Kinsley wraps her arms around me. I gently lower my arms and wrap them around her. I can feel her tears on my bare chest.

"Thank you," she says when she pulls away.

"You don't have anything to thank me for."

She smiles. "You saved her life."

I shake my head but don't argue with her. Now is not the time.

She studies my chest where a bullet scratched the surface of my skin causing a small wound. "You should have them look at that."

"No, I'm fine. I need to be here when there is news about her, and I don't want anyone to know that we were being shot at."

I see Santino and Killian walk over. Santino tosses me a clean shirt that he must have just bought in the gift shop. I put it on, and then we each take a seat in the waiting room and wait.

21

SCARLETT

I WAKE up to a pounding headache and four sets of eyes staring at me. I try to sit up, but Nacio and Kinsley both stop me on each side of my bed.

"What happened?" I ask, holding my pounding forehead.

"You passed out, Scar. Just a drop in blood pressure. You're going to be perfectly fine," Kinsley says.

I hate to even ask her, but I have to know. "And the baby?"

She smiles through her tears. "She is perfectly fine."

"It's a she?"

She nods and squeezes me tightly. Nacio hugs me as well, and then Killian and Santino join in on the fun. I don't know what happened while I was asleep, but somehow, everyone came together, much closer together than I ever thought possible.

Is there hope that our two worlds could survive together?

I wince a little when someone's arm accidentally collides with my head, and everyone moves off of me.

"Why does my head hurt so much?"

"When you passed out, you hit your head," Nacio says.

I can see the pain in his eyes. He thinks this is his fault. Although, if all I have is a cut on my head, I think I will be fine. He did what he could to save me.

A woman that I assume is a doctor comes in. "You're awake. How are you feeling?"

"Tired, and my head hurts."

"That's to be expected. Do you all mind giving me and Scarlett a few minutes alone, so I can do an exam?"

Killian and Santino immediately leave, giving me tight smiles before exiting my hospital room. But Nacio and Kinsley both stand firm on either side of my bed.

The doctor smiles. "I promise, I will let you both back in as soon as the exam is done. I just want to check her over again and give her an update on her condition."

"We aren't leaving," Nacio says.

The doctor looks to me.

"I'm really okay with them both staying."

The doctor frowns. "Fine."

She begins talking about my condition. It was just a drop in my blood pressure, and I should be fine going forward.

"You were probably just dehydrated," she says.

I nod, not letting on that stress probably caused the dizziness. She talks more, and I hear something about needing to stay overnight for observation.

"Scarlett? Scarlett, did you hear me?" the doctor asks.

"Yes. Sorry, what did you say?"

The doctor begins flashing a light in my eyes, and then after a moment, she seems satisfied that there is nothing wrong. I just wasn't listening very well. Instead, I was thinking about what a future would be like with all of us.

The doctor interrupts those thoughts again, "Would you like to see your baby?"

I smile. "Yes."

She brings in the ultrasound tech, and she begins setting everything up. She rubs cold gel on my swollen stomach, and before I realize it, a picture of my baby girl is on the screen. Nacio and Kinsley each squeeze my hand.

"She's beautiful," Kinsley says, sighing.

"Just like her mother," Nacio says.

I study the beautiful picture of the baby that is still thriving in my stomach, despite everything I have put her through.

"It's a girl? That's what I was told," I ask the technician.

"Yep. It's definitely a girl."

I smile. *A girl.*

The technician prints off some pictures and hands one to me and one to Nacio. "You two are going to make great parents. I can always tell the ones who are prepared from the ones who don't have their stuff together. You two are going to do great. You even have the support of great friends. I'll leave you alone now." The technician wipes the gel off my stomach before she walks out.

I frown because the technician has it all wrong. We aren't going to make great parents.

"Kinsley, do you mind giving Nacio and me some time alone? Just for a few minutes. You can go show the pictures to the guys."

She nods. "Of course." She leans down and kisses my cheek. "I'm so happy you are both okay."

And then she leaves me and Nacio alone in my hospital room. I wipe the remnants of gel off my stomach, that the tech missed, with a towel and then pull my hospital gown back down, so I don't feel so exposed.

Nacio gently strokes my hair as he sits next to me. "When you collapsed...I've never felt so afraid in my life. I'm so sorry. I should have caught you. I shouldn't have put you under that much risk. I should have protected you better than I did. I failed you."

"Shh...no, you didn't. You saved me, protected me. I'm fine, and the baby is fine. There is nothing more you could have done."

"I could have caught you."

I shake my head. "It doesn't matter. We are both here. We are all alive. That's all that matters."

He smiles and touches my stomach. "That was amazing."

"What was?"

"Seeing your baby on the screen. It was incredible."

"It was, wasn't it?"

He nervously looks down at his hand on my stomach. "I know we haven't talked much about what our future looks like or if a future together is even possible."

I nod. "I know there are so many things to figure out. One thing that seems to have straightened itself out is you and Kinsley."

"Yeah, I think she's finally come around to the idea of us."

"Good. I'm glad."

"I know we have a lot to figure out. Our lifestyles. Our jobs. I have a lot of explaining to do about my involvement with the FBI."

I nod.

"But, after seeing that picture of your baby, I don't think I could ever *not* be in your baby's life again. I know I'm not the actual father, but I can't imagine not being a father to your baby."

I frown. "Nacio...we need to talk about the baby. There are some things you need to know."

"All I need to know is that I love you and this baby"—he rubs his hand across my stomach again—"more than anything else."

"I know. But I need to tell you—"

He shuts me up with a tender kiss, making my words disappear just as easily as they came. I don't have thoughts until he pulls away and says, "I'm going to put a stop to this. I'm going to keep you safe. I'm not going to let anything happen to you or your baby."

"What do you mean?"

"I'm going to go talk with Reina. I'm going to end this."

I grab his arm. "No, just wait until I can leave the hospital, and we will go together."

"No, this is my battle. You need to stay here and protect our baby."

I love the sound when he says *our* baby.

"Stay here. You can turn her into the FBI. They can arrest her and put a stop to this."

He freezes, not ready to have this conversation with me, but he has to. "I'm not really a good guy, Beauty. You had me pegged the second you called me Beast."

"I know," is all I say because I know he doesn't have loyalties to the FBI.

The FBI might think he works for them, is loyal to them, but he's not. The FBI would never have been okay with him killing everyone he's killed.

"And, as much as I want to be a good husband, a good father, I'm none of those things. Not until I protect my family and set things right. Not until I become the good guy that the FBI, Killian, and Kinsley think I am."

"Nacio."

But he's already pulling away. He's already made up his mind. He's leaving me, and there is nothing I can do to stop him.

I grab his neck and pull him to me to kiss him, hoping that I can get him to stop thinking about risking his life to try to save mine. Instead, I want him to do whatever it takes to stay here with me.

He kisses me. And I think for a moment that there is no way he will be able to leave me after this kiss.

His lips move off of mine, and then he turns around so that he can't see me.

"Nacio! Wait."

He doesn't wait. He walks out the door, leaving me all alone.

I look around the room for my cell phone, but I don't see it anywhere. I find the Call button to call my nurse or doctor and press it over and over.

I consider getting out of bed and going after him, but I still have an IV in my arm. And wires are hooked up to my chest, monitoring my vitals. As much as I love Nacio, I can't risk the baby's health just to try to stop him. I doubt I would be able to stop him anyway.

A nurse rushes in. "Are you okay? Can I get you anything?"

"Sorry, I just need my friend Kinsley to come in. I'm sorry. I don't know where my phone is or any other way to get ahold of her."

She frowns. "I'll see if I can find her for you."

She leaves, and then I'm all alone.

If he thinks that leaving me here while he's putting himself at risk is helping to protect me, he's wrong. Because I'm sure my blood pressure has risen higher than what is safe. He's putting me in just as much risk while I wait here for him to come back.

Kinsley walks in the door. "Are you okay?"

"No."

"I'll grab a doctor. Hold on."

"No, wait. I'm physically fine. Nacio left. He's going to go see his sister to try to put a stop to this."

She nods. "I know. He told me before he left."

"And you let him go?"

"Yes, he needs to put a stop to this, Scarlett."

I sigh. "He doesn't know the full truth about the baby."

Thank God there is a chair behind her because she doesn't even look when she sits down. "He doesn't know?"

"No."

"So, he thinks..."

"Yep."

"He thinks he's protecting his future child by doing this, doesn't he?"

I nod. "That's why I can't let him do this. As much as he wants this child to be his and as much as I know he would make a great father and take care of it like it were his own, you know that this baby can never be his. He doesn't deserve to die for a child that can never be his."

"He's not going to die."

I take a deep breath. "He doesn't deserve to risk his life either."

Kinsley nods. "I'm sorry."

"It's not your fault. Just help me get out of here, so I can stop him. I love him, Kinsley. He can't die."

She nods again. "I'll help you."

22

BEAST

I OPEN the door to Reina's house in Chicago. I know she's here. I tracked her cell.

The whole way here, I should have been thinking of ways to convince Reina to stop this. Instead, all I could think about was Scarlett. How I want a normal, boring life with her where we can raise her baby together and not have to worry about who is coming after us to kill us. That's all I want.

But I'm not sure if, even after I convince Reina to stop trying to kill Scarlett and Kinsley, that is going to happen.

Scarlett wanted to tell me something about the baby. Most likely, the baby girl's father. I didn't want to hear it though. Not when I knew I needed to come here and protect her and her baby. I didn't want to hear that she'd decided to be with her baby's father.

Since I've spent time worrying about a future that I will likely never have, I have zero ideas on how to convince Reina to change her mind.

I walk in with my gun raised, prepared to shoot anyone who fucking works for Reina. I walk through the house and straight to Reina's office.

"Done killing my best men?" Reina says, not even bothering to look up from her computer screen.

I walk into her office with my gun still drawn. "I'm not done until your men are done coming after Scarlett and Kinsley."

"Why? Because you've gone soft on me and don't want to kill innocent women anymore? Please."

"No, because I love her."

She laughs. "She doesn't love you back. She got knocked up by some other guy."

"That was when she thought I was a monster. I'm not a monster anymore, Reina. I want to do better."

"You will never be anything else. You're holding a fucking gun in my face. I'm your sister. How does that not make you a monster?"

I don't lower my gun. I don't let her get to me.

"Reina, this has to stop. Just let it go, and move on. I love Scarlett. That's all you need to know to stop the hit you put out on her and Kinsley."

She cocks her head. "Nothing is going to stop the hit on Kinsley. She has to die. Showing that we don't take kindly to traitors is the only way anyone will respect my company and not walk all over us. And Scarlett doesn't love you back. Just let me kill her and put you out of your misery."

"Stop it," I say, walking toward her. "I don't care if Scarlett loves me back or not. I love her, so that's enough for you to put a stop to the hit."

"No. I love you, Nacio. I care about you. And I'm not going to let a bitch like her destroy your life. Just let me do my job."

I grab one of the chairs in her office and throw it hard against the wall. "You're not listening to me, Reina. I'm not asking you. I'm telling you what to do. I'm the one with the gun. I can kill you right here and take over the company if I wanted to."

She laughs. "You wouldn't kill me. I'm your sister. You've spent your entire life protecting me after you fucked up when we were kids."

I frown. "You're right. I did protect you. I've always protected you, and I'm sick of it. You don't get to keep hanging that over my head anymore. Not after you told me the truth."

"You don't know how to stop protecting me, Nacio. It's the only good part of you."

"Maybe I just want to protect someone who deserves it for a change."

She nods slowly. "Maybe, or maybe it's because you don't have the balls to just kill her like she deserves for getting knocked up by another man, especially this man in particular."

"Enough, Reina." I tighten my grip on the gun as I point it at her.

She smiles. "Just trying to help my brother out since she obviously hasn't told you who the father is yet."

I freeze. I don't want to know how she knows, and I don't want to hear it.

"Killian's the father, Nacio. She let that bastard fuck her and knock her up." She studies her nails. "I guess since he couldn't knock up his wife, he felt the need to spread his sperm around with any woman who would fuck him."

"You're lying."

She smiles as she looks back up at me. "Am I? Hmm...I guess you'll never know because that tramp will never tell you the truth."

"I should kill you," I say.

"You won't though. You should kill Scarlett and Kinsley. They are the ones who have betrayed you, not me."

"You don't get it, do you, Reina? I own you. I've been working with the FBI, but I've been doing it to protect you. I've turned in your enemies instead of you to the FBI. I've steered them away from you anytime they caught your scent and picked up your trail. I made sure you stayed alive. If you betray me, that's over. I'll turn you over to them...if I don't kill you."

She shakes her head as her phone buzzes in her pocket. She pulls it out and looks at the screen and then back to me. "That might be true, but in order to make threats like that, you have to have all the cards."

Reina glances past me, and my heart stops as I turn to look

behind me. One of Reina's men has his arm around Scarlett's neck, his other hand pointing a gun against her temple.

Fuck.

I can't keep my eyes off of Scarlett as he drags her into the room.

I'm sorry, she mouths to me.

I don't mouth or say anything back because I don't know how to get out of this situation. I could save myself and get out of here, but I don't know how to save her. Not without killing Reina.

But I already know Reina's play. She'll force me to put down my gun in order to save Scarlett, and then she will shoot us both. Reina doesn't give a fuck about me any more than she does Scarlett. And, if I'm no longer of value to her, if I'm no longer willing to kill for her, then I'm just a liability that needs to be taken care of.

But, if all three of us are going to die, I want to at least do one thing first that might bring Scarlett and me a tiny bit of happiness before we die.

I slowly lower my gun as I kneel down. I gently place the gun next to my feet and then slide it toward Reina.

"Smart move, Nacio. I knew you would do the right thing."

"I didn't do that for you, Reina. I did it, so I could do this."

I quickly reach into my pocket and produce the box before Reina's goon thinks I could be pulling out another gun.

I look up at Scarlett with a smile on my face because, if this is the last thing I do, it might be the best way to die.

I open the box, displaying a large engagement ring that I had designed weeks ago. I look up at Scarlett, into her glistening eyes that no longer show fear.

"Scarlett Bell, I'm so sorry.

"I'm sorry that I never found the time to ask you this before.

"I'm sorry that I couldn't find a more romantic time or place to do this.

"I'm sorry that it took me forever to admit my feelings for you. To admit that I had more than lust.

"I'm sorry that I didn't take you on enough dates.

"I'm sorry that I didn't have time to study every look on your face and every curve of your body.

"I'm sorry that I never got to spoil you properly like the woman that you are.

"I'm sorry that I never realized until recently how much I wanted your baby to be our baby. How much I wanted to be a family with just the three of us.

"I'm sorry that it took me too long to tell you that I love you.

"I know we don't have much time left, and I want nothing more than to be able to propose and ask you to marry me. And I'm sorry now that we will never get that chance.

"So, instead of asking you to marry me and then never being able to actually get married, I'm going to ask you a different question instead. I'm going to ask you to forgive me for being the beast that I am and ask you to promise that you will love me every second for as long as we both shall live. I love you, Beauty, and I can't imagine a better way to spend what I have left of my life than by looking at your gorgeous eyes when I die."

A tear rolls gently down her cheek, but I don't think it's an unhappy tear or even a tear out of fear. It's pure happiness.

"I'll love you forever even if forever isn't long enough," she says.

23

SCARLETT

I FUCKED UP. I realize that now in hindsight, but when I came here, I thought I would be able to protect Nacio. I thought I could convince Reina to leave us alone. To let us live.

Instead, I'm going to get us both killed instead of just me.

But it's all worth it. To see Nacio down on one knee, proposing to me, is one of the best moments of my life.

Now, it's going to end. I still have a gun pointed at my head, and Nacio doesn't know it, but Reina has a gun pointed at his head. I just hope that, when they kill us, they do it at the same time because I don't want to spend a second of what's left of my life without Nacio in it.

Nacio is still kneeling on the floor, and as much as I want to keep looking into his eyes for the rest of this short life, I haven't given up yet. I can't, not when I have a baby growing inside me.

I look into Reina's eyes. "I love your brother very much. I would never do anything to hurt him. I just want to protect him, just like you do."

I watch Reina lower her gun, and I see the pain and conflict in her eyes, but most of all, I see the love there.

"If you love your brother, then put a stop to this. End this," I plead.

I see Reina giving in. I see her preparing to put an end to this. And then I see her glance to her phone and lift her gun again to Nacio's head.

I don't know how I find the strength or if I just take the man holding me by surprise, but I break free of his hold in time to grab Nacio and protect him from getting shot.

"Please, don't kill him. Just spare him at least. I can die, knowing that he gets to live."

"If you are so worried about him living, then who the hell is this?" Reina thrusts the phone in our faces, but I don't have a clue who the men on the screen are.

"The FBI. They must have followed me here," Nacio says. "You need to get out of here now."

Reina looks at him, and I can see the tears there. "You would still try to help me, despite the fact that I threatened to kill the woman you are desperately in love with?"

"Yes. That's what you do for the people you love. You protect them, even when they don't deserve it."

Reina lowers her gun. "I'm sorry."

"No time for that. We need to get you out of here. Now," Nacio says.

He grabs Reina's hand and begins pulling her out of the office. The man who was holding on to me before at gunpoint has already left. He most likely ran the second that Nacio mentioned the FBI.

"Stay here," Nacio says. "I'll be right back."

For once, I listen to Nacio. I stay in Reina's office, and Nacio takes Reina somewhere she will hopefully be able to escape the FBI. Even though she might deserve it, I don't want her to end up in jail.

I don't want to think about Reina anymore though. I think Nacio and I are safe now. I think Nacio did enough to convince her that she doesn't need to go after Kinsley and me in order to protect Nacio. I think she knows we are on his side.

I walk over and pick up the box that Nacio left on the floor. He never got a chance to actually put the ring on my finger. It's a beautiful ring with little diamonds surrounding the large center one and continuing around the band. It might even be more beautiful than the ring he got me before.

I take the ring out of the box and study it but don't put it on. I want Nacio to be the first one to put the ring on my finger. I look inside the ring, and that's when I see the inscription, *Mine forever*. I smile. Forever just got a lot longer now.

I hear a noise outside the office, and I know the FBI is here. I look at the ring one more time before I step out of the office and come face-to-face with another gun in my face.

I automatically put my hands up. I'm really tired of my life being threatened every few seconds. "My name is Scarlett Bell. Reina, the woman you came here for, was holding me hostage."

The man slowly lowers his gun as he realizes that I'm telling the truth. "Let me get you out of here then."

He grabs ahold of my arm and begins guiding me out of the house. As we walk, I see more men pouring into the house. I just hope they come up empty.

He leads me next to one of their unmarked SUVs. He opens the door for me, and I climb in. "Wait here."

I nod as he shuts the door, and I keep my eyes glued on the door, waiting for Nacio to come back.

It takes a long time for him to emerge, but when he does, the sight I see is not what I expected. An FBI agent has Nacio in handcuffs, leading him to a different door.

I throw the door open and run to him. "What are you doing?" I shout to the FBI agent. "He's innocent."

The man laughs. "This man is anything but innocent."

"He works for you. He was trying to turn his sister over to you."

He shakes his head again. "This man was trying to deceive the FBI—again."

I stop trying to argue with the man. I walk faster until I can see Nacio's eyes one last time before he is shoved into the back of a car. "Nacio..."

"I'm sorry, Beauty. I'm not a good guy. I'm just a beast that never turns back into a man."

I reach out and kiss his lips, shutting him up. The kiss doesn't last long enough though because one of the other FBI agents pulls me off of him. I watch until he is placed in the back of a car and then driven away.

"What will happen to him?" I ask the FBI agent who pulled me off of him.

"He's going to prison for a long time."

"How long?"

"My best guess is life. That was his original sentence that we commuted if he helped us. Instead, he screwed us and probably killed who knows how many other people while he was out. He was never working for us. So, yeah, I think, even if he gets life, he will be getting off easy."

I freeze as I look down at the ring I'm still holding in my hand. Forever isn't such a long time after all.

24

BEAST

PRISON ISN'T such a horrible place. At least not the physical prison I'm in, where I'll most likely be spending the rest of my life. This time, I don't think I will be able to find a way out. The FBI has no reason to let me back out now that I've ruined their trust.

What's worse is what goes on in my head while I'm locked up here. The pain and suffering that comes with never being able to be around those I love.

But this time around, it won't be as bad. This time, I did everything I wanted to do. I saved everyone who needed saving. I saved Scarlett, Kinsley, Reina, and Scarlett's baby. I saved them all, and in turn, they saved me.

I can't be upset that I still have sins to pay for. I wouldn't change anything about these last few months even if it meant I could still be free. I would have rather spent the time I got with Scarlett then to have never gotten any time with her at all and be free.

For the millionth time in the past two months, I sit down at the table with a pen and paper in my hand. I need to write a note to set Scarlett free. I need to write a note to tell her that she needs to go live her life without me. That she needs to be happy. That I know that the baby is Killian's, and if he makes her happy, then I'm happy for her.

That I don't judge her for what she did or for hurting her best friend the way that she did. That I hope they can find a way to be happy.

The only problem is, I haven't been able to write any of those words down. Because, once I do, I'm afraid that it is going to be final. That, by writing her this note, I will be giving up and accepting my fate of living a lonely life here in jail while she lives a life without me.

I just can't. I'm too afraid that, once I do, I'll decide my life isn't worth living. But I could never do that to Scarlett. I could never hurt her like that.

"Marlow, come with me," an officer I don't recognize says to me just as I'm about to force myself to write words down on the paper.

I stand and follow. I've learned not to ask questions in jail and to just do as I'm told.

What surprises me though is when he takes me to a room where my lawyer is seated. I'm not supposed to have another meeting with my lawyer for a few weeks.

I sit down at the table across from him as he smiles at me.

"How are you doing?" my lawyer, Wendell, asks.

"Horrible. I'm in prison, most likely for the rest of my life. Why would you even fucking ask me a question like that?"

"Because today is your lucky day."

I narrow my eyes. "And why is that?"

"Because, today, you are getting out of here."

I suck in a breath, trying to remain calm. I've learned to never trust if I'm getting out or not until I'm actually out. And I think he must have me mixed up with one of his other clients.

"Your friend Killian talked to the FBI on your behalf and convinced them to give you a break. Convinced them that they couldn't honestly expect you to turn in your sister. Reminded them that you had turned in hundreds of other men in your time with them. And, he said, for that, you deserved for them to honor your deal. Plus, there is no evidence that you did any crimes while you were out. Nacio, you're free."

I shake my head. "That doesn't sound like free. That sounds like they want to continue to use me as their puppet."

Wendell frowns. "Maybe so, but at least you will be able to get out of here and go home every night to the woman you love."

I smile because I don't have the heart to tell him that isn't true. That the woman I love is secretly in love with and fucking another man.

True to his word, Wendell has me out of prison within hours of speaking with me. The FBI reminded me of our deal—that I basically have to work for them, but I will no longer be in prison unless I fuck up again.

I see Scarlett as I walk out of the building. I was expecting her. She's probably here to return the ring I gave her that she accepted under duress.

"Can we talk?" she asks.

I nod and then follow her across the street to a nearby park. She sits down on a bench, so I do the same, sitting next to her. She's wearing a gorgeous white dress. It hugs her now-large belly with her baby that she thinks is a secret but is no longer a secret.

"I wanted to give you this," she says, holding out the ring I gave her.

It's just as I suspected.

I take it. "Thanks." I look down at the ring that she will never wear. "You know, we don't need to do this. I understand. You said yes with a gun pointed to your head. And I didn't even ask you to marry me, not technically. Also, you don't need to tell me about the baby. I already know."

She frowns. "I said yes, and I meant it. I want to marry you, Nacio. I want to spend forever with you. I love you. And how do you know anything about the baby?"

"Reina told me that the baby is Killian's, so I understand if you don't want to be with me. That you would rather be with him. He's been on the straight and narrow for a lot longer than I have."

She slaps me.

I look at her in confusion.

"You think I slept with Killian?"

"You didn't?"

She laughs. "No."

"Then, whose baby is it?"

"It's Killian and Kinsley's baby."

"What? How?"

"I agreed to be their surrogate. After I left, I needed to do something good in the world, and helping them have a baby they so desperately wanted felt like that thing.

"The only thing I wanted was for you to understand that this baby wasn't ours. That you couldn't get attached to it because we wouldn't get to keep it. It's theirs."

I smile. "But we will make an awesome aunt and uncle to this baby." I touch her stomach.

She raises her eyebrows. "We will. Does that mean you aren't rescinding your offer to love me forever?"

"I'm not. Although you were the one who gave me the ring back."

"I just wanted you to be the one to put it on my finger."

I smile and get down on one knee in front of her. "Scarlett, my Beauty, will you marry me? Will you spend forever with me even though forever now could be a long time? Even though we don't know what the future holds?"

"Yes. And we do know what the future holds. It is us spending forever loving each other because, in the end, that's what happens. The Beauty and the Beast live happily ever after."

EPILOGUE

SCARLETT

MY HANDS SHAKE a little as I turn the handle on the door to my office at Beautifully Bell. I've been gone a long time. Too long. I haven't stepped foot in this office for months. Close to a year. I took six months off after I gave birth to Kiera, the beautiful baby girl that has brought so much joy to Kinsley and Killian.

I could have easily come back to work months ago. I should have, but I was scared and selfish. I wanted time to enjoy my niece. I wanted time to spend with Nacio. I wanted time to figure our lives out together. And I wanted time to come to terms with the fact that everyone now knows that I'm with Nacio. A beast. A monster. A killer.

I was scared to come to work in a world where everyone thought of my fiancé as a monster. I'm still scared. But I need to go back to work. I've been gone long enough and it's been torture not working. Well the last couple of months have been torture. I enjoyed the first few months with my niece and Nacio. But that slowly turned to boredom and then torture. I love my work. I love creating clothing and makeup that makes women look and feel beautiful. I love the control. I love pushing myself each day.

I turn the knob and walk into my office. It looks exactly the same but also different at the same time. Nothing has changed, all of my furniture has stayed the exact same, but I've changed. That's the difference.

I walk over to my desk and remove my coat and smile as I notice the small box sitting on my desk. I pick up the note that is attached and open it.

Just because I'm the Beast doesn't mean I'm the strong one. You have more strength than anyone I know. Now go use it to show the world just how strong you are Beauty.

Love -Beast

I open the box and find a gorgeous necklace with the inscription "You are my Beauty and my Beast." I wipe a tear from my cheek as I smile at the necklace. It's beautiful and it's just what I need today. I can face whatever people say about me. They can call me sick, a criminal. They can say that Nacio should be locked up in jail. I don't care. I'm strong enough to face them.

I put the necklace on over my black dress that I wore today. I feel like a beast in the dress and necklace.

I hear a knock at the door followed by, "Thank god you are back. I need a vacation."

I smile when I hear his voice. I glance up at Preston standing in my doorway his arms crossed across his chest. He's changed since the last time I saw him. He stands taller when he walks into a room. His voice is deeper and more in control of what he wants. He hasn't just survived these last few months without me, he's flourished and turned into an amazing vice president.

I smile. "You can take as long of a vacation as you need. You deserve it."

He steps into my office and closes the door behind him. "Nah. I don't really want a vacation. I just wanted you back. I missed you."

I get up from behind my desk and go over and hug him. "I missed you too."

Preston's phone vibrates and I let go of him and return to my desk. Preston talks for a minute while I pull up my email on my computer. I have thousands and thousands of emails. So many that with every second that passes the number ticks up higher and higher trying to process them all.

My eyes widen. I'm going to have to figure out how to just delete them all and start over. There is no way I will be able to get through all of them even if I spent all of my time going through them for the next year.

Preston ends his call and says, "You only have five minutes to answer your email, then you have a meeting with Madeline, followed by a meeting with—"

"Preston."

"What?"

I cock my head to the side. "You are not my assistant. You are my vice president. You don't need to rattle off my schedule to me anymore, that's way below your pay grade. Just because I'm back doesn't mean you go back to being my assistant. You've done great work since I've been gone and I want you to continue that work, not go back to being my assistant."

"But you need me and I need to go back to being your assistant. I miss you."

I shake my head. "You are not going back to being my assistant."

"But I want to work with you. I don't want to be stuck in an office on a different floor and never see each other."

I frown. I don't want that either. "You'll move your office next door to me then. I want you near me too. You are the best employee I have and one of my best friends. I want to hear your opinion about everything."

He thinks for a moment. "Done."

"Good. Now I just need to find a new assistant to help arrange all of that."

Preston frowns.

"Don't worry, whoever I hire I won't like as much as I like you."

"Good. Now until then I'm going to act as your assistant until you get back up to speed and find someone new."

"No, you are my vice president."

"No, I'm on vacation as your vice president. Today I'm just your assistant."

A knock at my door stops the arguing.

"Come in," I shout.

The door opens and Jake stands in the door. I frown. "I thought I made myself clear you were to find another job."

"You did and I did."

"Then why are you here?" I narrow my eyes at him ready for a fight.

Jake glances from me to Preston who is also giving him a dirty look. He slowly turns his gaze back to me.

"To say I'm sorry. For everything."

My eyes narrow in confusion. I was expecting a lot of things from Jake, but I never expected him to apologize.

He takes a step forward and Preston takes a step closer ready to step in between us if he needs to. Jake doesn't even glance his way.

"I know you're happy. I know you chose a man that is right for you. You obviously wanted danger and excitement, while I'm boring. I just couldn't stop myself because I've been in love with you all these years. I love you and that made me do all sorts of stupid things. Things I deeply regret."

He takes a step forward again.

"It's okay. I understand. I've done some stupid things I regret for love as well."

He shakes his head. "What I did was worse."

A small grin sneaks onto my lips. "I doubt that."

His eyes scan my body. "I just wanted to tell you I'm sorry, but I'm glad you're happy. I won't cause you any more trouble."

"You didn't cause me any trouble. Not really." Not compared to everything else I've been through.

"And I'm sorry for what I'm about to do."

I raise my eyebrows, but before I can realize what he is doing his lips are on mine. It's a short kiss. His lips barely brush mine before they are suddenly gone. Preston pushes Jake back.

"I'm sorry," he says with sad eyes as Preston pushes him out of my office.

I'm not sorry though because it felt like the closure he needed.

Preston returns to my office. "I'll tell security to make sure that Jake never steps foot inside this building again."

I nod, although I don't think it will be necessary. Jake won't bother me anymore. Reina won't either. The FBI won't. We have no enemies left. I can finally be happy. We can finally be happy.

"Come on Preston, we have a meeting to get to."

I walk out of my office no longer afraid of what people are going to say to me. I am the boss after all, if anyone disapproves of our relationship I can fire them. They don't deserve to work for my company anyway if they feel that way about me.

I plop back into my office chair after an exhausting and thrilling morning. Every person that I met with today was excited to hear about my engagement. They wanted to know all of the details of when we were getting married and what I would be wearing. Nobody cared who Nacio is or what he has done. At least not beyond the superficial level. I worried about our two worlds colliding for nothing. Everyone here is excited to meet him. I'll have to make sure he stops by the office sometime later this week.

I hear a knock on my door and I hope it's Nacio although I know it's not. He has been away the last two nights on FBI business.

"Come in," I shout toward the door.

The door opens and Kinsley comes in carrying a bag of take out and baby Kiera.

I jump out of my chair and run over and take Kiera from Kinsley's arms. She smiles at me as I grab her and spin her around.

"What are you two doing here?"

"We wanted to bring you lunch on your first day back," Kinsley says.

"Perfect timing, I'm starving."

"Good, because I brought lots of yummy Mexican food that I can't eat all by myself."

Kinsley walks over to my desk and begins unpacking our lunch while I carry Kiera over to the couch and sit down with her on my lap.

"You've gotten so big Kiera. I'm going to have to get you some more clothes since your old stuff won't fit much longer."

"You have got to stop spoiling Kiera, Scarlett. Her closet is already completely filled. I'm pretty sure she has more clothes than I do. If you get her any more, I'm going to have to find a second closet for her," Kinsley says.

I look down at my niece, who is grabbing onto the necklace around my neck and trying to put it in her mouth. "I can spoil her as much as I want. I gave birth to her, and I'm her aunt, so I get to spoil her."

Kinsley laughs. "Fine, I guess you do."

I kiss Kiera on the cheek for about the millionth time since she got here.

Kinsley pulls out some chips and salsa and brings it over. I dig in immediately as Kiera continues playing with my necklace while sitting in my lap.

"Are you still planning on having dinner with us tonight?"

I sigh. "Yes, I'm just not sure if Nacio will make it or not. He's working on a case for the FBI and I don't think he will be done and home in time for dinner tonight."

"I could tell Killian that it could just be a girls night tonight, just the three of us."

I shake my head. "That's okay. If Killian is there to distract you then it means I get more time with this cutie." I kiss Kiera's cheek again. "I just can't get enough of her."

"I know. It's why she loves you so much."

Kiera looks at her mom holding her arms out. She may love me, but she still knows who her mom is. She cries when I don't immediately turn her over to Kinsley.

"She's hungry," Kinsley says pulling out a bottle, I take it and then Kiera is happy to stay in my lap as long as I feed her.

"I'm just glad I don't have to deal with the three a.m. feedings like you do. I'm not sure I'm ready for that yet."

Kinsley smiles. "Well, she rarely wakes up in the middle of the night anymore. The first few months we brought her home were hard, but whenever you and Nacio decide it's time to have one of your own, you'll find a way to be ready."

"You think he will make a good dad?"

She smiles. "I think he will make a great dad."

I nod and think back to Kiera's birth. If he is anything like he was that day, he will make a great dad.

I lie in bed pretending to sleep so that Nacio will sleep. I don't think he has slept at all this week so far. Instead, he has been by my side worrying about all the possibilities that could go wrong when I deliver this baby.

I've been too uncomfortable to sleep much this week so he hasn't slept either. So instead of spending my night reading or watching TV or asking him to rub my back or feet I'm pretending to sleep so that he can sleep. But from the tightening pain in my stomach that is growing more intense by the second I don't think he's going to get much sleep tonight either.

Another contraction hits me and I know despite being one in the morning that I can't wait. I need to get to the hospital.

"Nacio," I whisper when the contraction is over.

He moans.

"Nacio," I say a little lighter as I push on his shoulder to get him to wake up.

He does, popping out of bed.

"Are you okay? Is it time?"

I nod. "It's time."

His eyes pop as panic fills his eyes. For just a second he stands frozen trying to figure out what to do and then the second passes and he moves into action.

He runs to the closet and grabs our bag for the hospital and somewhere along the way back to me he threw on some jeans and a shirt of his own. He slings the bag over his shoulder and then is on my side of the bed helping me stand up.

He starts guiding me out of the bedroom when I stop. "I need to change first."

He looks at me like I'm crazy. "I'm not wearing my pajamas to the hospital."

He frowns. "Yes you are. We need to get you to the hospital now and as soon as you get there they are going to have you change into a hospital gown anyway."

"But I look—"

He kisses me to shut me up. It works because I no longer care what I'm wearing when we stop kissing. Nacio begins leading me out of our apartment and into his Mercedes and then we are speeding toward the hospital as I have another contraction. He holds out his hand for me through the whole contraction as he says in the calmest voice I have ever heard, "Breathe. Imagine the pain leaving your body."

His words are exactly what I need.

The whole hospital stay he is exactly what I need. Through all twenty-two hours of labor. He held my hand. Said the right words. Got me ice chips. Made sure Kinsley and Killian were there and taken care of. He did everything perfectly until Kiera was born. Until the emergency, that I can remember more than the pain of giving birth.

"She's hemorrhaging," the doctor says.

"What?" I ask, but I never hear the doctor's response. I know she gives one because Nacio listens intently but the pain is too much for me to focus on silly things like words.

I scream while Nacio grabs hold of my hand. He says words, but again I don't hear them.

I begin to feel light headed after the immediate pain and hope that maybe I'll pass out so I don't have to deal with the pain, but Nacio grabs my face focusing my eyes on his and I know I'm not supposed to close my eyes. So I keep them open and deal with the pain with him. His eyes calm me even though I can see his mouth moving and I know he is probably saying something comforting, it's his eyes that stay so calm, so loving, that keeps me calm.

I don't know how long it takes to get the bleeding to stop. But it must because the pain slows. I can finally hear words again.

"The bleeding stopped. You are going to make a full recovery," the doctor says.

Nacio grabs hold of my head and kisses me hard on the forehead. When he steps back he finally lets in the fear that he was holding back from me. Intense fear at losing me.

We both cry as we grab onto each other. "I'm not going anywhere," I whisper into his ear.

I later learned that the hemorrhaging was bad. Some of the worst the doctor had seen and they were considering whisking me off to surgery to possibly have to have a hysterectomy. I might not have ever been able to have children of my own. I could have died. But despite Nacio knowing that, he stayed by me as my rock. Keeping me calm so that I could survive.

"What's going on with you?" Kinsley asks breaking my thoughts of the memory.

"Nothing."

She studies me. "Something is going on, I just don't know what it is yet."

I smile. "I'm not hiding anything from you. I promised you I wouldn't ever again."

She smiles, but I can tell she's still suspicious.

I turn my attention back to Kiera. I'm not hiding anything. You can't hide the truth when you don't know what the truth is yet.

———

BEAST

"Reina, I have to go, I'm kind of in the middle of something," I say into the phone that I stupidly answered instead of doing my job.

"Then tell me yes. Tell me that you will let me find you a new apartment for you and Scarlett. You two can't survive living in her apartment forever. It's dull and tiny and not yours. It will always be hers."

I sigh. She's not going to let this go until I give in and tell her yes. Although, I don't need a new apartment. Scarlett's apartment is more than adequate and I really don't care where I live as long as I have her with me; that's all I want anymore.

I hear a moan escape the throat of Clint, the man I tied up to a chair with duct tape. I smile. Scarlett may be all I want anymore, but I still crave the blood. I still need to let the beast out every once in a while and I can't believe Scarlett, or the FBI for that matter, lets me do it.

"I really need to go Reina."

"Then tell me you will let me pick out some apartments for you and Scarlett to look at this weekend? I have some fabulous ones already in mind and with the amount of money you two make you deserve the absolute best."

I laugh. "No, you want to make a killer commission. You don't actually care about where Scarlett and I live."

"I could waive the commission, finding the perfect place for the famous Scarlett Bell and her hot fiancé would help me sell more apartments and homes in the aftermath, but of course I'm not. Just say yes and I'll stop calling you every day."

"Don't you have plenty of clients and money already?"

"Of course, but it's ridiculous that I don't get to help my brother and his future wife find a home."

"That's because we already have a home."

"No, you live in her home."

I run my hand through my hair. There is no arguing with her. And I shouldn't argue with her anyway. It's been clear these last few months that what Reina enjoys is the control and power that comes with running a company. Any company that makes her money, it didn't have to be running a company that involves killing people. I should just shut my mouth and support her.

"Fine, we will go with you this weekend—"

"Yes!"

"But only if Scarlett says yes too."

"Oh, she will. No woman says no to looking for a new, fancy home."

I roll my eyes even though she can't see me and end the call. I put my phone in my pocket and turn to Clint whose eyes have grown wide showing the whites around his dark brown eyes. I can feel my excitement growing as his fear grows. *Who would have known that I would love torturing people for information just as much as I would like killing them?* Of course I've tortured people in the past, but nothing like what the FBI has me do for information.

I walk over to my box of tools I brought with me to extract the information that I need, although most of the time the most effective form of torture doesn't involve any tools. Still, using tools can be fun. I look to Santino, who has been standing, watching our prisoner. He is supposed to be helping me, but I don't need his help to get the info that I need.

"Leave me and Clint alone now Santino."

Santino gives me a dirty look. He hates it when I don't let him do the fun part of the job, but I feel the beast growing wild inside of me needing to get out. I promised Scarlett that I won't kill or hurt anyone that the FBI doesn't instruct me to. I'll use my dangerous desires to only fight evil, not become part of it. But it's been a while since the FBI has let the monster inside of me out. So I need to enjoy this, without Santino.

I raise my eyebrows at him and he storms out of the mostly empty warehouse.

I turn my attention back to my toolbox trying to decide where I want to start. I run my hand over the array of tools. Drills, knives, hammers, pliers. I pause over the pliers. I need this to last a while so I can let the beast inside run wild. It will help me control my urges in the future. Pliers are a good way to start. If he's really a life-long criminal, he won't reveal anything to me after a few pulled teeth and fingernails.

I pick up the pliers and then turn my attention toward Clint. I walk toward him as I slowly roll up my sleeves.

"I'm not going to lie to you Clint. I need this. I need this to last for hours so that I can control the beast inside me afterwards."

I stop in front of Clint and bend down so that I can look Clint in the eyes. "Can you do that Clint? Can you hold out answering my questions for hours? Or are you going to give in right away?"

Clint groans.

I smile. "Good."

I rip the duct tape off his mouth before I stand up.

Clint screams as soon as the tape is off.

"No one can hear you Clint."

He still screams. They always scream. It doesn't matter how strong the man or woman, when they look death in the face, they scream. They just don't know that I can't kill them. The FBI won't let me. Although, I'm hoping at some point I'll get someone that they want dead and not just information from.

I grab Clint's jaw to keep him from screaming. I crack my neck back and forth. "You're supposed to scream after Clint, not before."

I hold firmly onto his jaw keeping his mouth wide open and I push the pliers inside of his mouth. He struggles trying to close his mouth, but I keep his mouth firmly open as I reach to the molars at the back of his mouth and grab hold of the tooth with my pliers.

His scream gets louder as I make contact with the tooth and begin to pull slowly on the tooth and then suddenly yank it out in one swoop.

Clint screams in agony and struggles against the duct tape holding him to the chair.

I take a deep breath, as the adrenaline takes over my body. I love the feeling.

I punch Clint in the head hard to get him to stop screaming. He does, the shock of the punch to the side of the head enough to get him to stop long enough for me to ask him the question I'm supposed to ask.

"Who do you work for?" I ask even though it's a stupid question. I already know who he works for. He works for a drug organization that operates mostly in Japan and China. So I don't know what the FBI thinks they are going to get from this question. They can at least ask questions that will get better intel.

He blinks a couple of times and then spits blood in my face.

I smile. "Feisty. I knew you would last long enough to soothe the beast inside when I saw you. Let's try pulling another though just to be sure you are up for several hours of torture."

I grab his jaw again as he tries to pull away. He can't get away. He's mine for at least the next three hours. That's my prediction for how long he lasts before he spills his guts. It will be long enough.

I reach the pliers into his mouth, this time going for the molar on his right side instead of his left. I yank this one in one motion not giving him time to get used to the idea.

He screams again.

I close my eyes loving the sound. I crack my neck again as I think of all the things I can do next. The damage I can do.

My eyes fly open when the screaming stops. It's too early for him to stop screaming. Clint is lunched over in his chair. His head flops against his chest.

I sigh. So much for lasting hours of torture. Two teeth pulled and he already passed out from the pain. I grab his head and lift it up hoping he's still conscious enough that if I smack him in the face he will wake so that we can continue. When I lift his head though it plops back and it doesn't look like he's breathing. I place two fingers against his neck checking for a heartbeat that I can't find.

Dammit. "Santino!" I yell toward the door of the warehouse that he disappeared behind.

I run to the toolkit and pull out a knife and then begin ripping off the tape weary that he could be faking it to get me to remove the duct tape, but I've never seen anyone good enough to fake no pulse.

"What did you do?" Santino asks from behind me.

"Just help me."

Santino begins helping me untie Clint. When all the bindings are off we pull him to the floor and begin CPR. After a couple minutes pass, we both realize our efforts are futile.

"You killed another one? This is the second one in—"

"Three months."

"They are going to fire you. Or throw you in jail. You weren't supposed to kill him."

I roll my eyes. "I know I wasn't. It wasn't like I meant to either of the times. I yanked two teeth. How was I supposed to know that pulling two teeth would cause a heart attack or whatever this guy suffered from?"

Santino narrows his eyes at me trying to decide if all I did was pull a couple of teeth. "And what was your excuse last time?"

"The drill slipped."

"Please tell me he at least told you who he works for before he croaked."

I shrug. "We already know who he worked for."

"They are going to fire you."

I sigh. He's probably right. They weren't too happy the last time this happened. They didn't give me any jobs for three months. That's too long to go without hurting someone.

I pull out my phone.

"What are you doing?" Santino asks.

"I'm going to call Killian. He still has some pull with the FBI, maybe he can help."

I dial his number and wait for him to answer.

"What happened?" Killian answers.

I frown. "Nothing happened. Can't I call one of my closest friends for a chat?"

"No."

I exhale deeply. "Okay fine. I accidentally killed the guy I was just supposed to torture for information."

"Goddammit Nacio. Can't you at least try to keep them alive."

"I did. Honestly, I just pulled two teeth."

"I'm sure that's all that happened."

"Can you fix this?"

"Yea, but this is the last time Nacio. Next time you are on your own."

I smile.

"Are you going to make it to dinner tonight? Kinsley and I are having everyone over for dinner."

"Yea, I should make it back. It won't take long to clean up. It never takes long to clean up a dead body."

I can feel Killian frowning on the other end of the line.

"I didn't do it on purpose."

Killian doesn't answer. He just ends the call and I begin helping Santino clean up the body.

"You going over to Kinsley and Killian's tonight for dinner?"

"Yep and I'm bringing a date."

I raise my eyebrows. Dinner just got a lot more interesting.

———

SCARLETT

I get back to my apartment that Nacio now shares with me. I hear the shower running upstairs which makes me smile. I didn't think he would make it home tonight but I'm glad he's home and can go to dinner with me tonight. I've missed him these last couple of nights, but I know he needed this. I could see with every day that passed the beast inside him struggled to get out and he struggled to keep him buried inside.

Now I can tell him that Reina called wanting us to go look at apartments with her this weekend. And that I said yes. It's been something I have been wanting to do for a while now. Go apartment shopping, but I wanted to wait to tell him my other news first. Now is the perfect time for both.

I start heading upstairs to bathroom and in perfect timing Nacio steps out of the bathroom with a towel wrapped around his waist.

I stop walking to admire him with what I'm sure is a goofy smile on my face. "Glad you're home. I missed you." I walk over and kiss him on the lips.

When I pull away, I see the cut on his lip and the bruise just below his eye. It should bother me seeing the danger that he was in. The evidence that he just did something bad to someone else. It doesn't bother me though. It makes me happy to see him doing what makes him happy even if I don't fully understand it. At least now he is working for good instead of evil.

I know that is who he is, and I'm not going to try to change him. I have just learned not to ask when he comes home looking like he does now. I don't want to worry that he might die or get sent back to prison every time he leaves the apartment.

"We need to get dressed, so we can leave for Kinsley and Killian's dinner in twenty minutes."

Nacio smiles and then flips off the lights in the apartment. "How about I do naughty things to you first?"

I giggle as he kisses my neck. "We can't. We will be late," I whine as Nacio pulls my arms together and then above my head, like he did the first time we met. And I know that's what he wants to do—relive the excitement of that night. "We don't have time for that tonight. Haven't you had enough excitement for one day?"

"Yes," he breathes seriously into my ear. "I have. I'm tired of the same old excitement that used to control my life. I'm ready for a new kind of excitement."

His lips kiss my neck, and I moan.

"Yeah, and what's that?"

"The excitement that comes with getting married and starting a family."

I freeze. That sounds perfect to me, but I don't think he understands that it might not be as exciting as he thinks it will be. "That's normal though. We don't do normal."

"We do when it's an exciting adventure that we are both ready for."

I laugh. "Let's start with getting married first, and then we can do the whole baby thing."

"Fine. But that doesn't mean we can't enjoy the fun and excitement of trying."

I giggle again as Nacio tugs my arms high over my head. We are going to be late to our dinner, but I don't care. I get to fuck my fiancé in the dark while imagining our lives being filled with babies and boring but exciting things, like feedings at three a.m.

It sounds like the perfect way to start our forever.

"We are just going to have to move the wedding up quite a bit because...I'm pregnant."

BEAST

I'm going to be a father, keeps repeating in my head. I'm going to be a husband and fast, like tomorrow if I have my way, although I know Scarlett is going to want a big beautiful expensive wedding, not a quick court wedding. But I will give her everything she wants as long as she marries me now.

Killian opens the door to their apartment with a frown on his face. "You're late."

Scarlett blushes. "We are not that late. Only a half hour. That's not late."

Killian continues to frown.

"Lighten up Kill," Scarlett says walking inside. I follow her.

"I would if Nacio would stick to his job instead of taking things too far," Killian says.

Scarlett turns to look at me. "You killed one again?"

"Don't look at me like that."

"Like what?"

"Like you are disappointed in me. This one was not my fault. I barely did anything to him. He just didn't have the heart to hold up to torture."

Scarlett laughs. "Sure it wasn't your fault. Just like the drill wasn't your fault. It just slipped."

I frown. I should have never told her that story. I should have known I'd live to regret it.

I grab Scarlett's hand and guide her into the dining room that is already full of people. Scarlett lets go of my hand to greet Kinsley who immediately hands her a glass of wine. Scarlett takes it, but she's flustered. She doesn't want to tell people we are pregnant yet. She says it's too early and she wants to plan a quick wedding first, but I don't know how she is going to keep it a secret. I can already see Kinsley eyeing Scarlett suspiciously. I think she gives Scarlett alcohol every time just to test to see if she is pregnant. Scarlett looks across the room to me asking for my help. I just shrug. I find Reina and give her a quick hug before I take a seat next to Santino. Scarlett quickly makes her way back to a spot next to me as she tries to avoid Kinsley although from the smile on Kinsley's lips she has already guessed.

Kinsey knows she won't get any answers from Scarlett so instead she looks to me raising her eyebrows. I wink at her in response. Kinsley claps her hands together excitedly as everyone at the table turns their attention to her.

"I'm sorry. I'm just so excited to finally have everyone together. It's been too long," Kinsley says taking a seat as Killian brings out the last of the food to set on the table.

I lean over to Santino who is sitting next to an empty chair.

"So who is your date?"

He sighs. "She couldn't make it. Had a family emergency."

I roll my eyes. "Sure she did." I don't believe for a second that he actually has a girlfriend. It's been years since I've seen him with anyone serious.

Kinsley grabs her glass of wine and lifts it. "I want to propose a toast..."

Scarlett shoots daggers with her eyes at me thinking I told Kinsley about our pregnancy. I smile at her not caring who knows or what the rules are about when you are supposed to tell people. I hope Kinsley is announcing it to everyone although I doubt that she is.

"I'm so thankful to have every one of you in my life. New and old friends. We consider you all family now and no matter what happened in the past between us, I know that now we are all one family. To family." She raises her glass.

"To family," everyone says as we clink our wine glasses before all taking a sip. I watch as Scarlett awkwardly takes a sip as well, obviously worried about how she's not going to drink tonight.

I glance to Santino to my left. He's my brother. He's always been family but even still we haven't always had the perfect relationship but we know we will be there for each other no matter what. And if he is really dating someone we will all be happy to invite her into our world as soon as he's ready.

I glance past the empty chair next to Santino to Reina. She looks happy. Happier than I've ever seen her as she chats with Preston on her left. Who also looks happy although I don't know him well enough to know when he's not happy.

I glance to Kinsley and Killian. Both sitting at a table where at least three people have tried to kill one or both of them. They have been so forgiving. So welcoming over these last few months and I couldn't imagine ever killing them now.

I reach down and take Scarlett's hand in my lap that is shaking slightly as I whisper into her ear, "Don't worry about the wine. I'll drink it for you. No one will know."

She smiles.

I glance around the room. I would kill for anyone in this room and I can't think of living without any one of them. I have a family now. A real family that cares more about loving one another than killing. I glance down at Scarlett's stomach, and I have a growing family that is just going to get larger and larger if I have it my way.

I have a family. A family that forgives me when I mess up. A family that doesn't expect anything from me. A family that loves me. A family that is mine, forever.

The End

Thank you so much for reading!

Grab your FREE copy of Not Sorry here→<u>EllaMiles.com/freebooks</u>

FREE BOOKS

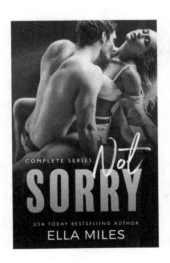

Read **Not Sorry** for **FREE**! And sign up to get my latest releases, updates, and more goodies here→<u>EllaMiles.com/freebooks</u>

Follow me on BookBub to get notified of my new releases and recommendations here→Follow on BookBub Here

Free Books

Join Ella's Bellas FB group for giveaways and FUN→Join Ella's Bellas Here

ALSO BY ELLA MILES

MAYBE, DEFINITELY SERIES:

Maybe Yes

Maybe Never

Maybe Always

Definitely Yes

Definitely No

Definitely Forever

TRUTH OR LIES (Coming 2019):

Taken by Lies

Betrayed by Truths

Trapped by Lies

Stolen by Truths

Possessed by Lies

Consumed by Truths

DIRTY SERIES:

Dirty Beginning

Dirty Obsession

Dirty Addiction

Dirty Revenge

ALIGNED SERIES:

Aligned: Volume 1 (Free Series Starter)

Aligned: Volume 2

Aligned: Volume 3

Aligned: Volume 4

Aligned: The Complete Series Boxset

UNFORGIVABLE SERIES:

Heart of a Thief

Heart of a Liar

Heart of a Prick

Unforgivable: The Complete Series Boxset

STANDALONES:

Pretend I'm Yours

Finding Perfect

Savage Love

Too Much

Not Sorry

ABOUT THE AUTHOR

Ella Miles writes steamy romance, including everything from dark suspense romance that will leave you on the edge of your seat to contemporary romance that will leave you laughing out loud or crying. Most importantly, she wants you to feel everything her characters feel as you read.

Ella is currently living her own happily ever after near the Rocky Mountains with her high school sweetheart husband. Her heart is also taken by her goofy five year old black lab who is scared of everything, including her own shadow.

Ella is a USA Today Bestselling Author & Top 50 Bestselling Author.

Stalk Ella at:
www.ellamiles.com
ella@ellamiles.com